DESPE

DUBAI

DESPERATE IN
DUBAI

AMEERA AL HAKAWATI

RANDOM HOUSE INDIA

First Published by Random House India in 2011
Seventh impression in 2012

Copyright © Ameera Al Hakawati 2011

Random House Publishers India Private Limited
Windsor IT Park, 7th Floor, Tower-B,
A-1, Sector-125, Noida-201301, UP

Random House Group Limited
20 Vauxhall Bridge Road
London SW1V 2SA, UK

978-81-8400-171-6

Typeset in Bembo by Jojy Philip

Printed and bound in India by Replika Press

For sale in the Indian subcontinent and middle east only.

To the women of Dubai,
who inspired me with
their strength,
their faith,
and
their stories

1

Lady Luxe has never sat so still in her life. She stretches her muscles as much as she can, given the restrictions of being in an aeroplane seat. However, after almost seven hours of sitting in one place she feels like bounding out of her seat and launching into a Jane Fonda aerobics routine. She wonders if the cute guy beside her would think she's nuts.

But the thought of the following day's headlines if she makes a spectacle of herself stops her. 'X heiress loses the plot' the expat tabloids would undoubtedly declare with undisguised glee, although the government-controlled ones would refrain from such vigour. 'Daughter of X publicly shames herself and her family' perhaps. If they haven't been silenced, that is.

She sighs, already missing London's grey skies, cool breezes, and the beautiful fragrance of freedom.

In London, Lady Luxe rarely felt the need to don a blonde wig over her thick, dark brown hair whenever she decided to have a little fun.

Nor did she bother with the blue contact lenses that masked her own hazel eyes, giving them an ethereal look. In London, her abaya hangs in her South Kensington closet acquiring the slightest sheen of dust, until it is time to board an EK flight back to DXB; her sheyla lies discarded somewhere close by. Her name is definitely not Lady Luxe. She is not the daughter of X, granddaughter of X, and niece of X. She is just plain Jennifer. She struggles to board the tube with everyone else, she stands squashed against sweaty commuters like everyone else, and in every restaurant she is served just like everyone else. She is completely anonymous; an ordinary twenty-something living a pretty ordinary life.

Shifting around in her seat and re-arranging her legs once again, Lady Luxe mindlessly flicks through the movie options and, for a fragment of a second, she toys with the idea of writing a screenplay about her family. A script full of dry British humour intertwined with colourful Gulf jokes; English with a splash of Arabic, just like her. However, she knows she will never be able to do this. Telling anyone about her father's mistresses, her mother's addiction to prescription drugs, her brother's fierce temper, and her own scandalous double life, will guarantee the X family's exile from the desert and her own head on a platter.

'Can I get you something to drink, ma'am? Some champagne perhaps?' The stewardess smiles at Lady Luxe, her pearly teeth even more distinct against the deep red lips that frame them.

Yes please. 'No thank you,' Lady Luxe murmurs, her throat dry, wishing she could. But she has already spotted four other Khaleejis in the cabin, and cannot risk having a drink in case they happen to know who she is. She snorts when she sees a man in the traditional Emirati white robe, the candoura, indulging himself in a glass of something clearly haraam, and wonders why society deems it is acceptable for Arab men to do as they please when God has set clear rules that apply to both men *and* women.

'Having a bad flight?'

Lady Luxe knew that the boy sitting next to her would eventually work up the courage to speak to her. He has been glancing at her every few minutes for the past seven hours.

'Not anymore,' she flirts, watching his cheeks turn pink with pleasure.

Recently graduated, he tells her that he has been headhunted by an American company in

Dubai to join a prestigious private equity firm. He shifts around in his seat, clearly not used to flying Business, and she finds this refreshingly endearing. As he continues to talk, she tunes out, concentrating on his hands instead. Small with long, delicate fingers, she wonders how niftily he could do undo the buttons on her Sevens and then quickly shakes the thought out of her head. She has got to stop being such a rebel.

'So where exactly is your office based?' she asks in an accent heavily punctuated with British, American and Arabic tones—the product of having being born and raised in Dubai, studying in an international school, and having an English mother. Her caramel complexion is also hard to place. She is too tanned to be from Iranian descent, too fair to be an original Emirati, and far too rosy to be Lebanese. Most people find it difficult to work out where she's from. Her hair and facial features also makes her stand out from most of her cousins, who, with their frizzy jet black hair subjected to countless Brazilian blowouts, dark brown eyes, and large noses (until they make the customary 'coming of age' trip to Lebanon to rectify it), envy her glossy chestnut hair, small, straight nose, and greenish brown eyes.

Although the combination is definitely appealing, attractive even, if you take in her lean limbs, small shoulders, and trendy clothes, Lady Luxe is not what you would call beautiful. But there's something mischievous about her wide smile, and something strangely innocent about her bright eyes, and together with her infectious laugh, the full package can be lethal.

'In Dubai International Finance Centre,' he replies, careful not to fumble the words.

She suppresses a giggle at his using the full name instead of the commonly used acronym, DIFC. Dubai is full of acronyms: DLC, DMC, JBR, JLT, MOE. The city that has grown so rapidly has an equally fast pace. No one even has the time to speak slowly, and pronouncing a title fully is a gross waste of time that could otherwise be spent partying or making money. 'It's obvious you're a newbie,' she says with a coy smile. *Do you need someone to help you out?* is the unasked question. She dares him with her eyes and his response is exactly what she expected.

'I could do with someone showing me the ropes,' he says hesitantly.

How predictable. 'Don't worry, there are plenty of friendly people who would be happy to assist you,' she replies, her voice warm with faux concern.

Lady Luxe doesn't mean to play mind games, but for some reason she just can't help it. From a young age, every word she has uttered has held an underlying meaning—whether it's negotiating for a new car, pleading for a new vacation, or asking for a credit card with a higher limit—she has always had to choose her words carefully to ensure the response she wants. Now, at twenty-three, it's not just her father or her brothers she tests her verbal skills on. Every man (or boy) that comes in contact with Lady Luxe never quite knows where he stands, what she wants, or what she's thinking. Most of the time, that's exactly how she likes it, but occasionally she wishes that a guy would just read her mind and give her what her subconscious desperately wants: a stable, uncomplicated marriage. No cultural issues, no second wives, just love. But everyone knows that such a thing doesn't exist. Not in an Emirati girl's life at least.

'Um, I hope so,' he replies, his disappointment obvious.

She takes in his sandy blonde hair and dark brown eyes with appreciation, but then looks away. She's not in the mood to continue playing with him no matter how attractive he is. It's not worth the risk. No matter what she does in London—the bars she visits, the clubs she stumbles out of at dawn, the men whose bedrooms she finds herself in when the cold British sun seeps its way in through the cracks in the curtains—in Dubai, she is Lady Luxe, and with a surname like that, she just can't afford to let her secret adventures become public.

She doesn't care about tarnishing her reputation and becoming unmarriageable. However, what she does care about is risking her life. Honour killings may not make the headlines, or even trickle into community gossip, but after what happened to her cousin, she knows better than to flaunt her escapades. So in Dubai she continues her good girl façade when she has to, and when the cat's away (in her case, her father) she plays. Hard.

It wasn't easy for Lady Luxe to persuade her father to allow her to study Fashion at the Central Saint Martin's College of Art and Design, one of Britain's most revered art institutions. It took her most of her life to make him accept that she wasn't interested in business administration, and then a full year of cajoling, pleading, crying, arguing, and hypothesizing to make him agree to her studying abroad. Eventually both her mother and uncle had to step in, explaining to her father the importance of her learning about her full heritage, of spending time with her mother, the importance of studying at a prestigious, historic college rather than an unknown Dubai establishment, as well as the benefits of learning how to be independent.

Lady Luxe's father was right to be concerned.

For three and a half years, his beloved daughter did everything she had only ever dreamed of doing, and more. Never particularly religious, God-fearing, or traditional, she utilized every minute of her freedom as if it were her last, knowing that eventually the time would come to an end and she would have to return home and continue living an unfulfilled double life.

'Well, I would kind of like it if you would show me around,' the Brit says hesitantly, the nervousness clear in his eyes.

'Would you now?' Lady Luxe replies, surprised. She had underestimated him. Against her better judgement, she pulls out a Mont Blanc pen, reaches over and takes hold of his hand. He freezes and she can sense that he has stopped breathing. She grins to herself. 'Here you go. That's my number. Call me if you need any help,' she says, scribbling down her second phone number—the one that serves one very clear purpose—on the back of his hand.

'Thanks. I will,' he replies, staring down at the number as if he is afraid it will disappear before he has a chance to commit it to memory.

As the captain announces the descent into DXB, Lady Luxe untangles her folded legs and hauls herself off her seat. Ignoring the Brit's bemused gaze, she scrapes her hair into a ponytail, rearranges her fringe and attaches a big, pink flower clip to the back of her head. Retrieving her Swarovski crystal encrusted abaya from the stewardess, she slips it on and loosely places her sheyla back on her head.

'Bloody hell,' the Brit chuckles, watching her in amazement. 'You look completely different!'

'That's the point,' she answers, sitting back down, this time folding her legs delicately, her gold Jimmy Choos peeping out from beneath the abaya's long hem. She looks across the cabin and sees a pretty girl with silky black hair perform the exact same ritual she has just completed. Their eyes connect and they smile wryly at each other.

Alighting from the plane, Lady Luxe says a quick, halal goodbye to the Brit, grabs her luggage that has been prioritized to come out first, and heads out into the humid Dubai night. The airport is freezing cold but the weather outside, despite it being the middle of January, is pleasant enough for light sweaters. Only in Dubai do you wear your jacket indoors and remove it outdoors.

Enjoying the warm breeze and the familiar smell of petrol by the taxi stand, she looks around for the chauffeur driven white Bentley Continental that usually picks her up from the airport. Instead, all she sees are the beige taxis waiting to pick up naïve passengers who are unaware that riding a taxi in Dubai is tantamount to suicide.

'Need a lift?' The Brit is back lugging a large, new suitcase, beads of sweat appearing on his forehead as he is confronted with the warm winter's night; his thick woollen polo neck and leather jacket completely inappropriate for Dubai's stuffy climate.

'Thanks, but I'm expecting someone,' she says, edging away from him and looking around quickly, hoping no one will notice the Emirati girl conversing with the foreign boy.

'A boyfriend?' he asks tentatively, taking off his jacket and slinging it over his suitcase.

'No. My driver,' she laughs, relaxing upon realizing that no one is looking in her direction.

'You have a driver? As in, a chauffeur?' he asks incredulously.

'So?'

'A bit precious don't you think?' He looks into Lady Luxe's hazel eyes, amused as they narrow in annoyance.

'You'll understand in a couple of months,' she says, a little peeved at his impertinence. 'Anyway, shouldn't you be catching a taxi?'

'Are you trying to get rid of me? Fine, I can take a hint. It's been a pleasure.' Giving her no time to react, the Brit leans forward, pecks Lady Luxe on the cheek and walks away.

Shit. She looks around, ignoring the disapproving gaze of the security guard, her heart pounding as she prays that her eyes don't fall on anything white, be it a candoura, guttra, or worse, her car.

Then she sees it. A hundred metres away, a white Bentley is waiting for her. Her heart thudding against her ribcage, she waits for the driver to step out and walk over to her, praying he did not see her with the Brit.

'Hi Mahboob,' Lady Luxe greets the Pakistani driver with a shaky smile as he hops out of the car and relieves her of her Louis Vuitton luggage.

'Salaam,' he replies abruptly, loading her bags into the car.

Without waiting for him to open the door for her, she yanks it open and sinks into the plush red leather seats. She wonders if she should say anything to him, implore him not to mention anything to her father *or* brother, or if she should pretend that nothing happened in case he hadn't actually seen anything. She opts for silence.

Mahboob skillfully manoeuvres his way through the lanes of traffic, over Garhoud Bridge and into Jumeirah—one of the most exclusive areas in Dubai, where only the nationals are at liberty to own property. Lady Luxe stares blankly out of the tinted windows at the blur of mismatched villas as they make their way to her sea-facing villa. It's only when she feels the wetness on her cheeks does she realize that she has been crying.

'Miss X, we are here,' Mahboob states the obvious as the gates of the villa glide open and he drives around the fountain and into the garage lined with a fleet of glistening luxury cars. He opens the door and sees the tears rolling down Lady Luxe's face.

'What's wrong, beta?' he asks kindly, handing her a tissue, which she accepts gratefully.

'Nothing, I'm fine.' Embarrassed, she climbs out of the car and rearranges her sheyla so that it sits perfectly over her head.

Mahboob opens his mouth to say something and then closes it.

'What?' Lady Luxe asks, walking over to the huge Berber style front door and looking back at him, 'I said I'm fine.'

'I...' He looks at her, his eyes filled with concern. 'I didn't see anything, okay?'

Lady Luxe says nothing, but thanks God silently for saving her...once again. Although she knows there will come a day when He will stop. And when that day comes, she doubts if she will be ready.

2

It has been an hour since he last called, promising to be home in twenty minutes. His dinner has turned stone cold and is almost inedible.

Not that he cares that his wife has been waiting for him on an empty stomach, reluctant to begin without him. Nor is he particularly concerned about the spread she has waiting for him—a leg of lamb roasted to perfection, stuffed aubergines with rice and minced meat, a salad, a yoghurt dip, saffron rice, and homemade lemon juice with mint. Daniel is, after all, so absorbed in his own life that he barely notices Nadia anymore. New haircuts are lost on him, sexy lingerie rarely rustles an interest down below, and tears just turn him into stone.

Nadia is painfully aware of it all.

She sits at the carefully laid dinner table in a simple red summer dress that she bought on a whim, hoping that her husband would notice it and pay a compliment. Long earrings dangle from her ears, and her crazy curly hair is loose and sexy.

She has had her monthly Brazilian, her legs are smooth enough to be in a Gillette ad, and her lips are painted a daring scarlet, matching her dress.

When Nadia first got married she didn't feel the need to make such an effort. She could walk around in faded flannel pyjamas with holes in them, and her husband would still look at her as if she were a priceless jewel. Now she finds herself spending more and more time on her appearance, desperately trying to catch his interest, wondering when and how she became so meaningless to him.

With each second that passes, Nadia is more resolved to make her marriage work. With her first class Biology degree from University College London and her Masters in Environmental Biology from Imperial, she is used to succeeding. When she married Daniel, she thought that she had also succeeded in finding the perfect husband. Sexy, attentive and deep, he wooed her with poetry that he had written himself, long, sensual love letters, and a willingness to massage her feet during balmy summer evenings in Regent's Park.

His spirituality had also drawn her to him. A recent convert to Islam, Daniel was yearning to learn more about the new way of life he had adopted, and his eagerness shone through from every pore of his translucent skin. Nadia was drawn to him like a beggar to a generous merchant.

She would have been happy to continue living in their dark basement flat in North London, while she continued her work as a consultant for an energy company, and he worked on the novel that would change the world. Her flat may have been tiny, but it felt like a proper home. Only a fifteen-minute walk from her sister's place, Nadia loved having her family nearby, she loved the fact that it was also in close proximity to the local mosque and the tube station. She didn't mind paying a slightly higher rent for the Zone Two address.

Daniel also seemed to like living in Highbury, unperturbed by the abundance of immigrants (after all, with his US passport and German upbringing he was a foreigner himself), the pigeon droppings that littered the pavements, and the regular muggings in broad daylight. The poet in him romanticized his life, and he fancied himself as a Renaissance writer struggling with poverty, as he strove to find a job and indulging in a passionate marriage with a beautiful North African woman. Until his jobless status slowly began to strip him of

16

his ego, his self respect and his sense of manhood. Every time he came across Islamic sayings, which emphasized the husband's duty to take care of his wife, reiterating the fact that the wife's income is purely her own and a husband has no claim over it unless the wife chooses to share it with him, he began to feel less like a man, a husband, or even a Muslim.

Daniel, being Daniel, kept the queasiness in his stomach and the loss of power in his limbs to himself. Then one day he announced that he had been offered a job in Dubai and he was hoping that Nadia would move with him.

At 9:36 pm, two hours and thirty-six minutes after her husband was supposed to be home, Nadia finally carves herself a piece of rock hard lamb, serves herself a small portion of limp salad, and ignores the stuffed aubergines—Daniel's favourite—altogether. By 9:49 pm, she has finished repeatedly rearranging the food on her plate, and gets up to wash her hands in the bathroom sink. Glancing at the mirror she realizes how pitiful she looks. She stares at her huge, black eyes rimmed with kohl, pale cheeks, pert cleavage, and slender arms and feels disgusted with herself. When she remembers the matching red lingerie underneath and the agony she went through getting waxed just for him, a wave of nausea washes over her.

Pulling off her new dress and underwear, she stuffs them all into the bathroom bin. Shivering, she wraps her arms around her thin body and looks at her naked reflection. Her collar bones are protruding and her skin is beginning to strain over her hips and ribs. She was never this thin. In fact, she used to relish her curves, enjoying feeling like a real woman; but after moving to Dubai she realized that she detested eating alone. The pounds slipped off as she spent less time eating and more time playing with the food on her plate.

Forcing herself into cotton pyjamas, Nadia makes herself a cup of green tea and climbs into bed with it. She opens her bedside cabinet and takes out a bundle of papers, anxious to remember why she married Daniel in the first place, and desperate to find a reason to continue trying. Choosing a leaf randomly, she begins to read.

Nadia, my angel, my saviour, he wrote one evening when they were on the brink of falling in love, when she was still unsure of the depth of his feelings.

I can't concentrate on anything—not my thesis, my lectures, or even my friends. Every time my mind begins to focus on what I came here for, my heartstrings tug it back to where it belongs—with you. When I embraced Islam, I thought I had finally discovered my purpose in life. I had found a sense of peace and solace that had warmed my soul with its radiance. But now even those intense emotions have been displaced. I live, I breathe, for you.

Liar.

She stares at the words written by a man consumed with love and longing and tries to understand how, in a little over a year, he has changed so much. She traces her fingers over the indentations on the page, running them over the small neat print, wondering if he would ever feel the same way again.

She falls asleep, the letter still in her hand, the lamp still on, and the cup of green tea still full, wondering if there is another woman in his life.

The next morning Nadia waits for Daniel to slip out of bed and leave the apartment for his weekly off-roading expedition before she opens her eyes and kicks off the covers. She counts to three hundred after she hears the front door close in case he comes back into the apartment. When the sound of his rumbling Nissan Patrol fades away, she climbs out of bed and starts making wudhu for Salaatul Fajr.

After last night's failed dinner, Nadia is too upset to make the first move to repair their wounded relationship and hopes Daniel will at least try to apologize. So far, he hasn't.

She finds that she can't concentrate on her morning prayers and stumbles on the words she has recited a thousand times. When she finishes, she sits still on the rug and clutches onto her turquoise prayer beads—a gift from her maternal grandmother in Marrakesh. She breathes deeply with her eyes closed, imagining herself in the Koutoubia Mosque. She misses Marrakesh, with its countless minarets and a spiritual fervour, which thrives despite the secular government's best efforts to tame it. She wishes she could walk through the labyrinth-like alleyways in Jamaa el Fna once again, or sit leaning against a pillar in the famous Hassan II Mosque in Casablanca. Although she is only half Moroccan (her father's side being Algerian) and had lived in Morocco for just a couple of years, she feels more Moroccan than any other part of her identity.

When the sun slowly begins its ascent into the violet sky, Nadia pulls herself to her feet and puts on the kettle. As the water boils, she makes the bed and then takes out her laptop with trepidation. Daniel hasn't bothered to buy his own laptop and uses Nadia's whenever he wants to check his email in the evenings or weekends. Last week though, she installed a keylogging device which tracks every password entered, and today she is planning on using the knowledge she will receive from it.

Nadia didn't want things to come to this but Daniel's behaviour is becoming increasingly suspicious. As well as being cold, distant, and indifferent, he also seems constantly on edge. He keeps his phone with him at all times, and when asleep he turns it off. She tried accessing it last week but it has been PIN protected. No one PIN protects their phone unless they have something to hide.

Opening the hidden program, Nadia pushes aside any guilt she is feeling and quickly scans in all the passwords which have been entered. His Gmail, Facebook, Myspace, Linkedin, and Twitter are all there. She copies and pastes them all onto a blank email and saves the draft, just in case she forgets them, and then logs on to his Gmail account.

Everything is kosher in Daniel's email and she feels a twinge of guilt for doubting him. There are emails from his friends and family in the US, work related messages, and some forwarded mail from her sister. Her eyes eventually fall on an email thread by someone called 'J'. Something doesn't seem quite right to Nadia. Who goes by a mere initial? She clicks on it, telling herself that as his wife it is her right to know about his potential interaction with women. The thread opens to show at least fifty messages exchanged between the two of them over the course of a few months. She doesn't want to doubt him yet; after all 'J' could just be a colleague or an old friend.

Half an hour later, Nadia is still sitting in the same position she was in when she turned on the laptop. She feels as if her bones are made of lead and she cannot move without experiencing a sharp pain in her head.

Daniel and 'J', it transpires, are meeting today. From their messages she can see their relationship unfold as if it were a movie. They both like to write and their emails are full of colourful stories and descriptions. Nadia has deduced that Daniel actually met 'J' at a club in London but she has recently moved to Dubai. They hooked up a few times in the UK before he met Nadia and renewed contact after he moved to Dubai.

The emails are littered with innuendos and the underlying passion of two people who want to be together but cannot. Daniel admits that he is married but 'J' doesn't seem to care. It is clear to Nadia that his unavailability has made him all the more attractive to her.

There are also pictures. 'J' in a bikini on South Beach, Miami. 'J' in an evening gown at a fancy party in LA. 'J' looking pretty in pink at a wedding at the Claridges.

'J' is tall, thin, with long, slightly wavy blonde hair. She is definitely attractive in a sharp, supermodel kind of way, with piercing blue eyes and a wide smile, but Nadia knows that she is much better looking.

Nadia's tea remains cold and untouched on the coffee table as the adjectives he has used to describe her play over and over in her head. *Sexy, smart, sweet, cute, lovable, beautiful.* Does that mean she is none of those things?

Reality slowly sinks into the numbness as she realizes that Daniel, *her* Daniel, is with another woman right now. What happened to their love? Their vows? Their promises?

Her hands begin to shake so she quickly logs out and climbs back into bed. Too scared to tell her family that her relationship with her husband is failing, too ashamed to confide in her friends, loneliness wraps itself around her as she buries her head under her pillow. The tears start slowly, but soon they are gushing out of her like a broken tap and her sobs are wracking her entire body.

Right now my husband is with another woman.

3

I know it's only been three weeks, and although it's far too soon to judge, I can't help but feel that moving to Dubai may have been yet another poor judgement call on my part. Yes, *another* one. In recent times I've somehow managed to perfect the art of making huge, life-changing mistakes. It's as if once you make a significant error, you can't help but make a zillion others, like dominoes falling over in succession. And when you're in the middle of all those tumbling blocks, it's impossible to get out.

Dubai was supposed to be getting out. It was supposed to help me move on from everything that happened in London and Delhi, to give me time to think about the mess I had made of my life, and hopefully give me the anonymity I needed to pave a new future.

But the shadows from the past follow me everywhere I go. Should I forget what I've done for the slightest second and have the audacity to actually smile, or feel an iota of happiness seep into my miserable soul, they are there, waiting, ready to close in, wrapping their darkness around me, and dispelling that single ray of light in one cruel motion.

It's amazing how much losing loved ones hurts. Even when you've chosen to leave them, the pain is indescribable. How do you begin to explain that sense of loss that leaves you so empty that a gentle breeze is able to knock you over? And how do you try and forget a sense of guilt so heavy that it slithers into your slumber?

Throwing the duvet off my body, I pull myself out of bed and climb into the shower, hoping that the cold water will snap me out of my current depressive state. As the water pummels down on my head, clearing my mind and injecting energy into my lethargic limbs, the shadows begin to fade. I make a conscious effort to stop moping around and venture outside for a change.

No more loafing around at home, Sugar. Get out, stick a smile on your face, and make some friends.

I'm feeling more like my usual, chirpy self when I eventually emerge from the bathroom. I was never the depressive kind. There was a time, not too long ago, when I was known for being the life and soul of every party. Everyone knew that a night out, or even a night in, wasn't complete until I got there with my off-key wisecracks and never-ending stream of jokes. But the old Sugar died in India and returned to England a mere fragment of her original self. The new Sugar is not only boring but also incapable of wearing a smile on her stiff face for fear it will crack and collapse in a pile of dust.

How will I ever make friends like this? Who on earth wants to be around someone like me?

No one, an annoying voice taunts.

'Oh shut up,' I grumble, making a face and pulling open my wardrobe door. Rifling through my meagre selection of clothes, I sigh and grumble some more. I miss my vast selection of jeans, t-shirts, tops, and hoodies, and I wish I had packed more when I moved out here. But clothes were the last thing on my mind as I stuffed random possessions into my small suitcase just one night before my flight. All I could think about was what I—*we*—had done.

I finally pick out a bright pink and white kurta, one of the few items of clothing that isn't huge on me, and wrinkle my nose as I hold it against me. The colours are far brighter than my mood, and I wish I could afford to go shopping to buy some new clothes. There's no chance of any shopping until I get my first paycheque, which is due in exactly eight days. So until then it's going to be a long week of wearing baggy, shapeless tops that scream 'I'm an Indian', even if I don't really look like one.

It's not that I don't *like* being Indian. I do. At least, I used to. In England, I never had any hang-ups about who I was or where I came from. Aside from the occasionally 'Paki' being yelled at me from not-so-subtle BNP supporters from nearby council estates, I felt the same as everyone else. Like I had a right to be there. I guess living in Stamford Hill, a cross between Gujarat and Jerusalem, helped me feel at home. Every other person in the vicinity was clad in black; either in a long abaya (or jabbo as we called it) and niqaab, or in a long black jacket and kippah. My little olive face was one of the hundreds, which occupied that small area in Hackney.

Here, the majority of the population is made up of those from the Indian subcontinent, but unfortunately we don't quite feel as if we belong here. It's not just because of the displacement issues you face when you live in a country you'll never be a citizen of. It's because in Dubai, Indians are considered to be second-class citizens. Right down at the bottom of the dung heap alongside the Filipinos and Africans.

No one has openly said anything to my face, but I feel it every time someone asks me where I'm from and 'England' doesn't quite cut it. They want to know where you are *really* from. In other words they're saying, 'Don't tell me that your complexion is from too much tanning, where is your *father* from?' And when you answer 'India', you can almost see the shift from respect to disdain in their eyes. At first, they don't believe me. They've never seen Indians with British accents, olive skin, and auburn hair before, but then they realize that it's not exactly something you lie about, is it?

After changing into my desi outfit and dusting a tiny bit of bronzer on my cheeks, I decide that the best way to cheer myself up is to go to the beach. Living next to the sea is still a novelty for me as the closest thing to a beach in London is Southend, which, with its dilapidated pier, murky waters, and Essex location, isn't quite as appealing as Jumeirah Beach Park.

The taxi gets me there in twenty minutes, and after parting with eighteen dirhams, I make my way through the park area and onto the sand.

All around me children are splashing about in the azure waters, teenagers are posing sexily in brightly coloured bikinis, and old Arab women, a stark contrast to them in their white headscarves and long skirts, are preparing hefty chunks of meat on metal barbecue skewers.

I lay out my beach towel, plonk down, and cross my legs. I take out my book but instead of reading it, I watch the people around me. I still can't get over the way Muslims here are so different from those back in the UK. Back home, being the gross minority, they're all united and overtly Muslim. Islam is a huge part of their identity and because they face a lot of difficulties getting accepted into mainstream society, they have a defensive nature. Here it's so much more relaxed; you see girls in hijab doing stuff you rarely see back home, such as smoking shisha, hanging out with guys, or going to concerts. I'm not sure why that is, but I'm guessing it has something to do with hijab being more of a cultural item of clothing than a declaration of faith or a religious statement.

I never used to notice stuff like this until I actually started thinking about wearing hijab, which wasn't until the day I boarded the plane to get here. In London, even though there is a pretty diverse Muslim community, I never really felt like I was a good enough Muslim to be an ambassador of Islam. And trust me, in hijab that's what you are. Everyone watches to see what you're doing and you get labelled as that 'Muslim girl' rather than the 'Indian girl' or the 'short girl' or any other part of your identity.

When I was mulling over the job offer I had received after applying for a few teaching positions across the globe, I made a conscious decision to be a better Muslim if I could. A kind of thank you to God for giving me the chance to start afresh in a new country with a pretty decent tax-free salary. I still haven't been able to take the plunge though. Every other day I take out the few cottons scarves I brought with me, and I wrap one around my head and wonder if I have the guts to go out like that. So far, I haven't been able to muster the courage, and to be honest, it's not just because I don't know if I'm a good enough Muslim, but also because I look so plain without my hair on display. My auburn locks are probably my best feature and without them visible, I'm just like any other plain Jane on the street.

I turn my attention back to the people around me, and my eyes fall on a group of girls and guys playing volleyball. I can't help but feel a slight twang of envy. Not because of what they're doing as I'm pathetic at all forms of physical exertion, but because they're having such a great time while I'm sitting here alone, watching on like the outsider that I am.

'Hey, wanna join us?' a girl calls out, catching my gaze and probably noticing the desperation in my eyes. She jogs up to me and I try not to ogle at her body in case she can see my stare through my Primark sunglasses and thinks I'm a lesbian or something. Her body is so golden, lean, and toned that I make a spur of the moment decision to join the gym and start exercising.

'Yeah, why not?' I reply, my mind still thinking of ways I can fix up my wobbly body, and before I know it I'm in the middle of this group of ten girls and guys, trying to play volleyball.

I don't hit the ball even once. It's pretty hard to when you run in the opposite direction as soon as it comes your way or worse, hold up your hands to shield your face. The opposition is too kind to exploit their enemy's weakest link and try hard not to let the ball come my way. So for the rest of the game I end up just standing around wishing I was wearing stronger sunblock and trying not to check out the hot guy opposite me. Which isn't easy, considering he has a golden body and instead of the usual coal coloured hair distinctive of most Arab men, his is a dark brown with stray strands of honey. With his intense eyes and strong yet gentle hands, he is definitely bad news for me.

Despite not really moving much, I feel exhausted when the game slowly rolls to an end. The goddess, who I found out is called Jennifer, saunters up to me and invites me to meet the group in the evening for some dinner and shisha. My tiredness disappears and I agree before the offer is taken away, like a child who has just been told she can have ice-cream for breakfast.

The taxi drops me off at Reem al Bawadi, a Lebanese restaurant that makes the Arabesque eateries in London's Edgware Road look bland in comparison. The exterior is lit up with twinkling fairy lights and as I walk up the short steps, I feel my heart pounding against my ribcage.

This is the first time I've properly gone out in the three weeks I've been here, and I feel like I've almost forgotten how to socialize. It's actually been *months* since I've voluntarily gone out with people. The only time I left my house in London was to go to my fortnightly Job Seeker's Allowance (JSA) appointment, and even in Delhi, when I wasn't holed up in my cousin's flat, wallowing in my self-induced misery, I was out on the balcony doing the exact same thing.

Taking a deep breath, I push open the door and step inside. The restaurant's interior is done up in typical Middle Eastern style with climbers dangling from its walls and ceiling, old Middle Eastern ornaments adorning every corner, live Arabic music accompanied by the faint hum of voices, and fragrant wisps of apple shisha wafting through the air. The atmosphere is so warm and reminiscent of how I imagine sticky summers in Beirut to be like, that I slowly begin to relax.

I spot the group and navigate my way around tables, chairs, and glass shishas, praying that I don't knock one over. I feel slightly awkward as I mumble 'hi' in a timid voice but even that melts away as Jennifer jumps up and exclaims, 'Sugar, hi, how are you?' in a loud, friendly voice and plants the customary kisses on my cheeks. I shake hands with everyone else and sit down at the nearest available seat. As soon as I sit down on the chair, bumping into my neighbour and almost knocking over a tall glass of a crazy looking fruit cocktail, I realize I'm sitting next to Goldenboy.

'Ahlan,' he says, smiling warmly.

It's the first time he's spoken to me. He's wearing a black shirt with jeans, and his beautiful tan, contrasting against his shirt, looks simply delicious. I look away, guilt gnawing at me. How could I even feel the slightest attraction for another man after all that happened? What kind of a shameless person am I? It hasn't even been two years.

'Thanks,' I reply stupidly, not knowing how else to reply to the greeting. 'Ahlan' means 'welcome' right? He is obviously confused by my answer.

'Keefik? Shu akhbarik?' he tries again, frowning slightly. Not with condescension, but befuddlement.

'Um…ana la atakallam al arabiya,' (I don't speak Arabic) I answer sheepishly in classical Qur'anic Arabic.

Jennifer, who overhears the awkward exchange, bursts into peals of laughter and explains something to the group in fast, incomprehensible Arabic, and soon they are all laughing.

'Sorry,' Goldenboy says with a grin. 'I thought you were Arab. You look Palestinian.'

'It's okay,' I reply with a shrug, secretly feeling thrilled. For some reason, I don't want him to know I'm Indian. I just want to be me, Sugar, without all those extra labels.

We don't say much else to each other through the rest of the evening and although I'm glad to be with people other than my host family, it's hard trying to have fun when everyone around you speaks a language you don't understand, and never had any connection with outside the mosque. Sometimes they look at my blank face and remember to translate jokes and anecdotes, and I force a laugh, a lot of the meaning and humour lost in translation.

That night as I lie in my bed, the drum beats still ringing in my ears, I feel a sudden pang of longing for my friends back home. I miss Yasmin's quirkiness, Farah's craziness, and Shakira's wit. But it was all my fault that I had to leave everything I had ever known.

Beneath the ache and the disorientation though, there is a warm comfort that heats up my entire being. I fall asleep thinking of Goldenboy's beautiful, copper coloured eyes with the tiniest specks of amber. And for the first time in almost two years, my sleep is uninterrupted. I don't wake up crying.

4

Leila suppresses a yawn as politely as possible as the fifty-three-year-old banker sitting opposite her bores her with 'witty' tales from the banking industry. He drones on and on, completely oblivious to the blank look on her face, the emptiness in her eyes, and the slump of her shoulders.

The date started off promisingly. He picked her up in a black BMW 7 series which may not be the calibre she has experienced before, but was just about good enough. He took her to Zheng He's—the Chinese restaurant at the Madinat Jumeirah—and booked a table outside, which boasts spectacular views of the Burj al Arab, illuminated in the warm, night sky. It wasn't the trendiest of venues, but was classy enough. Another box is mentally ticked. She can't decipher the cut of his dark grey suit and is unsure whether it is designer or not, but at this stage she doesn't really care. She may be desperate for a husband but unless he is filthy rich, she will never put up with such a selfish dinner partner who refuses to at least try and make an effort to be polite and charming. In Leila's opinion, men who aren't in the private jet league have no right to be so mind-numbingly boring.

'Excuse me,' she manages to say as soon as there is a pause in his monologue, and gets up to go to the restroom. 'I'll be back in just a moment.'

'No problem, sweetheart,' he drools, staring at her plunging neckline with his beady, blue eyes decorated with wrinkles. At fifty-three, he is older than most of the men she has ever dated but still far from her secret cut-off mark of fifty-nine and a half.

She narrows her eyes at him, smoothes down her beige knee-length cashmere skirt, and stalks off to the restroom in relief. She can feel his eyes on her ass and she wiggles it a little bit more. After all, he isn't going to get anything else tonight so he may as well get a good look at her infamous Lebanese trunk full of junk.

Plenty of heads turn as she saunters across the restaurant; the men appreciative and the women constantly looking for flaws or praying for her to stumble and reveal old, greying knickers. Or worse, flesh coloured Spanx.

Men always watch Leila move. Her walk is graceful and seductive, her shoulders always pulled back, and her head held up high. She moves as if she's walking the ramp in Milan, not across a restaurant, mall, or beach in Dubai. Leila is not overtly beautiful; her lips are a little bit too big (too much collagen), her nose is a little bit too sharp (an over-enthusiastic cosmetic surgeon), and her eyebrows are a tad too thin (no one to blame but herself). However, her big, blonde hair (courtesy of a fabulous hair stylist), smooth skin (La Mer and monthly glycolic peels), double Ds (a souvenir from Beverly Hills), and a firm behind (her maternal genes) more than compensate for her aesthetically-off facial features.

As soon as she is away from everyone's scrutiny, Leila whips out her mobile phone and hits speed dial number eight—her equivalent of 999.

'Sup shorty,' Lady Luxe drawls, answering almost immediately. 'It's only 10 pm so he's either tried groping your ass a little too early or he's taken you for a street-side shawarma. It's not good, is it?'

'It's not!' Leila whispers, afraid that the Old Fart may be skulking around outside the door, listening. She remembers that he isn't creative enough to think of something so adventurous, and he isn't Arab either, so the chances of him stalking her are very thin. She clears her throat and speaks at a normal pitch.

'Ya'ani…he's…just…so…boring!' she finally splutters, at a loss for a better adjective.

'That's it? Come on, habibti, you've dated worse,' Lady Luxe reminds her with a laugh. 'Remember the one who tried to impress you by…'

'I remember!' Leila snaps. 'But you don't understand. He's not only ridiculously boring, he's a pervert and keeps trying to stare down my blouse. I need to get out of here quickly!'

'Fine, I'll arrange something. Go back to the table and order some dessert for a change. It might sweeten you up. What's his name again? Or his phone number?'

'Old Fart,' Leila answers quickly and then hangs up. Re-applying her signature deep red Bobbi Brown lipstick and blotting her slightly greasy nose, she quickly checks for food lurking around in her bright, white teeth (courtesy of the Smile Clinic) and heads out of the restroom with dread. Directly outside the door stands a tall, handsome local man with a gleam in his small eyes.

'Marhaba,' he drawls in a deep voice, slowly looking her up and down and absorbing the curve of her hips, her tiny waist, and the swell of her chest.

'Hello,' she replies, quickly assessing him. His pristine white candoura is gleaming almost as much as his eyes, and he's wearing a Tag Heuer watch, and there is no wedding ring in sight.

'Here's my business card. Call me.' It's not a question, but a statement, and before Leila can reply, he stalks off leaving behind a faint scent of Oud. Not sure whether to be affronted by his assumption or complimented by the interest, she slips the card into her Gucci clutch (courtesy of a previous conquest, the Generous Geriatric) and drags herself back to her table.

Almost as soon as she sits down though, Old Fart's phone begins to ring and she sits up straight, her ears perking up with interest. He answers nonchalantly but his face quickly turns red with rage. Hanging up abruptly and spluttering something about an emergency, he gestures for the bill.

'I'm so sorry dear, but something has come up,' he says vaguely while signing the cheque. 'Here, take a taxi home.' He throws a hundred-dirham note on the table and disappears, leaving Leila half relieved and half pissed off. She hates taxis.

⊷

Half an hour later, Leila is sitting in Barasti with Lady Luxe, who is in her 'Jennifer' disguise—a long blonde wig and blue contact lenses—sipping a colourful cocktail and ignoring the feeling of disappointment from yet another bad date. She is one of the very few people who knows about Lady Luxe's alter-ego and is fully aware of her privilege. Although she is happy that she is trusted with the knowledge, she does wonder if she will ever have to use it as leverage. She hopes not. Despite the ten-year age difference (which she will never ever admit to, having gone to the length of swearing on her dead grandmother's grave, may God bless her soul, that she is still twenty-six), the difference in social status, upbringing, and religion, she actually likes Lady Luxe and enjoys her company. She's a lot less pretentious than the majority of her friends and despite her craziness, her heart is usually in the right place. They also have completely different tastes in men; Lady Luxe is still young enough to care solely about looks and charm, and thankfully the 'hoes over bros' philosophy has never had to be tested.

'So what did you do to get the Old Fart running out of Madinat Jumeirah like his wife's in labour?' Leila asks.

'I got his wife to call.' Lady Luxe shrugs nonchalantly, looking around her for potential meals in the form of sexy men.

'He has a *wife*?' Leila splutters, choking on her drink. 'The lying bastard! He told me he's divorced!'

'He is. Three times. But he's also married to the daughter of some Iranian businessman who knows my brother.' Lady Luxe spots her dinner and smiles cheekily at a tall, broad man on the other side of the bar. He smiles back at her and she averts her gaze. Her rule is to only make eye contact with a man once until he musters up the courage to talk to her.

Leila sighs as embarrassment washes over her, willing her face not to turn pink in shame. She has been in Dubai for nearly a decade and she still isn't able to spot the winners from the losers, the honest from the deceitful. The single from the married. Her last serious boyfriend turned out to be all three. A wealthy local businessman, he wooed her with orchids on her doorstep every Friday, lazy cruises aboard his private yacht in the weekends, and deeper into their six-month relationship, spontaneous weekend trips to the Shangri La Barr Al Jissah in Oman. Leila hadn't found it unusual that he never introduced her to his family—Arab men rarely did until they were ready to get married—and nor did she find it strange that he was always working. Maybe she just didn't want to read the signs; the way he would never let her look through his phone, the way he was never free on a Friday, and the way he would suddenly become withdrawn, his mind clearly preoccupied with something he would refuse to talk about. She was just too busy hoping he would be The One to take these signs seriously.

They broke up after Leila had received a hysterical phone call from a woman who swore by her entire clan, ancestors and descendents, that if Leila married her husband and became his second wife, she would poison her in her sleep. She never told any of her friends, including Lady Luxe, what the real reason for their break up was. Even now, she still pretends that she had grown bored of the tall, handsome, wealthy, and charming Emirati. She also resolved never to date a local guy again.

She has a sneaking suspicion that Lady Luxe, with her ability to find out everything—from how many fillings a man has to how many women he has slept with—knows the truth but hasn't told her for fear of hurting her, and for this, she is thankful. She hates being at anyone's mercy, hates appearing weak or vulnerable.

When Leila moved to Dubai, a brunette with a wonky nose, blemished skin, and B cup breasts, she never expected that she would grow into the kind of woman that needs a husband in order to feel accomplished. She thought that having a successful career and driving a BMW 3 series would be enough to make her feel content until Sheikh Charming came along. Over the years though, as most of her friends have settled down and started families, she has been feeling more and more alone. Dubai is, after all, a lonely, transitory place. It's hard to maintain relationships when people are always coming and going.

It is also full of temptation for men. The Las Vegas of the Middle East, women are available in all shapes and sizes and many are willing to sell their souls, not to mention their bodies, for the slightest bit of financial stability. The competition is tough for all women with high standards.

Towards the end of the evening, Lady Luxe disappears after receiving a booty call, and Leila decides to go back to her one-bedroom apartment in Discovery Gardens. Alone.

She walks into her empty apartment with tired eyes and a throbbing head. She longs for quiet evenings curled up on the sofa, leaning against a husband while they argue over what to watch on TV. She's had a lot of time to visualize her fantasies in detail. In her dream she's wearing pink cotton pyjamas and he's in shorts and a t-shirt.

She stands under the shower, trying to let the water numb the pain of having no one by her side. She goes through the motions of scrubbing her body clean with Bodyshop exfoliating scrubs, lathering her skin with moisturizer, and carefully applying a dab of Crème De La Mer to her face, careful not to use too much for fear of it running out too soon, and rubbing cream onto her feet, which are tired of being squeezed into tiny heels. Her beauty regime completed, she shuffles into her queen-sized bed in an old, faded white nightshirt. Face barren of makeup, she looks strangely innocent and young.

It takes her over an hour to eventually fall into a restless slumber.

5

As Lady Luxe looks down at the American Convert, admiring the hard lines on his body, she has the strangest urge to climb back into bed with him. She's not quite sure why she is wasting her time with someone she has absolutely no desire to have a future with, but there is something exciting about taking that which doesn't belong to her. And he tries so hard to please her. So when she is at a loss for a better way to spend the evening, she agrees to a little under (the) cover action.

Although it isn't the best she's had, there is something comforting about his droopy eyes and slight arms, and she enjoys being in his embrace. There was a tricky moment during the session though, when he became a little too enthusiastic and grabbed a fistful of her seven-thousand-dirham golden wig, which turned lopsided on her head. In his passion, he didn't notice and she quickly pulled it back into place, mentally cursing herself for having such a ridiculous disguise in the first place.

In that moment, fear crept inside her and the nagging voice that bugged her during the quiet hours of the night reminded her that her luck would eventually run out. What if he had pulled it off altogether and then recounted the story of the Arab brunette with the yellow wig to all his friends? Gossip spread like thrush in Dubai, and if even a whisper got out she would have no choice but to kill 'Jennifer'.

Carefully lifting his arm off her back, she slides out of bed. As she does, she catches sight of herself in his floor length mirror. Mascara smudged, wig askew, she looks like a Russian prostitute in the cold white light illuminating the room from the adjoining bathroom. She pulls on her skinny jeans and tight, white sleeveless top, stuffs her feet into her purple metallic Manolos, and hurries out of the eighteenth-floor apartment in Dubai Marina. As she passes the reception area, she makes sure to look completely straight ahead, familiar with the smirk that is likely to be on the security guard's face, and not in the mood to acknowledge it.

On her way back to Jumeirah in her nondescript black Porsche Cayenne Turbo with the equally nondescript five-number license plate (after all, no one forgets a double digit plate), Lady Luxe stops on a quiet road in Um Suqeim, retrieves her abaya from the back seat, and slowly puts it on. Removing the blonde wig from her hair, she places it in a plastic bag and leaves it in the back of the car, her handbag too stuffed to accommodate it. She takes out the prescription-free, purely cosmetic blue contact lenses, pops a mint into her mouth, and sprays a generous dose of 'Midnight Oud'—the new fragrance by Romano Ricci's quirky perfume brand, Juliette Has a Gun—all over herself. After meeting him at a fashion party in Paris, she has fallen in love with his charm and only ever wears his perfumes. During the day she is 'Miss Charming', in a club she is 'Lady Vengeance', and on a date 'Citizen Queen'. However, whenever she has to be herself—Lady Luxe—she opts for 'Midnight Oud', a mysterious, sexy fragrance infused with sandalwood, amber, and saffron.

Rubbing away the mascara from under her eyes, she reapplies her lip gloss and then continues her journey home, tuning in to Radio One as she always does, pleased to find her favourite presenter, Sheena, mixing old hip hop beats with newer pop numbers. The clock reads 2:45 and she is surprised as she had assumed it was far later.

Although she is thankful that her father is still away on business, her older brother, Mohamed, may be back from an evening entertaining voluptuous Moroccan women, and she has to be careful not to let him suspect that her own adventures are far more daring than his.

Passing through the security gates of her sprawling villa, she feels her heart shudder when she spots the study light on. Only her father ever enters the study at night. Parking between Mohamed's orange E-class Mercedes AMG, and her younger brother Ahmed's run-of-the-mill Nissan Patrol, she turns off the engine and takes a deep breath before getting out the car. She winces at the shrill beep when she locks it, acutely aware of every rustle around her, and wishes she wasn't in heels that will undoubtedly clatter across the marble hallway.

'Meno hni?' a deep voice calls out the moment her heels hit the floor, echoing in the sparse hallway.

'It's me,' she replies in English, her pace quickening as she makes for the stairs that are in the centre of the foyer, splitting into two at the top. He wasn't due back for another three days; even his PA had confirmed that he wouldn't be back until mid-week when she called her the day before.

'Come here,' her father says, his voice laced with ice.

Shit.

Taking another long breath, Lady Luxe composes herself and begins creating the stories she will have to tell. She enters the study and is engulfed by the intoxicating scent of bakhoor. A contrast to the rest of the contemporary décor in the spacious, airy villa, the study is painted a dark maroon and is lined with floor-to-ceiling mahogany bookshelves, full of first editions in Arabic and English. Her father is sitting on a large, dark green leather armchair smoking a cigar. He gestures for her to sit down on an identical chair next to him.

'Salam'alaikom, Baba,' she says, smiling brightly and sitting down at his desk facing him.

'Alaikom salam,' he replies, without looking at her.

They sit in silence for a while as he continues to inhale and exhale his cigar, and Lady Luxe wishes she could ask him for a draw herself as her palms begin to sweat.

'What is the time?' he asks after a while, finally turning his face to look at her.

'Almost 3 am,' she replies confidently.

'And what were you doing roaming the streets until Al Fajr?'

'I went to Maryam Al X's home. She has some ideas for my business.' At the mention of her business, Lady Luxe sees her father soften. Disappointed in Mohamed for not having a single entrepreneurial bone in his body, he is secretly proud of his daughter for creating an abaya label, putting together a business plan, securing funding (albeit from him), and gaining a steady stream of returning customers.

'What ideas does she have?'

Lady Luxe stares at her father, unsure as to what to say. Her pulse racing and her mind struggling to keep up, she keeps a straight face, well aware that she is hugging her bag to her chest so tightly that her fists are turning white.

'Lots,' she manages to say airily. 'She told me about her friend who is a website designer who can create a website for me, so we spent some time researching websites and so on. She also thinks that I need to cater to an international clientele.

You know, Khaleejis living in London or the US who wear the abaya, and she has a contact in London who can help me.'

'So you spent five hours talking about these two points?' Lady Luxe's father looks at her straight in the eyes and she looks back at him, anxious not to break her gaze and reveal her guilt.

'Of course not!' she laughs, still holding on to her bag for support. 'Baba, you know us girls. First we had dinner; they made delicious homemade pizza which I *have* to get the recipe for. Claudine's pizza is really lacking. Then we were chatting about...you don't want to know the details of who wore what to whose party do you?' She flashes her father a big smile and he visibly relaxes. She doesn't though. She is familiar with her father's temper and what he is capable of doing if his boundaries are pushed.

'Fine, but you know how I feel about you coming home late.'

'I know, Baba, and I'm sorry. I would have called you but I knew you were away, and you know how Mohamed is. He hates it when I disturb him when he's out so I didn't want to have to deal with that.' She continues gripping her bag, scared that if she releases her hands, they will start shaking. If she gives her father the slightest hint that she is less confident than she appears, he will be sure to pounce on her hesitation like a lion on its prey.

'Let me see your handbag,' he suddenly demands after a pause.

Shocked, Lady Luxe's mouth falls open slightly. 'Why?' she asks, buying time, her mind spinning as she tries to work out what is in it. Although she is relieved that she left the wig in the car, she still doesn't know what other incriminating objects may be lurking around in the depths of her large and very full Birkin. She's positive that there is a packet of Marlboro Lights somewhere amongst the makeup, spare shoes, sunshade, and spare sheyla, and she prays with every ounce of her being that there are no condoms.

'Because you have been clutching on to it like a mother with her newborn, and I am curious as to why you are so worried that I will see what is inside.'

'I'm not worried. I'm holding it because it's stuffed full of rubbish and I don't want everything to spill out.' *I really don't want everything to spill out.*

'Then hand it over. Let me see what you girls are carrying around with you these days and why you insist on lugging such huge bags with you.' His voice is jolly but Lady Luxe recognizes the hardness behind the façade and wordlessly hands it over.

She watches her father rummage through it with her breath stuck in her throat, and for the first time in her life she is thankful that it is full of junk. As he looks through the fabric samples, leaflets, jewellery and shoes, almost immediately, he comes across a pair of flimsy knickers. He withdraws his hand as if he has been burnt, and thrusts the bag back at her. Lady Luxe releases the air in her lungs. Her breath now steady, her heart rate slowing down, she feels indignant that her father has the audacity to question her like that, and the more she thinks about it the more annoyed she feels.

'I can't believe you did that, Baba,' she says, feeling a lot stronger knowing that he is now embarrassed. 'You see why I didn't want my things to fall out?'

'Be quiet,' he snaps. 'I don't care if you're working on your business, you are a lady and you will behave like one. If you wish to stay out later than 1 am, you will inform me or Mohamed of your exact whereabouts. Go to your room.'

She does, relief pouring out of every pore. As soon as she gets to her bedroom, she empties her bag onto her four poster bed. She finds a single, foil-wrapped condom as well as a tiny plastic bag of weed. She flushes them both down the toilet in her en-suite bathroom, her heart beginning to work overtime again. It was only her bag this time, but what if her father decided to check her phone the next? Although she has two, one for business, family, and friends, and another unregistered one for fun, he can easily come across the wrong one if he decides to make a habit of looking through her things.

Making space on her bed, she sits crossed legged, still in her abaya, and opens her 'fun' inbox. Her face turns pale as she comes across hundreds of dirty text messages from countless guys. She hits 'delete all' and decides to delete every new message which comes through. She does the same with the sent messages.

Tonight she has been lucky. But she knows that it's only a matter of time—or in her case, an investigative father—before her luck runs out.

6

Lady Luxe lazily opens her eyes and stretches out on her bed, enjoying the sensation of the soft, 100 percent pure Egyptian cotton sheets against her skin. For a moment, she forgets who she is, who she's expected to be, and who she wants to be, as she relishes the warmth of the glorious morning sun on her arms. The fear she felt when falling asleep has faded away entirely and she is already wondering what devilish acts she should commit after sunset. But before she does, she has business to attend to. Last week, she received a call from a woman who wanted a customized abaya.

Lady Luxe, unlike most couture abaya designers, offers a bespoke service which allows her customers to create their own abayas with her guidance. This freedom to play with her existing designs makes her popular with women looking for something unique and personal. Bounding out of bed, she has a shower and then wanders downstairs in three-quarter length white pyjama trousers and a shrunken pink French Connection t-shirt, which exposes a tiny sliver of torso. She is reluctant to get rid of it because it makes her feel like a teenager.

'Sabah al khair,' Mohamed mutters as she enters the bright, spacious kitchen. Very contemporary with its custom made Italian units, it looks like it belongs in a catalogue, and is nothing like the cluttered and cosy kitchen of her childhood.

'Good morning yourself,' she answers, sitting opposite him on the centre island counter, watching him devour his homemade waffles, courtesy Claudine—their competent European cook. 'Had a good night?'

'Yes.' He continues eating and flicking through the newspaper without looking at her.

'What did you do?' she tries again.

'I went out with my friends.'

'Where did you go?'

'What the hell is up with these questions? Are you mutawwa or something?' He finally looks up at her and scowls. 'You need new pyjamas. You look indecent.'

'Why? It's not as if there are strange guys here.'

Frowning, she takes a bite of the homemade waffles smothered in whipped cream, hot chocolate sauce, and fresh strawberries on the side. She has given up trying to be friends with Mohamed. He is only three years older than her but she feels as if there is a deep chasm between them. He is wearing a beige candoura and his briefcase sits on the stool next to him, almost as if it too were a very important person.

They sit in silence for a while, Lady Luxe enjoying the buttery fragrance of the waffles and Mohamed reading *Al Bayan*—the Arabic daily newspaper favoured by the Ruler—while Claudine tidies up after them, moving through the black and white kitchen like a mini tornado. He suddenly looks up, a sneer on his face.

'My friend took your number for his mother who wants something designed,' he begins. 'You're meeting her today, I heard. Don't mess it up. I don't want to be embarrassed in front of him.'

Lady Luxe stares at him. In just one year she has created and launched a successful fashion label, has showcased at the Dubai Fashion Week, has designed over fifty customized abayas as well as two ready-to-wear collections, and has made a tidy profit for herself. She is also in the process of signing a contract with the founders of X Boutique, who want to sell both her SS and AW collections. And half of this she managed to do while in London, flying back and forth for appointments and shows.

'Says the guy whose career in government is as menial and unimaginative as his noo noo,' she mumbles in Arabic under her breath, fuming. She is half-inclined to intentionally destroy the woman's abaya just to embarrass him.

'What did you say?' Mohamed growls, grabbing her wrist from across the counter and squeezing it hard. Although not obviously buff, his hours at the gym have paid off, and he can easily break Lady Luxe's arm in two. She winces at the force of his grip.

'Nothing!' she says defiantly. She doesn't have enough time to cover any bruises with concealor and foundation again with her client arriving in less than an hour.

'Good,' he says, letting go of her wrist and shoving her arm away from him as if it were contagious. Pushing his plate to one side, he leaves it for their maid Anna-Marie to clear up and exits the villa.

'Have a good day, habibi,' Lady Luxe calls out after him. Now that he has gone, she allows herself to rub her sore wrist, and asks Claudine for some ice in order to numb the tenderness.

Breakfast done, she changes into a pretty Tara Jarmon dress, sprays herself with 'Miss Charming', and scans her workspace to ensure everything is in place.

Previously a guest bedroom, her office is elegant and luxurious with its three off-white walls and black and white patterned feature wall. Together with the black velvet sofas, chrome bookcases, and turquoise and purple accessories, it is exactly how she always envisioned it to be. Her sketchbook and look book are out on the glass coffee table, next to the artfully arranged fresh lilies, which arrive every three days. On the opposite end of the room by the bay window, are the silver mannequins wearing her latest designs, while the closet is full of the older collections. Her coveted Abaya Designer of the Year award sits proudly on the marble mantelpiece, and next to it is the framed photo of her receiving it. She also has a file with cuttings from all the magazines and newspapers, which have featured her as a 'bright young thing'. These she likes to look through every once in a while.

'Miss Lady Luxe, Madame X is here,' says Anne-Marie, who always doubled up as her assistant whenever she has clients over.

'Salam'alaikom, khalti,' Lady Luxe greets the forty-something, robust woman with three kisses and gestures for her to take a seat.

They sip cardamom qahwa and browse the look book together, creating an abaya with the tiniest smattering of real pearls, talking fashion, beauty, travelling, and even social issues. Madame X's comments and suggestions impress Lady Luxe, and for once, she feels honoured to cater to the needs of such a charming and intelligent client. After two hours, Madame X has been measured, has chosen her fabric, and will come back in two weeks for a fitting when the abaya has been made.

Tired but exhilarated, Lady Luxe picks up her BlackBerry and BBMs Leila. Her father is away once again and will not be back for three days. She is, however, slightly wary and to ensure there isn't a repeat of last night's episode she sends both him and Mohamed a quick SMS saying she'll be out late.

That evening Lady Luxe meets Leila at the Cavalli Club. Having attended the opening party and exchanged business cards with Roberto himself, Lady Luxe isn't as impressed as Leila by the decadent, Swarovski studded interior. In an ode to its namesake, she is wearing a hot pink short, flowery Cavalli dress, which shows off her small cleavage and long, toned legs. Together with three-inch strappy Cavalli sandals in gold and her blonde wig, she looks lithe and sophisticated. With Leila by her side in a tiny black sheath dress, her hair tumbling down her back in loose curls and her eyes rimmed in thick kohl, every single man in the club has his eyes on them both. And the girls know it.

'So, what's the latest on Old Fart?' Lady Luxe asks as they sit in a small booth with a perfect view of the entrance.

'He called me a couple of times but I've been ignoring him,' Leila replies with a scowl.

'Loser,' they both say in unison and then smile at each other.

'Well, here's to the better hammour fish in the Gulf pacific,' Lady Luxe toasts, holding up her martini. They clink glasses, take delicate sips, and then survey the talent.

Lady Luxe spots a potential, and though she usually steers clear of Arab guys, she is willing to make an exception for him. Well over six-feet, with dark brown, messy hair and a complexion slightly fairer than hers, she guesses him to be Lebanese. She tells herself that this doesn't really count as Arab anyway. He looks young, around twenty-seven and she glances over at Leila hoping that she hasn't spotted him. She sighs in relief when she realizes Leila is preoccupied with the contents of her signature Gucci clutch.

'Okay, I've spotted a potential and I've seen him first,' she declares. As she does, Mr Delicious catches her gaze and flashes her a wide smile. He's wearing a plain white shirt over faded jeans and trainers, and she wonders how he managed to get in dressed like that. She shoots him a small, shy smile back and then looks away. *Let the games begin*, she thinks to herself with excitement.

'Hmm, yes, he is nice but far too boyish for me,' Leila says after checking him out. Busy trying to make eye contact with Lady Luxe, he doesn't even look at Leila, and she feels a twang of envy. Not at the way Lady Luxe looks—she knows she is far, far sexier—but because her youth is silently slipping away. Too boyish equals *too young*. She sighs and rummages around for her phone.

Having made eye contact a couple of times with Lady Luxe, Mr Delicious feels confident enough to introduce himself, and after saying something to his less fabulous friend, starts heading in their direction. Lady Luxe averts her gaze, pretending not to notice his approach, and instead says in a loud, overly-English accent as soon as he is within earshot, 'Yes, I totally agree that the UAE government needs to be made aware of the situation.'

Leila stares at her and Lady Luxe stares back, opening her eyes wider, trying to get the message across.

'What situation?' Leila asks stupidly.

'Yes, yes, I fully comprehend what you are saying,' she replies, almost shouting and nudging her sharply. 'IT REALLY IS A COMPLEX ISSUE THAT I BELIEVE WILL BE RESOLVED!'

'I DON'T THINK YOU DO COMPREHEND WHAT I'M SAYING,' Leila shouts back in confusion.

When Mr Delicious coughs and looks down at them, realization finally dawns and Leila hurriedly exclaims the poshest thing she can think of.

'Rightly so!' she yells in a strange accent and a massive smile. 'Gosh, you really are intelligent.'

'Good evening ladies, may I partake in this riveting discussion?' Mr Delicious asks, raising an eyebrow.

'We would be delighted to invite you to join us but I'm afraid the conversation was confidential,' Lady Luxe purrs, moving up to let him sit beside her.

Their thighs brush as he does and she gets a whiff of his cologne. Her stomach begins to tingle and a shiver runs down her spine. No man has had this effect on her in a long time and unlike most men he looks even better up close. His jaw line is sharp, his eyelashes thick, and his body seems to be tight and toned under the fitted shirt.

As the night progresses, Lady Luxe finds herself slowly becoming more and more drawn to him. They talk solely in English, so she still hasn't worked out where he is from, and his American accent hasn't revealed much either, given the number of American schools in Dubai.

The three of them laugh and joke together like old friends as they talk about books, films, music, and Dubai, with Mr Delicious' friend appearing ever so often to say a few words before disappearing back into the darkness for some ambiguous 'business'. When the DJ finally starts playing R&B, Mr Delicious stands up and pulls Lady Luxe to dance by their table since there isn't really a dance floor. She is conflicted as they start moving to the music—half of her desperately wanting to grind against him and re-enact Usher's 'Love in the Club', and the other half anxious for him to respect her and want her for more than just gratification. So instead of giving in to her wantonness, she dances prettily in front of him, careful not to shake her derrière too vigorously.

Towards the end of the night and countless drinks later, Mr Delicious takes Lady Luxe's phone from her hand and stores his phone number in it himself.

'I never ask for a lady's number,' he explains, 'and a real lady will never give it anyway. So here you go, Princess, the ball's in your court.' With that, he shakes her and Leila's hands gently, bids them farewell and disappears, leaving both girls in complete awe but also a little surprised. It's not normal for a decent Arab guy to just leave two girls alone in a club without offering to drive them home, or at the very least, seeing them to a taxi.

Lady Luxe watches his retreating back, her body on fire. She can't believe that they have spent an entire evening together and she doesn't know anything about him other than his name, the music he listens to, and the movies he likes.

Leila too, is stunned. Although Mr Delicious is very clearly uninterested in her, the few times he stared into her eyes, she felt a stirring in the pit of her stomach. She has never gone for 'boyish' boys before—that is Lady Luxe's style—but this one is charming, witty, friendly, and funny…and she also spotted a Rolex on his left wrist.

Half an hour later they are ready to leave, and Lady Luxe feels an odd pang of loneliness now that Mr Delicious has gone. They go to the restroom briefly and she hands over her Hermes clutch for Leila to hold while she pees. Leila takes out her best friend's phone from the clutch, scrolls through the contact list, and commits Mr Delicious' number to memory.

Just in case.

7

I don't know how I got through my first month at the English language institute with my sanity intact. Name learning, playing embarrassing ice-breaking games, and sitting in utter boredom during my lunch break with my dry sandwiches (the bread in Dubai is awful) in my hands and my iPod glued to my ears, is pretty much all I did.

Teaching English out here isn't much different from teaching it in the UK, except in London more than half my classes would be made up of Japanese students, and here, more than half are Arabs. I also had a pretty even ratio of men and women in my old class, but here my class consists mainly of men, who, once they got over the fact that I was Indian, began to notice my glossy hair and bright smile. I now have around six admirers who are constantly vying for my attention by cracking lame jokes and generally disrupting my class.

Alhamdulillah, I've made it to the end of the month, and I've received my very first salary.

I've also bought some new clothes, and now I'm getting ready to go and meet my one and only friend.

Yes, I have a friend! My best friend in London, Yasmin, has an older sister here in Dubai, and I met up with Nadia the day after I went out with that volleyball crowd. Contrary to the initial wariness of hanging out with my best mate's older sister, I actually had a really good time. We had a cheap dinner at the MOE food court due to my lack of funds (halal food everywhere is still a novelty for me so I'm refusing to touch veggies or seafood after twenty-three years of the stuff in London), and just being able to speak English without having to carefully enunciate every letter was amazing. Chilling out with someone who I've known for years and who can relate to more than just who I am, but where I'm from, made my insides warm up.

I was so grateful, that this morning I woke up to pray Fajr, my very first time, to thank God for his mercy. It wasn't easy though. When the alarm went off at four in the morning, I whacked the snooze button so hard that it went flying off my nightstand and crashed into the hard, tiled floor. The bloody thing didn't break though. It went off again ten minutes later, and I covered my head with my pillow in a pitiful attempt to ignore it, muttering profanities under my breath. I eventually dragged myself out of bed, grabbed the alarm and took the batteries out and started climbing back into bed. As I lifted one knee onto the soft mattress, I was conflicted. A part of me wanted to sink back into the warm sheets but the better part kept telling me that now that I had got up, half the battle was won; it was only a matter of a bit of water and a few minutes on the prayer rug and then I could jump back into bed and sleep for as long as I liked. I stood there for a couple of minutes and then I remembered that I had a reason to get up and pray. A shiver ran down my spine and it was enough to shock me out of my slumber.

Bleary eyed, I made my way to the bathroom and splashed cold water on my face. Every ritual I performed, from rinsing my mouth to washing my face, my arms, my feet, made me feel stronger and when I finally stood on the prayer mat, I felt like I wasn't alone. That God was looking after me.

After prayers, instead of going straight to sleep as I had originally planned, I felt inspired to actually move my body a bit. I ended up throwing on jogging bottoms and a baggy, long sleeved t-shirt and went for a walk on JBR beach. As I sat and watched the sunrise, the hues of pinks, reds and oranges all around me, feeling the warm sand between my toes and listening to the sound of the ocean lapping against the shore, I felt completely connected to myself and to my Lord. For the first time in a very long time, I felt there was hope.

The spiritual vibe lasted all the way home, while I ate my breakfast and showered. I did the whole trying-on-hijab thing for the millionth time, but wasn't strong enough to venture out of my bedroom in it.

When I turned on my PC and logged onto Facebook, it fizzled out as soon as I saw that I had a friend request from Goldenboy. I accepted it before the angel in me could persuade me to ignore the temptation, and then spent the next hour browsing through all his pictures, his friends list, and wall comments.

Once I'm done with my chores, I collapse onto the fresh sheets I had just made the bed with, and lie back with my eyes closed, wondering what to do until it's time to get ready to meet Nadia.

It isn't long before my thoughts drift back to Jayden, as they always do whenever I stop forcing them in another direction.

I've tried hard to forget him. To forget his hearty laugh, his deep brown eyes, his ability to make the worst situation seem okay. I've tried to forget the way we first met, when he smiled at me from across the university library. Not perversely mind you, but because I had just tripped over the shoelaces on my silver Adidas trainers. I had clutched the nearest bookcase for support, knocking over a potted plant in the process. The plant fell on the floor, strewing soil all over the carpet. I stared at it, horrified, and then tentatively looked up to see if anyone had noticed the goings on in the west corner. No one had. Except this boy who flashed a bright smile at me, revealing a single, lonely dimple on his right cheek.

I ignored the guy's piercing stare and started stuffing the soil back into the pot, and also attempted straightening the bent leaves, feeling sorry for the poor plant I had almost destroyed.

'Need some help?' A pair of pristine white Nikes stopped in front of me, and I looked up, past the loose jeans, the grey hoodie with the zip undone, past the smooth mocha coloured neck, and finally to that beautiful dimple. My stomach did a somersault.

'Um, n–no thanks, I think I've got it covered,' I stammered, picking up the pot and placing it back on the shelf.

'Alright,' he shrugged, about to turn away, 'but do up your laces before you buckle again. Oh, and nice trainers.'

I watched him swagger away, enthralled by the way his jeans hung perfectly on his hips, amazed by his confidence, and furious with myself for not replying with something remotely witty or interesting. And what was up with that stammer? I'd never stammered in my life. But of course the one time I did, it had to be in front of a gorgeous black guy with trendy clothes and a swagger that would have put Biggie, may god rest his soul, to shame.

I became an ardent library goer. Every day between lectures I'd visit the bright room, and sit in the same place I'd started to call the Plant Debacle, pretending to study. I actually ended up learning quite a lot during this time, with nothing but my books and my fantasies to occupy me.

When I was just about to give up on the library altogether and go back to my usual dossing ways, he reappeared.

'Knock over any plants lately?' he said, as I sat slumped in my chair, reading *Anna Karenina* for my literature class and drawing hearts on the pages.

'No,' I replied, slamming the book shut. I waited a moment to compose myself before I looked up at him and raised an eyebrow as indifferently as I could. 'Offered to help any damsels in distress lately?'

''Course,' he replied, grinning and showing off that dimple once again. 'Some girl dropped her food in the cafeteria yesterday and I offered to eat it off the floor.'

'That's disgusting!' I exclaimed. He started laughing, his laugh so infectious that I couldn't help but join him. It wasn't particularly funny but his fresh fragrance, Davidoff's Cool Water, his long limbs and his silky voice made me giddy with joy and I just couldn't stop laughing.

'If you two can't stop your hysterics then I suggest you leave the library,' the librarian hissed at us from the counter.

Still giggling, I gathered up my books and followed him out to the lawn, ignoring the dirty looks the more serious students were giving us. Placing his things under a tree, he gestured for me to sit beside him. We studied together for the rest of the afternoon. By this I mean I pretended to read *Anna Karenina* while imagining different scenarios of him seducing me on the grass. And him? He took out an Economics book and actually did some work.

Thus began a friendship infused with passion, laughter, and the underlying sense of something brewing deep within.

I'm meeting Nadia at a shisha place called Momo's tonight and I'm really looking forward to some stimulating conversation coupled with the subtle, smoky sweetness of double apple shisha. I'm wearing my one and only abaya, and I must say the layers of long, flowing black cloth really do make me feel like a million dirhams. Slipping it on over my jeans and t-shirt has transformed me from a cute, chubby, and slightly awkward Indian into a slim, graceful, and sophisticated Emirati. I've secured a garish flower clip to my head under the sheyla to give it the height at the back. My fringe has been styled such that it peeks out from under the light scarf and my eyes have been lined with MAC's smoulder eye pencil. I have dumped the usual ballet pumps for my one and only pair of three-inch heels.

Nadia glides up to me, looking like the epitome of Emirati beauty in an abaya scattered with black crystals, lots of mascara and even more glittery lip gloss, and gives me a quick hug and kiss outside Momo's. We laugh at how 'local' we look when neither of us even understand Arabic and walk into the restaurant.

I look around me and absorb the North African inspired décor. The high ceilings are covered with Moroccan lamps of different shapes and sizes, the light from their little holes playing on the burnt orange walls. The DJ is fusing traditional Rai music with pounding hip hop beats. A large projector on the wall is showing an old black and white Arabic movie, although the frames are barely visible in the dim light. And all around us locals, expats, and tourists lounge on low sofas along the walls or at the tables in the middle of the restaurant, puffing shisha or nibbling on Arabic mezzas.

'Gosh this place is stunning,' I say to Nadia in awe, unable to tear my eyes away from the seductive lights. We lean back against the cushions on the low seats and chat away, and I enjoy being able to talk without having to explain my every word or any references to London. I take my phone out to send Nadia some pictures of Yasmin that I have, and when I turn on my Bluetooth it automatically buzzes with an incoming message. Surprised, I look around me to see at least ten people playing with their phones. I ignore it but it buzzes again. Curious to find out what it says, I accept the message and then almost choke on my mocktail.

'Sugar, are you okay?' Nadia asks as I cough and splutter, tears filling my eyes and threatening to smudge the eye make-up I had painstakingly applied.

'Yes,' I gasp. 'Here, check this out.'

Handing over my phone to her, I watch her mouth turn into a huge grin as she reads the message that I know I will never forget.

I whant tel you you are so butfill. The message declares. *Take cer abuot you slef every one he dreem he have one like you 0509190889.*

Nadia cracks up and the two of us try to conceal our guffaws. I don't know what to be more outraged by—the atrocious spellings or the fact that some loser out there has the audacity to send such messages randomly without having the faintest clue as to who might receive them. For the next hour my phone consistently beeps with incoming messages and Nadia and I have a good giggle at the variety. Some send their numbers, some add corny messages, while others are more creative—one guy actually sends a picture of his torso with his number running across the middle. We just don't understand why guys would use Bluetooth to hit on girls they don't even know when they have mouths that can probably do a better job.

Our giggles are interrupted when a couple walk into the shisha lounge, hand in hand. Completely focused on each other, they take a seat in the corner of the room without looking around at all, and we can just about make out their faces in the shadows. I squint at the guy, trying to work out where I've seen him before. He's tall, bald, and slim bordering on skinny. The girl looks like any other white girl at first glance. She is tall, blonde, and is dressed in a tiny white summer dress, with her ample buxom spilling out of it. It makes me a tad annoyed; which part of 'dress respectfully in Dubai' don't these women understand?

The woman laughs and her face alters completely. And that's when I know where I've seen her before. I remember that smile from across a crowded table at Reem al Bawadi. It's Jennifer— the girl who introduced me to Goldenboy.

'Hey I know that girl,' I begin the same time Nadia opens her mouth to speak.

'Oh my God,' Nadia whispers and I look at her face to see that all the blood has drained out of it. I glance back at the couple and realize that the guy is Daniel, *her* Daniel, and the way he is looking at her suggests that their relationship isn't purely platonic. He's leaning across the table, his gaze fixed on her, and a tiny smile on his thin lips.

'Nadia,' I start tentatively, not knowing what to say or do. *Maybe they're just friends,* I tell myself, not wanting to draw conclusions.

'It's okay. I already know about this,' she says with a strained smile. 'I've read all their emails.' She is gripping her glass so tightly that I'm worried it will crack under the pressure.

'Do you want me to go up to them?' I ask, rage beginning to simmer inside me. 'I know her. Maybe she doesn't know he's married.'

'No, don't. I still haven't worked out what I want to do. And she does know.' Nadia's voice is tight and her clenched knuckles have turned white. She is staring at Daniel and Jennifer, watching him laugh with her, feed her some hummous with bread, tuck a stray strand of hair behind her ear.

I feel the pain radiating from her pores and I touch her arm, trying to transfer some of her agony to me. 'Let's go,' I say, unable to watch the two of them anymore.

Nadia agrees and we both get up to go. As we walk out of the restaurant I catch Daniel's eye, and he looks away to see who is with me. I see recognition dawn upon him when he spots Nadia, her gaze fixed straight ahead. He snatches his hand away from Jennifer's bare thigh. But it's too late. And he knows it.

8

Nadia hates herself for fighting for a man she is sharing with someone else, for trying to remind him of all the reasons they got married to begin with, and for desperately hoping that his infatuation with the sexy Jennifer is temporary. But as much as she is furious with herself for giving an undeserving man so much attention, a part of her feels proud that she is trying to salvage her marriage. She actually meant it when she swore 'for better or worse'.

When she was younger, perhaps more idealistic and a lot more naïve, tales of cheating husbands always made her resolve to never allow herself to linger in such a relationship. She was subconsciously brought up to believe that whenever a man did you wrong, you left him and preferably castrated him in the process. After all, that was what her grandmother did. And her mother. Twice. Divorce wasn't a taboo in her family; it was a tradition. Now it was her turn to be tested. Leaving Daniel would be so easy but staying with him would show the world that the women in her family were more than just divorcees.

This determination prevented Nadia from confronting him about the night she saw him with his girlfriend. Her pride stopped her from mentioning what had happened to Sugar during the drive home. She felt embarrassed and naked, as if all of her weaknesses had been exposed and she had nothing to shield herself with.

Sugar being Sugar, however, forced her to talk about what happened.

'I kind of know her, you know,' she admitted, breaking the silence as they drove through Al Sufouh, past the beautiful beachfront palaces belonging to various members of Dubai's royal family.

'Who?' Nadia asked sharply, turning to look at her friend.

'That girl Daniel was with. I don't know her very well but I've been out with her a few times. I have her number and stuff.'

Nadia said nothing.

That night she went home and crawled into bed without even scrubbing her face clean of the layers of makeup she had foolishly thought would repair her confidence and make her feel desirable again. She was convinced that Daniel would continue ignoring her, giving her time to work out her strategy, to assess what she really wanted out of her relationship.

But he didn't give her that time. Instead he came rushing into the apartment soon after and woke her up from her pretend sleep, claiming he had something to confess. Eyes wide with innocence, he told her a long and detailed story of his 'colleague' Jennifer who had just come out of an abusive relationship and needed a shoulder to cry on.

'Did it have to be your shoulder?' Nadia asked in a controlled voice, playing along.

'She has no one else, babe,' he explained earnestly. 'I just wanted to help her out, and I don't know, she was all over me and I didn't know what the hell was going on. I've told her that I can't help her anymore. It's not my place. Honey I'm so so sorry for doing this despite my better judgement. Please forgive me.'

Stunned by the lies her husband had told her so effortlessly, Nadia began to cry. Daniel, mistaking her angry tears as those of forgiveness, cuddled her and kissed away the black streaks running down her face. Soon they were clinging onto each othes bodies and weeping together—a tangle of warm limbs and hot tears. And with every caress, her resolve to hate him slipped away. As their bodies united, she felt like everything was going to be okay. He still wanted to be with her enough to lie about what he had been doing. Surely that was something?

Since then Daniel has come home every evening at 7 pm, an hour after Nadia, giving her just enough time to rustle up a quick pasta dish or stir fry. After dinner they snuggle up together on the large, L-shaped sofa to watch mindless TV, arguing over whether to watch MBC Action or Showseries. They don't talk much but neither minds the long silences. It is better than having to re-assess their relationship and try and figure out a way to save it. They don't make love for the next two nights though, despite Nadia going to bed in silky nightgowns, sexy enough to arouse even the most impotent of men.

On Wednesday, Nadia comes home early from work with a headache so intense that she feels as if her eyes will explode. She takes two painkillers and lies in bed with the curtains drawn until the headache begins to fade. When it does, she makes an effort to walk to the living room where she takes out her laptop, despite knowing that it will probably make her head feel worse.

She performs her usual ritual of checking her email and then her Facebook. *Don't be so masochistic,* she warns herself while entering his password and hovering over the log in button. She pauses for a few seconds chewing on her lower lip. She knows that it will only make herself feel worse. After a little deliberation, however, her curiosity gets the better of her and soon she finds herself opening the latest chapter in the Daniel–Jennifer love story.

It was so lovely seeing you again and I'm really sorry you had to leave so abruptly. Jennifer writes. *I can't stop thinking about you and I'm dying to see you again. Name the place and I'll be there.*

Bitch, Nadia thinks, scowling. *Just take a hint and take a hike.*

I'm sorry for rushing out like that. Daniel replies. *And although I'd love to see you again, things are really hectic at work at the moment so I don't think I'll be able to make the time.*

Nadia's pulse races in excitement. Although he hasn't even come close to ending this relationship with Jennifer, she feels as if she has won a battle.

He's choosing me, she thinks, the smallest smile beginning to play on her lips. She is relieved that she did not confront Daniel and that he has actually chosen her without her forcing the decision on him.

Her sense of peace lasts exactly an hour, after which anger and disappointment start bubbling inside her again. Just because he wasn't seeing her now doesn't mean that she could trust him, that their relationship would be okay in the end, that he would somehow fall in love with her again.

All it meant was that he had had a scare and was temporarily stunned into submission. She recalls Jennifer canoodling Daniel at Momo's, knowing quite well that he had a wife. Where was her sense of morality?

An idea hits her and at first she pushes it away. It is just asking for trouble and more pain. She was already at an emotional disadvantage merely by knowing far too much about her husband's affair. Most women only heard a name, read a text message, or perhaps saw a lipstick stain. Nadia, however, not only knew what the woman looked like, but was also aware of almost every little detail about their relationship. And it was eating away at her insides like a worm making its way through her system, leaving her hollow.

But the more she thinks about it, the more she wants to do it. Knowledge can be a curse. The moment you gain it, you thirst for more.

I'm already messed up, she justifies to herself. *How much worse can it really get?*

Before she can dissuade herself from making what she knows will eventually turn out to be a huge mistake, she takes out her phone and begins to compose a message to Sugar.

I want to meet her, she writes quickly. *I need to know who this woman is, S. It's killing me. I don't want her to know who I am though. Can I just be your friend? Not her lover's wife? Please make it happen. I need this.*

9

Leila hangs up the phone and slumps down on her cream-coloured IKEA sofa, her face in her hands. She stays in this position for ten minutes, her eyes closed, while she tries to regulate her breath. When her face starts feeling hot and sweaty, she slowly gets up, straightens her stained grey vest top and black velour jogging bottoms and shuffles to her fake Chanel handbag that is sitting on the tiny dining table next to a wilting bunch of flowers. She rummages around for her diary, flicks through the pages and when she finds September 14th she writes: 'Lara's Wedding' in tiny letters, pressing down on the page so hard that the imprint can be seen on the following three pages.

Lara, Leila's younger sister, has just been proposed to by her boyfriend of two years. The 2.8 carat solitaire on her finger is so heavy that she was barely able to hold the phone to her ear to tell her sister the good news.

'Mabrouk habibti!' Leila had exclaimed, visibly grimacing and resisting the urge to throw the phone at the wall in front of her. 'I'm so happy for you!'

Now as she stares at the date, which somehow seems more insulting in its written form, Leila fights the urge to collapse into tears. She repeatedly tells herself that she is not a failure. She has a good job, she drives a nice car, owns an apartment, and has hundreds and thousands of dirhams sitting in the bank. Lara on the other hand may be engaged, but she is also unemployed and still living with her parents. Besides, Leila also has a nicer ass, bigger boobs, and a smaller waist.

Leila's mother has never forgiven her fiercely independent daughter for moving to Dubai without her permission. It had taken the twenty-two-year-old Leila two years to persuade her overprotective, very Catholic parents to allow her to leave Beirut to complete the final year of her Bachelor's in Marketing in the US. Two years of arguing, crying, reasoning, and begging eventually made them relent but only to study and only for one year.

Only that year in Mandeville, Louisiana, wasn't half as glamorous as Leila had expected it to be. With barely a cent to her name, she waited tables almost every evening to get by, and had a non-existent social life. As soon as she completed her degree, she withdrew the little money she had managed to save and flew straight out to Dubai, the land of opportunities, all the while pretending to her parents that she was still in the US gaining a little work experience. When she eventually confessed that she was actually in Dubai after embarking on a flourishing career in real estate, her mother's first reaction was, 'Haiwana! Ya baghla! How will you ever find a husband if you carry on being so CRAZY? How will we ever find Lara a husband when her older sister doesn't care about HONOUR?' And every month since that day she reminds her daughter that independent, career girls always end up alone. So far, she's been right.

Sighing audibly, Leila grabs her iPod, ties her hair into a messy ponytail, and heads over to the gym on the top floor of her building. She is relieved to find that she is the only one there, as she hates having to worry about people spotting sweat patches under her arms. Thankfully the gym is usually empty. Although ideal for those wanting decent yet inexpensive accommodation in a not-extremely-bad location, half the apartments in Discovery Gardens are still uninhabited. The recent rent decrease has meant that those who can afford it have moved to more happening locations such as Jumeirah Beach Residence or the Marina. Leila may like appearing wealthy in public but she doesn't believe in throwing away money on rent.

Sticking her iPod into her ears, she starts jogging on the treadmill to old Amr Diab tracks, and with every step she takes she feels another stab of envy at the way her shy, sensitive little sister who everyone thought was too simple to find a decent man, has bagged a fiancé before her.

Leila remembers standing in the middle of Sheikh Zayed Road ten years ago absorbing the construction, the growth, and the sheer potential in the city with excitement. Young, naïve, and full of hope, she was certain that she would find a dashing prince, preferably a Westerner, who would sweep her off her feet and whisk her away to a place that was protected from war, where she would fall asleep to the comforting sound of owls hooting, not bombs falling. But somehow she could never make a relationship last longer than a couple of months. Every man she had ever dated just ended up disappointing her.

Her thirty minutes of jogging over, she slows down to a brisk walk, perspiration dripping down her hairline and tickling her forehead, when she suddenly realizes that in her bitterness she hasn't paid much attention to Lara's wedding itself. The wedding where she will probably have to be the single, lonely, and very desperate maid of honour—the focus of everyone's pity.

'Shit!' she shouts as an image of herself in a fuchsia pink taffeta dress blinds her temporarily, and she stumbles on the belt of the treadmill and falls down hard on her knees. Rolling off to the bottom of the machine on her knees, she somehow ends up on flat on her back. Gasping for air, she squeezes her eyes closed, her legs throbbing in pain.

'Are you okay?' a concerned voice asks as she lies on the ground, not moving.

Too embarrassed to open her eyes and face the man who has witnessed her yell an obscenity and then fly off the treadmill, Leila keeps her eyes closed, cursing herself for being so absorbed in her thoughts. *Maybe he'll think I've fainted*, she thinks to herself, trying not to let her eyelids flutter.

'Dude, I think she's passed out,' an American voice says from somewhere to her right. 'Shall we call an ambulance? Concussions can be serious.'

Leila, who has no medical insurance, has no desire to be sent to hospital and billed crazy amounts for a fake concussion. At the same time, she has no desire to face the men either. She is acutely aware that with no makeup, unwashed hair, and her tattered vest, she looks like she belongs in a trailer park. *Get lost and leave me alone,* she thinks, desperately trying to transmit this thought telepathically.

'I don't know. Let's see if we can wake her up first,' the first voice replies in Arabic. 'Go and get some water.'

'No!' Leila cries out without thinking, her eyes flying open. The last thing she wants is water washing away her carefully drawn eyebrows.

'You're conscious!' The second voice exclaims.

'Nooooo,' Leila whimpers, not looking at the boy. She flutters her eyelids a little, pretending to be woozy and tries to sit up. 'Nooo,' she says again, unsure what else she can say to make her sound ill and weak.

'Can I help you up?'

Rolling her eyes into focus, she is startled to see that he is actually rather good looking. But his watch is cheap, and she has no desire to waste time with a man she will not marry. She has learnt the hard way that the clock never stops ticking and spending time with an unmarriageable man does nothing but age you and make you less attractive for the next.

'No thank you, I'll be fine,' she says, getting up quickly and running out of the gym without looking back. She moves with surprising agility for someone who has supposedly just fainted, but she doesn't really care any longer. She just wants to fall in bed and cry. How could her younger sister get married before her? Before she went ahead and accepted that ridiculously large ring, didn't she stop to spare a thought for her older sister who was aching to get married?

Unlike Mrs Saade's unfair analysis of her daughter—that she is far too interested in her career to settle down—Leila has tried absolutely everything to find a husband. At first, Leila tried finding a husband the normal way—through work, friends, and family. She dated colleagues and their friends, but all the men she came across seemed to be after just one thing, and upon discovering that she cherished this one thing even more than the antique gold necklace her dead grandmother had bequeathed her, dropped her faster than a piece of hot coal.

By twenty-five she had yet to be in a relationship that lasted more than a month. Western men, it transpired, just didn't believe in women holding onto their cherries, and her virginity either proved to be a turn-on or a turn-off, depending on how kinky the man secretly was. They believed physical closeness to be an integral part of their journey together, not the final destination. But Leila had been brought up to believe that her virginity was her most valuable asset, and to give it away would render her cheap, promiscuous, and dishonourable.

Fahd was the first Emirati she had dated and everything Leila envisioned for herself when she moved to Dubai. He was the epitome of perfection: kind, generous, good natured, and funny. One night after she caught him flirting with another girl when she surprised him at work, jealousy bloomed within her like a thorny rose and she threw the biggest tantrum of her life. Leila screamed until her throat was hoarse, until makeup ran down her face like a dirty, muddy stream, mixing with the water seeping out of her nose. She cried until she began to hiccup, accusing him of cheating on her, playing with her emotions, and only pretending to love her. She pushed him out of her apartment and told him never to call her again. Like most fights between lovers, she never meant a word of it. She expected him to come straight back. After all only the day before, she had made him his favourite Lebanese dishes— tabbouleh, sambousek, kibbeh, bamia—which they ate before making love, for the first time.

'I love you,' he had said the next morning, after they fell asleep in each others arms on the living room rug. He traced his fingertips over her bare stomach, as light as a cloud resting on a mountain, and watched the goose bumps form on her smooth skin. 'I love you, Leila. Every part of you. Even that fart you did last night.'

'Shut up, hmar,' she replied, turning pink with embarrassment, her heart bursting with love.

'I said I loved it!' he laughed, trying to pin her down on the floor and she pretended to struggle as she stared into his baby face, his huge, dark eyes, his beautiful smile. She suddenly softened and pulled him closer to her, letting go of all her barriers once again.

That very evening, after catching him flirting with his colleague, they had their first major fight and she had forced him to leave. A couple of hours later, when she had finally calmed down and began to feel rather silly for overreacting, she waited for him to call. To apologize. To send flowers. To beg her to take him back.

But he didn't.

An hour turned into a day, a day turned into a week, and eventually Leila swallowed her diminishing pride and called him. With complete indifference, Fahd told her that he was engaged to his seventeen-year-old virgin cousin. She dropped the phone as if it had scalded her and stumbled into the bathroom where she retched into the sink. Nothing but acid came up and she clutched on to the sides for support. His green toothbrush still sat next to her purple one; his shaving foam stood right next to her deodorant. She eventually let go of the basin and fell to the floor, silent tears pouring down her face as all her dreams, all her plans for the future disappeared into the night sky. Along with her naiveté. The twenty-six-year-old Leila had finally grown up.

10

Lady Luxe waves goodbye to her father and then closes the front door, pulling off the big black shawl that she has wrapped around her head and body as she does so. Whenever she ventures out of the villa, even if it's just to get something from her car or to sneak in a cigarette, she is obliged to cover herself up completely in case there is a visitor in the grounds, male staff walking around, or a pervert with binoculars hiding in a palm tree. Leaning against the door, she pulls out her phone from a pocket in her loose, khaki combat trousers and checks it once again in the impossible hope that Mr Delicious has contacted her.

'How can he call you if he doesn't have your number?' Leila had quite rightfully asked her the previous day, when Lady Luxe called her to complain.

'I don't care,' she snapped. 'He should find a way! What the hell did he mean—the ball is in my court? It's he who has balls not me, so he can bloody well find a way of calling me!'

Hanging up the phone, she had stormed on to her balcony and smoked three Marlboro Lights in a row. In her frustration, she accidentally let the last butt fall to the garden below, which happened to be where her father was taking a phone call. She heard him pause in the middle of a sentence, and she instantly ducked back into her room before he could look up and see her.

Shitshitshit, she thought to herself as she ran silently across the upstairs hall way, barefooted, straight to her seventeen-year-old brother's room.

'Knocking is common courtesy,' Ahmed mumbled as she burst in.

Unlike Lady Luxe's room, which exudes her personality perfectly with its hot pink feature wall, pale silver muslin hanging from the four poster bed, and the plasma screen conveniently set up on the opposite wall, Ahmed's room gives absolutely nothing away at first glance. The walls are a neutral beige, the sheets on the double bed are white, and there are no posters or pictures hanging on the walls or sitting on the bedside cabinets. However, upon examining the contents of his bookcase it is clear that Ahmed is nothing like his older siblings. The shelves are weighed down with books on Arab history, Middle Eastern politics, interpretations of the Qur'an, narrations from the Prophet's (Peace Be Upon Him) companions, and thick volumes on Islamic jurisprudence. At the top of the bookcase, above all the other items, sits a small, worn out Qur'an.

'Sorry, habibi, but you have to help me,' Lady Luxe implored, grabbing Ahmed and yanking him out of his swivel chair. 'Please go and stand on my balcony and pretend you were smoking before Baba comes up. Please!'

Pulling him by the arm, she half dragged Ahmed to her room, lit another cigarette and then shoved it into his hand. She ran back into his room, picked up the first book she could lay her hands on and sat pretending to read. Soon she heard her father's slow, steady footsteps go up the marble stairs and into her room and she strained her ears, trying to listen.

'And what do you think you're doing-' her father began as he entered her room.

The pause, Lady Luxe figured, was him discovering Ahmed awkwardly leaning against the railings with the cigarette sitting uncomfort-ably in one hand, and prayer beads in the other.

'Hi, Baba,' Ahmed replied in a strangled voice. 'Are you looking for my sister? She's in my room if you want her.'

Without a word, her father turned on his heels and marched into Ahmed's room, flinging open the door.

'What are you doing in your brother's room?' he asked suspiciously, seeing his daughter sitting crossed-legged in the middle of the neat bed reading a book.

'Reading,' she replied in the most nonchalant voice she could muster.

'Reading what?' he asked, coming closer to look at the book.

'This.' Not knowing what she had hurriedly chosen, Lady Luxe held it up and showed her father the jacket.

'*The Muslim Marriage Guide* by Ruqqaiyya Waris Maqsood?' he read, the disbelief evident in his raised voice. 'You want me to believe that you're actually reading a Muslim *marriage* guide?'

'So?' Lady Luxe retorted defiantly, slamming the book closed. 'I need to be prepared, don't I?' Glaring at her father's impassive face, she realized she would have to change tactics if she wanted him to believe her. She softened her voice and relaxed her frowning eyebrows. 'I'm sorry for freaking you out, Baba,' she started, casting her gaze down in faux sadness so convincing that it could have competed with Leila's fake Karama handbags. 'It's just that...well, seeing as Mama isn't even Muslim and lives in another continent altogether, I don't really have anyone to talk to about these things. It's too embarrassing to speak to anyone else about it so I was looking through this to see if I want to borrow it from Ahmed or not.' She looked up at her father with the tiniest amount of water in her eyes, not enough to seem crocodile-like but enough for him to notice.

'Yalla ya bnayti, I'll let you continue,' he said sheepishly after a moment, his voice now soft. Looking down at his beautiful, strong daughter, he wondered whether the absence of a female role model had affected her. Perhaps it was time for him to get married again. Patting her shoulder in an unusual display of affection, he left the room and Lady Luxe sank back into the pillows in relief. A moment later Ahmed reappeared, a scowl on his face.

'I can't believe you just did that. You know I think smoking is haraam!' he chastised indignantly.

'And what's that you're reading? The guide to marriage? Maybe you should try this instead.' Picking up a book on seeking forgiveness from God, he tossed it over to his sister who smiled sweetly back at him.

'You know I love you,' she said, jumping out of bed and hugging him. 'Thanks. I owe you one!'

'More like a million,' Ahmed muttered as she skipped out of the room, still holding the book that had saved her life. *May God save her soul,* he prayed, watching her retreating back.

After the close call with her father, Lady Luxe spent the rest of the day hanging around the villa moping. Whenever she bumped into him, she would look at him with hurt eyes and say very little. Until dinner, that is, when he became annoyed and told her to get over it. She slumped back to her room and occupied herself with staring at her phone and Googling Mr Delicious as she had been doing all week.

Lady Luxe doesn't stalk—not in real life, not on Facebook, and not even on Twitter. In fact, she always turns her dainty nose up at undignified girls who gawk shamelessly at their crushes' pictures online, and constantly track their Twitter updates on their BlackBerries. Desperation, Lady

Luxe believes, is an unsightly disease which strips women of their sexiest asset—mystery. Or so she righteously claimed until she became a victim of the ailment herself, with the only antidote being a lifetime spent with the very cause of her sickness. Mr Delicious's entry in her life had swept her off her feet and for the first time in her twenty-three years, she had begun to feel the sweet pangs of infatuation. And though she would much rather don a pair of Crocs than admit it, she had been stalking him online ever since. She has found his Facebook profile and spends a few minutes every day looking at the only picture of him she can, her mouse pointer hovering over the 'add friend' button. She refuses to send him a friend request though. Everyone knows that adding a guy on Facebook is the cyber version of asking him out. She has also refrained from doing anything with his number, other than staring at it, willing him to miraculously find a way to track her down, despite the fact that he doesn't even know her real eye colour, let alone her name.

Chi @ the Lodge tonight? The message appears while Lady Luxe is sprawled over her bed flicking through *Ahlan* and sighing in relief as she realized that Jennifer has still managed to evade the society pages. She is surprised by Leila's choice. Although she enjoys the occasional night out at Chi, her friend tends to prefer upscale venues where she can meet wealthy men over places with good music you can actually dance to. It's been a while since she's been to a club and actually danced her heart out instead of just posing prettily. And she could use a distraction from stalking Mr Delicious.

Currently on a G6 to China, her father is definitely far away enough for her to have a long night of brazen fun. Chi is notorious for its shamelessly thirsty men, and tonight that is exactly what Lady Luxe needs—full on flirting without the usual pretentious mask of sophistication.

Sure…will come and collect you at 11 pm, she writes swiftly, and jumps out of bed, heading over to her dressing room. She wants to wear something that is comfortable enough to dance in, yet sexy enough to make sure the spotlight is on her, not Leila.

Looking around the dressing room, she notices that there isn't much space left for new purchases and wonders whether or not she should clear out the clothes she hasn't worn for a while to make space for new ones. The dressing room, designed by Lady Luxe herself, is a haven for fashionistas and shopaholics alike, with its luscious thick, cream carpet, hot pink walls, and white furniture. A spectacular floor-to-ceiling display of nearly two-hundred pairs of shoes is one of its primary attractions, the others being the clothes rails which are weighed down by everything from glitzy party dresses and elegant ball gowns, to heavily adorned jellabiyas, abayas, and even the odd Manish Malhotra sari.

After much deliberation, she chooses a sleeveless black sequined top by Anna Sui that she picked up in New York and pairs it with black twill shorts by Marc Jacobs and her favourite Gina sandals—silver leather, studded with diamantes. Big silver hoop earrings and matching bangles complete the diva look and she grins, laying out all the ensemble on her bed.

Lady Luxe jumps in and out of the shower and after moisturizing her entire body with La Mer face cream (she hates the clinical scent of the body cream), she carefully applies body shimmer all over. Skin now soft, supple and glowing, she deftly applies MAC primer, foundation, and pressed powder and then blends silver and black Sephora eye shadow on her eyelids. The result is stunning, transforming her into a model fresh out of the pages of a fashion magazine.

Squeezing into her outfit, Lady Luxe adds her final touches—a metallic pink Sephora lipgloss created with crushed pearls, sprays herself with Romano Ricci's Lady Vengeance and then slips an abaya over her head. Wrapping a sheyla around her face to hide the golden wig, she grins at her reflection and grabs her tiny purple leather Zufi Alexander clutch (Zufi and Lady Luxe go way back, both being hot young Dubains in the fashion industry), to complete her look. As an afterthought, she sends an SMS to both her father and Mohamed as she clatters down the marble stairs, ready for some action. Neither bothers to reply.

•●

'Going like that?' Leila giggles when Lady Luxe pulls up in front of her building, still in her Emirati gear. 'I'd love to see what the bouncers make of you!'

'Well hello to you too!' Lady Luxe answers, flinging open the door. She jumps out of the car and whips off her abaya, like Clark Kent transforming into Superman, revealing her daring outfit underneath.

'That's better,' Leila grumbles, absorbing her friend's glamorous outfit and smoky eyes with envy.

Fully aware that a designer ensemble compared to an ordinary outfit is like the difference between sashimi at Nobu and a fillet-o-fish burger at McDonald's, she unconsciously tugs at her Top-Shop leopard print boob tube dress and runs her fingers through her big blonde hair.

Smug, Lady Luxe smiles and says nothing as she slips back into the car and turns up the stereo. *You ain't got nothing on me,* she thinks to herself as she flies down SZR, completely ignoring the flashing speed cameras as she whizzes past. Wasta, which loosely translates to 'who you know', goes a long way in Dubai, and her father knows enough people to ensure that his children never get charged for speeding, parking, or even minor car accidents.

Leaning back in her seat, Leila remembers the first time she met Lady Luxe and wonders if she will one day look back and regret the effort she made to secure their friendship. It was one of those rare afternoons when she decided to treat herself to some quality pampering after selling a huge villa on the Palm and receiving a hefty bonus. Instead of grabbing a quick, cheap, and temporarily satisfying massage at her local beauty salon, she pushed money-saving thoughts to the back of her mind and went to the Burj Al

Arab instead. Although the thought of blowing a thousand dirhams on a massage at the Assawan spa was painful for Leila with her frugal ways, it turned out to be one of the best investments she had ever made.

Assawan is not the prettiest of spas; in fact, with its garish red and gold colour scheme, it is the complete opposite of what most people would find soothing. She made this comment to a thin, attractive woman who was lounging by the infinity pool overlooking the Arabian Gulf. The girl laughed and, connecting instantly, they began talking. On discovering that the Emirati was one of the exclusive few to have an annual membership at the thirty-thousand dirhams a year health club, not to mention the hefty thirty-thousand dirhams joining fee, Leila knew that there was a reason why fate had brought her to Assawan, and not Talise at Al Qasr or Cleopatras at Wafi. So she laughed and joked with her while they swam and ended up getting a coffee at Sahn El Dar afterwards. Sitting amongst the opulent luxury whilst sipping freshly brewed Earl Grey and nibbling on buttery scones, Leila realized that the attractive local girl with the diamond encrusted Cartier watch and patent Prada peep-toes could quite possibly be her passport into the world of rich, handsome, and powerful men.

Leila was right. In the past two years, during Lady Luxe's long holidays in Dubai, Leila has been to exclusive gala dinners, sat front row at fashion shows, attended restaurant openings, and movie premiers, all the while being chauffeured around in a Bentley, Porsche, or Ferrari. She has also come close enough to her to be introduced to Jennifer, thus expanding their activities to clubbing, drinking, posing and the occasional Bunning.

They can feel the pounding bass even before they reach Chi, and Lady Luxe slips into an available parking spot before screeching to a halt. They both slide out of the car, aware that the men who are currently being denied entry are staring at them in appreciation. As they do, Leila grabs Lady Luxe's arm and pulls her into the heaving club, hoping that their night out can help her forget Lara's impending wedding and her own lack of anything even resembling a husband.

Surprisingly the atmosphere at Chi isn't as Lady Luxe remembers it to be. It used to be full of pervy, sex-starved men who wouldn't bother feigning sophistication or aloofness as they ogled freely at all women, squashing their protruding nether-regions onto unsuspecting girls' derrieres while 'dancing'. The music, however, is good enough for Lady Luxe to be willing to brave the uncouth gestures of vile men with a tendency to invade personal space. Tonight, there seem to be more Western people than usual and the DJ is spinning a mix of R&B, hip hop, funky house, and good ole Brit pub songs. Lady Luxe smiles, pretending she is actually in London as she and Leila squeeze their way through hoards of sweaty clubbers. They find a place right in the centre of one of the dance floors next to a group of single men vaguely moving to the music and begin dancing to Sean Paul. A blur of gold, the fake blondes look spectacular together and soon two brave men from the group edge their way over to them. In the darkness Lady Luxe doesn't get to see much of what they look like so she grabs the taller one's hands, assuming he is the better catch and pulls him towards her. She spins around so that he is behind her and leaning forward, does her legendary, crowd-pleasing Beyonce butt-shake.

'Aiwa,' he calls out, pleased, and she freezes mid-shake.

She knows that voice. Too afraid to turn around, she continues dancing with him behind

113

her but this time with breathing space between them. Gut squirming, head spinning, and palms sweating, she sneaks a look at the guy Leila is dancing with. Unable to make out his features clearly, all she can discern is that he is a little shorter than the one trying to squash up behind her, and is wearing a huge cowboy hat. She doubts that Leila will mind parting with him, so when the DJ mixes a bit of Lady Gaga, she spins around again, drops to a squat and as she flexes back up, grabs Cowboy's hands and presses herself against him. The tall guy, now left facing Leila, laughs amicably and begins to dance with her instead. Out of his line of vision, Lady Luxe sneaks a look in his direction, her face turning green with nausea and her insides crumbling as her suspicions are confirmed.

Dressed in dark blue Emporio jeans and a plain black Gucci shirt, Mohamed, her brother, is holding Leila's hands and dancing with a big cat-that-stole-the-cream grin on his face. Feeling utterly disgusted with herself, Lady Luxe cannot believe that she had just shown her brother her infamous butt-shake from a proximity that could be deemed incestuous, had either of them been aware of the identity of the other.

Resisting the urge to throw up, Lady Luxe looks over at him again just to make sure her eyes are not deceiving her. A second glance confirms what she already knows and she racks her brain for ways to exit as discreetly as possible. If she vanishes Leila will realize something is wrong, and she cannot let her sly, gold-digging friend know who her dance-partner really is. She can just picture the look of evil pleasure on Leila's carefully made-up face if she realizes who it is who is currently being captivated by her fluid dance moves. She curses herself for coming to such a slimy place, one her brother would naturally thrive in, and wonders if she should just grab Leila and run.

'Can I wear your hat?' she asks Cowboy with a broad smile, dancing vaguely and trying her utmost to keep her back to Mohamed. Thankfully, Leila's plentiful curves are enough to occupy his vision and she catches a quick glimpse of him with his arms on either side of her while she gyrates against him.

Ugh, she thinks, swallowing another desire to puke. No doubt Leila has spotted his Breitling watch and from an outsider's perspective, Lady Luxe reluctantly concedes that Mohamed can be perceived as handsome. Unlike Ahmed who is thin and awkward, Mohamed takes after their father with broad shoulders and a rugged charm. His black, wavy hair, worn long, and curls at the nape of his neck, and his pseudo-beard is perfectly trimmed. 'Sure!' Cowboy bares his braces at her and whips off his hat.

When his curly black hair is exposed she recognizes him as Mohamed's colleague, having once caught a glimpse of him in their home when he 'accidentally' stumbled into the ladies' quarters. She feels dirty for dancing so close to him but knows that this proximity is the only way she can hide as much of herself as possible. She pulls the hat over her head in an attempt to disguise herself further, and continues dancing with him, sneaking peeks at Mohamed and Leila whenever she can, and praying fervently that her brother is happy enough with Leila and doesn't bother trying to gawk at her instead. 'Jennifer!' Leila calls out to her, untangling herself from Mohamed's embrace and skipping over to her.

Shitfuckshit. Panicking, Lady Luxe turns her back on her and facing a short, fat man who cannot believe his luck, and hops around in a very un-Lady Luxe like manner. She can't let Mohamed see her face. As long as he has seen her golden mane and nothing else, he will never suspect that she is his sister.

'Leila, wassup,' she growls without looking around and deepening her voice by an octave. Huffing, Leila stomps around until she is facing her and squints at her strangely. But she is accustomed to her friend's sudden bursts of weirdness and shrugs it off as another one of her games.

'I'm going to go home with Moe,' she breathes excitedly, her eyes bright with lust. 'Thank you for swapping with me! He is so cute!'

'But Leila–' Lady Luxe squeaks, losing the deep voice. 'You never go home with guys from clubs! How can you marry him afterwards if you sleep with him first? You know what these Arab men are like!'

'I'm sick of playing games. I haven't had a good lay in so long and I'm just going to go with the flow. See you later!' With that, she walks back over to Mohamed and only looks back to shout 'and get rid of that disgusting hat!' before she disappears.

Lady Luxe doesn't know whether to be relieved or horrified. Although she is thankful that she can finally breathe now that her brother has left the scene, she cannot wrap her head around the fact that he has left with Leila. The same Leila whom she has tried so hard to keep away from her family, has been careful not to divulge any personal information to. Leila, who wants nothing more than to marry rich. Sick to her stomach, Lady Luxe's desire to party has been well and truly murdered.

Shoving the sweaty fat man away from her, she smiles apologetically at Cowboy.

'Cowboy, I have to go,' she shouts over the music.

Cowboy, who watched her exchange with Leila but thankfully didn't catch much of it, looks crushed. 'Don't go,' he implores, following her through the club as she pushes past the thronging crowd to escape. Bursting out into the fresh air, she takes big gulps of it, feeling lightheaded and dizzy. She just wants to get home as quickly as possible and when Cowboy pleads, 'Stay a little longer,' she sighs in frustration.

Realizing that he is likely to stand there begging for a long time, Lady Luxe decides that the only way to get rid of the over-enthusiastic Emirati with a bad taste in hats will be to show him some light at the end of the tunnel.

'Take my number and call me,' she says briskly. Grabbing his phone, she dials her 'fun' mobile line and lets him save the number. She gives him a quick peck on the cheek, smiles, and gets into her Cayenne.

Cowboy watches her long legs and small behind in awe. 'I love you!' he yells as she reverses her car. She blows him a kiss and then drives away. When she is out of his sight, Lady Luxe grimaces, pulls the hat off her head and throws it to the back of the car, along with the wig that is beginning to make her head hot and sweaty. She can't believe that right now, Leila is probably performing all sorts of Godless acts with her older brother and she pounds the steering wheel in frustration. She makes her usual pit-stop to change and leaves the wig in the car, along with the hat and shoes that are now pinching her toes. Spraying a generous dose of Midnight Oud all over herself to mask the smell of smoke, she continues her drive back home, feeling sick the entire time.

Peace washes over her as the electronic gates to the villa open. She just wants to scrub Jennifer's face and Cowboy's sweat away, crawl into bed and forget that this disastrous night ever happened. She hurriedly parks her Cayenne next to Lady Penelope—a gift from her father when she won the 'Abaya Designer of the Year' award—and jogs up to the villa barefoot. She feels nervous as she slowly opens the heavy wooden door, but is relieved to find her home still and quiet, despite it being just 1 am. She drags herself up the stairs and into her bathroom where she pulls off the outfit she had so carefully put together and stuffs it into the bin with distaste. She will never look upon it favourably again. Climbing into the shower cubicle, she puts it in 'monsoon' mode and stands under the pelting rain, allowing it to soothe her nerves.

Mohamed, she assumes, must go through women as swiftly as she goes through bottles of Evian. She is certain that he will discard Leila like a broken toy once he has slept with her and the thought pacifies her. *She won't know who you are to him. They won't even exchange dialogue other than monosyllabic grunts during the deed,* she reassures herself as the water pounds down on her head and numbs her headache.

After showering, Lady Luxe sinks into her soft sheets feeling far more relaxed than she did a couple of hours ago. *He won't even remember her name and she has sworn off Emirati guys,* she repeats to herself. The repetition lulls her into a slumber, but just as the sandman calls, her phone beeps interrupting her restless stupor.

Squinting at the screen she realizes it is a message from Leila and she hurriedly opens it hoping that it's a rescue call which, for once, she would be only too delighted to attend to.

But it is not.

This guy is amazing. The short text message declares. *And if I'm not mistaken, the feeling's mutual!!!*

11

If there is one thing Leila is good at, it is making a man want her with every inch of his being, although she has yet to perfect the art of making him continue loving her once she has opened the gates to the promised land. Of course, she also hasn't managed to master the art of making him love her enough to propose to her after giving in to his desires. But if there is one thing she *can* do, it is to make him want her, yearn for her, and chase after her with a longing comparable to an addict's cravings.

Leila knows exactly what to say, and how to say it, to ensure that Mr Maybe calls her the next day. She also knows how to behave in order to guarantee a follow up date. In fact, she has the first six weeks down to a T(for Temptation). She tempts, seduces, solicits, flirts, snubs, implies, and entices to within an inch of her life. And finally, numerous flowers, chocolates and occasionally jewellery or shopping expeditions later, she gives in and shyly accepts an invitation back to his home. In white lacy underwear, she trembles with an innocence so convincing that even the head sister at her old convent school would have believed that she had held onto her chastity as tightly as she held onto her purse strings.

After swearing off Emirati men with their double-standards, multiple wives, and strange bedroom habits, Leila had no intention of wasting her time or skills with Moe from the club. They hadn't danced long before he suggested they go somewhere quiet to 'talk' and although he wasn't clad in a candoura, Leila was certain that he was an Emirati of Iranian descent, and therefore, Mr No Way. However, for the first time in a *very* long time she decided to indulge in a night of unrestrained pleasure with an attractive man wearing an even more attractive Breitling.

To her surprise, after struggling through the crowd of sweaty dancers and stepping into the sticky night, Moe slid his arm into hers and took her for a walk through the backstreets of Oud Metha. Slightly nervous, she wondered if he would attempt to make a pass at her in a dark alleyway and concluded that if he did, she deserved it after agreeing to leave with a stranger in the first place. But he didn't. Instead, he took her to a juice bar and they ordered fresh watermelon juice, which she laced with vodka. They sat on the wall outside sipping the cold, refreshing drinks and talking about their aspirations and their families, careers, and friends. The conversation was the longest, most sensual foreplay the ever-so-slightly tipsy Leila had indulged in. Every word he uttered made her insides melt into a mushy pool of hormones, every smile made the hair on her body prickle in anticipation, and every accidental touch sent a shiver down her spine.

She had never felt so alive before.

So, in the middle of a sentence, fuelled by alcohol and desire, Leila grabbed Moe's hand, pulled him into an alleyway, and did exactly what she was fearful that *he* would do. And she didn't even feel ashamed. She didn't care that the Rules dictated that she should withhold as long as possible, that any previous thoughts he may have had of marrying her were now shattered. There was no way that he would allow the mother of his children to be the sort who could put Russian prostitutes to shame with her moves.

It's not as if an Arab guy would ever go looking for a wife in a club, so I've already struck out. Why not live a little? She told herself. He didn't know her name, so he couldn't stalk her on Facebook and send messages to all her friends telling them that she was a ten-dirham ho. He didn't know where she lived, so he couldn't turn up on her doorstep at 3 am, pissed out of his face, demanding a repeat. And he didn't know where she worked, so he couldn't embarrass her in front of her colleagues either. All in all, she was safe.

'When can I see you again?' he gasped, wiping his clammy hands on his thighs.

'Let's not make any promises,' Leila purred, with a smile. She flicked her hair over her shoulders and began to stride away, her heart beating with the thrill of her lewd behaviour. 'Wait,' Moe called out after her, jogging to catch up. 'Give me your number at least!'

'Come on,' Leila grinned cheekily. 'We all know that decent Arab girls don't give out their numbers to strangers.'

'I think we've long passed those awkward formalities, ya helou,' he grinned back. 'Now give me your number, yalla.'

She gave him the number, smiled one last dazzling smile, and then sauntered away with her head held high and her derriere wiggling professionally as she flagged down a taxi. She stumbled in and made sure not to look back. It had barely even pulled away before her phone beeped with a message.

Can't wait to see you again, ya omri.

Giggling at his blatant bullshit, she hit delete and then sent a message to Lady Luxe instead. Oh how good it felt to feel desirable once again, although it was hardly the kind of attention she was looking for. She smiled all the way back to Discovery Gardens, all the way up the lift, down the corridor, right up until she reached her apartment and was confronted with loneliness once again.

Pushing thoughts of Lara aside, she teetered over to her bed and collapsed into it, sighing at how wonderful her life was. And before she could get up to clean her face or change her clothes, she fell into a deep sleep.

The next morning Leila is woken up by the sound of her ringing phone. Yawning loudly she forces her eyes open, and sees Lady Luxe's name on the caller ID. Looking down at her bedraggled self, still in last night's clothes, she rubs an eye tentatively and then looks at her finger. It is black with mascara and eyeliner. Confused, she answers and then holds the phone away from her ear as her friend's shrieks hurt her already pounding head.

'Why are you screaming?' she eventually manages to croak, after the yells subside and she can bring the phone back to her ear.

'I can't believe you went off with a random guy like that! A stranger from a dodgy club who could have done all sorts of humiliating and degrading things to you just because you are a woman. And because he was obviously local and you know what local guys are like!'

'Excuse me?' Leila snaps, her head spinning. 'Habibti, please correct me if I am wrong but surely you are aware that it is *you,* not *I,* who disappears with nameless men from clubs only to be treated like a glorified prostitute.'

'It used to be,' Lady Luxe replies, her voice rising again. 'But now you seem to want in on my game! Meaningless encounters are MY thing, not yours. That's why I was so worried about you!'

'Hold on a second,' Leila interrupts, her head still throbbing. Is Lady Luxe actually accusing her of going off with a man from the club? She racks her brains but cannot for the life of her remember what happened after she had left Chi. Ordinarily, she would had scoffed at the accusation but she has woken up in a leopard print boob tube dress hitched up to her hips, with her makeup still intact, and is therefore in no position to be self-righteous. 'What are you saying exactly? Be clear.'

'How much clearer do you want me to be? One second you're all up against that local guy, the next second you tell me you want to leave with him, and then a few hours later you text me declaring your undying love for him.'

'Shit,' Leila mutters, as realization dawns upon her. She vaguely recalls a man's sweaty palms in her hands. She remembers walking through Oud Metha's unkempt streets, remembers adding vodka to their watermelon juice, she remembers her feet blistered from the long walk. Then she remembers pulling the tall, rugged Emirati into a dark alleyway and fumbling with the buttons on his Levi's…and then…

'OH MY FUCKING GOD!' she screams in horror. 'Oh no! Please no! Please say I didn't!'

'Didn't what? DIDN'T WHAT?' Lady Luxe screams back. 'Leila…don't tell me-'

'I did! I did!' Leila cries down the phone, the weight of her actions looming down on her.

What if the police had caught them? She would have been locked away and then deported, but not before her name was splashed in every single newspaper in the UAE. Another horny foreigner caught making a mockery of Dubai's rigid rules. Her life would have been over.

'You got married?' Lady Luxe wails. 'Where did you find a sheikh to do it? Since when did Dubai become Vegas? La hawla wa la quwwata illa billah!'

'Married? No! I wish!'

'What? You didn't? If you didn't marry him then exactly did you do that you regret so much?'

'I gave him a…' Leila swallows nervously. 'In an alley.'

'That's it?' Lady Luxe almost weeps in relief. Her breath steadies itself and she smiles shakily. Leila has shown her brother the true extent of her trashiness. He will never take her seriously now and this little problem will be over before she can say Alf Mabrouk.

'What do you mean that's it? I am not YOU. I don't do these degrading, classless things!'

'Well, my dear, clearly you do.' With that, Lady Luxe hangs up and Leila sinks back on her pillow, bile creeping up in her throat.

She manages to drag herself out of bed and looks at her bedraggled condition in shock— her hair sticks up in all directions, her eyes are swollen and her foundation is cracked. Sighing, she pulls off last night's outfit and then steps under the shower.

Her phone rings as she finishes, and wrapped in a towel, she walks over to it and squints at the caller ID, wondering who on earth 'Moe' is.

'Hello?' she answers.

'Hello, my beautiful angel,' a deep voice drawls. 'I can't stop thinking about you.'

'And why is that?' she asks, stalling for time. Moe? Surely he isn't the guy from last night?

'Because those lips of yours are incredible and I can't wait to find out what they can do to the rest of me.'

Shit, she realizes in horror. He is the guy from last night, and he obviously likes her sudden slip into promiscuity. And wants more.

'What? Ew! No way! Don't call me again!' she gasps, and then hangs up, feeling queasy. She can't believe she gave him her number. Clearly she wasn't thinking right. It was all Lara's fault for getting engaged and rubbing her single status in her face.

A minute later the phone rings again, and this time she rejects it without answering.

During the next hour, Leila's phone rings thirteen times and each time she ignores it till the ringing stops. Hopefully, Moe will get the hint eventually and stop calling. She isn't interested in embarking on a meaningless relationship, which will end in disaster and make her feel like an old hooker past her prime. She doesn't want to invest time and effort on a man who will not marry her. Especially when her sister is about to get married and she is hoping to go to her wedding with a fiancé on her left arm, and a *real* Chanel bag on her right.

He doesn't.

Habibti answer the phone. Is the first message.

Habibti, don't be shy. It's okay. Don't be ashamed. You didn't do anything wrong.

Ya 2lbi, don't burn my heart like this. I can't stop thinking about you. You have stolen my heart. Come here and give it back to me.

7araam! You are killing me like this! I am nothing without you. Your beauty makes the moon look ugly. Your smile makes the sun look dark. Your skin makes pearls seem dull. Yalla. Call me back!

Ya 3omri, why are you teasing me like this? I miss you. Yalla answer the phone, my patience is going. I can't live without you.

With each overtly expressive message, Leila's resolve to change her number grows. Why won't he just leave her alone?

If you don't answer the phone now I will call my friend in Etisalat and find out who you are. And then I will come to your home and wait outside the door until you open it.

At this last message Leila panics and answers. Moe seems unperturbed by the fact that he has had to threaten her in order to make her yield to his advances. She wearily accepts his dinner invitation, unsure as to how to deter him. Arab men, especially Emirati men, do not take kindly to rejection, so she will have to think of a better strategy to make him give up. She knows this won't be easy though. These are the same men who think an open car window is an invitation to start heckling. So what does a you-know-what in an alley mean? Leila doesn't even allow her imagination to wander down that avenue.

She gets ready for dinner as if she is going to a funeral. She slips on a pair of formal grey trousers, a black blouse and ties a black and white silk scarf around her neck, trying to cover as much of her skin as possible. If she were Muslim, she would have wrapped it around her head in an attempt to deter him further. She dusts the tiniest amount of powder on her nose, blusher on her cheeks, and a little bit of mascara. No lipstick or gloss, or anything that implies that she has made an effort to dress up. Of course, she could have gone without any makeup on, but for Leila that would have been sacrilege. She forgoes the usual dangly earrings for plain studs and pulls her hair back into a neat bun. *I look like a school teacher,* she thinks with a grimace. Grabbing her 'Chanel' handbag, she slowly makes her way down to the restaurant, dread festering in the pit of her stomach.

She pulls up at Madinat Jumeirah the same time as Moe, and is surprised to see that he is driving a Mercedes AMG with a two-digit license plate. She suddenly remembers his Breitling watch from the night before and his expensive Italian shoes. *So they were real,* she notes approvingly. At least she is being harassed by a rich Emirati and not the poor 'just moved out of the desert and have been given a villa in Jumeirah by the Government' type.

They park next to each other and he takes her to the Caviar House & Prunier—the finest seafood

133

and caviar restaurant in Dubai. As they take their seats outside directly opposite the illuminated Burj Al Arab, letting the deliciously creamy, perfectly salted Caspian caviar melt in their mouths, Leila has an epiphany. Moe is being attentive, complimentary and sweet, in short the perfect gentleman. He drives an expensive car, wears expensive clothes, and clearly has more money than he knows what to do with. She knows that she has had bad experiences with Emiratis before but that was when she was naïve and looking for a Sheikh Charming who would whisk her away on an Arabian stallion. Now she knew better than to expect monogamy, loyalty, or even honesty.

Moe may already be married, but even if he were, was it so bad to become someone's second wife? After all, her clock is ticking and she is old enough to know that fairytales do not exist. What's so bad about marrying a man who will provide her with her own luxury villa, a limitless credit card, and a Maserati, and who she will not even have to see very often? She can be married and yet free to do as she pleases. Is that *really* such a bad deal?

'You look beautiful by the way,' Moe says to her in his mixed British–American–Arabic accent and she begins to warm up to him. The icy demeanour she has adopted all evening melts away as she realizes what she has to do. Maybe his motives are a little shady. Maybe he just wants her for a bit of fun on the side. Or maybe he's looking for a dishy number two now that he's fulfilled his familial obligation of marrying some ugly, buck-nosed, hairy cousin his family chose for him. Either way, she has nothing to lose; besides she doesn't exactly have suitors queuing up in front of her door.

She smiles shyly at him. 'Thank you,' she says sweetly, looking down. Her sell-by date is fast approaching and she knows exactly who should pluck her off the shelf.

12

Nadia can't pinpoint the exact moment when her marriage took a bitter turn—when Daniel stopped asking her about her job, stopped sharing with her his plans, or stopped talking about the future. In the beginning he relished having time to read, to study Islam, to explore London, and would recount a lecture he had attended or show her a book on Sufism he had found. After a while though, he stopped going out, stopped reading, and spent all day and night on the internet looking for employment. His excitement turned into resentment; he hated the weather, the pace, and even the pigeons. When he ran out of problems he had with the UK, he would move onto her family or even her—her exhaustion after a long day at work, the housework that piled up and had to be tackled on the weekends, her lack of interest in the kitchen.

During one fight when he brought up the stack of laundry still sitting in the basket and the amount of pizza they consumed on a weekly basis, Nadia, her voice shaking, retorted, 'I'm the one who's at work every day with an hour-long commute each way. Since you're the one sitting around at home, why don't *you* do it?'

He fell silent. The anger that had been simmering in the air died as if a bucket of water had been thrown over it. He turned on his heels and walked out of the flat into the winter streets without his coat.

Nadia collapsed onto the kitchen chair regretting the words that she so carelessly flung at him. A little part of her remained angry though. As sensitive as the subject was, the fact did remain that he was the one at home and should therefore have been the one tidying up and cooking. She shouldn't have to do everything. She was being made to feel guilty for not fulfilling her 'wifely' obligations, but the sad reality was that neither was he. According to Islam, it was his duty to provide her with a roof over her head, to put the bread on the table. Not hers.

After the fight Daniel stopped complaining. In fact, he stopped talking altogether. He spent more time alone and no matter how hard Nadia tried to give him a shoulder to lean on, he refused to acknowledge it. Terrified that her marriage was failing because of its uneven dynamics, Nadia stopped talking about work and spent more time in the kitchen, attempting to restore some balance into their relationship.

The silence became louder and louder until one Sunday morning he told her that he had been offered a job. In Dubai. A job he had already accepted without even asking her.

What Nadia hadn't realized about her husband at that time was that he rarely spoke about the inner battles he fought daily. He was skilled at translating lust into love and then conveying it. But that was it. All other turmoil and conflict was buried under an indifferent façade. So, although he had finally broken down and admitted his resentment, he didn't reveal the extent of his emotions—his bitterness at marrying someone more educated, more intelligent, better looking than him, and his inexplicable need to feel wanted, powerful, and desirable.

Nadia, like any other wife who wanted to save her marriage, quickly agreed to move to Dubai, despite the brilliant opportunities coming her way in London. She blamed herself for not acknowledging Daniel's restlessness and bitterness until it was too late, for not doing more to make him feel strong and worthy. Weighed down by the burden of her guilt, she pushed thoughts of her career, her family, her life, and her home to the back of the mind and went about arranging the move with robotic precision.

Despite the steady degeneration of their relationship and the clear indicators of his impending—if not existing—infidelity, Nadia still clung to the tiny shred of hope she had left. She would remember their dizzying courting days, the lazy Sunday mornings, and his eloquent love letters, and tell herself that all that love couldn't have just disappeared. It was this fragment of faith that kept her heart beating. It also kept her from poisoning Daniel's meals.

'What are your plans for today?' Daniel asks, walking into the bedroom and raising his eyebrows at the sight of his wife still in her pyjamas at three in the afternoon.

'I'm going out with Sugar and some girls tonight,' she replies, forcing her face into a smile in order to reduce the chances of him suspecting that she is up to far more than he can imagine. 'I'm thinking about having a facial and getting my nails done beforehand though.'

'Oh okay, so you don't mind if I go to the cinema with some friends then?' he asks, walking over to the bed and planting a kiss on her cheek.

The physical contact makes her squirm, and she tries not to let her feelings show. 'Of course not!' she replies with a cheerfulness she does not feel, doubting that he would choose a movie over girls in a bar. 'Have fun!'

As soon as he leaves the room, Nadia returns to her thoughts. She will be meeting Jennifer tonight, but she's already having second thoughts about the rendezvous. All she knows is that she needs to meet her, talk to her, understand who she is and what she wants with her husband. She needs to know who she's dealing with.

She gets ready carefully, knowing that there is a chance Jennifer will know who she is. After her mani–pedi and facial she feels fresh and revived, and she decides to wear her favourite LBD, which she knows make her look tall, thin, and fabulous. She throws a bright pink shrug over her shoulders to cover her arms, a pink silk scarf, and black skinny jeans. She slips her feet into black patent heels and applies thick eyeliner to her eyes, shimmery blusher to her cheeks, and for a change, hot pink lipstick. Stepping back to observe the complete look, she feels guilty for looking so sexy when the concept of hijab is to be modest in public. She tells herself it is only normal to want to look good when coming face-to-face with one's nemesis.

Despite knowing that she is in top form, the long taxi ride to Zuma ends all too soon for the nervous Nadia. Her stomach in knots and her throat dry with anticipation, her legs shake as she climbs out of the cab and waits for Sugar to arrive. What on earth was she thinking orchestrating this torture mission, and why didn't Sugar refuse to do it?

'Hey, sorry I'm late,' Sugar says, jumping out of her car and almost tripping over her four-inch heels as she hands it over to the valet. Her auburn hair perfect and shiny, she is wearing dark blue skinny jeans and a loose silver sweater, and looks fresh and happy. 'I had *so* much to do today. Well, Jennifer and her friend Leila are already at the table. Shall we go up?'

'I...I don't know if I can do this anymore, Sugar,' Nadia squeaks. 'What's wrong with me? Why am I being so masochistic?'

'It's not masochism; it's curiosity. But you know what that did to the cat so it's up to you. If you want to bail it's fine, I'll go up alone.'

'No, if I leave now I'll always wonder, and I'll always wish I had. Come on, let's just go.'

Taking a deep breath, she recites *Allahu Akbar* with each step as she follows Sugar up the stairs, silently praying that she doesn't make a fool of herself.

Sugar spots Jennifer and giving Nadia's hand a final squeeze, walks up to the table. Nadia trails behind and almost chokes on her own saliva when she sees Jennifer up close. Her blond hair is smooth and falls in perfect waves on her shoulders, her golden skin is flawless, and her eyes are so blue they are almost unreal.

'Hi! I'm Jennifer. It's nice to meet you,' she greets Nadia in a mixed American-English-Arabic accent, leaning over to kiss her on both cheeks.

'Nadia,' Nadia croaks in response, feeling dizzy.

The difference between Jennifer and her pictures is comparable to that between a gramophone and a Dolby surround sound system. With an ache in her heart, Nadia understands exactly why Daniel is drawn to her. Everything about her, from her tinkling laugh to her wide, white smile, her perfect posture and dainty fingers, ooze class and sophistication. She is wearing a beautifully cut, black off-shoulder dress with a thin gold belt tied at the waist, emphasizing her svelte figure. A Cartier watch sparkles on her left wrist and an understated diamond bracelet caresses the right. Long earrings fall from her ears, shining the way only quality diamonds can, and Nadia feels like throwing up right there on the table.

Next to Jennifer the other girl, Leila, looks like a cheap wannabe. Her style distinctly Lebanese, she is wearing a tight, leopard print boob tube and leather trousers, her bottle-blonde hair is absolutely huge and her talons are long and scary. Nadia can see from the way Leila looks at Jennifer that the friendship is as sincere as a politician's smile. There is clearly a lot of underlying tension between them. Nadia makes a mental note to make an effort to befriend Leila. She is sure she will come in handy someday.

The girls talk, laugh, eat, and drink (well, Jennifer and Leila drink, and Sugar and Nadia make do with mocktails), and Nadia realizes that if Jennifer wasn't the woman dating her husband, the two could actually have been friends. She is smart, witty, and definitely more than just a pretty face. Nadia understands Daniel's fascination but what she cannot comprehend is Jennifer's interest in him. What did a twenty-something rich, sophisticated fashionista want with her ageing, balding pauper of a husband? It just didn't make any sense.

'Well, what did you think?' Sugar asks as they wait for the valet to return her car. Jennifer's Porsche Cayenne is predictably the first to arrive, and she and Leila hop in and wave goodbye, shouting promises of meeting again soon and then zoom away, leaving Nadia feeling worse than ever.

'She's a goddess,' she replies quietly. 'Who the hell am I to even attempt warring with her?'

13

I thought living in a country where I barely know anyone would be easy. I assumed I'd make friends at work and I'd have people to go out with if I wanted to, and that I would be okay pottering around by myself the days I stayed at home. I really wasn't expecting this ache in my heart whenever I had an interesting experience. I never knew how long evenings could get if you had no one to share them with. The novelty of solitude wears off pretty quickly when you have it forced upon you.

To make matters worse, Nadia has been avoiding my calls ever since that evening with Jennifer. I tried calling her a couple of times but I think she just needs some space to herself while she works out what to do with that skinny rat she married. So until then, I'm officially friendless.

I hear the front door of the apartment close and I wander out of my room in my mismatched pyjamas, thankful to have a bit of space where I can walk around however I want without worrying about modesty. I slide open the balcony door and step out onto it, basking in the sun and enjoying the feeling of the wind in my hair and the sun on my bare arms. I'm dying to get a full body tan but I still haven't made it to the Ladies Only day at the beach, and doubt I ever will as it's on a Monday and I'm at work then. Dubai Ladies' Club is far too much of an extravagance for my meagre teacher's salary so until I get a Monday off, I'll have to make do with tanning my arms and my face only.

My hosts are a very lovely South African couple and their adorable two year-old daughter. They've been really kind to me, letting me use their PC, taking me to the mall and even to the mosque. If I wasn't on my period, I would have gone for Friday prayers at the Springs' Mosque today where the khutba is translated into English, but Muslim women cannot pray when they are menstruating. Some girls see this as a holiday period when they can do what they want without having to stop five times a day, make their wudhu and submit to God. To be honest, I used to be one of them until I started praying sincerely and with concentration. Now I revel in the chance to connect with my creator and if I miss a prayer, I feel disorientated. It's also a lot easier in Dubai where every mall has a prayer hall and there are mosques on almost every dusty street corner. In the UK though, I had friends who would pray in the most bizarre places—the beach, the park, a museum, a train station—whenever it was time and I always thought it was a little extreme. Now I realize that they just believed that nothing should get in the way of their five minutes with God, that those little breaks within the day kept them in tune with their spiritual selves, offering a little clarity amid all the confusion.

Instead of going to the mosque, I log into Facebook to check out Goldenboy's page and see what he's been up to. I learn that on Monday he was painting, on Tuesday he felt sick from all the shisha, on Wednesday he was bored at work, and on Thursday he was looking forward to clubbing with his friends. Today, he is still recovering from last night. I feel a twinge of jealousy as I go through his photos and see all the sexy girls he's friends with, with their big boobs and bootylicious bums, who he was no doubt dancing up against last night. *He's completely wrong for you*, I tell myself self-righteously in order to make myself feel better. The truth, however, is that until I underwent my religious awakening I was a hard core reveller myself and would direct lost tourists in London using clubs, bars, and pubs as landmarks.

Browsing through his 'clubbing' photo album and getting more and more annoyed with every passing frame, by the pictures of him grinning with loads of pouty skanks by his side, I decide that he clearly isn't the kind of guy who fears God. In fact, he's probably the kind who sleeps around with any girl who's up for it.

'Hi!' A message pops up on my Facebook chat, interrupting my thoughts and I turn red when I see that it is Goldenboy himself. After working myself up into a frenzy with my stupid imagination, I feel a little annoyed with him, wondering how many of my speculations are true.

'Good morning,' I reply stiffly.

'How are you?'

'Fine thanks. You?'

'Sleepy!'

'Too much clubbing?'

'Too much everything!'

'So go and rest.'

'I'd rather chat with you.'

When he says that my stomach begins to flutter and I forget that two seconds ago, I thought he was a male harlot. I tell myself not to get worked up over nothing as usual and just play it cool. He's just being nice. We continue talking and I'm pleased to see that he's actually funny and friendly without being overtly flirtatious. We have a light-hearted conversation without finding out anything about each other, until he asks me the dreaded 'where are you from' question.

I'm a North Londoner through and through, and everything from my accent to my trainers shouts out where I'm from. Well, it used to anyway. Lately, I've been called an Emirati, an Egyptian, a Palestinian, a Pakistani, and a few things in between. Everything except British, because with my olive skin and Muslim ways, I can't possibly be from the UK.

In a bid to add a bit of variety to this tedious inquiry, I've started making up answers to the question. I never thought I'd do that again, not after the terrible faux pas I made back in London when I couldn't be bothered to go through the long-winded truth behind my Arabic name after an exercise class. Inspired by the Yaser Arafat scarf wrapped around my neck, I pretended I was Palestinian and I thought I got away with it until some know-it-all asked me about the elections.

What elections? I remember thinking. I didn't have a clue what she was talking about, so I gave the most ambiguous answer I could think of.

'It was surprising,' I said at last.

'Oh really?' she answered, raising her eyebrows. 'I thought it was quite obvious that Hamas would win.'

Oops. So she was talking about the Palestinian election, not the local ones.

'Maybe to us, living in the West,' I explained mysteriously. 'In Palestine, the general feeling amongst the people is confusing.' I then legged it as fast as I could.

When I first moved here, I would answer truthfully when people asked me where I'm from, but after going through the routine around a hundred times, the conversation has become extremely tedious. Saying I'm from the UK isn't good enough as it only explains my accent, not my colour. Then there's my Arabic name. So I have to explain that my grandparents moved to the UK from India many years ago, but no we're not Hindus, we're Muslim. This explanation makes me fall from grace immediately.

'Where do you want me to be from?' I answer in the end, diverting the question away from me and back to him.

'I don't care,' he replies. 'It would be quite cool if you were from another planet though. I've always wanted to make friends with an alien.'

I laugh and before I can think of a witty reply, he writes, 'Would you like to go to the cinema tonight?'

Would I like to have the chance to spend time with an actual person rather than a computer? Hell yeah! I resist the urge to pump my fist in the air like they do in American movies.

'Sure, why not?' I reply coolly. 'I'll meet you at Ibn Battuta Mall at 8 pm.'

'Aren't you going to give me your number?'

'You don't need it. Let's pretend we're from an era where people actually show up when they say they will. I'll meet you by the cinema. Bye!'

Before he can change his mind, I log out of Facebook and sit staring at the PC for a few minutes. *Is this a date?* I wonder nervously. *It can't be a date. It's just a meeting with a friend,* I tell myself. *Who happens to be a guy. An attractive guy.*

But no, this is different. I need friends. I can't just sit around alone all the time. I push the queasiness aside and focus on the matter at hand which is a mission in itself. I have about four hours to beautify myself without actually looking like I've made an effort.

By 7:30 pm, I've finally finished my regime. I'm wearing my favourite magic jeans again and a loose purple jersey dress—casual enough for the cinema and dressy enough in case Goldenboy suggests dinner afterwards. And deep down, I'm hoping he will. My hair sits in glossy waves just below my shoulders, bouncing as I walk. I hail a taxi feeling gorgeous and confident although I can feel the butterflies buzzing in my stomach.

I spot him standing outside the cinema, by the big wooden ship in the China Court of the mall and wave at him. Although I prefer Mall of the Emirates (MOE) to Ibn Battuta as the atmosphere is friendlier and warmer, there's no doubt that the latter is stunning to look at, especially for first timers. Immortalizing the journeys of the famous Arab traveller, Ibn Battuta, each section of the mall follows a different theme. The India court with its elephants and ornate pillars feels like the inside of a Moghul palace whereas the Persian court, with its imposing dome and intricately decorated ceiling, is exactly how I imagined the interior of the stone mosques in Tehran to look like.

I can barely prevent myself from grinning widely as I walk up to him, trying not to stare at his perfect biceps and muscular body beautifully contoured against the fabric of his black T-shirt. We shake hands and I wonder what he will think if I don't let go of his hand. I do of course, although reluctantly, relishing the warmth of his touch, and he gives me a quizzical look which immediately makes me look away and study the crêpe menu.

For the next two hours I am in agony. I'm dying to lean against him and feel his arm against mine and I have to apply every ounce of self control in order to restrain myself. I've never been this attracted to a guy before and I begin to wonder if God is testing me more now that I'm trying to be a good Muslim. If I had met him in my pre-enlightened days, I would have been delighted by all the sexual tension knowing that it would bear some fruit eventually. But now I'm beginning to wish he were ugly and smelly so that I didn't have to be subjected to this masochistic torture. So I spend the entire film holding my breath and muttering the occasional swear word under my breath.

The movie ends with me having no clue what happened so I avoid making small talk about it afterwards. He invites me for dinner at the Marina

Walk which though I'm dying to accept I politely decline with a dainty yawn, claiming that my self-imposed curfew hour has been reached. In the two hours I spent not watching the film, I had plenty of time to analyse all possible outcomes of my newfound 'friendship' with Goldenboy, and I'd decided that it was simply not worth the risk. I didn't leave everything behind just to make the same mistakes all over again. And despite the chemistry between us my wounded heart wasn't ready for anything big right now.

So, hoping my sudden holier-than-thou strategy will deter him and render me a geeky loser, I insist that I have to go home and that I am usually in bed by 10 pm.

'Are you sure?' he asks, eyebrows raised.

No I'm bloody not, I think, but with every second I spend with him, my barriers are becoming weaker. I've only been a 'good' Muslim for a couple of months. It's much too soon to test the waters. So this is what Edward Cullen must have felt like every time he saw whatshername, I think wryly.

My plan doesn't appear to have worked though. There is newfound respect in his eyes as he realizes I'm not like all the other girls he knows, that I'm not just going to drop everything and run off with every hot guy who appears to be interested in me.

'Next time then,' he says. It's not a statement, but a question, and I don't know whether to laugh or cry, to feel flattered or to run a mile. I get the feeling though that the faster I run, the harder he will chase. And in all honesty, I don't want to run. A part of me is craving his friendship if nothing else, hoping that platonic relationships do exist between girls and guys who are attracted to each other. But then, that's what I thought the last time, didn't I?

When Jayden and I became friends, I didn't analyse every situation like I do now. I was different then—more carefree, adventurous, open to new experiences. My parents aren't strict Muslims; my mum doesn't even wear hijab. But they're strict Indians. At times they think they're still in Gujarat not Stamford Hill, with the way they go on about the community, and their honour. When I'd come home late (by late I mean 11 pm) my mum would be waiting by the door of our eight-bedroom terraced house, hissing, 'What would people think if they saw you coming home in the middle of the night? Jaldi, go to your room before your father realizes you're not home!'

Despite my parents' steadfast traditions, I still managed to find ways to do what I wanted. I'd pretend to be staying over at a friend's house, revising, when really I'd go out clubbing. I'd leave our house in baggy trackies and hoodies and then remove the hoodie when I turned the corner to reveal tight t-shirts or sleeveless tops underneath. I'd even pretend to fast in Ramadan—waking up before the crack of dawn and feasting on a heavy sehri and then indulging in a sandwich on my way to college or uni. I clubbed, I partied, I had boyfriends, I ate haraam food and I wore revealing clothes. Just like everyone else I knew.

I knew that if my dad ever caught sight of me with a boy, I'd get beat. Not serious enough to inflict deep injuries, but enough to teach me a lesson or ten. I didn't resent him for it— he rarely hit me—but when he did, I'd accept it unquestioningly. It was a normal part of my, and all my Asian friends', upbringing. If my dad ever found out that I was in love with someone though, I didn't know how he would react. Perhaps he would send me back home on the next Air India flight like my Uncle Jamil did to my cousin Sumaiya, or he would throw me out of the house like Uncle Yahya did to Atia, another of my cousins. Either way, the outcome wasn't appealing, but for some reason I wasn't scared. I thought I was invincible.

My dad's wrath didn't stop me from befriending boys; all it did was make me more careful. Most of my cousins are around the same age as me so we'd hang out together and we were all friends with guys. There were no secrets between us because there was no reason to hide anything. There was one unspoken rule though, that none of us would dare to ever consider breaking. We could date Asian guys—Punjabis, Bengalis, Pakistanis—but never, ever a white boy and definitely not a black one.

There was no future with either race, no prospect of marriage, and therefore, all liaisons with them would appear slutty.

And no girl in my family was a slut.

That's why when Jayden and I starting hanging out in the library together, I kept our friendship away from my cousins. Anyway, we were only studying together, I reassured myself. There was nothing wrong with that. Plus none of my cousins went to my university so the chances of them seeing us together were slim. But of course, the world is small and North London even smaller.

It was naïve of me to think I could get away with it.

My memory suddenly takes me from the beginning to the end. A shudder runs through my body. I remember the look on my cousin's face when I told her my secret. I remember my dad turning his face away in grief, my mother's tears. And I remember the police sirens in the distance. The clink of the handcuffs in the night.

My palms begin to sweat. I can't do it again.

14

Lady Luxe slumps back in her chair with a grimace, ignoring the quizzical look the young woman at the next table gives her. For the past week she has had to endure Leila gushing about Moe taking her to swanky restaurants and bars, long descriptions of his orange Mercedes, and painfully intimate details about his full lips that always know exactly how to probe, nibble, and tingle.

Little does Leila know that it was she, Lady Luxe, who helped Moe choose his car, that his full lips have been inherited from their father, and that the expensive restaurants and bars will not even cause a tiny dent in his bank account.

'So now I've decided to just go with the flow, you know? I want to live a little, to stop worrying about finding The One and have a little fun with The One-I'm-Settling-For instead,' Leila explains to Lady Luxe with a cheesy grin on her face. She is looking happier than she has in weeks; there's a glow on her face, a twinkle in her eye and even the small creases on her forehead seem to have been smoothened out.

'Right,' Lady Luxe answers non-committally, taking a sip of her Moroccan mint tea, and when that doesn't soothe her nerves, a long drag from her double apple shisha.

After Leila embarked on this love affair with her older brother, Lady Luxe decided to abandon her Jennifer persona until further notice. She simply cannot risk bumping into Mohamed again, and with Leila constantly trying to run into him, she is afraid that she may not have a choice. No matter how real her wig looks, or how stupid her brother is, he is certainly astute enough to recognize his own sister should he come face to face with her in broad daylight. And that is a predicament Lady Luxe plans to avoid like swine flu. So she's been putting off meeting Leila with lame excuses of work and family affairs.

Tonight, after relentless hounding by Leila, Lady Luxe has finally agreed to meet her as her original, abaya-clad self at QDs, the outdoor Lebanese restaurant at the Park Hyatt Hotel. Although relatively atmospheric, with its cosy, majlis-like tents strategically placed around the restaurant, the corny 1980s classics playing are getting on Lady Luxe's nerves almost as much as Leila's incessant chattering. She has a sudden urge to jump aboard one of the yachts moored nearby and disappear into the horizon.

'But I haven't done it with him yet, you know,' Leila confides with a gleam in her eyes. 'I'm going to hold out as long as possible, but it is *so* hard to resist when all I want to do when I see him is...'

'I'm surprised he hasn't forced you into it seeing as you threw yourself at him the first time you met him. He really is one of the good ones.' Lady Luxe interrupts snidely, nausea rippling through her. This is exactly the kind of conversation she refuses to tolerate and is one of the reasons why she was so unwilling to meet Leila. Lady Luxe hopes that her brother will just become bored of his Lebanese lover before she has a chance to join the dots and use Lady Luxe's secrets as a lifelong leverage.

Lady Luxe often has the urge to run away to another country, change her name and adopt a whole new persona. This desire occasionally fades away though. She enjoys having a kind, fun younger brother to play Wii Sports with, she relishes the sweet moments when her parents acknowledge her existence in a loving way, rather than just trying to control her or attempting to impart their very different beliefs on her, and there are even times when she appreciates her last name as well. Whenever she has a little run-in with the police, for example, she always drives home feeling relieved that she does not have to endure their law enforcing efforts in the same vein as ordinary people do.

Then there are moments when she can barely stomach her life, her family, her existence; when a newspaper implies that her success lies purely in her name, not her talent nor her hard work, or when her older brother decides to exercise his authority. With every slap, pinch or shove, her hatred towards him grows stronger, so much so that she has recently started to fantasise about adding cyanide to his tea. She finds it ironic how she loves her step-brother more than her real one. That she is closer to the brother who attends the Jumeirah Islamic Learning Centre in his spare time than the one who enjoys the same hobbies as her.

And then there are the times when she returns to Dubai feeling cold, confused, and lonely, after another 'bonding' session with her mother in London. Lady Luxe's mother, whom she calls

Isabel, doesn't try to hide her distaste for all things Middle Eastern. After making the dreadful mistake of falling in love with an Emirati man in the 1970s and sacrificing her home, her culture, and her family in order to be his esteemed wife, she realized that she was expected to sacrifice not only her freedom but also her personality. Her husband, when he was her boyfriend, was fun, easygoing, and modern. He drank like a fish, travelled like a gypsy, and swore like a sailor. Having boarded at Sandhurst in his youth, like most of his family, he went on to read PPE at Oxford. She was the cute, preppy, Literature student notorious for her endless legs and quick wit, and he was the proverbial tall, dark, and handsome foreigner with wads of cash and an open-topped Aston Martin.

She found his accent endearing, his quirky habits cute, and his jealousy sexy. He found her sarcasm funny, her temper endearing, and her tiny shorts sexy. They soon became inseparable, spending hours together, smoking weed, and listening to Bob Marley. They would talk about how much they despised social norms, their rigid, traditional families, the ugly glares on peoples' faces when they realized that this pretty English rose was frolicking with a dark-skinned Bedouin.

All the while, their fingers and limbs entwined, a beautiful contrast of milk and honey.

Isabel thought it would be exciting to move to the UAE, to embark on a marriage rather than a career, to don an abaya over the shorts and become a Muslim. Her husband's religious piety did not extend beyond Ramadan and she assumed he would not expect any more from her.

Hell broke loose when he returned home with his not-so-blushing, definitely non-virgin bride. Isabel's devastated in-laws cried, screamed, spun lies, and threatened to die, all in an attempt to break up the relationship. Their efforts only made the stubborn English girl try even harder to assimilate, to win over their hearts, to cling on to her husband.

They eventually conceded that he could remain married to his harlot so long as she respected her new religion and culture. She would not work, would not go out unaccompanied, would never leave the home without her face fully covered, and would never, *ever* do anything that could tarnish the family reputation. Oh, she would also have to be willing to share his body and heart with another wife—an Emirati wife from a wealthy and prestigious family—if he still wanted his inheritance.

As time wore on, however, everything that the two had found attractive about each other became a constant source of irritation, anger, and bitterness. Isabel's sarcasm turned from funny to rude. Her temper ceased being endearing—it became disrespectful. And her tiny shorts were more shameless than sexy. Her husband's jealousy became unbearable, his quirky habits uncivilized, and his accent irritating.

When his wife disappeared on a sticky, summer night with their newborn daughter, leaving behind not just her husband, but their first born as well, Lady Luxe's father's heart and pride were shattered. He tracked her down, took their daughter from her, and then proceeded to marry the first woman his family suggested in order to soothe his nerves and placate his parents. They had one child together and he divorced her soon after, preferring the company of mistresses whom he didn't have to endure on a regular basis.

Thus, the X family consists of an English woman who dislikes the Middle East, an Arab man who detests the West, an innocent Emirati woman caught in the middle of a vicious feud, and their children; a curious mix of two cultures and two women, desperately trying to juggle each aspect of their personality and their family, unable to fit in perfectly in either world.

'...and then I said, 'no habibi, I want it to be special, and your tree of desire will bear many fruits if you water it with some patience.' And then *he* said, 'my tree of desire is so big that I am afraid it will die unless it is watered by you!'

Snapping out of her dream like state, Lady Luxe tunes back to Leila's droning.

'How cute,' she mutters, scowling. 'Anyway, did I tell you that my cousins are coming to town?'

'You're interrupting my love story to talk about your cousins?' Leila asks, annoyed. 'Either your sheyla is heating your brain so much that you don't know what you're doing, or you're insanely jealous and can't bear talking about my perfect man.'

'Jealous? Ha! Why would I be jealous?' Lady Luxe scoffs, raising an eyebrow.

'Quite simply, I have a man. And you don't. And you feel threatened because he's Emirati and he chose me instead of you. And you probably want to marry him.' Leila leans back in her seat with her arms folded across her chest, her mouth set and fire flashing in her eyes.

Lady Luxe looks back at her friend in distaste. No woman wearing tight white jeans and a tighter pink t-shirt should have that sort of contemptuous attitude. Leila has been dating her *brother* for five minutes and she has already developed airs and graces. Imagine if she actually, God forbid, married him? She would be positively unbearable.

'Carry on deluding yourself, my dear. To him you are nothing but a piece of stale meat wrapped up in pretty paper. The sooner you realize it, the better.'

There is a pause while Leila processes what Lady Luxe has said, and then she gasps and holds a manicured hand to her mouth in shock.

'You really are a spiteful little bitch aren't you!' she says, standing up abruptly. 'If you don't mind, I have to go and meet my *boyfriend* now. The one you're jealous of. Try and steal him from me and see what I do!'

With that Leila stalks off, her three-inch shiny hot pink sandals clattering away until she disappears from sight. When she can no longer hear her shoes or smell her strong perfume, Lady Luxe lets out a sigh, knowing that she had just made the situation worse. There is nothing like the threat of competition to make a woman cling onto her man even more. If Leila was only interested in having fun with Moe before, now she was determined to prove Lady Luxe wrong. She would no doubt pull out all the stops to ensnare him in her web.

#&$^@&! Lady Luxe curses in Arabic, feeling completely drained. She takes another long puff of her shisha and releases the smoke slowly out of her mouth, her mind tired from all the scheming. She wishes she could just go home and curl up in her PJs. For once she just wanted to be herself— no labels, no expectations, no demands.

But she can't.

Instead she has to go home, swap Lady Penelope for her Cayenne and head over to DXB Terminal three to collect her crazy cousins, Moza and Rowdha, who will be in town for a week. Although she usually enjoys their monthly visits, when they swoop into town to attend Rowdha's laser hair removal treatments and indulge Moza's shoe fetish, she can be sure her life will be put on hold. And right now, she just can't afford to stop thinking about Leila and Moe. She needs to hatch a plan to end their little relationship before it explodes in her face.

'Where the hell have you been?' A voice demands as she runs into the villa to change her shoes, her feet tired from being squeezed in a pair of black Blahnik's. She stops in her tracks and turns around to see Mohamed standing in the foyer, having just exited the kitchen.

'I was at QDs with my friend,' she answers quickly, flashing him a smile. Reluctant to start a fight just before she has to go out again, she decides it is better to remain polite and informative.

'Which friend?' Mohamed asks, leaning against the white wall, almost camouflaging into it with his pristine white candoura. She stares at him, wondering what, aside from the obvious monetary fascination, Leila finds so attractive.

'Leila,' she replies simply, watching his expression carefully for any hint of recognition. His face remains impassive.

'Where is she from?' he continues, his gaze unrelenting. She unconsciously fiddles with her scarf, wondering where the questions are leading.

'She's Lebanese. Is there a problem?' Although Lady Luxe's voice is steady, inside, she is beginning to feel queasy.

'Lebanese? You're befriending Lebanese women now are you? What a great way to portray our family name.'

Lady Luxe is agog at his hypocrisy, and she forcibly bites her tongue. 'Is there anything else

169

you would like to interrogate me about? I'm running late.'

'Don't be impertinent or you won't go wherever it is that you're going at all. Didn't Baba tell you to ask my permission before you went out in his absence?'

Lady Luxe feels her blood begin to boil and she breathes in slowly, trying to soothe her temper.

'Actually, no,' she manages to say, her voice shaking and her mouth contorted into a grimace. 'He told me to inform you of my whereabouts, which I did, this morning. I told you I was meeting a friend for dinner, and I also told you that I have to go and collect Moza and Rowdha from the airport, which I would be happy to let you do yourself if my impertinence prevents you from allowing me to leave the house. I sincerely hope your important admin career doesn't require you to pay much attention to detail.'

She spins around on her heels and begins walking up the stairs, blood throbbing in her ears, wondering if her tenacity will go unacknowledged. But before she can even reach the fourth step, Mohamed grabs her hair from the back, where it is wrapped around a flower clip, and yanks it hard. Her head snaps backwards, her eyes stinging with tears of pain and anger. 'Let go of me!' she gasps, trying to wriggle out of his grasp.

'Not until you apologize for being such a bitch,' he snarls, his grasp tightening, causing her to yelp in pain.

'Let go!' Lady Luxe can feel the skin on her neck stretching so much so that her throat constricts, and she wonders how far he is willing to go to get an apology out of her. She is too proud to let her knees buckle and knows she will never give in, not like this.

'Say sorry.' He says quietly, his eyes narrow and cold.

'No!'

'Hammoudi! What are you doing?' Lady Luxe looks up to see Ahmed at the top of the stairs, staring down at his older sister struggling to breathe in horror.

'Teaching your sister some manners,' Mohamed hisses. With one final yank, he lets go of her and shoves her away from him. She collapses on the stairs, her breath coming out in gasps, strands of her hair sticking to her sweaty face.

Without a word, she picks herself up and with trembling knees, walks up the stairs.

'Ukhti, are you okay?' Ahmed asks, reaching out to her.

She brushes his hand away and walks into her room, slamming the door behind her. Leaning against it, she hears the muffled sounds of two brothers fighting; one for the respect he has not earned and the other in defence of some-one weaker.

Lady Luxe washes her face, dabs on moisturizer, sprays a little Miss Charming and then plasters a smile on her face. She checks her reflection. Her eyes are a little red and her plain face looks young and vulnerable. Grabbing her handbag, she slips her feet into comfortable trainers, counts till five and then walks out of her room.

The stairway is empty and she looks down at the hard, cold Italian marble, wondering what it would look like with splatters of red, or what it would feel like to have her head smashed against it. Because if Mohamed finds out about her other existence, about the amount of men she has slept with, about the fire she has played with, no doubt it will come to that.

Water fills her eyes again, but this time in fear, not pain. She can never let him find out.

15

Nadia is at work pretending to write a report on post-recession oil prices in the Gulf. Anyone looking her way would think she is intent at her work, but her mind has been on every subject other than oil for the past four hours, and beneath the flitting thoughts is an uneasy sense of guilt. Not because she is on the brink of leaving her husband or because she is experiencing failure for the first time, but because last week, when she picked up the phone to call her mother for advice on what to do, her fingers began dialling a different number altogether.

'Hello?' he answered, in his deep voice. The familiarity of his voice, together with the warmth in that single word brought instant tears to Nadia's eyes. She opened her mouth to speak, but instead of words, sobs began to pour out.

'Nadia? Is that you? What's wrong?'

After months of battling with her problems alone, those simple words uttered by someone she knew genuinely cared for her, instilled a sense of peace in her heart. She wiped away her tears on the sleeve of her worn long-sleeved shirt and forced herself to calm down.

'I don't know what to do,' she finally whispered. Clutching onto the phone as if it were his hand, she closed her eyes remembering his scent—pine trees mixed with cinnamon. It was an odd combination but one that reminded her of her youth in Qatar; playing knock-down-ginger in their compound in Doha, dancing to Michael Jackson's tapes, and her very first kiss. It had been over a year since they last spoke, her union with Daniel encouraging her to steer clear of her first love. But now the barrier she had hastily built between them to protect herself, her husband, and her marriage, had a self-inflicted crack in it.

Nadia was just ten years old when her father, a computer engineer during the IBM days, was offered a lucrative job in Doha. It wasn't difficult to persuade his wife to join him on an Arabian adventure. Nadia's mother weighed her choices— she could either raise her three daughters in a two-bedroom, ex-council flat in London Bridge, or an eight-bedroom villa in Qatar. Like any woman who had always dreamt of a beautiful family and a comfortable life, she agreed and quickly found herself living the proverbial over-indulgent expatriate life.

They assimilated into compound life easily— discos on Wednesday nights, potlucks on Thursdays, picnics on Fridays, pool parties, sailing trips, glitzy malls. Their life was so different from the one they had left behind in London. The cloudy skies were replaced with painfully bright ones, the long queues at the post office waiting to cash child benefit vouchers were a thing of the past, and there were no longer the daily battles in the Underground or lugging prams on to buses. There were drivers and maids to do all that. It was easy to fall in love with life in the Gulf.

And it was easy to fall in love with Yusuf as well.

The only other Anglo-Algerian family in the compound, Yusuf and his younger brother Tahir spent hours with Nadia and Yasmin, riding their shiny bicycles on days the weather was mild and playing cards whilst lying on the cold, tiled floors in their homes when it was too hot to venture outside. Everyone always joked that the two brothers would end up marrying the two sisters because they were so perfect for each other.

However, the perfection ended with their teenage years, when their biggest fights were based on who wanted to watch which movie. After Nadia's parents separated and her mother moved back to the UK with the girls, Nadia lost not only her father, but the first boy who had stirred her heart, and the first boy who had made her cry in secret because he chose to dance with another girl on a Wednesday night.

The evening before she was forced to close a beautiful chapter in her life, Yusuf pressed his inexperienced lips against hers and swore that he would come for her as soon as he could.

But then Yusuf's family moved back to the US. The more immersed he became with his new life, the more he lost what attracted Nadia to him in the first place. He stopped praying, started drinking, began catching up for all the time he had lost while living in a religious state. Clearly, he no longer had time for the girl waiting for him on the other side of the Atlantic. Like two pieces of driftwood in the ocean, they floated further and further away from each other. Their breakup was an unspoken, mutual understanding that neither needed to articulate.

When Nadia and Daniel got engaged, Yusuf, who heard the news from his brother before he heard it from Nadia, was devastated.

'You were supposed to wait for me!' he slurred when she answered his call at two in the morning.

'Wait for what? For you to sow your wild oats? To stop having fun at uni? To stop the parties, the clubs, the drinking?'

That was the last time they spoke, almost two years ago. But when Nadia called him last week, all their differences seemed irrelevant and deep beneath his cynicism and her pain, they were still Nadia and Yusuf, the young lovers separated by fate.

They spoke for almost five hours. At first about Nadia's problems then about Yusuf's own issues. He spoke of his white American girlfriend who didn't understand him, his inability to balance both parts of his identity, his sense of displacement. They joked about setting his girlfriend up with Daniel. They analysed the steps they had taken that lead them to their respective situations, what they could have done to avoid all the heartache. The conversation was like a glass of ice cold water —clear and fresh—and Nadia drank it all, like a traveller in a desert stumbling across an oasis. Until, during a moment of comfortable silence, Yusuf mused, 'Why didn't we end up together,

Nadia? You know we were always meant to be with each other. You know I'll always love you.'

Nadia snapped out of her reverie. She was married. Yes, to a cheating bastard but that didn't give her the right to stoop to his level. That didn't mean she wanted another man professing his love for her. Bidding Yusuf a hasty farewell she hung up, her hands shaking.

As if her life wasn't confusing enough without adding Yusuf, his feelings, and their joint baggage to the equation.

Pressing that little red button may have ended their conversation, but it didn't stop her from constantly wondering about Yusuf and whether he would still want her after her relationship with Daniel came to an inevitable end. If he had grown into the man she always hoped he would be. His messages to her have only succeeded in confusing her further.

Maybe all this happened so we could end up together the way we were supposed to, he wrote to her that morning. *This time I'll wait for you, like I wanted you to wait for me.*

She had wanted to wait for him and she *had* waited, all those years. But with every year that passed another part of him changed, until he became virtually unrecognizable. Almost everything she ever loved about him faded away and although a piece of her heart would always be with the first man who took it, she had doubted that they had a future together.

Was she wrong?

When six o' clock finally arrives, Nadia grabs her bag and leaves the office as fast as she can before her manager can ask her about the incomplete report.

Damn Daniel for putting her in this position, for abusing her love and trust, for ruining their marriage for an affair with a rich, stunning blonde. Nothing, not even an end to the affair, could heal her wounded heart. All she wanted to know was *why* Jennifer was interested in him. What was she getting out of the relationship? And when if ever, she was planning to move on.

Nadia can't be bothered to walk home and opts for a taxi instead, but as soon as she climbs into the slightly foul smelling vehicle that comes to screeching halt outside her office building in Internet City, an idea strikes. There is one person who, if she played her cards right, could provide her with not only the answers to her question, but the solution to her problem. She pulls out her phone and dials a number.

'Leila? Hi, it's Nadia. We met the other day at Zuma with your friend Jennifer and my friend Sugar?'

'Oh hi Nadia,' Leila replies, surprised at the call.

'Sorry to bug you, but I'm near Discovery Gardens and I remember you saying that you you've got some apartments for lease there. If you're not busy, would you mind showing me some? I'm looking to rent a one bedroom with a balcony.'

'Sure, I've just finished working for the day so I can be there in about ten minutes. How about we meet at Ibn Battuta Mall and drive there together?'

'Sounds great! See you soon.'

Hanging up, Nadia leans back against the seat and asks the driver to take her to Ibn Battuta instead. Maybe now she will get the answers she is looking for.

16

When I declined Goldenboy's dinner invitation last week, I wondered how he would react—whether he would be turned on or off by my good girl façade. I was hoping it would turn him off, thus making the decision to stay away from him easier, but he's been sending me messages almost every day and inviting me out every other day. I can't help wondering if he's just enjoying the thrill of the chase though. I've heard the rumours about Arab guys—about the way they fall in love at the drop of the hat and fall out of it just as quickly. How they will profess their love for you with an eloquence that will sweep you right off your feet, and how they will drop you like a hot potato the moment you become another notch on the bed post. I hope against hope that Goldenboy doesn't fall into that category. But then at the same time, a part of me hopes he does. Because his presence in my life is dragging me through feelings I never thought I'd have again.

As I lie in bed on Saturday morning, I try to tell myself that my relationship with Goldenboy is nothing like my relationship with Jayden. That I'm not the same Sugar I was back in London. That if we happen to fall in love, I will never make the same mistakes I made the first time.

What are we doing today?

The message alert startles me and I look down at my phone and smile at his use of 'we'. I have already seen Goldenboy twice this week. A few days after the movie we went to a shisha lounge where we sat talking about work and other mindless things while sharing a double apple shisha. While we chattered away, I suddenly found myself wondering how much he earned. Don't get me wrong, I wasn't trying to suss out his eligibility as a husband. I'm just really curious about pay discrepancies in Dubai. I can't believe that people get paid according to their nationality, not because they have more experience or have earned that salary. Unless you count a maroon passport as hard work, that is. This 'hard work' will often get you a hefty tax-free salary, a generous accommodation allowance, school fees allowance, medical insurance, annual flights home, and all other necessities that your salary won't have to pay for. Others will probably get paid a quarter of that.

I didn't realize that I had actually voiced my thoughts out loud until he looked at me strangely.

'What?' I asked, puzzled by the surprised look on his face.

'Well salaries are personal things,' he said, raising his eyebrows. 'Are you trying to find out if I'm a good catch?'

'No!' I exclaimed, taking a long puff of shisha in a lame attempt to give him something other than my eyes to look at.

He told me anyway and I kicked myself for asking him when I learnt that he earned less than me. He then asked me how much I earned and I was torn between telling him the truth—a few thousand dirhams more than him or lying—to make him feel better. We already had an awkward conversation when he found out that I didn't have to re-take my driving test in order to get a UAE license, and that I just had to submit the relevant UK documents and wait in a few queues. He on the other hand, being from Syria had to invest hundreds of dirhams in lessons and tests, despite holding a licence for much longer than me, and for being experienced in driving on the right hand side of the road.

'You Brits get away with everything over here,' he said, half jokingly.

I was a bit unnerved by the twinge of annoyance in his voice, unsure of what to say. Should I apologize for being British? Should I feel guilty about having certain things made easier for me?

'It's not because I'm British, it's because it's really difficult to get a driver's license in the UK so they know we've already been thoroughly trained.' I defended.

'Unlike me, you mean?' he said quietly.

'No, I didn't mean that,' I began, but he looked away and I wondered if our nationalities would be a constant source of bitterness on his part and guilt on mine.

This wasn't the first time I had issues with clashing cultures in a relationship. I remember the day Jayden had borrowed his brother's Beemer and rolled up on campus like he was some kind of G, blaring hip hop out of the open windows, the ground shaking under the force of the subwoofers.

'Aight shawty, wanna ride?' he purred, pulling up next to me, wiggling his eyebrows.

'I ain't that kinda girl,' I teased, flicking my hair over my shoulders and pretending to be offended. He continued following me and I gave up the pretence, laughing as I walked over to the car.

A group of Asian girls with massive hoop earrings and tight jeans stopped to stare, expressions of shock disfiguring their otherwise pretty faces. It was obvious that they couldn't believe that the fittest guy on campus had just stopped his pimped out ride to let in the clumsy coconut girl who never spoke to them.

I never ignored the Asian gang at Uni out of spite, but I guess after hanging out with my cousins in the weekends and spending evenings with my family, I was all Asian-ed out by the time I got to Uni and preferred meeting people from different cultures instead. For me, Uni was supposed to be about making new friends, broadening horizons, and going out of my comfort zone, so I made an active effort to get to know those who weren't from my part of the world.

Plus, the Asian girls at Uni just weren't my cup of masala chai. Some of them were living away from home for the first time, others were in a mixed-gender environment for the first time and they just didn't know how to handle the freedom that they were suddenly granted. I wasn't perfect myself and I did my fair share of messing around, but these girls had a sort of wildness about them, and it unnerved me.

'Slut,' one of them hissed at me the moment I got into the passenger seat. Her taunt felt like a physical assault and I took a deep breath, nerves clawing at my stomach, before turning around to see who it was. All five of them were whispering, looking at me like I was a prostitute being picked up for a quickie.

Was what I was doing really deserving of that label? But before I could think of a retort, the driver's door was flung open and Jayden stepped out of the car, towering over the group in his six-foot frame.

'Is there a problem, ladies?' he asked, his tone pleasant but the steely glint in his narrowed eyes saying otherwise.

There was a silence as he continued to look down at them, looking more than a little imposing in his black hoodie over a tight white vest and dark blue jeans sitting loosely on his hips, his trademark diamond stud decorating his left earlobe. Most of the time I wished he didn't look like such a hoodlum and made more of an effort to look respectable but that chilly Autumn morning, I was quite happy that his bark was far worse than his bite.

The girls remained silent and Jayden smiled, his lanky arms folded casually over his chest.

'Good. I thought not. But disrespect my girl again and there's gonna be beef.' Turning around, he swaggered back to the car, revved up the engine and we drove away, my heart hammering in my chest.

'J, do you really think it was a good idea to intimidate them like that?' I asked eventually as we left the de Havilland campus behind us and drove through the quiet Hatfield streets and back into London through windy A-Roads.

'Me? Intimidate them? Surely you jest,' Jayden joked as he leaned back against the leather seat and casually placed his left arm across my shoulders, using his right to control the steering wheel.

'Come on J, not everyone knows that you're not a thugged out G but a sensitive nerd who smashes all his exams,' I said with a laugh, leaning over to yank the baseball cap off his head. 'Maybe you could try losing that diamond stud…'

'I'm not going to change my style just because people are too ignorant to look beneath the surface,' he snapped, snatching the cap back. 'Yes I'm black, yes I like my gangster rap, yes I prefer my jeans baggy, but that doesn't automatically make me a thug.'

'No, it doesn't, but bullying a bunch of girls does!' I retort unfairly. For some reason his self defence irritated me, perhaps because I was tired of people thinking I was going out with a rude boy. I turned to face him, about to argue more, but the sadness in his eyes stopped me from continuing.

'So you would prefer me letting them get away with that remark, just because you're with a black guy?' he asked, glancing at me.

As always, his puppy dog eyes melted away my irritation and a twinge of guilt gnawed at me for making him feel bad. He did, after all, come to my rescue. 'You have to let me fight my own battles,' I said softly, leaning over to nestle my head in the crook between his arm and his chest. 'Trust me, I know how to handle Asians. Setting my boyfriend loose on them wasn't the right move.'

'Sugar, there were five of them. Were you really gonna take them on?' he replied, softening against my touch.

'Next time, let me find out,' I whispered.

We sat in silence for a while, listening to the hum of the engine as we eventually entered London, the tension between us slowly melting away. We could never stay annoyed with one another for long and soon, we were laughing and joking like we usually did. We spent the rest of the drive singing along to an old Beenie Man song about a Beemer and trying to match it with reggae dance moves.

After the awkward conversation with Goldenboy, I tried to avoid sour subjects, so when we went for our next shisha session, I deliberately kept the conversation light.

We went to Elements, an arty restaurant at Wafi City, a mall modelled on Ancient Egypt. I'd never been to Wafi before and I was amazed by the colourful glass pyramids and the intricacy of the Khan Murjaan souk, with its huge stained glass ceiling engraved with Arabic calligraphy and the strong scent of bakhoor tickling my nose. The gorgeous open air restaurant hidden within the souk was exactly like the old houses in the ancient backstreets of Damascus. But because the Khan Murjan restaurant was a little too noisy, with the live band playing old Arabic songs from the Seventies and Eighties, we opted for Elements instead. As we sat down on the low, mattress-like seats in a corner of the room, I resisted the urge to snuggle up to him.

He was sitting close enough to me for me to inhale his fresh, clean scent. He smelt like soap, detergent, and a bit of musk all rolled in one. The combination was intoxicating, and I found it hard to focus on anything other than him. As we waited for our mint and grape shisha to arrive, we looked at the brightly coloured oil paintings adorning the walls.

'See that red one? Technically it's incorrect as the shadows should be on the other side,' he explained. 'Look, let me show you. Do you have a pen and some paper?'

I pulled out my organiser and handed it to him along with a pen, and he opened a blank page and began drawing on it. While he was sketching, he explained the way light and dark colours should appear on a canvas, the rules about placing objects on different parts and other complicated rules that I wasn't particularly interested in. I was more interested in the way his strong fingers gripped the pen, the way his hand moved fluidly over the page the way his eyebrows came together in concentration.

Oh man, I thought to myself as the true depth of my lust became apparent to me. I couldn't even watch him draw a box without feeling like my knees would buckle. How could I possibly stay friends with him?

That evening I drove home feeling depressed, the absence of his presence making my loneliness in Dubai all the more apparent.

17

Leila dashes out of her apartment teetering in her five-inch Louboutins, thrilled to have found a pair similar to the ones Christina Aguilera wore in 'Burlesque,' and slams her front door shut without locking it. She wiggles over to the lift and grins as she looks down at her fabulous new shoes with delight, like a kid who's just been handed a massive ice-cream. It's been three glorious weeks since the incident in the alley, and they have possibly been the best three weeks of her life.

In the last 21 days, Leila has been to dinner with Moe nine times and each time, the bill has come to more than a thousand dirhams. The first time, it was close to three thousand, the same amount that Leila budgets for her monthly glam expenditure— manicures, blow dries, facials, and massages. They have been clubbing four times, during which they lounged at a VIP table, sipping on Dom and making small talk without actually dancing. Just like Leila imagines celebrities to do. They have been to the cinema once—Gold Class of course—

where they spent more time canoodling on the reclining leather seats than watching the movie, they have gone for shisha and coffee a couple of times—Leila enjoys making subtle innuendos with the shisha pipe and her lips, and shopping twice. During these shopping trips, whatever Leila 'oohed' over—just clothes and accessories thus far, since it seemed too soon to peer through Damas' sparkly windows—miraculously appeared at her apartment the next day by an express courier. She was in heaven.

'Habibti, weinich enti?' Moe growls down the phone as she exits the building and fumbles around in her new white, calfskin, Chanel quilted bag for her keys—the same one that Lady Luxe has in three colours and for which ordinary people usually have to wait in line for. His voice is smooth and deep, and she feels a thrill down her spine, although she's still not sure whether it is him or his money that excites her more.

She can't believe her good fortune. Not only is Moe attentive, sweet and generous, he is also chivalrous. He opens doors for her, refuses to let her spend a single dirham when they are together and always makes sure that she reaches home safely.

Of course, Leila is not completely delusional and knows that a major part of his fascination with her stems from his desire to peel away her expensive clothes and go where she has implied that no man has been before. She knows that once he has had her, his fascination with his Lebanese 'virgin' will disappear like a sweet dream in the morning and she will be left feeling cold, empty, and alone. She's determined to make the most of her time with him. She knows that their days are numbered, despite her silly denial to Lady Luxe; what's more, she is angry that her friend forced her into declaring that her relationship with the handsome Emirati was more than a temporary, mutually beneficial affair. She knows perfectly well that there is nothing more to it. But she wishes there was.

'I've just left my apartment,' Leila replies checking her reflection in the building's glass door approvingly. She is wearing a cream coloured chiffon dress with bronze embroidery from the boho boutique, Antik Batik, that she had borrowed a long time ago from Lady Luxe and accidentally-on-purpose forgotten to return. At first glance, she appears to be modestly dressed; the kaftan has long sleeves, it is loose and it falls just above her knees. But on closer inspection, and no doubt Moe will be analysing her every move, it transpires that her dress is the tiniest bit transparent, that the neckline occasionally slips, displaying a smooth, tanned shoulder, and a pale pink bra strap. She has pinned her hair up, but has left loose tendrils framing her face, begging to be tucked behind her ears and her makeup is subtle, giving the illusion that she isn't wearing any at all. In actual fact, she is wearing most of MAC on her face: primer, concealer, tinted moisturiser, a brief brushing of studio fix, mineralize bronzer, a tiny dab of gold pigment on her eyelids, brown mascara, a little bit of brown eyeliner to define her eyes, eyebrow pencil to bring out her otherwise non-existent eyebrows and her favourite lip plumping gloss—Sexy MotherPucker. The result of her entire look seems completely natural and effortless, not the outcome of six outfit changes, an hour's worth of careful makeup application and another hour of hair styling. Perfect for an afternoon wandering around JBR, browsing the designer boutiques and sipping coffee at an Italian café by the beach.

'Yalla, hurry. I miss you.' Moe says and Leila hangs up putting on her new Chopard sunglasses.

She makes sure that she is always the first to hang up, that she never calls him first, only returns calls if she absolutely has to, and often lets him call twice before she actually answers. She also ensures that she never agrees to meet him until she has checked her schedule, after which she feigns unavailability and offers an alternative after some probing.

The games she is forced to play to maintain his interest in her are physically and mentally exhausting. As she drives out of Discovery Gardens and joins Sheikh Zayed Road, blaring Fairouz on the music system like all of Lebanon in the morning, she feels an unexpected urge to just let down her hair and be herself. She wants to wear denim cut-offs and an old t-shirt. She wants to run a comb through her hair before pulling it into a haphazard ponytail. She wants to call her boyfriend whenever she gets the urge to hear his voice, to answer with a huge smile when he calls her, wants to send him cute messages telling him she's missing him. She wants to curl up in bed with him and fall asleep in his arms, to drop the façade, to stop constantly watching her words, her actions, her expressions and just be herself. Leila Saade. Not Leila the Lebanese Temptress.

But she can't. Because the last time she did, the time she actually thought what was happening went beyond the surface, she found out the hard way that it was not. That the Leila with no makeup, no barriers, no inhibitions, simply wasn't what he wanted. It was too real for him.

As always, JBR is buzzing. The car park is packed full of Hummers and Corvettes, the occasional Lamborghini and Ferrari providing tourists with glamorous holiday photos. The walkway is full of people; mothers pushing strollers, lovers holding hands, teenage girls in tiny summer dresses showing off their lean, golden limbs, students sit at tables with their laptops, while families busy themselves at the market stalls. It is just as the developers envisioned it to be—a vibrant, family-friendly promenade parallel to the ocean, where people can relax, dine, and shop while absorbing the fresh sea air and basking in the sun.

Leila spots Moe sitting at an outdoor table at Paul's but to her dismay sees that he is with a friend. So much for a romantic afternoon. Pasting a smile on her face, she saunters up to the table and greets them both breezily, allowing them to stand up to return her 'marhaba'. Moe pulls a chair out for her and she sits down, smiling sweetly at him, irritation clawing at her insides. He could have at least told her that he would be bringing someone.

Moe is wearing a white candoura and white guttra. With his RayBan aviators he looks young, trendy, and sexy, and his good looks melt away the iciness Leila felt upon seeing his friend. For once, she is actually happy to be seen with her date. She usually has to persuade herself that it is the size of a man's wallet and not his looks that matters. She has dated fat men, old men, balding men, ugly men, smelly men, obnoxious men, and even short men, all in the pursuit of monetary satisfaction. After all, they're all the same when the lights are off.

'You look beautiful as always, my angel,' Moe declares gallantly, taking her hand in his. 'Leila, I'd like to introduce to my good friend, Humaid. Humaid, this is my...Leila.'

'Nice to meet you,' Leila says, acknowledging Moe's inability to refer to her as his girlfriend and giving Humaid the once over.

Humaid too is in a candoura, a dark brown one, with a beige guttra messily wrapped around his head. His complexion is a lot darker than Moe's and bits of curly hair peep out from beneath the head wrap. He isn't ugly and could be considered to be attractive had he been sitting next to someone less good looking. There is something familiar about the glint in his eyes, and she feels as if she has seen him somewhere. Nervousness buzzes in her stomach. *Please don't let him be someone I've hit on before.*

'Actually, we've already met,' Humaid answers with a knowing smile. Leila's own smile falters as she struggles to remember where. 'At the club, remember? We danced together before you decided to go off with Moe instead.'

Recognition finally dawns on Leila, but Humaid continues talking good-naturedly. '… and you don't know how much I regret letting you go that night!' He winks at her and both he and Moe start laughing, their guffaws causing her to turn red with anger.

'Now, now, don't insult my girl,' Moe chastises vaguely as he gets up to answer a call on his BlackBerry, leaving Leila to fend for herself.

'Humaid, as lovely as you are, you are clearly not in the same league as my darling Hammoudi, so there's no way you would have gotten anything that night.' Leila replies scathingly, giving him a look so evil that it would have made a weaker man shrivel up in fear. Humaid, however, simply laughs. She cannot believe that Mohamed has completely ruined their so-called 'romantic' Friday afternoon by inviting his buffoon of a friend.

'If you say so, habibti,' he replies sarcastically. 'As it happens, I'm actually more interested in your friend than the favours you bestow on mine. The sexy Syrian girl with the long blonde hair and breathtaking dance moves that was with you that night. She hasn't returned a single one of my calls and I'm getting impatient.'

Although Leila is thankful that the spotlight is finally off her and the 'favour' he is referring to, she cannot believe that he has sought her company only to enquire after Lady Luxe.

'Perhaps you should take the hint then,' she says, raising a perfectly drawn eyebrow, willing Moe to come back to her and rescue her from his evil friend.

'If she didn't want me to call, she wouldn't have given me her number. She's just playing hard to get. Why is it that you Arab girls make things so difficult for us?'

'Difficult how?' Leila asks, biding time. He has a point. Why did Lady Luxe give her number to him if she didn't want to speak to him? No doubt it had something to do with another one of those complicated games she likes to play. If their relationship was as it used to be, Leila would have excused herself and then called her friend to tip her off, but after the way she scoffed at her relationship with Moe, Leila is convinced that Lady Luxe regrets handing him over to her and wants a slice of the Expensive Emirati Pie for herself. This is treachery beyond Leila's limited tolerance threshold, and she decides that an ad-hoc response to Humaid's questions is ample payback.

'It's the games you play!' Humaid exclaims earnestly. 'You want us to chase you based on the subtlest of signals. Why can't you just be clear and tell us yes or no? Why do your 'no's actually mean 'yes but I can't tell you for fear of looking too easy?'

'Well maybe it's because you actually like playing games. If a girl reciprocated your interest, how long would you remain interested?' Leila answers articulately, folding her arms across her chest in defiance. The nerve of the man, accusing all Arab girls of playing games when clearly he revelled in the excitement of the chase.

'Well your Syrian friend was definitely interested,' Humaid says confidently. 'Have you forgotten the way she practically snatched me away from you? And not only did she give me her number, she also took my hat! Right off my head! How many more signs do I need? I love Syrian girls! They're so original and classy, not easy like you Lebanese.'

Leila holds back a snort, unsure whether to be further aggravated by his comparing her to her more traditional neighbour, or thrilled that she has the upper-hand over him.

'Sorry to burst your bubble, habibi, but your sophisticated Syrian is actually an Emirati,' she says snidely, putting both Humaid and Lady Luxe in their places in one, swift move. *Check.*

'What?' Humaid is shocked and the look on his face makes Leila regret the words that maliciously poured out of her. She shifts around in her seat, unsure of what to say next.

'My apologies for that long phone call, it was actually my father.' Moe reappears at the table and sits down, squeezing Leila's hand as he does. She almost weeps in relief, hoping that Humaid won't continue the conversation in his presence. She squeezes his hand back.

'Ahlan,' she simpers, beginning to relax. In Leila's eyes, Moe is practically perfect. His eyes are rimmed with thick eyelashes, his nose is nothing like the typical Emirati nose—it is straight for one thing—and his strong jaw is covered with the hint of a beard, adding to his masculinity.

'I'm not being a very good host tonight am I, habibti?' he continues, smiling warmly at her. 'I'll make it up to you, don't worry. What have you been talking about?'

'Oh noth-' Leila begins.

'Apparently Leila's Syrian friend is Emirati!' Humaid interrupts. 'The nerve of the girl, pretending to be Syrian like that! She even spoke in the Syrian dialect. Don't tell me the blonde hair isn't real?'

'Of course it is. She dyes it that's all,' Leila answers quickly, panicking and sitting up straight. She lets go of Moe's hand, glancing at him to gauge his reaction.

He tuts, shaking his head in disapproval.

'Emirati girls these days are a disgrace,' he declares righteously. 'She is obviously of very poor breeding. No girl from a good family would behave like that.'

Leila looks down in humiliation, aware of the unintentional implication. 'Well anyway, she's not interested,' she says, trying to repair the damage she has caused. 'She's really not that bad. She doesn't date guys. She just likes to have fun.' There is a short pause while the two Khaleeji men comprehend what Leila has said, and she relishes the silence, hoping that the conclusion will be to drop the subject like a hot falafel.

'Make her interested,' Humaid says quietly, a steely note in his voice. *Check.* There went the queen.

'How am I supposed to do that?!' Leila squeaks, the colour disappearing from her face.

'Tell her that I know she's Emirati and I know her phone number. It won't take that long for me to find out who her father is. Tell her to spare me the hassle. And tell her that I don't like girls who play games.'

Leila looks over at Mohamed for help, but he is uninterested, pressing buttons on his BlackBerry instead of paying her any attention.

'Humaid, she really isn't that pretty in the light,' she says nervously, desperately clutching at straws. 'Just forget about her and move on. A good looking guy like you can get any girl, so what's the point of chasing after one who won't give you the time of day?'

Humaid doesn't answer immediately. Instead, he looks over at the uncomfortable Leila who is fidgeting in her seat and wonders if she has feelings for him, and is jealous of his interest in her friend. His chest swells with pride.

'Khalas, we'll talk about it later,' he says reassuringly, grinning at her.

Leila lets out a conspicuous sigh, glad that the game of chess is over but oblivious to the reason why Humaid has temporarily stopped hounding her. She is certain that he will forget about Lady Luxe as soon as another reasonably attractive female pays him an iota of attention.

'Anyway, it was lovely seeing you again Leila. You are just as beautiful in the sunlight as you were under strobe lights. I'll be in touch! Yalla hammoudi, nshofach bokra. Bye!'

Leila watches Humaid's back as he walks away and finally stops tapping her feet, which she had unconsciously been doing the entire time he was there. She glances over at Moe who is still playing on his BlackBerry and frowns. He looks up and notices the annoyance on her otherwise pretty face, which, for the first time since they've started dating, she doesn't bother to disguise. Irritated and stressed, Leila has had enough for one afternoon and now wants nothing more than to just go back home and work off her aggravation in the gym. Her romantic date—the one that she spent more than *two* hours preparing for—has been more like a police investigation and she is tired of feeling like a criminal.

'Sorry, I'll just be a minute. I'm arranging a few important matters with my father,' he says apologetically.

'You know what, you carry on doing that. I'm sorry for getting in the way of your important business. I'll see you later,' Leila gathers up her belongings but Mohamed places a hand on her arm to stop her as his phone rings.

'Yes, Baba,' he says into his phone, pleading Leila with his eyes to have patience. 'No, I didn't have a chance to talk to him about it again today but we'll schedule something for next week, earlier perhaps. I'll let you know. Salaam.'

He hangs up and takes Leila's hands in his. Still annoyed she looks away and takes a deep breath. If she was planning on marrying him she would have shown more patience, but as she knows that their relationship will die out in a few weeks she doesn't see the point of acting like an angel. Sure, she doesn't mind pretending to be innocent or uninterested, but that was it. He had to know that her time was valuable and no man, no matter how rich, had the right to waste it unless he was planning on putting a ring on her finger.

'Habibti, don't be angry,' Mohamed implores, stroking her face.

She stiffens, hoping he won't ruin her makeup. 'I'm not angry.'

'Yes you are, and I deserve it. It's just a little family thing I have to contend with.'

At the mention of the word 'family', Leila's ears prick up. Moe, like most Emiratis dating illicitly, has been extremely secretive about his family. She still doesn't know his last name, where he lives or what his father does, and is gagging to know more about her mystery man other than his first name, which he shares with 90 per cent of the Emirati population.

'Like what? What is more important than me?' she demands to know, exaggerating slightly, excited at the prospect of knowing more about his personal life.

'Well my father wants me to find a suitor for my sister,' he says, gesturing for the waiter and ordering another coffee. Leila leans forward in anticipation, like an eager student, almost wishing she could take notes.

'And?' she says impatiently as soon as the waiter leaves.

'And I'm thinking of introducing Humaid to her. Purely in a professional setting of course.'

'What a fantastic idea!' Leila exclaims with a broad grin on her face. If Humaid is introduced to Mohamed's sister, perhaps then he'll stop pining after Lady Luxe and she wouldn't have to worry about incurring her wrath for blurting out her secrets.

'Really? Do you think so? What did you think of Humaid?' Mohamed asks.

'I think he's very intelligent and charismatic,' Leila lies smoothly, reaching out to brush a strand of hair out of her face and then tingling at Moe's touch as he stops her hand and does it for her.

'Hmm...I don't know how serious he is though. He certainly likes his women, but then, we all do, don't we? I don't expect any man who marries my sister to be content with just her. Marriages need mistresses to keep them fresh.'

'Oh yes, I agree,' Leila nods dishonestly. *After all, I won't be the wife who has to worry about your affairs. In fact, I will probably be the mistress.*

'You do? That's refreshing.' Moe looks at Leila with newfound respect, a smile playing on his lips.

'Well, marriage is a very boring institution don't you think? No man can ever be satisfied with one woman, and accepting this fact is healthier for *all* parties involved.' Leila is astounded at how quickly the lies pour out of her mouth, anxious to continue persuading Mohamed to allow Humaid to meet his sister.

'I agree wholeheartedly,' Mohamed says with genuine enthusiasm. 'Though I doubt my sister agrees.'

'Why? What is she like?'

'Very…fiery,' he answers, stroking his beard thoughtfully. 'She's very intelligent, slightly arrogant, and extremely rude. She needs someone who is able to control her and keep her in line. I think Humaid would be able to do that adequately. And he is, of course, from a suitable family so they may be a good match. My father seems to think so anyway. He thinks she's becoming far too independent so we're planning a meeting between them soon.'

'Will your sister agree?' Leila asks curiously.

'Oh yes, if my father tells her to, she will have to. She will have no choice.'

Leila grins happily, leans forward, and gives Mohamed an unexpected kiss on his cheek. She is thrilled that she has managed to salvage the situation between Humaid and Lady Luxe, *and* learn more about his family in the process. She really is cleverer than Lady Luxe gives her credit for.

'But anyway, in case things don't work out… After all, he may not even like her…he needs something to keep his mind busy,' Moe continues, his eyebrows knitted together. 'Ensure that your friend is willing to cater to his needs.'

'What?' Leila's grin freezes on her face.

'Yes. This Emirati friend of yours needs to be taught a lesson. She can't just dance with a man in such a provocative way, give him her number, and steal his hat without expecting to give anything in return. I can't stand teases. She needs to know that there is a price for everything.'

'There is?' Leila gulps, her voice almost inaudible.

'Yes. There is. Nothing in life comes for free, my dear Leila. Yes, the matter is solved. Humaid will meet my sister soon, in the next couple of days anyway, and he will meet your friend soon after. He really is a good friend of mine and if he is to be in my family, I want him to be happy. I trust you understand how important it is that you arrange that?'

Mohamed looks at Leila, and her breath gets caught in her throat as their eyes connect. She notices something beneath the apparent warmth that she never paid much attention to before. Ice.

'By the way, habibti, I forgot to mention how marvellous your handbag is. It wasn't easy to get hold of it without waiting on that ridiculous list.'

Leila looks down at her pristine white handbag and her toes curl in fear inside her new Louboutins.

'Thanks,' she manages to whisper. *Check mate*.

18

Lady Luxe lies back in her bed and wills herself to get up, activating the snooze option on her Vertu phone to give herself another ten minutes of uninterrupted rest—something she never thought she would crave for at the age of twenty-three.

Is this what getting old feels like? she asks herself, rolling over on her stomach and covering her head with her duck-feather pillow in an attempt to block out the bright morning sun.

It has been a week since her crazy cousins, Moza and Rowdha, stormed the UAE like two Swarovski crystal encrusted tornadoes. And since their arrival, Lady Luxe has had no more than four hours of restless sleep every night, the result of which has prompted two pink, sore pimples to form on her otherwise flawless complexion. Dousing said spots with tea tree oil last night, Lady Luxe stared at her reflection in the mirror— at her dehydrated skin, the faint shadows under her tired eyes and her limp hair—and scowled furiously. The nightly shenanigans were not the only things that were playing havoc on her health though. It had been over three weeks since Leila started dating her brother and she had expected their perverse little affair to have run its course by now. But it hadn't. In fact, it had not even peaked yet, with Leila withholding access to her rose garden with surprising resilience.

After their argument at QDs, Lady Luxe has refused to ask Leila a single question about her blossoming relationship and in turn, Leila has kept her chips close to her, barely mentioning Mohamed's name during their few conversations, leaving Lady Luxe with nothing but her overactive imagination to piece together the puzzle. She has imagined all sorts of chilling scenarios: running into Mola, her new name for the gruesome twosome, and Leila subsequently blackmailing her for the rest of her pitiful life or perhaps bumping into her as she makes a hasty exit at 5 am from their villa. This particular thought sends chills down Lady Luxe's spine, waking her up completely. When her phone rings again, instead of switching it off, she looks down and sees that it is Rowdha calling her, and not her alarm.

'Hello?' she mumbles, her head still under the pillow.

'Wake up tart,' Rowdha demands in her thick British accent. 'We've got *loads* of stuff to do today. Be in JBR by 3 pm.'

Lady Luxe mumbles an incomprehensible profanity and Rowdha hangs up the phone, knowing that she won't have to call her reliable cousin again.

Moza and Rowdha, like their first cousin, were also educated in the UK, although unlike her, they didn't just complete their degrees there. When Rowdha was thirteen and Moza eleven, their mother decided that they were far too dependent on their maids, and that they needed to learn more about the side of their heritage that was often overlooked. Thus, she packed away a scowling Rowdha and a teary Moza to Cheltenham Ladies' College to learn about the British culture, to refine their accents, and to become a little more independent. Their father, Lady Luxe's uncle, was always more liberal than his younger brother. He too had married an English woman, but one he remained happily married to without taking on further wives even after twenty-five years of marriage. Moza and Rowdha, however, were compelled to wed Khaleeji men despite their own father's preference and ended up marrying two Saudi brothers whom they met while holidaying in Evian Les Bains.

Contrary to the stereotypes of Arab women miserable at the mercy of vindictive Khaleeji men, both sisters were relatively content with their choices; Moza's husband happily helped his wife to open her own beauty salon in Jeddah, while Rowdha's encouraged her to complete her MBA at Harvard.

Rowdha was never at want for anything, but did wish she saw her husband a little more often. But his time was limited, especially since he had recently taken a new wife when she refused to bear any more children for fear of ruining her figure—after all, she had worked extremely hard to get back into shape after the birth of her son and daughter. She was far from upset by the marriage though, polygamy being a reality in many Khaleeji women's lives. In fact, she enjoyed the extra freedom it afforded her. Having mothered two children, her duty was fulfilled and she was more or less left to her own devices. She spent her summers in Chelsea with her children, her autumns on the Upper East Side, her winters in Riyadh, and her springs in Montmarte. Her kids, currently home-schooled by a range of tutors and raised by a score of maids, were left relatively unaffected by their mother's tendency to take flight whenever it took her fancy.

Moza's husband was different—he felt that his hands were full with the one wife and one son. However, he too was happy to let his wife to travel without him whenever she needed to, completely oblivious to the extent of her beauty, and even accusing her of paranoia the rare occasions she complained that the men in the streets were undressing her with their eyes. Even if he wasn't watching her, other men certainly were, for Moza is the exact definition of beauty. Her complexion is as smooth as freshly whipped butter, her smile is radiant, and her eyes are constantly alight with mischief. Slightly chubby, with a voluptuous bosom to match her equally generous lips, she is never at want for male and female admirers alike.

Rowdha, too, has the same, cheeky glint in her eyes, her caramel complexion is clear and even, and her tiny frame almost gives her an elfish look. Together, they are unstoppable, as they speed down Jumeirah Road in their white Porsche Panamera, and give sidelong glances through the half open windows to all the ogling Emirati men who pull up beside them in their Range Rover Sports and BMW X6s.

For the past week, Lady Luxe has accompanied them as they race various cars on their way home from shisha evenings in Fudos, their favourite hangout next to Mercato Mall. Fudos, in Lady Luxe's opinion, is a true, undiscovered treasure, completely misrepresented in the *Time Out* description. It is perhaps the only shisha restaurant that actually serves really good Thai, Japanese, Italian, and Lebanese food, together with live music, karaoke nights and the occasional group of shaami men bursting into a spontaneous debka dance around the joint.

The restaurant is also full of local men, who have a tendency to stare relentless at any attractive woman until she accidentally catches his eye. After this unfortunate coincidence, which the Emirati will undoubtedly view as a divine sign, he will continue staring in the hope that she will turn on her Bluetooth and communicate with him further. Or worse, he will hold up his number on an electronic screen, willing her to memorise it, or at the very least, glance at it, thoroughly embarrassing himself in the process. Emirati men, however, are incredibly thick-skinned when chasing their prey, and usually never take no for an answer. They firmly believe that a woman who ignores their attention is simply feigning indifference. They understand a downward gaze to be a pretence of chastity, an open car window an invitation to sinful acts, and a direct look a declaration of lust.

The last time they went to Fudos, Lady Luxe had a man grab her long gothic-style abaya sleeve in the restroom, an intrusion that exceeded the usual kind. The basins in the restroom are the type that is shared with the adjacent male restroom, the mirror acting as a wall between them, leaving ample space to play paper-rock-scissors under.

Outraged by the audacity, she yanked her sleeve back, stuck her middle finger up under the mirror and yelled 'piss off you perv', before stalking out of the restroom. Returning to her low, black sofa in the corner of the room, usually reserved for regulars, she repeated the incident to her cousins who laughed raucously in response, neither of them displaying much decorum when it came to their giggles. Moza's laugh was infectious, and Rowdha's was hearty, inviting all around them to stare in curiosity. Lady Luxe laughed along with them, relieved to be around girls who actually understood her. It had been so long since she let down her sheyla and relaxed, without having to worry that an acquaintance would work out who she was. If she happened to be spending her evening with a distant friend who *did* know her family, she knew that her antics would be all over the grapevine before she even got home. It was a lose-lose situation.

'No one gets what it's like to be us,' Rowdha said knowingly, taking a long drag of her grape and mint shisha. 'The Westerners find us exciting since they're always curious to know what lies under the sparkling black outfits and high rise villa walls, excited when we befriend them, and boasting about us as if we're ornaments on a mantelpiece…'

'Hear, hear!' Lady Luxe nodded in approval, raising her mint tea glass and eyeing up a cute local with big eyes. He caught her eye and she looked away, not wanting him to hold up his number.

'The Arab expats detest us, angry that although we're all essentially from the same family, God has blessed us with wealth and they have been incapacitated by war, famine or poverty,' Rowdha continued, clearly on a roll. 'Some of them simply look down at us, proud of their ancient history, viewing us as ignorant Bedouins who have just escaped the desert and come into wealth and prosperity due to no talent of our own. And then there are our own people, testosterone-charged teenagers, moralistic middle-aged women, boring old cows or traditional tarts. Not easy to find a good friend among those.'

Moza and Lady Luxe nodded in agreement, taking drags from their shisha pipes.

'Even in our community, there's a stark difference in values and beliefs,' Lady Luxe added thoughtfully. 'If we become friends with a girl from a lesser-known family, there's a chance that she's only looking to increase her own social network, and will bitch about us the moment our backs are turned. It's so hard to find a true friend who isn't there just for the novelty, who isn't looking for a scandalous bit of juicy gossip to talk about over tea with her real friends, who has had the same Western educational influence, is from a successful family, is on the same wavelength. And isn't religious.'

'It's bloody impossible,' Moza interrupted. 'If I didn't have you two, I don't know what I'd do.'

She took Lady Luxe's hands and held them in hers. 'Habibti, you have to be careful about who you hang out with over here. Your father has a lot of friends but he also has a lot of enemies. There are lots of people who'd kill for a bit of information about his only daughter. I know you're still young and having fun. I know that it's been hard for you to come back to Dubai. But you really have to be careful.'

Lady Luxe said nothing but her chest constricted with fear and grief. She wondered if she could still abandon her alter ego or if it was already too late.

That night, she excused herself from their nightly drive up and down Beach Road looking for fast cars to race and climbed into her Cayenne alone with just her thoughts for company. On reaching home she collapsed into bed and eventually drifted into another light sleep, the slightest noise—a car horn, a footstep, a sneeze—waking her up and reminding her of the precarious tightrope she has been naively balancing on.

How long before she would fall?

'Good morning, freak. What happened to your head?' Ahmed greets Lady Luxe playfully as she enters the kitchen in her old pink pyjamas, inhaling the glorious scent of homemade buttery pancakes. Her brown hair, usually straight with the slightest of waves, stuck up in all directions and her fringe sat nowhere near her forehead. She couldn't be bothered to run a comb through the tangles and decided to relish in the temporary liberation of not caring about her appearance. 'Sabah al khair, geek,' she replies with a smile, ruffling his jet black hair as she passes him and taking a seat opposite him on the kitchen table. 'What happened to your face?'

'Good morning, Miss X,' Claudine says stiffly with her ever-so-slight French accent, preparing Lady Luxe's plate of pancakes with chocolate sauce, whipped cream, and strawberries and placing it gently down in front of her. 'Would you like me to pour you some juice?'

'No thanks Claud, I think I can manage that myself,' she laughs, grabbing the jug of freshly squeezed orange juice and pouring it into a glass, giving Claudine a quick grin.

They eat quietly, flicking through *Al Bayan* together and Ahmed occasionally steals a strawberry from his sister's plate when he thinks she's not looking. She lets him as she always does, pretending not to have noticed.

'I'm not going to be home for dinner by the way,' Lady Luxe announces, licking the last of the chocolate sauce off her lips in satisfaction.

'You're not?' Claudine turns around to look at Lady Luxe in surprise her neat eyebrows raised quizzically. 'But what about the guests, Miss X?'

'What guests?' Lady Luxe asks, grabbing Ahmed's last strawberry as payback for the ones he's been sneaking from her plate and stuffing it in her mouth before he can protest.

'The family your father has invited in the evening, just for coffee I think but still, you need to be home early. I think you need to call him and speak to him before you make plans for the evening. It sounded important. He wants me to make nine different kinds of snacks.'

'Nine!' Lady Luxe exclaims.

'Is he inviting Sheikh Mohamed or what?' Ahmed jokes, getting off the stool and stretching in his black 'One Ummah' t-shirt and baggy grey tracksuit bottoms. He walks over to the sink and begins rinsing his plate, while Claudine hurries around the kitchen, checking the glistening white cabinets to ensure she has all the correct ingredients for tonight's feast.

223

'Not exactly,' Claudine begins awkwardly, clearing her throat. 'Well, how shall I put this? You see, your father thinks that perhaps it's time you were introduced to some…suitors,' she finally manages to say, the French touch to her otherwise British accent like a dust of icing on a Victoria Sponge.

Lady Luxe's smile freezes on her face.

'What?' she whispers, her heart plummeting.

'Oh yeah,' Ahmed chimes in. 'I think I heard Mohamed mentioning something to Baba.'

'Who is he?'

'A friend of Mohamed's,' he replies, making a face. 'Humaid, I think. Baba's cut his trip short especially for this. He should be here in an hour and the guests are going to get here around six I think, before dinner anyway.'

'Shit,' Lady Luxe mutters, cursing herself for telling her father she had been reading marriage books. He obviously remembered her little lie and decided it was the right time to display paternal concerns. 'But today? Why today?'

Ahmed shrugs and Claudine disappears into the kitchen from where delicious aromas have already started wafting out.

'I'm going to call Baba,' Lady Luxe announces at last, pulling her BlackBerry out of her pocket and seeing Leila's missed calls for the first time. She drags herself up the stairs and slams her bedroom door shut, even though there is no one around to listen to her angry outburst. Her phone beeps again Leila calling for the third time, and Lady Luxe grudgingly answers. She really cannot stomach Leila's childlike boasting about her brother today.

'Shu?' she says rudely.

'Where have you been? I've been calling you for days,' Leila moans on the other end.

'My cousins are here, remember? I've been busy with them,' Lady Luxe snaps, throwing herself onto her bed and scowling.

'Okay, well anyway, I was wondering if you want to go out tonight? As in *out?* It's been so long since we did something fun.'

'No thanks,' Lady Luxe says curtly. 'I'm too busy. Family stuff.'

'Well what about tomorrow night? That wig hasn't seen the moonlight in so long, it's probably getting eaten by moths. What do you say?' Leila continues, her insistence grating on Lady Luxe's nerves.

'Sorry, I can't. You know my cousins are here, I'll be busy till they leave.'

Leila senses Lady Luxe's reluctance to go out with her and has a vision of Moe looming down over her, all her new designer goods in his hands, and finds her palms beginning to sweat a little. 'When are they leaving?' she asks in a small voice.

'I don't know. Look Leila, to be honest, I have no intention of being Jennifer again,' Lady Luxe relents, the ice melting away at Leila's persistence. 'I'm twenty-three years old now, I have a lot of family shit going on. I can't mess around anymore. Besides, I'm getting bad vibes about it all.'

Leila listens in horror wondering how she is going to deliver the goods to Humaid if Jennifer goes AWOL. For good. She decides to come clean. Lady Luxe has always been up for a laugh and may even consent if she's honest.

'Okay, the thing is, do you remember Cowboy? That guy you were dancing with at Chi? The one you were all over and whose hat you stole?'

'Yes. I remember,' Lady Luxe answers, wrinkling her nose in distaste. 'I had to shower for an hour to get his strong perfume off me. He's been calling me and I've been ignoring him.'

'Oh. Well. How about we go on a double date? Mohamed and me and you and Humaid? Just for a laugh?' A desperate edge appears in Leila's voice and Lady Luxe notices it.

'NO!' she says firmly. 'I'm not interested in hanging out with *any* Emiratis. You know how I feel about that. Hang on, what did you say Cowboy's name was?'

'Humaid. He's actually really sweet, why don't you give him a chance?' Leila says quickly, mistaking Lady Luxe's question as interest.

The blood drains from Lady Luxe's face and she experiences a fresh wave of nausea sweep through her body. 'Look Leila, I never want you to mention his name again okay? Jennifer is gone for good, the old me is gone for good, and that's that. Just let it go!'

'Fine!' Leila snaps finally getting annoyed. 'Do what you want. But just to let you know he knows you're Emirati and he has your phone number. He said he'll phone his friend in Etisalat and find out who you are if you don't meet him.'

'Whatever,' Lady Luxe scoffs. *As if I was stupid enough to register my dodgy number in my own name.*

'And he also has your Cayenne's licence plate number,' Leila lies.

Lady Luxe stops breathing. Her licence plate number? Her cars were registered in her father's name.

'It's not that easy,' she manages to say, trying to keep her voice level.

'It is for people with wasta,' Leila retorts, struggling to keep the power with her. 'He's serious. He was going on and on about you and...'

'How did he find out I'm Emirati?' Lady Luxe suddenly asks. 'You told him didn't you?'

'No I didn't...' Leila protests.

'Right.' Lady Luxe cuts in. 'I'm not meeting him, so you can tell your new best friend to fuck off.'

She hangs up and sinks back against the pillows. Her phone beeps again and she looks down wearily to see she has a message from Mohamed. *Wanker*, she thinks to herself, opening it.

My friend Humaid is coming round tonight with his family to meet you. Make sure you make an effort and look respectable. Baba's coming home early.

'Argh!' she screams out in frustration, throwing her phone across the room with all her strength. It smashes against the wall and falls to the hard tiled floor. Humaid wants to meet her *and* Jennifer? If he really knew her licence plate number and wasn't bluffing, then she was well and truly screwed.

She might as well start choosing who to bequeath her possessions to.

19

Nadia leans against the wall, one hand casually placed on her suitcase's handle and the other unconsciously gripping her leather handbag. Her long, beige cardigan is creased after being stuffed in a suitcase for over ten hours but despite the extra layer, she still feels a little chilly.

She looks on at the hoards of people at Heathrow's Terminal Three, observing the bustling crowds with a sense of peace in her heart. Colourful Asian women shuffle along in their traditional salwar kameez and saris, thick woolen shawls wrapped around their shoulders; a group of trendy Japanese students with paper straight hair and funky tights giggle together while taking photographs; and the occasional hijabi smiles at her in commiseration.

The airport is shabbier than she remembers, the décor dated and dull, the people devoid of the tiniest hint of glamour. There are no flowing black abayas gliding along the floor, no clouds of perfume lingering in the air or glistening white candouras catching her eye.

Dubai, despite being in the depths of economic ruin, is like a well-to-do woman who may have recently lost her fortune but projects the illusion of wealth with her classic jewellery and well-kept hair. London on the other hand, is more like a working class woman who is simply too busy trying to organise her life to bother with taming her unkempt curls or manicuring her chewed-down nails.

'Nadia!' There is a flurry of red and Nadia looks up to see Yasmin rushing towards her in a bright red coat and her signature punk boots. Yasmin throws her arms around her older sister and Nadia hugs her back, a little of her sister's energy transferring to her.

'I'm so glad to see you,' Nadia whispers.

'I'm glad to see you too but you don't have to strangle me,' Yasmin jokes, her voice muffled by Nadia's cardigan. She breaks away and looks up at her sister, her smile faltering as she takes in her pale skin, dark circles, and protruding cheekbones. Yasmin, usually the more poorly-looking of the two with her death-white skin and fragile frame, looks radiant in comparison.

'You don't look like someone who lives in a sunny country,' she notes, taking hold of the suitcase and beginning to walk towards the busy Underground station.

'Well you know what they say about too much sun exposure. I don't want to end up getting skin cancer or worse, ageing too quickly!' Nadia replies lightly, navigating her way around the crowds of people queuing up to buy train tickets.

The long stuffy journey home down the Piccadilly Line is uneventful and other than the occasional strange look Yasmin gives her, it is almost as if she never left. Almost, not entirely, as she is now seeing everything she has seen before through new eyes. She never really noticed the conflicting smells in the Underground—soot mixed with perfume, food, and body odour—nor had she paid much attention to the controversial advertisements. Her eyes fall upon a particular advert, one that appears to be quite bland at first glance, until she actually reads the writing and realises that it promotes atheism through denouncing the existence of God. She recoils as if she has been electrocuted. Shaking her head, she tells herself to snap out of it, that the bubble that she has grown accustomed to has well and truly burst. She isn't in Dubai anymore. She is no longer a religious majority. She is back to being a minority, an immigrant, and occasionally, a 'terrorist'.

After the initial shock of realising that she is no longer in a country that caters to Muslims wears off, she begins to enjoy watching the diverse mix of passengers entering and alighting the train. She also enjoys the fact that on the tube, there is no hierarchy. There are no first-class compartments, no one is better than the other, no one but the elderly, pregnant, or disabled gets priority.

Yasmin stares at her sister, opens her mouth as if to say something and then closes it again, worry etched all over her face as she contemplates whether or not to confront Nadia.

'What?' Nadia says eventually, tired of watching Yasmin's mouth open and close like a goldfish.

'Nothing,' Yasmin replies quickly.

'Well stop staring at me then,' Nadia snaps, turning her face away.

'Okay fine, it's not "nothing",' Yasmin retorts. 'I don't know how to say this so I'm going to be blunt. Why do you look like shit?'

'When did you start saying 'shit'?' Nadia asks, mildly surprised, 'I thought you always refused to swear and said s-h-i-t instead?'

'That's not the point so stop changing the subject. Nadia, you look like death. I've never seen you look so awful in my whole life. Even your skin has broken out and I know that only happens when you're stressed. So can you tell me what's going on?'

'Nothing's going on,' Nadia lies, looking away. 'If you don't mind, could you continue your interrogation later? I'm kind of tired.'

Nadia leans back against the soft blue seats and rests her head against the glass panel on her right, careful not to catch her sister's eye. She feels a pang of guilt at being so abrupt with Yasmin but really cannot bear the idea of discussing her pitiful life there and then.

He's promised he'll change, that we'll go for counselling together, she thinks, trying to calm herself. She struggles to remember Daniel's contrite face as she waved goodbye to him at the airport and wonders if he is enjoying her absence. She knew that leaving him in Dubai for ten whole days without her was like leaving an alcoholic alone with a bottle of rum. But the truth was, she wanted to see whether the bottle would remain untouched until she came back, or if she would return to find it opened, or worse, completely empty.

'Wake up! We're here!' Nadia opens her eyes slowly and lets them roll into focus.

Yasmin is standing, balancing precariously, as the train grinds to a halt while trying to prise her sister's fingers open so she can pull the suitcase off the carriage. Nadia blinks rapidly, letting go of the case and staring at Yasmin as she manages to yank the case off the train. Still disorientated, she slowly gets up as the driver instructs the passengers 'to mind the doors' just before they close. The train lurches and she falls backwards onto the passenger sitting next to her.

'Oh!' she exclaims, trying to pull herself up. Yasmin is already on the platform, shooting evil looks at her, as the train moves away, leaving a slightly dazed Nadia on someone's lap.

'I'm so sorry,' she mumbles, her face as red as a beetroot as she pulls herself up. She turns around to apologize but is momentarily at a loss of words as she stares at the good looking stranger.

His skin is dark, his eyes a warm brown and his shoulders are broad and muscular. 'No worries,' he replies, his voice as smooth as a bar of Galaxy chocolate, causing Nadia to blush even more. 'I'm sorry that you missed your stop.'

'It's okay,' Nadia says, a genuine smile appearing

on her face and she takes the seat opposite and tries not to stare at him too much. 'My sister will just have to wait a little till I find my way back.'

'Oh right, you've just come from the airport. Will you know your way back to Arsenal?' He looks straight into her eyes and she notices tiny flecks of gold sparkling among the coffee brown of his eyes. His mouth is full and soft and she has to drag her eyes away.

Half tempted to lie and pretend that she doesn't have a clue how to navigate her way around the London Underground and solicit help from the handsome stranger in the process, Nadia forces herself to admit that she is actually British and lived in London for many years before she moved to Dubai.

'So you're a half Moroccan, half Algerian Brit with an American accent who lives in Dubai?' he says just as the train slows down again.

'I guess that sums me up,' Nadia answers, reluctantly getting up to leave.

'Somehow, I think there's more to you than that,' he replies with a half smile. 'And if you wouldn't mind letting me find out, I'd like to meet up with you while you're here. Can I give you my number?'

235

As tempted as she is Nadia takes a deep breath reminding herself that in God's eyes, she is still a married woman, regardless of her husband's vile ways.

'Thanks but I'd better not,' she says as the carriage doors open. She gives him one last smile and steps off the train, their brief encounter making her feel warm inside. Maybe her life wouldn't be completely over if she and Daniel parted ways. *Maybe I'm not as awful as Daniel makes me feel.*

'God, you need to get with it,' Yasmin chastises Nadia as she reaches Arsenal station.

They lug her suitcase up the ramp, eventually emerging onto the quiet street where the station sits in between a row of small, terraced houses, like a shiny silver coin among a pocket full of coppers. The sky is bright blue, decorated with the occasional wisp of cloud and Nadia shivers, pulling her cardigan tight around her body, unused to the cold breeze.

'Didn't you bring a coat?' Yasmin asks as they turn the corner into Quill Street, the council estate rife with Bengalis, with the Ziani family being one of three Arab families, unless you count the Somalis, in which case, they are one of twelve. The houses are made from yellow bricks, a welcome change from the dismal brown of most council estates and there are children on the streets with their colourful bikes; the girls in gaudy frocks or cotton kameezs paired with frayed jeans, their slick, oiled hair glistening in the sun. As always, there is a scent of freshly cooked curry in the air and Nadia's stomach rumbles. She can't remember the last time she had a full meal or even wanted to.

'Why would I own a coat in Dubai?' Nadia retorts, following Yasmin into the bright apartment. The fragrance of buttery rice greets them and Nadia inhales deeply, her stomach growling once again. She pops her head into the small kitchen, her eyes falling on the table that saw many family meals, but now looks more like a magazine rack, with various journals and papers adorning it.

'Gosh, things have really changed since mum moved back to Morocco,' she notes, pulling off her white trainers and tossing them next to Yasmin's collection of more interesting footwear in the hallway.

'Well, seeing as you lot pretty much left me alone here, what did you expect? The flat to still look like a family house?' Yasmin snaps, her sharp tone causing Nadia to stare at her in surprise. The sisters look at each other in silence; the older wondering if her baby sister really was okay with living all alone in a big city, and the younger wondering why her big sister looked so tortured.

Nadia leaves the kitchen, already feeling despondent. Her old home just didn't feel the same without her mother's laughter and warmth and she is worried about the distant look in Yasmin's eyes. She has been so wrapped up in her own life, her own problems, that it never occurred to her to find out if her little sister was okay.

Guilt weighing her down, she drags herself up the stairs, pushes her old bedroom door open and enters, glad to be home despite the changes.

She isn't prepared for the rush of emotions that follow, the wave of nostalgia, the tightening in her throat as tears begin to gather in the corners of her eyes. The small room, painted cream during the days when magnolia was the hottest thing in home décor, looks almost the same as it did when she left home and moved in with Daniel. She takes a deep breath and closes the door before walking over to her bookcase, the shelves laden with university textbooks and old CDs. On the top shelf is a picture of her and Yasmin during their Qatar days. Nadia stares at her fifteen-year old self. Her eyes were big and bright, her smile open and unassuming, her skin fresh, and supple.

Moving over to the full-length mirror by the window, she looks at herself, thirteen years later. Her eyes are beginning to sink into their sockets through lack of sleep, her once round face is now gaunt and strained, her cheekbones protrude like an iceberg and her complexion is dull and lifeless.

'Nadia! Come down and eat!' Yasmin calls from the bottom of the stairs and Nadia is thankful for the interruption. She has come to hate looking at herself.

It has been three days since Nadia came home and she has realized that she actually missed navigating her way around pigeon poop and occasional dog droppings on the pavements on her way to the train station. She has also missed being able to walk to places rather than take taxis or coerce Daniel into taking her. But more importantly, she has missed having family around her.

Although it has only been seventy-two hours since she landed in London, she can already feel a huge shift in her emotional and physical well-being. She has been sleeping through the night without waking up in panic. She has been eating three balanced meals, and even the odd snack instead of skipping most of them and relying purely on breakfast cereal to ensure she has enough energy to move.

Even her relationship with Daniel seems to be improving. He's been calling her every evening to say how much he is missing her and that he can't wait for her to come back to him. Every morning she receives a text message proclaiming how sorry he is for all the hardship he has inflicted on her. And every time she hears from him, another pebble of hope joins the little cluster she has collected. She wonders if one day, she will have enough to build a wall around them again.

Feeling tired after her day of shopping Nadia has a bath, changes into flannel pyjamas, and makes herself a mug of hot chocolate, feeling sinful after taking a sip of the thick, creamy cocoa but tells herself that she needs to gain weight. She sits on the soft, faded canary yellow sofa, and sinks into the cushion, her hands clasped around her mug to keep them warm. She glances over at the bookshelf, wondering if she should pick up one of Yasmin's books to read, but then decides against it. She's not in the mood for anything heavy.

Taking out her laptop, she tells herself she will only check her own emails and not her husband's, although in her heart she knows she will have a peek eventually. He had of course changed his passwords, oblivious to the fact that Nadia used her key logging device to learn all of them again. He still thinks that he had accidentally chosen Google chrome to save all his passwords and Nadia is glad that he was inventive enough to reach his own conclusion without delving too deep into the reality.

As she browses through the various forwarded mails in her inbox, she comes across one that she has refrained from opening for a week, and as such, has not even opened it yet. However, the pangs of loneliness, together with the nostalgia she is experiencing being back at home, finally make her give in.

7obbi my love,

I understand why you feel compelled to ignore my messages and calls. As always, you have been far better than the men in your life, so it is only natural that you would respect your status as someone's wife despite the fact that he disrespects his own status as a husband.

All I want to say is this—I am willing to wait for you however long it takes, just like you were willing to wait for me all those years ago. But please, I need to know, should I wait, and should you leave your undeserving husband, should fate open the doors for us again—would you be willing to come back to me?

Just reply 'yes' or 'no' if you cannot bring yourself to write anything else. And if it is the latter, I will respect your decision and will omit myself from your life.

Yours,

Y

Nadia's hot chocolate is now lukewarm, but she takes a sip of it anyway. Yet another decision she needs to make. Another option to add to the mess that is her life.

She cannot help but feel annoyed as she re-reads his self-indulgent words. He was always dramatic. Why is he putting her through this torture when he knows she is suffering enough? Couldn't he have waited for her to come back to him instead of forcing a decision out of her?

She hits 'reply' and with her fingers poised on the keyboard hopes for some kind of divine sign that will guide her. Would replying in the affirmative count as cheating? Would it stoop her to Daniel's level? But replying in the negative would cut off the last, fragile tie she has with her childhood love.

Nadia's phone beeps with an incoming text message. She is relieved at the interruption and gets up to retrieve the phone. Upon seeing Daniel's name on the screen, she lets herself out onto the veranda and leans against the cold brick wall, pausing to watch a train go by on the rail tracks behind the flat, before she eventually musters up the courage to open it. Although Daniel has been messaging her every day, each time she sees his name, her heart thuds with fear. She never knows what to expect. It could be anything from an apology to a talaq.

Whatever the message is will decide what your answer to Yusuf will be, Nadia tells herself, closing her eyes for a fleeting moment.

Hey babe, just wanted to see how you're doing. I'm still missing you, still wish you hadn't left me. But then, it's good you did. It's reminded me that I didn't know what I had…until it was gone.

Nadia smiles and heads back indoors. Feeling more self-assured and confident than she had ten minutes before, she reopens her laptop and sends

Yusuf a resounding 'no'. Things between her and Daniel were finally looking up. He was willing to change and he realized what he had being doing was wrong. For her to tell another man to wait for her wouldn't be fair to her marriage.

Within seconds she receives a reply from Yusuf. A simple 'okay'. No flowery words, no profound testaments, just a four-lettered, two-syllable goodbye. Instead of feeling as though a weight had been lifted off her chest, Nadia feels an immense sense of loss, as though it were the end of an era.

Nadia is tired of crying lost tears. She logs out of her email and logs on to Daniel's, hoping that the contents will affirm that she has made the right choice.

Her eyes flickering through the various names, she learns with relief that there is nothing there. Feeling a little guilty at doubting him she is just about to sign out when an email from Jennifer comes through. Heart beginning to sink, she opens it quickly and reads the short message:

Last night was amazing. Thank Wifey from me for leaving you all to me ☺

Nadia's head begins to throb and she pauses a moment, holding her head in her hands and pressing her temples, wishing the pain would go away. There is a picture attached to the email, and she recoils in horror when she opens it. Before she can recover from the shock of seeing the pornographic image, another message from Jennifer comes through. Daniel must be using his mail at the same time as her. She smiles wryly at the irony. She is finally connected to her husband, finally on the same page. Just not in life.

You're welcome, babe, and thanks for the pic, I didn't even know you took it! Let me know when you want some more ;) She's gone for a few more days so let's make the most of it!

Nauseated, Nadia pushes her laptop aside and runs to the bathroom where she vomits into the toilet bowl, her stomach aching with every contraction until there is nothing but bile. She continues to throw up, her mouth stinging with acid, water running down her nose, her eyes bloodshot, her knees sore on the ice-cold tiled floor.

He wants to screw her while I'm away. He sent me a message telling me he missed me and then emailed her to arrange more of what he got last night.

Her body eventually stops heaving, and she lies on the bathroom floor for some time, the coldness soothing her burning skin, breathing heavily. She gave up her life in London for this. She gave up her dignity for this.

She gave up Yusuf for this.

As the weakness subsides, rage begins to take control over her body. Holding onto the toilet seat, she hoists herself up, washes her face and brushes her teeth, glancing at her reflection as she does.

Something has died in Nadia's eyes. The softness has been replaced by steel. She is sick of being a pushover. She will never let any man make her feel weak again.

She goes back to the living room and curls up on the sofa once again. But this time, instead of letting grief overcome her, she focuses her emotions on her anger instead. Daniel has taken advantage of her one too many times.

This time she will get her revenge.

20

I had another nightmare last night. I keep having them every other week like an alert on my phone, reminding me of what I've left behind and what I'm trying to achieve.

Last night's choppy, static dream was so intense that I can still feel the tightness in my chest as I let out a silent scream. I can still feel my head spinning as the walls closed in around me and I collapsed in a heap of limbs on the ground, the sound of sirens clawing at my ears. That was when I woke up, my breath heavy, beads of perspiration clinging to my skin. I dragged myself out of bed and stumbled to the bathroom where I made wudhu with cold water, my eyes still heavy with sleep, my movements slow with fatigue. After I finished the last step, washing my feet up to my ankles, I stared at my reflection, at the dark circles under my eyes, my lifeless skin, the water dripping down my face and my neck, leaving wet patches on my Snoopy nightshirt. I looked exactly as I felt—cold, lonely, and miserable.

Heading back into my bedroom, I wrapped a scarf around my head, pulled on my dressing gown and stood on the prayer mat. It wasn't even time for Fajr, so I prayed the optional night prayers instead. I prayed for Allah to ease my parents' pain, their heartache, their disappointment. I prayed for Allah to forgive my brother for his anger and frustration, to instill peace in his heart, patience in his mind. The last prayer before I fell asleep was for Jayden, wherever he is; for Allah to accept his soul into the garden of eternal peace and happiness.

Hours later, the phone wakes me up. I slowly open my eyes to find myself lying on the prayer mat, and my dressing gown covering me like a blanket.

'Hello?' I manage to croak, my throat dry, acutely aware that I sound disgusting first thing in the morning. 'Sabah al khair,' Goldenboy replies, his voice smiling.

I smile back, wondering if he too can feel my expressions through the phone. 'Sabah al nour,' I reply, trying my best to pronounce the guttural sounds properly. Arabic is definitely a beautiful language, but so difficult to learn and even harder to enunciate accurately.

'Why are you smiling?' he asks, and I grin even more.

'Because you called,' I say without thinking. The second I say it, I regret it. I'm supposed to be the cool, suave girl from North London. Not a sickeningly adoring teenager.

'Because you woke me up, I meant,' I hastily add, trying to redeem myself. 'I forgot to set my alarm. So I'm happy I didn't oversleep.'

'Well get ready. I'm coming to collect you,' he says, oblivious to my embarrassment. 'I'll be there in an hour.'

'Where are we going?' I ask, panicking.

'It's a surprise. Just dress comfortably, okay? See you soon!' With that, he hangs up and I sit still for a moment.

Persuading myself that my relationship with him is legit and nothing like what happened with Jayden, I get into the shower. I throw on a pair of loose, frayed jeans, trainers, and a long sleeved mustard cotton jersey top that just about covers my bum.

Excitement flutters in my stomach as I get into Goldenboy's blue VW Scirocco. The sun is bright, but the air is surprisingly fresh, cool enough to open the windows and drive along the motorway. I connect my iPod to the sound system and introduce him to Coldplay. I can't help but sing along to 'Yellow', and I see him watching me from the corner of his eye, smiling as he leans back against the seat and controls the wheel with his left hand, his right elbow leaning comfortably on the arm rest.

Goldenboy is wearing aviators, white linen trousers, and a dark blue Armani T-shirt and I have a sudden urge to touch his leg to see if I can feel his skin through the thin linen. Obviously I don't though, and I play with my iPod to divert my thoughts elsewhere.

'You're so different from all the girls I know,' he suddenly says, turning the volume down.

'Really? Why?' I ask nonchalantly, secretly pleased. 'I don't know. You just are,' he says quietly. 'You seem so comfortable with yourself and you're so open. What you see is what you get. There are no secrets.'

My face turns pink at his inaccurate analysis and I turn my face towards the window so that he can't see how uncomfortable he has made me. I wish I had no secrets.

But the reality is that I do. I have a secret that grows every single day, one that I will never be able to forget because it breathes the same air as me. It was created from within me. And then it was torn away from me.

The day we came home from the hospital and back to my cousin's dingy flat in Karol Bagh, I saw Bhen staring at me like she couldn't wait for me to get on the next flight back to Heathrow. She left us alone for almost an entire day, too scared of my emotional outbursts to come too close. So she watched me—us—from afar, and I could smell the desperation on her. As her distress grew, so did mine and I stared down at my angel, my breath stuck in my throat. I couldn't believe that I had agreed to it all.

That night, I stepped out onto the balcony and stared down at the city beneath us. All around us was life. Cars horned, men cursed, children cried, women sang, lights twinkled, onions fried, chillies stung. The laughter, the spices, the blurs, was all evidence that even if my world stopped spinning, life would go on.

Inside my room there was life. An amazing bundle of joy who would have to grow up without me. It didn't mean that I didn't love her, or didn't want her. It meant that I was able to look beyond myself and give her what was best for her; a stable family life, doting parents, and the chance to learn who she was without the stigma of being 'the girl whose black father was killed by her uncle'.

We continue driving down the motorway, leaving the glitz and glamour of Dubai behind us and join a much smaller dual carriageway. The desert is on either side of us and occasionally we drive pass a few dirty, dusty roadside shops. This is the first time I'm venturing out of Dubai and already I feel like I'm in another world. One that is actually real, not a mirage of all things new and shiny. As we get further away from the city, there are fewer people and vehicles on the highway, the signs are in a different language and brown mountains loom ahead. I stare at them in awe, excitement rippling through me.

'Welcome to Jebel Hafeet,' Goldenboy declares. 'I thought we could have lunch in the oasis. Do you like the surprise?'

'I love it!' I exclaim, my eyes shining and a huge grin on my face.

As much as my relationship with Jayden was thrilling and exciting, it wasn't particularly romantic. He never actually took me anywhere different, not unless he wanted a quiet spot to make out with me, in which case we went to various lonely parks and cemeteries. I know, how morbid. Neither of us had a car, we relied purely on our Oyster cards to get about and we didn't have much money either, so we couldn't go anywhere remotely exotic, unless you think graveyards could fall in that category. There was a hidden one just off Stoke Newington High Street that was quite peaceful. The grass was unkempt and there were loads of trees and foliage covering the headstones, providing ample privacy. I should have realized that any relationship that blossomed in a place rife with dead bodies was ill-fated.

Even our nikah was basic. We had dragged three of our friends to East London mosque and the Imam performed the ritual in a bland monotone. I wore a simple shalwar kameez and Jayden wore a shirt and jeans. My dowry was my Argos ring, which I wore around my neck on a delicate gold chain. Afterwards, we went for lunch at Tayyabs in Whitechapel, and I barely ate a thing, sick with guilt and trepidation. This certainly wasn't the wedding I had envisioned for myself. A marriage is supposed to be a joyous occasion filled with love and blessings. Not a secret union between secret lovers.

The oasis is nestled amongst the towering, sandy coloured mountains, a luscious splash of green in otherwise arid landscape, and we choose a spot close to a little stream. Goldenboy has actually not only packed a fabulous picnic of Arabic bread, grilled chicken, roast potatoes, hummous, baba ghanouj, fattoush, and lots of fruit and drinks, but he has remembered to bring a blanket, cutlery, and even a thermos of mint tea *and* a shisha. There are other families around us, barbecuing fragrant cubes of lamb and preparing salads, and others sitting around drinking tea. Goldenboy strikes up a conversation with one family in Arabic, and the next thing I know, they've sent a lot of grilled goodies in our direction. I love the Arab hospitality, how they are so generous with their time, attention, and material possessions. I can't imagine being invited to join in someone else's family picnic in Springfield Park. In fact, they'd probably nick our stuff when we weren't looking.

When the sun sets, we hear the adhaan in the distance and Goldenboy asks me if I want to pray behind him. I readily agree and he stands in front of me and begins leading the prayer. His voice is sweet and melodic and I feel a rush of emotion stir my very soul as he recites various verses from the Qur'an. We finish praying, get the shisha ready, and relax under the stars, smoking the fragrant double apple shisha and sipping on mint tea. I wish I could stay like this forever.

'I haven't seen these many stars in a long time,' I tell him, looking up at the clear black sky. I lie down on my back and try to count them, encouraging Goldenboy to do the same. He seems to be taking the task quite seriously. All I want to do is roll over and place my head on his chest and listen to his heart beat and then confide in him my secrets, my hopes, my fears. My story. I wonder how he would feel if he knew everything about me, if he would still want to be friends with me. Or if he would reject me, hold me in contempt, and lose all respect for me.

I have had to learn the hard way that the people who you think love you unconditionally, actually only love the idea of you and when you fall from grace, they no longer want you. The idea they had has been shattered and the real you—the naked, vulnerable you—simply isn't good enough. I came out here hoping for a fresh start with people who don't know my sordid past. I wonder how long I can keep it like that.

Goldenboy turns his body to face me, his expression thoughtful. My heart starts to pound and the metre between us suddenly feels like nothing. After all, he is close enough to touch me. The possibilities between us are endless.

I break away from Goldenboy's gaze and look away, turning my body away as I do so, my palms beginning to feel clammy. I don't want Goldenboy to suffer the same fate as Jayden. He didn't deserve what my family did to him, and the only thought that offers me some comfort is the hope that he has found peace without me.

And me? Every day I wake up with an overwhelming sense of guilt. I should have known that nothing can remain hidden forever. I shouldn't have trusted my cousin with my life-changing secret. I shouldn't have started anything with Jayden knowing that my family would never accept him. I should have known better.

Then there's the confusion. Was giving my baby away the right thing to do? Would she grow up to resent the mother who, she would think, abandoned her? Would her parents even tell her the truth? Would she know about her mixed heritage? Would they tell her that after I returned to England, I stopped going out, stopped talking and eventually stopped eating because I missed her so much? Would they tell her that I ended up in hospital, attached to a drip? That I had to resort to counselling to keep my sanity intact?

Or would they just tell her that I didn't care? That I didn't want her? That it was easy to let her go?

Maybe that's why Goldenboy's arrival is such a relief. I finally have something, someone, who numbs just a tiny bit of the pain.

21

Lady Luxe is certain that if she does all she can to make Humaid like her, *really* like her, he won't bother pursuing her alter ego. She is certain that once subjected to her subtle yet intoxicating feminine wiles, the hussy with the blonde hair will become an obsession of the past. Of course, there is always a chance that he really is a complete a-hole, in which case, he will probably want the best of both worlds.

And if he did turn out to be a bastard like most men (with the exception of Mr Delicious of course, whom she still pines after) she has, with a little help from her trusty cousins, Plan B. Just in case.

In an attempt to test the waters Lady Luxe sends Humaid a text message, asking him to meet Jennifer at six, knowing quite well that he will be too busy with the real her to comply.

His reply comes almost immediately: *I would love to habibti, but unfortunately I have some family commitments. Can you please do me the honour of postponing it to 9 pm?*

Bastard. The politeness aside, the creep was planning on meeting a prospective bride at six, and a prospective shag at nine. The things men did to get laid never failed to surprise Lady Luxe, although admittedly, it worked in her favour when she was the one looking for a little action.

'Don't be so hypocritical,' Moza chastises her, brushing magic powder on her cousin's dehydrated skin to make her look young and fresh. 'It is *exactly* the kind of thing *you* would do.'

'No it bloody isn't,' Lady Luxe snaps, trying not to move her facial muscles too much. 'If I decided I wanted to get married the Emirati way, I'd stop messing around in an unIslamic way. I wouldn't have my cake, eat it, and then try another.'

'Right,' Moza replies uninterestedly. 'Anyway stop moving around. I'm trying to sort your face out here. When did your complexion become so terrible?'

'Since Leila and my bloody brother became "Mola".'

'Well that's no reason not to take care of yourself. Now open your eyes, let me admire my handiwork.'

Lady Luxe slowly opens her eyes and lets them roll into focus on Moza's frowning forehead and her own tiny reflection in Moza's critical brown eyes. 'Well?'

'I really do have magic hands, don't I? Go and check yourself out.' Moza steps back to allow Lady Luxe to climb off the bed, smiling proudly as her cousin floated past in a jade silk jellabiya courtesy of their friend, fashion designer Rima, creator of the haute couture brand, Rimalya.

Lady Luxe peers into the mirror and tries not to let her jaw drop open in awe. Gone is the tired old hag from that morning and in her place is a beautiful, vibrant young woman with perfect creamy skin with a hint of gold, cat-like eyes amid hues of green, and glistening lips. Her fringe is then blow-dried to perfection and she places a purple chiffon sheyla loosely over her head, matching the purple beads on her jellabiya and slips her feet into Gina sandals. Her favourite diamond bracelet rests on her dainty wrist and a generous application of Romano Ricci's Midnight Oud completes her look.

'He'll never be able to resist me like this,' Lady Luxe grins, running over to Moza and throwing her arms around her. 'Where's Rowdha?'

'She's out getting some supplies for Plan B.'

'Okay great. Although I'm getting the feeling that Plan A will work just fine.'

The two cousins smile at each other, slightly nervous, as they wait for the doorbell to ring. Downstairs in the ladies reception room Lady Luxe's aunts, Maryam and Fatima, her father's older sisters, were waiting to greet the groom's party, taking the place of her mother and her deceased grandmother. Not that they would have stayed at home, had Lady Luxe's mother and grandmother been present.

Aunt Maryam and Aunt Fatima were like characters from a Roald Dahl book. The epitome of selfishness, Maryam the divorcee and Fatima the widow stopped at absolutely nothing to get what they wanted. Be it a home renovation, a new car, or a new sister-in-law, they were constantly on the phone with their younger brother, whining, moaning, and emotionally blackmailing him in their nasal voices until they got what they wanted. They weren't in the least interested in finding a good match for their errant niece, but they were interested in maintaining the family reputation. They needed to be assured that Humaid is from a respectable family and that he is able to display good conduct in public.

'Sis, they're here,' Ahmed declares in a loud stage whisper, knocking on Lady Luxe's door and then sticks his head around it before she even acknowledges the knock.

'What? I didn't hear the door bell,' Lady Luxe whimpers. 'What car have they come in?'

'A white Merc G350, two digit plate. I saw four figures in black and then him. He's sitting with Baba and Mohamed in the men's living room and I think they'll let him come and check you out after you go and sit with the ladies for a bit. That's what Baba said to Mohamed when you were getting ready anyway.'

'Oh man. I'm dreading this,' Lady Luxe moans, leaning against Ahmed for support, hoping that she will succeed in making Humaid forget about Jennifer and save herself from more drama.

'Don't worry hon, you'll be fine,' Moza says reassuringly, giving her cousin's arm a tight squeeze. 'They won't let you sit alone with him, so I'll be there the whole time. I won't make it obvious that I'm listening to your conversation, but if he gives you a hard time, I'll step in, okay?'

'Okay,' Lady Luxe answers in a quiet voice, trying to calm down and not think of all that could go wrong. Humaid was *not* going to find out that his blushing virgin bride was the same woman he danced with at Chi. Mohamed was *not* going to find out that his sister was far from the innocent girl he thought she was. And Leila was *not* going to find out that her 'best friend' was her lover's sister. Everything was going to be fine.

'Miss X? The guests are here and your aunts are asking you and Miss Moza to come downstairs,' Anne-Marie says timidly from the door. 'Oh Miss X! You look beautiful!'

'Thanks Anne-Marie, we'll come down now,' Lady Luxe replies, composing herself and holding her head up high. 'Ready, Moze?'

'Yalla, let's go.'

With Moza leading the way, the pair make their way down the staircase, their heels clattering on the marble, announcing their arrival long before they actually reach the living room door.

Ahmed trails behind them. 'Have fun,' he says wryly, leaving the women at the foot of the stairs and heading into the study.

Moza takes a deep breath and pushes the heavy wooden door open, the clouds of musky bakhoor swirling around them.

'Salaam'alaykom,' she greets the unknown faces. 'My name is Moza, I am Lady Luxe's cousin, her father is my father's younger brother,' she says with a sombreness that makes Lady Luxe choke back a snort.

The ladies' living room in Lady Luxe's home is very different from the minimalistic décor of the rest of the house, with the exception of her father's study of course. Lady Luxe had designed the room to look like an old Emirati house, with sandy coloured walls, thick Persian rugs and low, red and black Majlis style furniture. She had collected the ornaments scattered around the large room from her travels across the Muslim world; leather floor lamps and colourful glass chandeliers from Morocco, ornate ceramic bowls from Turkey, an antique iron birdcage from Tunisia, colourful wall hangings from Cairo, ornate mother-of-pearl encrusted coffee tables from Damascus. The eclectic combination, instead of appearing in conflict, felt like a free-flowing story, each piece holding a special beauty, each artefact telling a different tale, each colour complementing its neighbour.

'Salaam'alaykom,' Lady Luxe says with faux shyness, following Moza into the room and casting her gaze down, lifting her extremely long and fake eyelashes a little to glance surreptitiously at her surroundings. There is a low murmur as all of Humaid's female relatives appraise Lady Luxe's slim frame, her generous height, her hazel eyes, and her straight posture, mumbling 'helou' to themselves as they continue to stare.

Lady Luxe's aunts sit together, dressed in their abayas in preparation of Humaid's arrival, and adjacent to them, along the wall opposite the door, sit four women, also in abayas.

'Alaykom Salaam, habibti, how are you?' One of the women exclaims, as Lady Luxe glides over to greet them all personally, shaking hands and kissing their cheeks.

'Oh!' Lady Luxe exclaims, recognizing her to be her recent client. *So this was why Mohamed warned me not to mess up his friend's mum's abaya.*

'Yes, I didn't want to intimidate you that time by telling you that I am Um Humaid,' she replies with a smile. 'Plus I didn't want you to feel obliged to give me a big discount. Sit down ya bnayti, you look very beautiful Mashalla, Mashalla.'

Lady Luxe continues looking down, smiling small smiles occasionally and answering questions about what she does and what she studied with such sweetness that she almost gets a sugar rush. She feels a lot more comfortable knowing that Humaid's mother was her intelligent client, and actually wishes that her son wasn't such a loser. If Humaid had been half-decent, she would have actually considered selling out to the farce that was also known as marriage.

'Did you say you studied in London?' Humaid's fat aunt asks in disapproval, her eyes narrowed and her thin lips pursed spitting out the word 'London' like a bitter cardamom pod.

His grandmother remains silent, her piercing stare unfaltering as she clutches prayer beads in her wrinkled right hand and mutters prayers under her breath. Her face is covered by a bronze burqa and her eyes are watery, as if they have seen much sorrow in their years.

'Yes, khala. My mother lives there so I stayed with her,' Lady Luxe lies in a quiet voice, omitting the fact that her mother only visited her South Kensington apartment once a month for her Harley Street trips and preferred living in her cottage in Hampshire the remaining twenty-eight days of the month. She peers over her long eyelashes and adds woefully, 'I do miss her terribly.'

'Yes, poor child, she had to grow up far too quickly,' her Aunt Maryam interrupts. 'However, as a consequence, she is very responsible. You should see her with her younger brother. She is marvellous.'

'Isn't her younger brother actually her half brother?' The Evil Fat Aunt asks.

'Oh, it depends on your definition. My niece loves him terribly, he really is like her own,' Aunt Maryam answers without skipping a beat.

'But isn't he the product of her father's second marriage?' The Evil Fat Aunt persists. 'And didn't he divorce her soon after?'

'Well, you know how it is,' Moza interrupts smoothly. 'My uncle, like many men, is so very difficult to please as you all know. But if there is one woman he is happy with, it is his daughter.'

Before they could continue, Anne-Marie rushes into the room and announces that Humaid will be entering in a few minutes. There is a flurry as half the women in the room readjust their sheylas, Lady Luxe's older aunt, Maryam, holding the end of it over her mouth, covering herself further.

'Salaam'alaykom,' he announces loudly, sauntering into the room and flashing a wide smile at the women who sit in wait of his arrival, feeling a little like the Prophet Yusuf the day all those women chopped off their fingers.

Dressed in a plain white candoura and messily wrapped white guttra, he looks simple yet oddly attractive, Lady Luxe notes with interest. His eyes are big and dark, and his mouth full and generous.

Grabbing a cushion, he places it opposite Lady Luxe. 'I hope you don't mind if I sit here while we talk?' he asks to no one in particular, plonking himself down on the cushion and folding his legs.

'Of course, habibi, you must get to know your prospective wife as much as you can in the next twenty minutes, because the choice you make now will either make or break your entire life,' his mother replies, laughing.

All the older ladies join her in giggling, making a big show of not watching the couple, but clearly hanging on to every word.

'How embarrassing,' Humaid says quietly, smiling at Lady Luxe while she pours him fragrant Arabic qahwa with steady hands. 'I'm Humaid by the way.'

'Ahlan w sahlan,' Lady Luxe answers with a small smile, catching his eyes for a moment and then looking away like she believed a chaste virgin would do.

They begin to talk quietly, trying to ignore the women around them who are desperate to hear what they are talking about. Had they managed to overhear anything, they would have been disappointed to note that the conversation barely got beyond their favourite movies, music, and food. Lady Luxe is surprised to learn that Humaid loves watching documentaries, that his favourite music is rock, and the one dish he can eat over and over again is Phad thai with prawns.

'You're not how I expected you to be,' Lady Luxe concedes towards the end of their fairly enlightening conversation.

'And how was that?'

'Shallow. Conceited. Unoriginal.' she says bluntly.

'Well you're not what I expected either,' he retorts with a smile.

'And what was that?'

'Boring. Stupid. Unattractive.'

They laugh together, causing all the women to turn and stare at them with huge smiles on their faces, while Lady Luxe covers her face with her hands in embarrassment, playing her part to the hilt. Her attempt at feigning innocence seems to have worked as all the ladies nudge each other and whisper about how attractive her naiveté is.

'Aiwa,' Humaid's older sister calls out from across the room, winking conspicuously, causing Lady Luxe to blush some more.

'I think your aunts seem to approve of me. Does that mean I can take your number?' Humaid asks with a slow smile taking in Lady Luxe's pink lips and ready smile with lust, aching to know what is hidden beneath the loose folds of her gown, whether the rest of her body is the same caramel colour of her face and whether the rest of her will turn pink beneath his touch like her cheeks.

'Sorry Humaid, but I've never given my number to a guy before.' *You already have it, you nerd.*

'Oh okay. Well can you make an exception?' *If she gives her number to me after a little persuasion, it definitely means that she's ready to give it to anyone.*

'No I can't, sorry. If you need to get hold of me, you can always call my brother Mohamed and pass a message on.' *You know Mohamed right? The same guy I danced with at Chi?*

'Sure, I understand.' *This girl really takes her reputation seriously. Perfect wife material. But maybe not that much fun.*

The conversation draws to a close, hurried up by Humaid's mother who feels that they are

270

beginning to overstay their welcome even though most of the snacks Claudine had whipped up remain untouched. Lady Luxe bids farewell to all the smiling ladies, kisses them affectionately on their cheeks and then excuses herself from her aunts' chattering as they analyse the evening's events, claiming she has a headache.

Pulling her sandals off her feet and running up the stairs with Moza close behind, she shuts the door to her bedroom and grabs her Vertu phone, willing it to beep with a cancellation message.

'Girl, you were *wicked* down there,' Moza gushes. 'Seriously, if I were a bloke looking for a missus I would so propose to you. It was an Oscar worthy performance!'

'Really?' Lady Luxe asks, playing with the phone and praying fervently.

'Really,' Moza says with confidence. 'Look, he only just left and it's only 7:30. Give it another ten minutes, I'm sure he'll cancel. He was so besotted by you.'

Putting her phone on loud, Lady Luxe goes to the dressing room and changes into comfortable tracksuit bottoms and an oversized hoodie. Pulling her hair into a ponytail, she goes back to her bedroom to find that Moza has taken off her abaya and is lying on the bed, flicking through the TV channels.

The minutes drag by slowly, so slowly that Lady Luxe decides to join Moza in watching mindless TV. They settle on the Style Network, criticizing most of the costumes that appear on the catwalk and claiming that they could do much better themselves, until suddenly there is a beep from across the room.

Lady Luxe jumps out of bed, tripping on Moza's abaya and ends up falling on the tiled floor on her knees.

'Ouch!' she yells, clutching her knees in agony and dragging herself to her desk where she left the phone. She opens the message straightaway.

I'm running a little late. See you at Atlantis at 9:15.

'Shit!' Lady Luxe cries out, half tempted to hurl the phone across the room like she did with her BlackBerry, but the fact that it is a limited edition piece and is adorned with tiny white diamonds prevents her from doing so.

'Shit indeed,' Moza echoes, a worried look on her face. 'Plan B it is then.'

22

Nadia finds solace in the fact that Daniel has no idea that his wife, though in another country, is fully aware of the sordid affair he has embarked on. He doesn't have a clue that his wife is merely buying time until she returns to Dubai before she unleashes the true extent of her fury on him and that bitch Jennifer who gave him his first, delicious taste of infidelity, all the while mocking her for not being able to satisfy her own husband.

It is this feeling of empowerment, of having the upper hand that gives Nadia just enough peace of mind to fall asleep at night; albeit an uncomfortable, restless kind of sleep that never lasts more than an hour or two. And during her waking moments, she plots her revenge. Whether lying in bed and staring up at the ceiling adorned with glow-in-the-dark stars or ploughing through a painfully quiet meal with Yasmin, Nadia cannot think of anything other than seeking justice.

Before Daniel metamorphosed into a lying, cheating, scheming son-of-a-bitch, Nadia took pride in her ability to rationalise with serene detachment. But months of emotional abuse have taken their toll on her personality and she has recently discovered a side to her that previously remained dormant. The initial hurt, pain and self-loathing has worn off and in its place sits a cloud of bitterness.

'What do you want to do today?' Yasmin asks as she enters the dim kitchen to find her sister standing at the sink and staring out of the window, her view obstructed by the faded lace curtain intended to afford them a degree of privacy from their neighbours.

'Something that involves lots of walking,' Nadia replies, turning around and offering her sister the slightest of smiles. 'In two days I'll be back in the desert, back to using a car instead of my legs and back to the sweltering heat. Let's make the most of what London has to offer.'

'Camden or Covent Garden?' Yasmin asks with forced cheerfulness, taking note of the sadness in Nadia's eyes but trying to pretend that it has gone unnoticed. 'Or somewhere else? It's your day, you decide.'

It has not been easy for Yasmin to ignore Nadia's frailness since she has returned, but whenever she opens her mouth to say something, she takes one look at her sister's sunken eyes and snaps it closed. As they tidy up the breakfast mess, she makes a conscious decision to force herself to ask her sister what the hell is going on, regardless of how the answer will make either of them feel. After all, they are family. They are supposed to help each other in times of need, irrespective of whether or not help has been sought.

An hour later, the sisters are walking arm in arm through the colourful stalls in Camden Lock, weaving their way through the crowds of people while Nadia tries not to stare at the punks with their fluorescent hair and piercings, the Goths with their pale faces and black attire, or the hippies with loose, flowing shirts and baggy trousers.

Their hands full with all the shopping they've done, Yasmin and Nadia finally sit down to devour their rich cheese crêpes in silence, grease dripping down their fingers. Nadia tries her best to enjoy herself, but she cannot. The memories of Daniel and the life she's left behind are still too fresh in her mind.

Noticing the frown on Nadia's face, Yasmin takes a deep breath and before she loses her nerve, begins to speak.

'Nadia,' she begins, nervous at the prospect of upsetting her sister, 'I know something's wrong.' She falters as Nadia's expression changes from wistfulness to wariness but ploughs on regardless.

'Wait, let me finish,' she says, avoiding her sister's eyes. '*Please* don't pretend that everything's okay when it's not. I *know* something's wrong. I don't know what it is, but I know that it's bad enough for you turn into…*this*.'

Yasmin reiterates her point by gesturing at Nadia's painfully thin body, her sallow skin, her sunken eyes, and the worry lines creasing her forehead like carvings on a stone statue.

Nadia looks down and says nothing, shame and panic rising within her. She was hoping that Yasmin would never work up the courage to ask her what was wrong. She was hoping she wouldn't have to admit to her younger sister that she had failed.

'Please,' Yasmin implores, taking her sister's hands in hers and finally looking into her eyes. 'Tell me what's going on. Maybe I can help you, maybe I can't. Either way, talking about it will make you feel better.'

The silence stretches itself around them, strengthening the wall Nadia has built around her.

But Yasmin, who is equally stubborn, refuses to let go of Nadia's hands or break eye contact. She doesn't understand why her sister won't confide in her.

'You're my sister. I love you. Seeing you like this without knowing why is killing me,' Yasmin pleads. 'Is it work? Too much pressure? Friends? Loneliness?'

There is still no response from Nadia and Yasmin feels her temper ignite. How is she supposed to help if she doesn't know what is wrong? She remembers all the times Nadia was there for her; through their parents' divorce, their subsequent remarriages, the second divorces. She helped her through years of being dragged from one country to another, constant bullying at school. Yasmin remembers the way Nadia would prise her emotions out of her, relentless in her pursuit to know what was going through her unstable mind.

Yet here she was. Unyielding.

Nadia, oblivious to her sister's emotions; struggles to breathe as claustrophobia overcomes her.

Please don't make me say it.

'What is it Nadia?' Yasmin continues, her voice hard as her frustration grows. 'What is it? Are you bored? The luxurious Dubai lifestyle not good enough for you anymore?'

Nadia snaps out of her trance as if a bucket of water has been thrown over her head.

'Boredom?' she scoffs, yanking her hands out of Yasmin's grip, her eyes narrowed in disdain. 'You think mere boredom can do this to me? You think that I *want* to have my baby sister staring at me with her big eyes like I'm some kind of freak show?'

'What the hell is it then? What is so awful that you can't even tell *me,* your own flesh and blood?' Yasmin retorts, her tone matching her sister's. Although she feels guilty for pushing Nadia to this level, she is also relieved that the wall is beginning to crumble and that she is finally getting some answers.

'You just don't get it, do you?' Nadia hisses, standing up. 'You think I *like* looking like this? That it's somehow escaped my notice that I've aged ten years in the past ten weeks? You think I came to London for pity? For an interrogation? I came here for *peace* God dammit, Yasmin! I just wanted a break from wondering about who my husband was cheating on me with now. What I did to make him hate me so much. What I was supposed to do with my life now. There. I said it. Happy?'

Blinded by tears she stumbles forward, knocking over one of their shopping bags. Yasmin reaches out for her but she shoves her hands away, grabs her handbag and walks away, her pulse thumping in her ears, drowning out all the noise around her. She sees nothing as she pushes through the crowds of people, eventually breaking into a run, everything around her becoming a blur.

'Oi watch it!' a voice cries out as Nadia slams into a passerby, almost knocking him over. He grabs her waist just before she falls to the ground. Her body presses against him and the shock prevents her from pulling away immediately. Panting heavily, she mumbles an apology and then disengages herself.

'No worries love,' he replies, watching her with amusement as she attempts to straighten up still mortified. 'Hang on a second,' he adds, staring intently at her face. 'Haven't we met before?'

The shamefaced Nadia finally brings herself to look at the man insisting on conversing with her, and then does a double take as recognition dawns on her.

'You're the guy from the tube,' she says without thinking and then curses herself for letting him know that she remembers him. Her anger dies down immediately, replaced by extreme embarrassment. She wills her face not to turn red as she looks down at the pavement, unable to meet his piercing gaze, staring at his feet instead.

'So you remember,' he grins, puffing out his chest. 'Seems like you can't stay away from my lap.'

'If you say so,' Nadia responds, not knowing what else to say. Her heart is still beating a little too fast, whether due to the physical exertion or the sudden appearance of this good looking stranger, she's not quite sure.

'Anyway, I'm sorry once again,' she says indifferently. 'Take care…' Hoisting her bag onto her shoulder she begins to walk away.

'Hey, hang on a second,' he calls out, jogging to catch up with her. 'Don't you think you owe me a drink at least?'

'For what?' Nadia glances at him sideways without slowing down, resenting the intrusion but also beginning to enjoy it. It has been so long since she allowed this kind of attention. And although she feels a twinge of guilt, the gold band on her ring finger suddenly feeling like lead, she pushes the uneasiness aside and reminds herself that her husband is currently sleeping with another woman.

'For what? For physically assaulting me, not just once, but twice!'

'Does it look like I drink?'

'I don't know. I never judge a book by its cover.'

'Well I don't.'

'Not even hot chocolate on a cold winter's day?'

Nadia stops walking, Camden Town tube station now right in front of her, and looks at the stranger, unsure of what to say. Most of her wants to laugh off his advances without a second thought but another part of her, the part that longs for some kind of male attention, the part that needs to feel desired, tempts her into reconsidering his offer. Maybe he can help her forget about Daniel, at least for an hour or two, if nothing else.

'You know what? Why not? But you're inviting me.'

'It would be my pleasure, m'lady!'

For the first time in weeks, Nadia breaks into a genuine smile as they walk into the warm station, and for the first time in months, she feels like a woman.

○●○

'Are your eyes always this sad?' Prince Charming asks Nadia as they walk through Regent's Park, their hands stuffed into their coat pockets, and their noses red from the chilly March wind.

'Of late, yes,' she replies, surprising herself with her honesty. Prince Charming is far easier to talk to than she expected and she finds herself admitting things she would never admit to someone she actually knows. He doesn't even know her name, nor she his, but she finds this sense of anonymity strangely liberating.

'Of late? What century are we in?' he teases, and she shoves him in response, feeling shy all over again. During these three, short hours, she has barely thought about Daniel and her thirst for revenge. In those three hours, London has burst into colours. Through the grey, she is noticing the vivid green grass, the splatters of bright yellow as spring's first daffodils emerge from the ground, the blue sky decorated with tufts of cartoon-like clouds.

And then there's the chocolate of Prince Charming's skin, the specks of gold in his coffee coloured eyes, his soot coloured hair. It is easier to forget Daniel, who is teetering on the brink of baldness, when she is next to someone far superior in the looks department.

It's a shame he's not Muslim, she thinks for a fleeting moment before shoving the thought into a dusty corner of her mind. She cannot allow herself to open a door of possibilities. *It's just today,* she tells herself. *Nothing more. You don't need more complications in your life.*

There is a familiar sound in the distance and Nadia stops mid-step and mid-thought to listen.

'What—' Prince Charming begins but she hushes him, her eyes closed.

'Shh…can you hear that?' she whispers.

'Hear what?'

'That voice in the distance? It's so amazing. Listening to it you'd think we were somewhere in the Middle East, yet here we are in a public park in the middle of London.'

'The adhaan you mean?' Prince Charming asks and Nadia opens her eyes in surprise.

'That's very culturally aware of you,' she half-teases, secretly impressed. 'You must know that it's time for prayer then. Mind if we go to the mosque so I can pray?'

They start walking towards the minaret in the distance. It is partly hidden by the trees surrounding the mosque, and when the golden dome is finally within sight, Nadia stops again to devour it with her eyes. Prince Charming watches her in amusement, and she catches him looking at her and shrugs helplessly.

'It's just so beautiful!' Nadia says, smiling sheepishly and turning to face the minaret again. 'I know it must seem weird to you, and I don't even know how to explain it myself, but right now, I'm in a pretty dark place and my faith is the only thing that's keeping me going.'

She stops talking and glances at Prince Charming from the corner of her eye, wondering how he will react. There is no disgust, pity, or even confusion in his eyes though. Rather, he appears to be deep in thought, so she continues, searching deeper within herself to articulate what she is experiencing.

'Just when I'm about to fall, something happens to remind me of why I was created. Like I'll see a mosque or hear the adhaan, or come across a verse in the Qur'an that touches me and suddenly it's like everything will be okay again.'

They reach the entrance to the courtyard and pause for a moment. Nadia wonders if Prince Charming will wait for her outside or whether he is curious enough to venture into the peaceful grounds with her.

'I'll let you in on a secret,' he says, his voice light but the look in his eyes strangely serious.

Nadia says nothing and waits for him to continue, assuming that he will confess that he has been inside a mosque before.

'I converted to Islam a few years ago.'

Nadia stares at him in shock. This is definitely not the confession she was expecting.

'Erm, okay,' she says eventually, unsure whether to be pleased or troubled by this short, simple admission of fact that has suddenly and drastically altered the dynamics between them. Until now, there had been no possibility of anything ever happening between them. It was supposed to be nothing more than a beautiful afternoon between two strangers who would never cross paths again. It was this lack of possibility that Nadia found so liberating, and that allowed her to behave so uncharacteristically.

'Don't look too thrilled,' Prince Charming says wryly, noting Nadia's wary expression.

'Sorry, it's just…I didn't expect it.'

'Well why don't you go and pray and I'll do the same. I'll meet you back here in about fifteen minutes?'

They walk together through the spacious courtyard and part ways when they reach the foyer of the mosque. Nadia slips into the women's section, taking off her black cashmere coat and unwrapping her grey hijab as she does so. Rolling up the sleeves of her slightly fitted black woollen jumper and taking off her boots and socks, she sits on a stool and begins performing the ablution, the hot water instantly warming her cold skin. She dries her face, arms, and feet using tissue paper, then wraps the scarf back around her head and pins it in place before climbing the stairs to the prayer area.

The women's prayer hall is almost empty, with the exception of a couple of Arab-looking women sitting on the floor with their backs against the wall, reading the Qur'an. Nadia looks around the room at the familiar thick blue carpet, the glistening chandeliers, and the magnificent dome, engraved with verses from the Qur'an and remembers the times she would come here to get away from whatever was bothering her. It used to be her secret hideaway, her respite from the outside world. The emotions connected to the room are intoxicating, and Nadia blinks back the tears from her eyes.

The imam begins the prayer, his melodic voice filling the hall and Nadia joins the line of women in prayer as they follow the imam through all the various motions. As her forehead touches the soft carpet she feels tears rush to her eyes again.

When the congregational prayer is over, Nadia holds up her hands and offers her personal supplications to God, begging him to help her through the darkness, to give her the strength to leave Daniel and to give her a sign that the future holds some form of happiness for her.

She sits in prayer for over an hour and it is only when her phone beeps with an incoming text message that she remembers that there is someone waiting for her outside. She tries to get up quickly, but her legs seem to have been turned to wood having sat in the same position for so long. Hobbling over to the shoe rack, she somehow manages to put her boots back on and then stumbles down the stairs, hoping that Prince Charming hasn't given up on her and left.

Rushing out into the courtyard, her coat still in her hand, Nadia is confronted by the ice-cold wind as she looks around the empty area for Prince Charming, cursing herself for forgetting all about him. Her scarf flailing in the wind and the tip of her nose already turning red, she struggles to put her coat back on, her heart already beginning to ache with loneliness.

Don't be such an idiot. You only knew him for a few hours, she tells herself as she does up the buttons with cold, stiff fingers.

Shoving her hands back into her pockets, she slowly begins to walk towards the road, each step laden with a newfound emptiness, one that was different from the emptiness she felt the day before.

'You're leaving me after making me wait for an hour?'

Nadia turns around to find Prince Charming jogging up to her holding his coat in his hands with a bewildered expression on his face.

'Oh, you're still here? I thought you had left,' she mumbles, her heart skipping a beat. His presence breathes fresh life into her.

'You didn't think I was going to stand out in the cold all that time did you? I was in the bookshop. Anyways, it's freezing out here. Let's go and get something to eat. You up for it?'

'Yeah, why not,' she concedes, still trying to remain impassive while acutely aware that this was beginning to take a dangerous turn.

Oh screw it, she thinks as they walk up Park Road, past rows and rows of grandiose apartments.

Prince Charming stops outside Mumtaz, an Indian restaurant near the mosque that Nadia has never been to before, and gestures for her to follow him inside. As they open the door they are welcomed by a blast of heat and Nadia takes off her coat before she begins to perspire. As she does so she notices Prince Charming running his eyes over her body with appreciation. They make eye contact and he blushes, embarrassed. 'Nice jumper,' he says sheepishly, looking away.

Turning red herself, Nadia hurriedly plants herself on her chair and clears her throat, anxious to change the subject.

'So why did you become Muslim, and more importantly, why didn't you say anything to me sooner?' she says, hoping that the question will dampen the charged atmosphere.

'Do you want the long answer or the short answer?'

'How about short and if it's interesting you can tell me the long one later.'

'Alright here it goes. I met a Muslim girl when I was at Uni and we started dating, I fell madly in love with her but she wouldn't go all the way as she was a bit strict like that. Hormones, love, and a little bit of interest in Islam inspired me to convert, so I did, and we got married in secret.'

Prince Charming pauses and looks at Nadia, who stares back at him in astonishment.

'It's like something out of a movie,' she says genuinely intrigued. 'Go on, tell me more.'

Prince Charming laughs and takes a sip of sweet lassi. He licks his lips and Nadia tries not to stare at them by focusing on his nose instead.

'Okay, so we got married in secret and obviously did everything married people do. Well, not really as it was a secret so I couldn't exactly meet her family or anything.'

'And then?'

'One night, completely out of the blue, her brothers and her cousins came after me, beat the crap out of me and pretty much left me for dead. Here, look at this.'

Prince Charming stands up and much to the horror of the rest of the customers, lifts up his white hoodie to reveal a long, deep scar across his taut torso. Nadia stares at it.

'It's beautiful,' she says simply, looking away. 'So what happened next?'

'Her brother was arrested, but he got out of it as he obviously had a million alibis and they didn't have enough proof that it was him. And then she disappeared.'

'Oh my God. They didn't *kill* her did they?'

'At first I thought they did something to her. I went crazy looking for her everywhere. But then I heard that she left town and that she didn't want anything to do with me. I didn't want to get in touch or track her down in case her family did something to hurt her. And that was it. The last time I saw her was a day so normal I don't even remember what happened, or what we did, or what she was wearing.'

'That's so sad,' Nadia whispers, touching her chest with her hand. 'So you went through all that for nothing?'

'Yeah that pretty much sums it up.' Prince Charming feigns indifference but it is obvious to Nadia, from the slouch in his shoulders and shadow in his eyes, that he's still hurting. She leans over and takes his smooth hands into hers, and he looks at her in surprise, but she says nothing.

'So what's your story?' he says, his voice husky, pulling his hands away.

'Long or short?'

'Short of course.'

'I met a guy. Fell in love. Got married. Moved to the other side of the world to be with him. Then found out he's been cheating on me pretty much from the word go. Only he doesn't know that I know and I'm working out what to do about it.'

'Ouch. That's harsh.'

'Yeah.'

Nadia and Prince Charming eat the rest of their meal in silence, barely tasting any of the food, both lost in their own thoughts.

'You know, it's so weird how we know so much about each other but we don't even know each other's names,' Nadia says after a while, breaking the comfortable silence they had fallen into. 'Somehow, it doesn't seem to matter though.'

'How come you never asked me before?' Prince Charming asks, raising his eyebrows.

'I didn't see a point,' Nadia admits, her voice quiet.

'And now?'

'I see a point.'

There is another silence as Prince Charming weighs Nadia's words.

'Well,' he says eventually. Nadia looks at him in trepidation, wondering what he will say.

He's going to tell you to forget about it. You're still married. He doesn't want you. You have too much baggage.

'How about we start again then?' he says with a smile, holding out his hand. Nadia laughs in relief, and accepts his handshake with enthusiasm.

'Alright, love? I'm Jayden. Jayden Lynch. And you?' he says in his most charming voice.

'Nadia Ziani,' Nadia replies with an exaggerated coy smile, trying not to laugh.

'Pleasure to meet you Nadia.'

'The pleasure's mine, Jayden.'

Nadia and Jayden burst into laughter and this time it is he who reaches across the table and takes her small, cold hands into his. The warmth of his touch runs through her veins and she smiles at him, hoping he doesn't let go.

He doesn't.

Instead, he draws her hand closer to him and brings it slowly up to his lips.

23

I have moments when I absolutely love living in Dubai and lately, they're not as few and far between as they were when I first moved out here. I still have major issues with a lot of things—the blatant discrimination, the hierarchial system and lack of transparency—but I've realized that since I'm stuck here for the duration of my contract, I may as well enjoy what I can, while I can. It's not all doom and gloom. I love the abundance of halal food, pampered lifestyle (I went to the salon to get a mani and pedi *again* after twenty-four years of never being bothered) and I love the fact that one can pray just about anywhere, something that definitely beats having to pull over at a service station or take refuge behind a tree.

In ode to this realization, I have decided to take the plunge and rent a car. I've never owned a car before and relied mainly on Travelcards to get around London.

I stand there in the dimly lit basement car park, staring at the rented Toyota Yaris and wondering how I'm supposed to drive the fragile little thing around this monstrous city. Sheikh Zayed Road in particular scares the hell out of me. Nevertheless, muttering verses from the Qur'an under my breath, I decide to see if I can make it from JBR to the Springs in one piece.

I slowly drive out of the car park and as I do, I think back of the first time I sat behind a wheel— the day Jayden brought his brother's BMW to our Uni and we had the run in with the Asian rude girls. Lost in my thoughts, I accidentally take the Jebel Ali/Abu Dhabi exit, my memories interfering with my limited sense of direction.

'Damn you Jayden for messing with my mind so much,' I think, as I drive on to Sheikh Zayed Road and wince as I join the traffic.

After some time, I actually begin to enjoy the drive so I roll down my windows and turn up the radio, relishing the sensation of the wind ruffling my hair. I plod along at ninety kilometres an hour, and when I get used to the road with its six lanes on either side, I tentatively begin switching lanes. It isn't long before I am weaving in and out of the cars like a pro, wondering why I am the only one who seems to know what the indicators are there for.

In the UK, the motorways generally operate by a uniform rule—drive on the left unless you need to overtake—and very rarely do you see people hogging the fast lane. Here though, anything goes when it comes to roads. You can overtake, undertake, intimidate people by coming right up to their bumpers and flashing your headlights until they move out the way, and ignore indicating altogether. You can speed down the slow lane at one hundred and eighty, and you can cruise down the fast lane at hundred—until someone comes up behind you and forces you to move out of the way, that is. I realize that driving in Dubai requires a lot more concentration than in London; you have to be aware of everything that is around you at all times and you have to expect people to undertake you or swerve in front of you without signalling. You can even do bizarre things like reversing around a roundabout when you miss your exit without anyone batting an eyelid.

As soon as I become comfortable with driving, I start thinking about that autumn day in London again, and no matter how much I try to delete the memories from my mind, I can't. I even try thinking about my dilemma with Goldenboy instead, but that doesn't help either. The scent

296

of the upholstery, the feel of the steering wheel between my nervous hands, the sensation of finally being in control, all resonate with that morning with Jayden.

We ended up in Alexandra Palace, one of our favourite hang out spots in North London. Jayden parked by the ice rink and we walked to the actual palace and sat on the walls, feasting our eyes on the magnificent view in front of us. We could see miles and miles of London in the distance; tiny grey buildings, baby towers, all against the backdrop of a typical English blue-ish grey sky. We sat huddled together, the chilly breeze surrounding us. He wrapped his arms around me and his warmth filtered through my denim jacket and my white hoodie, heating up my skin. We didn't talk much as we sat there, just absorbing the amazing view and enjoying each other's proximity.

Until I began to wonder how long our relationship would last. What would happen after Uni was over and my parents undoubtedly began enquiring into suitors? It had only been a couple of months since we technically got together and neither of us had uttered the dreaded 'L' word. I was probably the only girlfriend in the world who adored her boyfriend but hoped he would never work up the courage to say it. That four-letter word would change everything. And I wasn't ready.

To avoid voicing my growing sense of uneasiness, I jumped off the wall, grabbed Jayden's hand and pulled him back to the car. Thinking he was about to get 'things', he happily obliged, but instead, I slid into the driver's seat and asked him to teach me how to drive. Jayden being Jayden, readily agreed without asking any questions.

The next day, a group of Asian boys who weren't from our Uni turned up in Hatfield. When Jayden walked out of the campus, earphones glued to his ears, completely oblivious to the group that was waiting for him, they pounced. By the time they were finished, Jayden lay in a broken heap on the floor, his entire body covered with bruises, his white t-shirt smeared with red.

None of us realized that this was only his first run-in with overprotective Asian boys. The worst was yet to come.

I've been driving for about forty-five minutes now and don't have a clue where I am. I know that I need to somehow go back the way I came, but every time I reach an exit, I end up driving just a little bit more. Although I'm just cruising along in a straight line, I'm enjoying the experience.

The scenery has changed and so has the road—it's now a reddish colour and the signs are describing places I've never heard of, or been to. The mosques on the roadside are beautiful, and for some reason, seem more magical than those in Dubai. Huge structures of stone with intricate domes, they look like something out of *1001 Arabian Nights* and I'm tempted to pull over and explore.

My mobile phone rings and I answer it without checking the screen, not wanting to tear my eyes away from the road ahead of me. I'm supposed to be using a handsfree kit, but whatever. People here don't even wear seatbelts and their kids jump around in the front with no care in the world.

'Hello?' I mumble, my eyes focused on the road ahead.

'Hi.'

I recognize Goldenboy's voice instantly and I curse myself for not screening the call. I have been yearning to hear his voice again and just hearing that one-syllable greeting has already melted my heart. At the same time, after our trip to Al Ain, I'm too scared to talk to him. I'm worried that he'll wear down my barriers until I forget everything I vowed to do, or not to do, to avoid my previous mistakes.

The initial nervousness I felt wears off, so I park at the next service road, push the seat back and fold my legs as we talk, getting comfortable. Our conversation is as sweet as his broken English. I love the way he mispronounces words. I love the way he tries to find alternative methods to explain himself when he doesn't know the word. And I love the way he occasionally arranges his sentences the Arabic way rather than the English one. Everything about him is so endearing and all I want to do is snatch him, wrap him up in cotton wool, and place him high up on a mantelpiece, so I can stare at him forever without breaking him.

'Where are you?' he suddenly asks, and for a moment, I forget that I am sitting in my car in a petrol station, somewhere between Dubai and Abu Dhabi, not snuggled up in bed next to him.

'Um, I dunno. Somewhere near Abu Dhabi I think,' I answer absentmindedly, wishing I were by his side.

'Abu Dhabi! What the hell are you doing there? Are you alone?' His tone is angry and I frown, wondering why he's sounding so angry.

'What's your problem? What's wrong with Abu Dhabi? And who cares who I'm with?' For some reason, I don't want to tell him that I'm alone but want to let him think I'm with another guy. Okay, it's not 'for some reason'. It's because I want to see if I can make him jealous.

It bothers me that we still don't know what we mean to one another. Which doesn't make sense really, as I don't even want to know what's going on. Putting a label on 'us' means defining us. And when something has a definition, it needs a purpose, a path. I'd rather not be forced into a box I'm not ready to climb into. Yet, at the same time, I want him to *want* to put us in a box. And then close the lid.

'Tell me who you're with!' he demands, his voice still raised.

'No,' I answer, pissing him off further. I can hear him breathing heavily down the phone and I wonder why he's so annoyed. I've never seen this side to him and I can't imagine why he's being like this.

'Tell me, Sugar, or I swear to God I'll come and find you and kill him, whoever this kalb is,' he finally says.

I burst out laughing at his threat and my giggles deflate the charged atmosphere like a pin to a balloon.

'Don't laugh at me,' he mutters petulantly. 'I just feel jealous okay?'

'Well don't. I'm not with anyone, silly. I'm driving by myself.'

'You're *alone*? In Abu Dhabi?' His voice begins to rise again and I sigh. He senses my irritation and starts again, using a different tactic.

'It's not safe,' he says, his voice softer now. 'What were you thinking driving all that way by yourself? What if something happens to you? What if you need help? What if your car breaks down?'

'Don't worry, I'm perfectly capable of looking after myself. And Abu Dhabi is hardly a dangerous place.'

'You don't know that. What if your car breaks down and a man comes pretending to help you and kidnaps you?'

'I'll knee him in his you-know-what,' I joke.

'Astaghfirulla. Why are Western girls so independent?' he laments, half to himself and half to me.

I contemplate telling him off for being so quick to judge and then decide that we've had enough

302

drama for the afternoon. 'Look, you need to calm down,' I say with as much gentleness as possible. 'Don't get so worked up about things.'

'I'm sorry,' he apologizes in a voice so quiet and regretful that I can't help but smile. His passion is actually quite endearing. 'But I'm an Arab guy, Sugar. You have to know that about me. I'm not Western.'

'It's okay,' I reply, shaking my head and still smiling. There is another silence and I wonder if all Arab men are so over-protective. I wonder if his attitude will be stifling later and then I decide that I quite like having a knight in shining armour. I'd rather he protect me than abandon me altogether.

'It's just…I can't bear to imagine you with another guy! It's the worst thing in the world for me,' he suddenly bursts out, surprising me again.

'So don't then,' I answer glibly, trying not to take the conversation so seriously. We *still* don't know what we mean to each other, but he feels he can just come out with whatever he wants, whenever he wants.

'Sugar…I was wondering something,' he begins hesitantly.

I become tense immediately, not liking the sound of what he is about to come out with. 'What?'

'Have you had a boyfriend before?'

The question shocks me and I feel my face turn red, first with shame and then with anger. Who does he think he is, asking me personal questions like that when he hasn't even made his feelings clear?

'I don't think that's your business is it?' My voice is curt and I intend it to be that way.

'That means "yes" doesn't it?' he replies quietly.

'No it doesn't, it means it's not your bloody business!'

'So does it mean "no"?'

'Look, you're just a friend, nothing more,' I begin, my blood boiling again, 'You have no right to be asking me such personal questions.'

I know I'm overreacting but I can't seem to control myself. I feel so annoyed with him for making me feel so shameful all over again. I wonder if my past will ever let me be free.

'I'm just a friend? That's it? Do you act like this with all your male friends then?'

Although he sounds hurt, all I hear is the implication that I am loose and then I lose it. I shout and I cry. I can't seem to control myself. I'm sick of being judged, sick of being labelled, sick of running, hiding, pretending.

'Just leave me alone!' I eventually gasp, before hanging up the phone, tears still streaming down my cheeks.

My heart is aching and my hands are trembling. I want to tell him that I've fallen for him. I want to tell him that he is my only ray of sunshine, my only glimmer of hope, in this strange city. Amongst the thousand things I want to tell him, there is one thing I definitely don't. And that's my past. It is clear from his questions that if he ever found out about my sordid history, he would never give me a second glance.

A shiver runs down my spine and I burst into a fresh flood of tears, a sense of hopelessness overcoming me. Does it mean that every guy I ever meet will strike me off his list because I made some mistakes in the past?

My phone rings and I ignore it, still crying. It rings three more times and each time I will myself not to answer. I don't know what I will say if I do. I don't know whether to come clean, I don't know whether to lie. I don't even know if I want someone as traditional as him in my life.

With each ring though, my resolve wears thin and I wonder if I should just answer and give it a go anyway. He doesn't have to know everything about my past. Not yet anyway. Maybe we could just be friends? The thought of losing him forever numbs me. I don't know what we are doing, where we are going or what will come of it. But I do know that I'm not ready to let him go completely. I can't.

I decide that if he calls once more, I'll answer. But if he doesn't, it's over.

The minutes pass and I calm myself as I wait. The tears stop rolling, I stop hiccupping and shaking. I wipe my face with a tissue and blow my nose, feeling better after letting it all out. My heartbeat rises in anticipation as I wait for the phone to ring once more.

Half an hour later, I'm still sitting there with the phone in my hands. He doesn't call back.

24

Jennifer climbs out of the Porsche Cayenne, teetering in cheap white stilettos. She snaps her chewing gum loudly, pulls up her grey skinny jeans in order to avoid exposing an unsightly bum crack, and flicks her long, blonde hair over her shoulder. Readjusting her gaudy silver boob tube, she looks back at the other two who are still fiddling around with their sheylas.

'Don't worry, everything's perfect,' Moza assures her, following her out of the car, looking ridiculous even by Dubai standards in her huge Chanel sunglasses at nine in the evening.

Lady Luxe is next, her face completely covered in an opaque niqab, with only her eyes peeking through the slits in the cloth. Handing over the car to the valet outside the hotel, she joins her cousin in walking up to the entrance of the huge salmon pink building. What the architect was smoking when he conceived the idea is anyone's guess. She hasn't been here since the grand opening night party and quite frankly, the colourful structures and the shoddy finishing have left her unimpressed. It is the last place anyone she knows would expect her to grace, and therefore absolutely perfect for tonight's rendezvous.

'As fine as a chav can look, you mean?' Rowdha, dressed as Jennifer, jokes, blowing a big bubble with her gum in order to soothe her static nerves.

'Dahling you'd put any Sharon or Tracy to shame,' Moza says in an over-exaggerated poncy accent, following her sister into the hotel. 'Now just remember, we'll be right there the whole time. We'll give you around fifteen minutes with him before Exhibit A, then we'll send over Exhibit B ten minutes after that and the final showdown will happen when you give us the go ahead.'

'And remember that he doesn't know a single thing about Jennifer other than the fact that she's an Emirati, she dances like Pussycat Doll, and she drives a black Cayenne,' Lady Luxe adds, excitement rippling through her veins. The evening's previous drama, combined with the knots of anxiety in her stomach and countless sleepless nights, has suddenly caused an unexpected reaction within. Adrenaline has replaced the tension and she feels sharp, strong and in control, much like her previous scheming self. So she can't do much about Mola at present, but she *can* do something about that sneaky little bastard Humaïd. He isn't the only one with contacts at Etisalat, nor is he the only one with wasta. In fact, she is far higher up in the food chain and tonight, he will have to learn the hard way that no one messes with Lady Luxe. Especially not a horny, pubescent Emirati with far too much money and not enough class.

'Got it,' Rowdha says. 'So I can basically say or do whatever I want. Yalla, I'm ready for this. I'm going down, see you later.' She suppresses the urge to leg it back to the car and walks away, her long blonde wig swishing behind her and her heels clattering on the pink marble floor.

Moza and Lady Luxe sit down on a bench by the colourful statue of a sea amoeba and say nothing for a moment, absorbed in their thoughts.

'Do you think this is going to work?' Lady Luxe finally asks, breaking the silence. Although she is no longer riddled with fear of having her entire life exposed, she is still on edge. She is relying on Plan B to solve the Humaïd issue once and for all, and if it does work, then she can go back to concentrating on bringing Leila down, something she has been dying to do ever since the annoying, gold-digging cow hoisted herself on a throne.

'Actually,' Moza replies slowly, 'I do. It's obvious what kind of guy Humaid is. He's two-faced and shallow like the rest of them. By the time we're through with him, he'll never show his face near your house again.'

'Ameen to that,' Lady Luxe hails, standing up and stumbling slightly, unable to see properly through the tiny slit in the cloth. How women cover their faces on a daily basis is beyond her comprehension. Already she feels as though she is being smothered. Besides, hiding a face like hers from the public would be a great pity, she decides. She simply cannot imagine being so anonymous, or not having men constantly admire her. Nor can she imagine a world where she is a nobody.

'You should have just worn sunglasses like me,' Moza says, looking far more graceful as she stands up. 'They'll be easier to take off later as well.'

'I'd rather be a clumsy munaqqaba than an extreme fashion victim,' Lady Luxe retorts, making her way down the long hallway and concentrating on watching where she is going. She realizes that in niqab, she cannot simply look down with her eyes; doing so results in her vision being obscured by cloth so she moves her head to see her feet. They walk slowly for a couple of metres before

Moza stops in her tracks, causing her cousin to bump into her.

'Watch it,' Lady Luxe complains. 'I can't see properly as it is.'

'Look, there they are!' Moza whispers urgently, pulling Lady Luxe behind a glittery gold column. 'In the lounge. Look!'

Lady Luxe peers around the column and sees Rowdha sitting on the far end of the glitzy room, facing the entrance. Humaid is sitting opposite her, dressed in the same outfit as that afternoon. *Bastard*, Lady Luxe thinks again with hatred.

'So what shall we do?' she whispers, unable to tear her eyes away from the pair, desperately trying to read Rowdha's impassive facial expressions. 'Hide here until it's time?'

'Well we can't exactly go in there like this,' Moza replies, also trying to see what is happening between her sister and Humaid. 'We'll stand out like prossies in a mosque. Let's just wait here.'

'Okay, let me send some BBMs,' Lady Luxe murmurs, forcing her eyes to look away, her heart pounding in anticipation. 'Almost time for Exhibit A.'

Rowdha sits next to Humaid feeling more uncomfortable than she does at her quarterly smear tests. As much as she enjoys talent spotting and the occasional flirting, this is the first time in five years that she has left her home in something so revealing, not to mention tacky. With her post-baby figure, it isn't exactly flattering either. Even back in her slightly wilder days, her antics were always conducted in Western countries, never, ever in Dubai. She cannot understand how her cousin can plonk a wig on and then mess around practically in her own back garden. That girl has far too much courage. If she had been more sensible in her choice of venue and the company she kept, they wouldn't have been in this precarious situation in the first place.

Her palms clammy, Rowdha fidgets in her seat, pulling up her top to reveal less of the mother-of-two cleavage and tries not to make her awkwardness so obvious.

This is also her first (and last, she swears) extra-marital 'date', something she never dreamt she would do. Although her presence is not voluntary, and nor is it really a date, she can't help but feel as if she is doing something terribly wrong. She tries to tell herself that she isn't cheating, but sitting there at the Atlantis with another man who is trying to let his knee touch hers, she gets the distinct feeling that her husband wouldn't agree.

'You look a little different today,' Humaid notes, his eyes flickering over Rowdha's thicker eyebrows, her bigger mouth, her rounder face.

No kidding, Sherlock, she thinks to herself, suppressing a yawn and trying to follow the bimbo/slut brief she has been given.

'Really? Well, you did see me in the dark,' she giggles, chewing her gum loudly. 'But then, most guys do see me in the dark. I hardly ever go out with guys during the day. I don't look very pretty in natural light.' She says this with such a straight face that Humaid actually believes the statement to be true. Weird, definitely, but true all the same.

'Is that so?' Humaid leans forwards, unashamedly trying to look down her top. 'You look fine to me.'

He is close enough for Rowdha to smell his spicy oud, and she moves back as much as she can, another wave of guilt rippling through her. *Please God, forgive me for this*, she pleads, taking a sip of her tea.

'So how come you've taken so long to get back to me?' he asks, his gaze still fixated on her chest. Rowdha shrinks further into herself, feeling completely naked. How women walk around wearing next to nothing is beyond her. She makes a mental note to ask her promiscuous cousin how she brings herself to wear such skimpy clothing, assuming she gets out of this mess relatively unscathed, that is.

'You know how it is. So many guys, so little time,' she laughs, discreetly wiping her palms on her jeans. 'I mean, all of last week I had to like, you know, go out with this Saudi guy who pays for all my plastic surgery. And then the week before there was this American tourist who wanted me to 'show him around', if you get my drift. This is like, literally the first free night I've had in a *long* time.'

'Oh.' For once, Humaid is speechless. *Is she a prostitute*, he wonders, partly intrigued, partly repulsed.

'Are you a...' he begins, his voice rising in indignant excitement.

'No!' Rowdha laughs, slapping her thighs. 'Well, not literally. I don't charge but I do accept gifts, if you know what I mean.' She winks at him, and he feels his tea rise up his oesophagus. What happened to the classy girl from the club? After all that time he waited for her to finally yield to his pursuit, he was expecting a woman with a little more decorum. But then, what did he expect from a club-whore whose best friend liked to assault innocent men in dark alleys?

As they continue to talk, Rowdha dropping more and more references to previous 'boyfriends', Humaid starts to wonder if this is all a big joke, if Jennifer is actually *trying* to put him off. Surely no woman—prostitute or otherwise—would behave with such indignity in public unless she had an ulterior motive.

'Leila told me you're Emirati,' he states, narrowing his eyes and looking at her face for a change. The accusation comes like a drawn gauntlet and Rowdha wonders whether to admit she is, or to lie a little more.

'Oh Lord no!' Rowdha exclaims, choosing the latter and guffawing loudly.

'That's what she said,' he protests in defiance, scowling.

'That's what she *thinks*,' Rowdha improvises conspiringly. 'Actually to be honest, my father is Emirati. My mother is Sri Lankan. She was his housemaid.'

'Your mother was a housemaid?'

'Yes, but it was a very long time ago. We actually have a history of maids in the family. My grandmother and great-grandmother were both maids back in Sri Lanka.'

'You're half Sri Lankan?'

'So?'

Humaid leans back in this seat, clearly exhausted by the conversation, finally beginning to realize that Jennifer isn't worth his time at all. However, after all those days he spent fantasizing about her, along with the pent-up sexual energy following the meeting with his future wife, he wonders whether to just screw her and leave her anyway. She is practically a prostitute anyway and probably won't be too difficult to lure into his car. But there is no way he will actually pay for her services—with money *or* gifts. No, after wasting his thoughts and his time, she owes him this. And he always makes sure that his rights are fulfilled.

Rowdha is also shattered. The story-telling was a little fun after she got over her initial sense of guilt, but now it is just plain tiring. She hasn't told so many stories since her children were younger, demanding bedtime tales before going to sleep and even that was a chore. She is hoping however, that the plan is working and

Humaid is too disgusted with Jennifer to pursue her further.

'Jennifer! Darling! How are you?' Rowdha looks up to see a small, Filipino man with high cheekbones and short, spiky hair stride over to her. He is wearing a bright pink shirt and tight jeans, and as he comes closer, she notices that the tips of his hair are ice-blonde.

'Jose!' she squeals, jumping up from her seat and throwing her arms around him. 'Oh my God, it's been *so* long!' She beams at him and playfully ruffles his hair, more relieved to see him than he can possibly imagine.

'Who's this?' Humaid asks sharply, a little put out by the interruption, just as he was about to entice Jennifer into accepting a ride.

'Humaid, meet my old friend Jose,' Rowdha gushes, still grinning. 'Jose, this is Humaid. My boyfriend.'

Humaid almost chokes on his drink.

'Nice to meet you,' he splutters, too shocked at Rowdha's statement to be insulted by the presence of a Khaneeth.

'Jose, you have to join us,' Rowdha declares, pulling his slender arm and forcing him into the seat beside her.

'Oh, I don't know,' Jose says, smiling a bright, toothy smile and covering his baby face with his hands. 'I don't want to impose…'

'You're not imposing, you *have* to stay for a bit.'

'Okay, if you absolutely insist,' Jose huffs, sitting down and putting his arm around Rowdha's shoulders. 'So tell me darling, how *are* you? As in, how are you *really*?'

'I'm fine,' Rowdha says, imploring him with her eyes to be quiet.

'You're such a strong little thing,' he continues with raw emotion, pulling a silk handkerchief out of his pocket and dabbing the corner of his right eye.

'It was just a cold,' Rowdha says through clenched teeth, pretending to be annoyed. She pretends to kick Jose under the table, deliberately kicking Humaid instead.

'Ouch!' Humaid exclaims, bending down to rub his sore ankle. 'What the hell was that for?'

'Sorry, my foot must have slipped,' Rowdha says quickly, throwing Jose a quick warning look, one that is not missed by the increasingly suspicious Humaid. 'Anyway Jose, don't you have somewhere you have to be?' she says, all the warmth in her voice gone as she stares daggers at him.

'Right. Yes. I better go. Hope your..."cold" goes away soon,' he says with a huge wink.

Humaid stares at Jose's retreating back in confusion. Although he is not the sharpest knife in the drawer, he is perceptive enough to realize that there is something going on—something he is not supposed to know. Jennifer is obviously sick, but is trying to hide it from him. He rubs his swollen ankle again, befuddlement written all over his otherwise attractive face.

'What's wrong with you?' he asks, more out of curiosity than genuine concern.

'Nothing!' Rowdha snaps, folding her arms and looking away.

They sit in stony silence for a while, Humaid trying to understand exactly what was going on while Rowdha suppresses the smile that is aching to form on her scowling lips. The tension is thick enough to slice, and Rowdha is enjoying his obvious discomfort.

She opens her mouth to begin talking, but before she can, there is a sudden movement in the lounge, and she looks up to see a vaguely attractive girl in a plain black abaya descend upon her table.

'Can I help you?' Rowdha asks politely.

'Galeelat al sharaf,' the girl hisses in Arabic, hatred clouding her dark eyes.

Man, this girl is good, Rowdha thinks to herself, looking forward to seeing what would happen next. 'What's your problem? Do I know you?'

'What's going on?' Humaid intervenes weakly, his head beginning to pound. All he wanted was to spend time with the sexy, fiery little thing from the club, but the girl who snatched his hat and danced with him was so different from the one who now sat opposite him. This girl wasn't fiery, she was rude. She wasn't sexy, she was annoying. And she definitely wasn't a little thing. In fact, she seemed to be a lot older than he expected. He sighs, wishing he hadn't wasted so much time on her, but reluctant to let her go completely without getting *anything* in return.

'You may not know *me*, but you certainly know my husband don't you?' The girl spits, bringing her face so close to Rowdha's that she can smell her cigarette breath. 'Don't try to deny it. I recognize you from the picture he has, you cheap whore.'

'I don't know what you're talking about,' Rowdha says defiantly, glancing over at Humaid who is looking shocked all over again.

'Don't fucking lie to me!' The girl screams in English. The other guests in the lounge turn around to stare, but the girl either doesn't notice or doesn't care. 'Don't fucking insult me anymore! You gave him herpes you dirty bitch! And now I have it too!'

There is a stunned silence while the other guests stare in open-mouthed horror. Rowdha says nothing, her face turning red. The girl is so convincing that she almost feels as if she actually does have the disease. Humaid's face also begins to turn red and then green.

'I hope you rot in hell,' the girl chokes out, her eyes wild with fury. She turns to leave but then stops, turns and then spits on Rowdha's lap before striding away.

Rowdha doesn't know whether to laugh or cry. The girl was amazing but here she is, sitting with a stupid jerk in an outrageous outfit, saliva on her lap and the entire lounge ogling at her as if she were one of those ugly monkeys from Al Ain Zoo with their bums hanging out.

'What the hell,' Humaid mutters, his hands shaking. 'You have *herpes*?'

'Yes,' Rowdha says in a quiet voice, looking down. 'I don't know how I got it or where it came from. That's why I didn't want to meet you. I didn't want you to get it. It's so painful and so sore. I have blisters all over my–'

'Okay! I get it!' Humaid interrupts, bile rising to the back of this throat. To think he almost…

'I'm so upset!' Rowdha chokes, her voice beginning to wobble. 'I don't know what to do!' Before Humaid can respond, she gets up and plants herself on his lap, wrapping her arms around his neck and sobbing into his chest.

'Get off me,' Humaid mutters in disgust, trying to disentangle himself. The evening has been nothing like he had expected it to be and he no longer knows what to do. Should he push her to the floor and leave? Wait for her to stop crying and then leave?

'What do we have here?'

The voice is familiar and Humaid is almost too scared to look up. He has had enough drama for one evening. His eyes focus on a pair of sparkly sandals, an abaya hem grazing them gently. With baited breath he looks up, his eyes moving past the length of the abaya and up to the girl's face. When he sees who it is, all the blood drains from his face. The innocent girl he was thinking about marrying looks at him with undisguised

322

disappointment. Her cousin stands next to her, disapproval etched all over her face.

'You should be ashamed of yourself,' Moza says, venom lacing her words. Her phone ready in her hand she takes a picture of Humaid sitting there with a blonde bundle on his lap. 'I'll be sure to show this to Abu Mohamed.'

'Wait! I didn't do anything! She just...' Humaid struggles to push Rowdha off his lap, but she clings on even tighter, her body heaving with laughter masquerading as sobs.

'Goodbye,' Lady Luxe says softly, before turning on her heels and walking away, Moza close behind her.

'You stupid bitch!' Humaid yells, pushing Rowdha off his lap. 'Look what you did!'

'What did I do?' she cries. 'You're the one who's been hounding me for weeks! I didn't know that you're married.'

'I'm not! I was…Oh forget it.' Humaid gets up, throws a five-hundred dirham note on the table and walks away without looking back.

25

Leaning against the door and listening to the footsteps of the delivery man on the other side disappear, Leila holds the package in her hands for a few moments, wondering what it could contain. The last time she went 'shopping' with Moe, she pointed out various things in Dubai Mall's fashion avenue that had taken her fancy, but none of the things she had 'oohed' and 'aahed' over were small enough to fit in a parcel that size.

Although Leila is accustomed to receiving gifts from generous suitors, she still gets a tingling sensation in her stomach every time she is bestowed with a package, whether it comes wrapped in pretty paper, adorned with bows, in its original packaging or, as of late, in a plastic courier packet.

Unable to suppress her curiosity, she runs over to her slightly dusty kitchen table and plonks herself onto a fragile IKEA chair. The scissors are still lying on the surface from three days ago when she opened a pack containing a luxurious

La Perla underwear set in pale pink with a note saying 'When will I get to see you in these?' She grabs them and cuts the package open as neatly as possible.

Inside the plastic packet sits a flat box with the hair-prickling Damas logo glistening in the centre. Shaking with excitement she opens the box to find a stunning white gold necklace encrusted with what appear to be countless brilliant cut diamonds. Her breath stuck in her throat, she lifts the creation out of its velvet surroundings and gapes at it in awe before running over to her full length mirror and placing it against her smooth, tanned neck. It sits perfectly on her collarbones, as if it were created especially for her and she turns her body to examine it from all angles. The ice sparkles in the sunlight and a shiver runs down her spine.

This is it, she thinks to herself as she studies her reflection, knowing how amazing she will look once she wears it with a more appropriate outfit. It's time to give in to his needs.

Leila has had enough experience with generous men to know that it is unlikely to get better than this. A diamond on her finger is almost certainly out of the question so she will make do with them glittering on her neck instead, and give a little something back before things turn sour. She is perfectly aware of the fact that every gift comes with a price, and only last week she was forced into almost betraying her friend in an attempt to stay in Moe's good books. The time for her to get out with her gifts while she could, had arrived.

For the first time since she embarked on her precarious relationship with Mohamed, Leila picks up her phone and dials his number. She no longer cares about appearing to be too interested, too eager, too easy. In fact, she would rather control the way their relationship degenerates than allow him to dispose of her like an empty cigarette carton once he has had his way with her.

"allo?' he answers, dropping the 'h' in the typical Arabic way.

'Keefak, habibi?' she purrs back, still looking at her reflection and tentatively touching the necklace with her finger tips.

'You like it.' Moe states.

'I love it,' she answers with sincerity, beaming. She imagines his chest swelling with pride and for once, allows his ego to inflate as much as it wants.

'It is exquisite,' she adds. 'Thank you.'

'So when can I see you wearing it?' he demands impatiently, raising his voice over the sound of traffic.

'Whenever you want,' is her coy reply, a small smile playing on her lips.

There is a stunned silence as Moe's heart begins to thud. During their entire courtship, Leila has remained stiff, stern and, for want of a better description, positively prudish. There were moments when Moe would wonder if he had imagined their first physical encounter, whether the entire scenario was a figment of his imagination.

'Now?' he suggests quickly, as if he is worried she may take back her promise.

'No, not now. Tonight.' Leila affirms, still staring at her reflection. She may be grateful but certainly not so grateful that she is willing to drop everything to go and cater to his whims. 'Come and collect me at 8 pm. See you later…'

With that, Leila hangs up the phone and then gently takes off the necklace, placing it back inside the box, as carefully as if it were a newborn baby. Turning on the taps in the bathtub, she fills the tub with fragrant bath oils and when the temperature is just right, climbs in and closes her eyes. She was ready to give Moe a night he would never, ever forget.

Leila is wearing a pale pink satin dress so tight and so low that her breasts are almost spilling out of its embrace. She is also wearing her new diamond necklace, although the spectacular creation is struggling to compete with her cleavage. Every single man in the restaurant is aching to catch a glimpse of Leila's bosom as she wriggles past them, until they realize that her rear assets are just as generous. Every woman is shooting her down with death stares, their eyes fixated on her sparkling necklace.

In ode to the occasion, Leila's hair has been professionally blow dried and is sitting in soft, sensuous waves down her bare back and her makeup, courtesy of the MAC counter at Ibn Battuta, is simply smouldering. Everything about her—from her silky blonde hair to her tanned golden skin, her slender neck surrounded by a cluster of glittering diamonds and her tiny waist, is screaming for attention, and oozing with sexiness.

Quite naturally, the Emirati man who has the pleasure of escorting the sex siren is being tantalized by her in a manner he never anticipated. Not even his overactive imagination, fuelled by late night television, could have conjured up the stirring sensation in his loins

They are dining at Atmosphere at the Armani Hotel, Burj Khalifa and Leila can quite honestly admit that she has never been to a more exquisite restaurant in a more stunning location. High up on the 122nd floor of the world's tallest tower, the decor is classy and understated and everything from the attentive maître d' to the delectable cuisine, oozes sophistication.

From the moment Leila slid into Moe's orange AMG, she has been all over him like a rash, touching his knee, stroking his face, clinging to his arm. Now at the restaurant, she is staring at him through half-shut eyes as she slowly licks her lips before taking the straw in her cocktail glass between them. Moe almost chokes on his Chardonnay and tries to compose himself, wiping his clammy palms on his dark brown candoura. Leila pretends not to notice and licks her lips slowly and deliberately.

Although Leila was originally only pretending to be like a cat on heat, the longer she plays the role, the more real the feelings become. Now she too is desperate to get away from the crowd of people and spend some quality time alone with the man who she knows is about to slip through her talons.

She analyses Moe's handsome face and realizes that she will miss him. Over the past few weeks he has become the only constant in life. With Dubai still recovering from the economic crisis and the subsequent crash of the real estate sector, Leila's career has taken a gigantic plunge. She has been getting paid late, her commission percentage has been reduced, and she is highly unlikely to receive a bonus. She had sworn never, ever, to touch her savings, but if things didn't improve, she would be forced to.

If her turbulent financial status wasn't bad enough, Leila has also noticed with horror that her body is changing. A fine line here, a wrinkle there, a sun spot, an ache. Although hours of Yogilates has kept her muscles supple and flexible, she just doesn't move with the same agility she did a decade ago, her face just doesn't hold the same youthful glow, and no amount of gym, microdermabrasions, or sneaky visits to clinics in Jumeirah can prevent time from taking its natural course.

But her love life, as always, is turbulent, exciting, promising, painful and most of all, uncertain. With Moe soon to exit the scene, she will be left alone. All over again.

Leila wonders when that defining moment in her life was, the moment when she traded her naiveté for cynicism, when her innocence was stripped away from her, when she realized that there was no such thing as a 'happily ever after'. She wonders if she should pin all the blame on Fahd, who taught her that no man wanted an imperfect woman and no Arab man would marry a 'loose' girl. Or maybe she should blame Michael, the American who falsely made her believe that fairy tales did exist.

She met Michael in her second week in Dubai and for the naïve twenty-three-year-old Lebanese girl, it was a dream come true. Not only was he intelligent, attentive, and respectful, but he was also American. And not the kind of American she had encountered while studying in Ohio either, but a native New Yorker who drawled, dropped his r's and wore Italian shoes. The fact that he was ten years her senior made him all the more appealing.

Although Leila had youth on her side, she was certainly lacking in the looks department and it wasn't long before Michael dropped a few hints about his fascination with blondes during a post-movie dinner. Mortified, the brunette hastily booked herself into her local salon and emerged three hours later with a gorgeous yellow mane.

As the weeks progressed, Michael's dissatisfaction with his girlfriend continued to grow. Fuelled by their lack of physical intimacy and her commitment towards maintaining her virginity, Michael expressed his frustration through degrading Leila whenever possible. He commented on her acne-prone skin, persuaded her to see a dermatologist, made subtle remarks about her B-cups, and laughed at her very Middle Eastern nose. He even made fun of her accent that was tinged with Arabic and French. The more he 'joked', the more Leila withdrew into her shell. Her confidence deteriorated with every comment and she was desperate to do something right.

Then, two months into their relationship, came the inevitable day when he invited her for dinner at his apartment. She happily agreed, stunned that a man was willing to cook for a woman.

The putrid stench of his alcoholic breath on her face, the wildness in his eyes, the aggression of his touch, plagued her at every moment for weeks after. How could she have understood the situation so wrong? How could she have expected a man to respect her monogamous choice?

You fucking tease. You've been fucking using me and giving nothing back. You fucking ugly bitch.

His voice continued ringing in her ears, long after she had managed to extract herself from him after kneeing him in the groin, long after she had stumbled to the lobby of his apartment, her dress torn and her arms bruised. And long after the bruises faded away.

When she gave herself to Fahd, three years later, her mind wandered back to Michael and her refusal to submit to him. Sometimes during her darker moments, she wishes she had.

The Michael incident, coupled with Fahd's betrayal, taught Leila an invaluable lesson: with the exception of her future husband on their wedding night, virginity had no value to absolutely anyone, least of all herself. And that was if he happened to be an Arab. With simple surgical procedures readily available for women wanting to repair their hymens in order to dupe their unsuspecting husbands, even that wasn't a big deal anymore. She realized that her body was her own, what she did with it was her business and what was more important was the illusion she portrayed of herself. For it was this illusion that she had complete control over.

'Shall we go?' Moe's tentative question, coupled with the longing in his dark eyes, is a welcome distraction from Leila's painful memories, and she nods. When the bill is settled, Moe stands up and for the first time in their relationship, offers her his arm. Leila feels another stab in her heart. Would this be the last time? She accepts it graciously and stands up.

Leila extracts herself from Moe's embrace, his gentle snores assuring her of the depth of his slumber. As she lifts one heavy arm he stirs and she stiffens, her heart beating quickly. The last thing she wants is him waking up and pretending that he still wants her there after finally achieving his goal. She would rather his last memory of her to be beautiful, strong and sexy, not weak, cowardly, and ashamed.

She smiles as she recollects the look on his face when he unzipped her dress and let it fall to the floor. His eyes moved up and down her body, savouring every inch of her lean body and smooth skin, and lingered on the pale pink lingerie that he had bought her. Then, he left her in nothing but the diamond necklace.

It was a night neither of them would ever forget.

She finally manages to sneak out of bed and looks around the room for some clues as to who Moe actually is. She still cannot believe that he has brought her home instead of taking her to a fancy hotel, and she relishes the opportunity to snoop around.

Mohamed's bedroom is like the stereotypical bachelor pad, and needs just a mirrored ceiling to complete the look. The walls are a plain grey, the furniture black and the accessories a cold chrome. The bed is possibly bigger than any of the beds Leila has ever slept in, and a gigantic zebra print rug sits at its foot. On the wall opposite is a sixty-inch plasma screen and below it is a water feature that is more annoying than soothing. There are no photos on the nightstands and no pictures on the walls. Nothing to divulge who the real Mohamed is.

Leila gathers all her clothes, tiptoes across the room, and opens the bathroom door, hoping it doesn't creak. Thankfully it glides open with ease and she locks the door firmly behind her.

The bathroom is just as sleek as the bedroom with stark black and white tiles and a huge shower. There is a corner tub which Leila assumes is a Jacuzzi, and she wishes she could fill it up and just soak there for a while. It is a definite upgrade from her own little bathroom in Discovery Gardens and she sighs audibly, wishing she had been blessed with better fortune.

Leila peeks inside the medicine cabinet but is disappointed to find that all it contains is toothpaste, floss, mouthwash, shaving lotion, and aftershave. She closes it and stares at her reflection. The girl staring back at her looks tired and weary. Makeup is smeared all across her face and her hair has lost its grace.

Tearing her eyes away from her pitiful appearance, she sits down and opens her gigantic handbag, glad that she didn't use the new Chanel. As beautiful as it is, it wouldn't have been able to hold a pair of leggings, a long t-shirt, deodorant, a hair brush, ballet pumps, face wipes, moisturizer, and her wallet. Not to mention her perfume, makeup bag, and keys.

Leila gets to work with the face wipes and cleans off every scrap of makeup before rinsing her face quickly and moisturizing it. She moves diligently, afraid that if she stops moving, the void that Moe had temporary filled will resurface, leaving a dull ache in its place. She focuses on getting dressed as quickly as possible so that she can go home and forget that Moe ever existed.

Exiting the bathroom as quietly as she entered, Leila takes one last look at Moe's peaceful expression and turns away before tears begin to form in her eyes.

Stop being such a wimp, she thinks as she forces herself to open the bedroom door and step out into the deserted upstairs hallway. She is glad she had enough sense to bring rubber soled shoes that will reduce the chances of her waking him, or worse someone else, up. All the doors in the hallway are closed and although Leila is dying to peep into some of the rooms, she controls herself in case there are any other people living there, despite Moe promising that no one else was at home.

Walking down the magnificent marble stairs and absorbing the crystal chandeliers and intricate stained glass window, Leila wonders if she has made a terrible mistake by approaching her relationship with Moe as nothing more than a little fun on the side. Had she put up the innocent act a little longer, had she packaged herself as the perfect wife, perhaps he would have wanted her enough to marry her? She stops at the foot of the stairs and looks around her at the beautiful artwork and ornate marble with wonder. Imagine if she could wake up to such splendour every morning.

But no. She met him in a club, for God's sake. She had accosted him in an alleyway. Their relationship was doomed before it had even begun. Leila tells herself that she made the most of her situation. She has a fifty thousand dirham diamond necklace in her shopper and is obviously better off than she was when she met him. And she hardly wasted any time either. Straightening her back and holding her head up high, Leila decides to just go home and enjoy the memories she has created instead of skulking around the villa wondering about what might have been.

The front door is heavy and creaks as she pulls it open and steps out into the cool, desert night. Inhaling deeply, she looks back at the enormous villa and smiles. This will be one interesting story to tell her daughters one day.

A roar fills the garden and Leila jumps, almost dropping her bag. She spins around and then squints as a bright light shines on her face. Like a deer caught in headlights, she freezes, wincing at the intensity of the spotlight, terrified that a guard with a gun is about to shoot her down.

The lights turn off and so does the deafening roar, leaving Leila in complete darkness and silence once again and she blinks rapidly, trying to adjust her vision, her ears still ringing. The hairs on her arms begin to prickle, and as her eyes adjust to the moonlight, she realizes that the lights belonged to a car. And not just any car either, but what appears to be a Ferrari.

Staring at the familiar car but still not registering where she has seen it before, she tries to see who is in the driver's seat, the tinted windscreen preventing her from doing so. Perhaps it is Moe's parents back early from their vacation. It is too late to hide behind a palm tree and all she can do now is walk away as gracefully as possible. How she hates walks of shame.

Feeling more than a little awkward, she quickly begins shuffling towards the gate, but as she passes the Ferrari, she realizes with a shock that it is pink. Stopping in her tracks, she stares at it again, not caring that it could be Moe's father. Something just doesn't feel right. A million thoughts begin racing through Leila's confused mind and through the dark tints, she eventually makes out the silhouette of a woman. Still disoriented, before she can control herself, she raps on the window. There can't be only one pink Ferrari in the whole of Dubai…but then, she has never seen more than one before.

Anger begins bubble inside, and Leila raps on the window again, this time with her fist not her knuckles. *It can't be her,* she desperately tells herself, panic racing through her system. When there is no answer, she tries the door and it swings open, revealing exactly who she was afraid she would find.

Her face red with fury, Leila clenches her fists and forces herself not to react until she knows precisely what is happening.

'What the *fuck* are you doing here?' she manages to hiss as Lady Luxe, the woman she once described as her friend, stares back at her, with eyes full of guilt.

26

From the moment Lady Luxe awoke to the brutal wails of her alarm clock, she was confronted with a nervous sensation in the pit of her stomach, warning her of the events that were yet to occur.

After dragging herself out of bed, she bumped into Mohamed, whom she could barely look in the eye following the staircase incident. He muttered 'salaam' to her, their brief encounter putting her off her breakfast. Dismissing Claudine's offer of poached eggs with salmon and hollandaise sauce, she changed into a plain abaya coupled with a hot pink sheyla and went to meet her cousins who were due to fly out that evening.

Moza and Rowdha, anxious to remain in Dubai where they could pretend to be single and carefree instead of married mothers, spent the entire morning wailing about their husbands and children and how they didn't want to return to Saudi. Bored of their endless moaning, Lady Luxe tuned out and listened to the low hum of conversation around her instead. Anything to take her mind off the growing sense of unease she was experiencing.

'What the hell's wrong with you?' Rowdha demanded after a while. 'Why are you being so bloody depressing?'

'Can't you be a bit sympathetic for a change?' Moza scolded, taking Lady Luxe's hands into hers. 'Ignore her, habibti. She's just pissed off because we're going back to Saudi tonight. Now tell me. What's wrong?'

'Nothing,' Lady Luxe mumbled, pulling her hand away and staring out of the window at the happy people walking by, enjoying Dubai's beautiful spring weather. Mothers pushed prams, children whizzed past on scooters, and lovers strolled by, hand in hand. Everyone seemed so carefree and relaxed. Everyone but her.

'What exactly about your over privileged life is upsetting you today?' Rowdha continued, almost as if her sister hadn't spoken. 'What? It's true! Look at you. You're young, beautiful, healthy, rich. You live in a gigantic villa, you drive a Porsche *and* a Ferrari, and to make things worse, you're even a successful businesswomen. So please, enlighten me. What exactly about your life is so shitty that it warrants this kind of behaviour?'

Lady Luxe remained silent, knowing that what her cousin said was harsh but true. She didn't want to try to explain that she was always disorientated, that she never, ever felt truly comfortable, even in her own home. *Especially* in her own home. She didn't know how to describe the ache in her heart whenever she heard a British accent, came across a picture from her student days in London or felt a drop of rain.

But most importantly, she didn't know how to adequately convey the fear that was slowly creeping its way into her, warning her that things were about change. And she didn't know which was worse. To be beaten by Moe, kicked out of the family for good, or killed in order to protect their honour.

'Nothing,' she said shortly. 'My life is great. And so was Hend's, I'm sure.'

There was a discomforting silence.

It had already been five years, yet a mere mention of the circumstances that lead to Hend's disappearance was enough to send shivers down the spines of all the girls in the X family.

The product of a consanguineous marriage, Hend was both her father's sister's daughter and her father's cousin's daughter. She was bright,

343

fun loving, and feisty, and when Lady Luxe is being honest with herself, she acknowledges that there were great similarities between them both.

Externally, they could not have been more different. Hend's hair was jet black and unruly, her skin was a smooth mocha and her eyes were framed with the thickest, darkest eyelashes Lady Luxe had ever seen. Unlike Lady Luxe's slight, athletic frame, Hend had a curvaceous body that could rival the likes of J-Lo and Beyonce, and she loved to show it off in skin-tight glittery gowns whenever they went to weddings. She was loud, she was smart, and she had no qualms about speaking her mind. Everyone knew when Hend was in the room.

Beneath the lively exterior however, was a deep sadness that only those extremely close to her could detect. When all the cousins would get together and joke about their other family members, amid the laughter and giggles Lady Luxe would find Hend staring into the distance. When their eyes met Hend would always smile at her younger cousin, but even as a teenager, Lady Luxe was aware that the smile was hiding a sorrow that could not be articulated.

When news of Hend's disappearance made its way to Lady Luxe's ears, when rumours of Western boyfriends, stolen chastity, and shameful acts travelled through the grapevine, everyone knew exactly what had happened. But no one had the nerve to say it.

They stopped visiting Hend's house, and for a while, the inhabitants of the house stopped visiting everyone else. When they finally made their way back into the community, all mention of Hend stopped. It was as if the parents had raised two sons and no daughter.

Two years later, Lady Luxe paid a visit to her sick aunt whose health had completely deteriorated following the disappearance of her only daughter. Dark circles rimmed her eyes, her sallow skin was sickly and thin, and she had lost most of the hair on her head. Towards the end of the customary visit, Lady Luxe claimed to need the toilet. Ignoring the bathroom door altogether, she slipped past the wandering maids, crept up the stairs, and sought out Hend's bedroom.

She pushed open the door and stepped inside, bracing herself to be assaulted by memories of her missing cousin. But she didn't have to, for the pink walls were now a clinical white, the countless photographs were nowhere to be seen, and there was not a single pretty ornament in sight. It was as if Hend never existed.

Feeling nauseous, the twenty-year-old Lady Luxe turned away and closed the door softly behind her. Tears falling down her face, she ran back downstairs and for the first time in two years, confronted her aunt.

'Where have all of her things gone?' she demanded upon returning to her aunt's bedside, unable to contain her emotions.

Her Aunt looked over at her niece and saw in her hazel eyes her own tempestuous daughter.

'Habibti,' she began, her voice quivering with undisguised pain, 'There is no place in this family for shame. Not one member, even those who profess to love you, will spare a girl who soils our name with dishonourable acts. Never forget that.'

Later that night, Lady Luxe winces as her car door swings open and Leila glares down at her, her eyes wild with uninhibited rage.

For almost a month, she has spent every waking moment—and occasionally, even sleeping moments—worrying about the day her friend will discover the truth about her relationship with her boyfriend, either through a mistake of Lady Luxe's own, or some carelessness on Mohamed's part. She has plotted and planned, lied and avoided, and even persuaded her cousin to pretend to be her alter ego in order to ensure that the subject of her nightmares will never materialize.

And now, for the first time in her life, Lady Luxe finally understands what God meant when He said in the Qur'an that He is the Greatest Planner.

No amount of scheming or hypothesizing had prepared her for this moment. In all the scenarios she has imagined, one thing she never expected was for her mindless brother to actually be disrespectful enough to bring his girlfriend to his father's house. How difficult would it have been to hire a hotel room for the night, or even take her to one of the many other family villas scattered around the city? But no. For all his lectures on honour, shame, and dignity, Mohamed was really nothing more than an ignorant adolescent, ruled by the anatomy on the lower part of his body, completely oblivious to the consequences of his hormone-induced actions. And it is her, Lady Luxe, who has to pay the price.

Staring back at her friend with a thudding heart and a dry throat, she suppresses the urge to drive away with the door still open and instead, persuades herself to climb out of the car as gracefully as possible, trying hard not to let her legs wobble. She takes a deep breath and turns around to face her furious friend.

Leila's face is contorted with anger, but beneath the fire, Lady Luxe knows there is a deep sadness. Once again, she fell for the charms of a wealthy, handsome, and enigmatic man who lacked the most crucial ingredient that made a relationship: loyalty. And once again, Leila was embarrassed in front of Lady Luxe, who had warned her against such predators right from the start.

It is this pain, this shame, and this humiliation, that Lady Luxe knows she will have to exploit in order to protect herself. After all, everyone knows that all is fair in love and war.

'You fucking bitch,' Leila begins, her body heaving as she visibly tries to control herself, her rising voice shattering the previous silence. The watchman's light turns on and Lady Luxe begins to panic. The last thing she needs is Mohamed waking up.

'You fucking back-stabbing bitch,' Leila continues, the intensity of her venom causing spittle to
spray out of her mouth. 'Of all the guys in Dubai,
you *had* to go and dig your claws into the *one* guy
who was mine!'

'Control yourself, you silly tart,' Lady Luxe
snaps with slight defiance. 'Why are you staring
at me like I'm some kind of traitor when *you're*
the one who is imposing on *my* territory?' *It is my
territory,* she justifies to herself. *Although not in the
way I am implying.*

'What?' In an instant, Leila's voice plummets
to a whisper, the blood draining from her face.
She clutches onto the Ferrari for support, her
knees almost buckling from the shock. Surely she
doesn't mean what she thinks she means? Her
mind spinning, she stumbles, and Lady Luxe is
forced to grab her before she falls to the ground.

The contact between her hands and Leila's
quivering body sends guilt shooting through Lady
Luxe's body, and she swallows, trying to push the
intense feeling of unease aside.

'Look Leila, it's not a good idea to talk here.
Let's go for a drive,' she finally says, letting go of
her friend. Leila doesn't reply, so she ushers her
friend into the car and looks back at the watchman

349

who is watching her intently. She gives him a quick smile and a wave before slipping into the driver's seat, igniting the engine and rolling out of the grounds.

The street is dark and quiet, with the dim streetlamps providing only enough light for stray kittens to observe their surroundings. The only sound to be heard is the Ferrari, which slices through the silence like a knife through butter. In the distance, the silvery grey Burj Khalifa juts into the cloudless sky, standing tall, proud, and imposing; a reminder of Dubai's extravagant past, precarious present, and imminent future.

Lady Luxe glances over at Leila who is staring straight ahead, almost as if she is in a trance. She looks away, guilt poking her again and continues to drive. She has a good idea what Leila is thinking and it is exactly what she wants her to think. But if things are going the way she is planning, why does she feel so terrible?

They reach Dubai Marine public beach without a single word uttered between the two of them during the entire journey. Lady Luxe pulls over next to a group of young Emirati boys sitting on the low wall, playing traditional Khaleeji music on their white Land Cruiser's sound system. She ignores their stares and kicks off her shoes, rolling the legs of her jeans up to her shins.

'Let's walk out onto the sand and sit here for a bit,' she suggests, looking back at Leila who is still inside the car. Lost in her own thoughts, Leila obliges without uttering a word. She too takes off her shoes and follows Lady Luxe onto the sand. It is cold underneath the clammy soles of her feet and she welcomes the contrasting sensation.

Dropping to the ground, Lady Luxe draws her knees to her chest and looks out into the ocean. The beach is unusually quiet, but at 3 am on a Thursday night, she guesses most people are either sleeping soundly or wandering drunk out of one of Dubai's many clubs. Watching the waves glide over the shoreline, she stares into the black sea and hugs her knees tighter to her body. What was she going to say?

'So? Are you going to tell me what's going on?' Leila finally ventures, unable to handle the suspense any longer. She looks over at Lady Luxe, who has a strange expression on her face, one that Leila has never seen before.

Lady Luxe, knowing that whatever comes out of her mouth next will determine her immediate fate, mulls over the various explanations one last time before she takes a deep breath and clears her throat.

'Mohamed is…' she begins hesitantly. Leila's anxious face has distorted into a mixture of pain and anger, and Lady Luxe's words get caught in her throat. Should she confess the truth and relieve her of her pain, or should she lie to protect herself? Whatever she says, she is inextricably connected to Mohamed now, and whatever she says, Leila will have the opportunity to blackmail her. However, if she *does* lie and profess to be a girlfriend, there is a small possibility of Leila being angry enough with Mohamed to cut him out of her life once and for all. If she tells the truth, that she is only his sister, Leila may still believe she has a chance with the handsome Emirati and use her new-found knowledge as lifelong leverage.

'…my husband.'

'What?' Leila feels as she if has been punched in the stomach and she struggles to breathe.

'We got married about a year ago, while I was still in London,' Lady Luxe continues with more confidence. 'Things were going fine until I discovered that he was cheating on me the entire time I was studying. He doesn't know I know, but after I found out, I stopped being loyal to him.'

Lady Luxe cannot look Leila in the eyes for fear of revealing the truth, so instead, she stares at the sea and digs her toes further into the sand. *Please just accept what I say and then leave me and my family alone.*

'W–why didn't you tell me something sooner?' Leila asks shakily, remembering the night they came across Moe and the way Lady Luxe practically shoved him on her. So that was why she couldn't get away fast enough. That was why she was so condemning of their relationship. And that was why she had been avoiding her like the plague and had refused to meet the two of them together.

'What was I supposed to say?' Lady Luxe retorts, her voice dripping with sarcasm. 'The guy you mauled in the alleyway was actually my husband? You should know me better than that, Leila.'

'Turns out I don't know you at all,' Leila replies quietly, looking straight at Lady Luxe.

She believes me, Lady Luxe thinks with sheer relief as she stares back at Leila's confused eyes that are brimming with tears. 'I'm sorry,' she says simply.

Leila accepts the sentiment with a nod, completely unaware that her friend is not apologizing for hiding her marital status, but for lying about it.

'Me too,' she says after a while, digging her toes into the sand and wrapping her arms around her cold body. 'Listen…I kind of need to be alone right now. Do you mind if I just hang out here by myself?'

'Of course not,' Lady Luxe answers without pausing. 'I'll see you soon okay?' She is thrilled at the opportunity to exit, but before she leaves, she leans over and gives her friend an unexpected hug. *I'm sorry,* she says silently before she hoists herself off the ground and walks to the car, leaving Leila's dejected silhouette behind.

27

Nadia looks around Dubai International Airport, at the shiny floor, bright lights and huge Rolex clocks, and actually feels happy to be there. For the first time since she moved to Dubai, she actually has a reason to be here. After all, it would be difficult to execute her plan in another continent.

It is her desire for retribution that stopped her from being too sentimental about leaving Jayden. Although neither had put a label to their 'relationship', their eyes as they said goodbye to one another said it all. Nadia had to force herself to think of Daniel and her plan throughout the flight so that she didn't dwell on Jayden's ability to make her laugh until her sides hurt, the way they talked without pausing for breath, the way he somehow managed to inject life into her.

Yasmin noticed the change in her the moment she came home that evening. Instead of shutting her out like she had done for most of her trip, Nadia walked over to her sister and hugged her tightly before sitting her down and telling her the entire painful story.

'I can't believe the son of a bitch did all this to you! And I can't believe you never told anyone! Watch when I get hold of him! How come Sugar didn't tell me? What kind of friend does that?'

'The kind I trusted with my secret, Yaz,' Nadia said calmly. 'Look, just relax okay. I have it all under control, I know exactly what I'm going to do, and don't worry, I've already started moving on with my life.'

'Oh really? How? All week you've been walking around like an orphan. Look at you, you look like...' Yasmin frowned and stared at Nadia's face in confusion. 'What the hell's happened to you? How come you don't look like a corpse?'

'I've met someone.' Nadia confesses, smiling from ear to ear.

'What? Already? When? Where? Can I meet him?'

'A couple of days ago, here in London, and no, you can't meet him. It's far too soon to introduce him to family. Right now, we're just friends, but I have a good feeling about this and I'd like to let things unfold naturally.'

Nadia spent the next two days hanging out with Yasmin during the day, and saw Jayden during the evening. She loved the way she felt when she was with him, the way he made her feel as if everything would be okay, that she still had a chance at happiness, her life wasn't over because the man she had believed to be her soul mate was actually someone who was worth *less* than what was stuck to the soles of her shoes. He never asked her questions about Daniel or her problems, and she didn't ask him about his own issues either. They just enjoyed each others' company without the extra baggage, and Nadia welcomed the respite. She talked enough about her problems with Yasmin. Being with Jayden was like receiving death row pardon.

Their last night together was laced with sadness.

'Keep in touch, yeah?' he muttered gruffly after walking her to Quill Street.

'I will,' she whispered. Just as she was about to turn away, she stopped, threw her arms around him, and buried her face into his chest. He hugged her back, and they held each other so tightly that she could almost feel his heart beat through the layers of clothing.

When they finally let go of one another, Nadia walked away without looking back. It hurt too much to see him standing there, alone, at the bottom of the hill. Even if nothing came of their new-found friendship, she would always remember him as the man who had restored a little of the self-worth that her husband had spent months hacking away at.

'Nadia! Over here!' Nadia looks around the glistening terminal and is surprised to spot Daniel waiting for her. She had assumed she would be taking a taxi like she usually did, and wonders what inspired the sudden chivalry. He runs over and grabs her in a bear hug, lifting her off the ground and spinning her around.

'Man, I've missed you,' he says, his voice muffled as he buries his face into her scarf and inhales her scent.

'I missed you too,' she lies smoothly, pulling away. 'Come on, let's get out of here.' She walks briskly towards the exit, and Daniel tags along behind with her suitcase, a confused expression on his face. There is something different about his wife, in the way she moves, the way she carries herself. He had grown accustomed to the shadows under her eyes and the slight stoop in her shoulders. Now, however, she stands tall and straight with her shoulders pulled back. Despite having disembarked from a seven-hour flight, she looked fresh and rested.

'So what have you been up to for the last few days?' Nadia asks once they're in the car and on the way home, looking out of the window at the tall buildings dominating the landscape in order to avoid looking at his face.

'Oh not much,' he replies breezily. 'You know work, desert, the usual.'

Nadia almost laughs out loud at 'the usual' and fights the urge to ask him if 'the usual' involved cheating on her with ex-lovers. Instead, she continues staring blankly out of the window, her mind ticking.

'How was your vacation?' he asks her.

'Friends, family, the usual,' she answers back. 'Are you looking forward to going to the States on Sunday?'

'I am actually. I mean, I wish we had more time together, but my mom needs me, and I'm excited about seeing everyone again.'

Nadia can't believe that she used to be so crazily in love with the man sitting beside her, that there was a time when she felt the earth stopped spinning whenever he entered the room. Although hatred heats her veins, she knows that the masochistic part of her still loves him. But the love has faded away into something almost insignificant, and the other emotions she feels towards him—anger, resentment, disgust—are far, far weightier than that drop of love.

At least he would be leaving in a couple of days and she wouldn't have to endure his presence for much longer.

They pull into the car park outside their building and Nadia looks around at the trees lining the path, the boys playing basketball in the courts opposite her kitchen window, the cats strolling in the street, wondering if she will miss it all when she leaves. She climbs out of the car and tells herself to snap out of it. Now is not the time for nostalgia.

'Listen, do you mind if I go to sleep for a couple of hours?' Daniel asks as they enter the apartment. 'I couldn't sleep last night and I'm really tired.'

'Sure, no worries,' Nadia smiles sweetly at him and gives him a peck on the cheek. 'Go and have your rest. I can imagine how tired you must be.' *After partying and sleeping around all week.*

As soon as Daniel disappears into the bedroom, Nadia pulls off her headscarf, pulls out her laptop, and begins the long task of sending every incriminating email in Daniel's inbox to herself, and then deleting the evidence from his sent items.

When she is certain that he is fast asleep, she tiptoes into the bedroom and takes his phone from the nightstand and puts it on silent. Turning back to her laptop, she smiles each and every time she presses a button. It takes her just ten minutes to execute the first part of her plan, and when she is finished, she puts Daniel's phone back and makes herself a cup of green tea.

Her phone beeps with an incoming message, and she grins when she sees it is from Jayden. For the next three hours, while Daniel sleeps in the adjacent room, Nadia and Jayden exchange messages as she co-ordinates the rest of her plan. The messages start off being innocent and friendly, but it isn't long before they take on a more flirtatious nature and Nadia feels a rush of guilt mixed with pleasure. She knows that technically what she is doing is wrong, but she can't seem to help herself.

Anyway, I'm going to leave Daniel tomorrow so what's the big deal, she justifies when she finally says goodnight to Jayden and makes her way to the shower, making sure to take the phone into the bathroom with her.

Leaning against the door, she swiftly deletes all the messages and then changes Jayden's name in her phone to Jane, just in case Daniel manages to look through it without her knowledge and as she does, she feels another stab of guilt. She has never been so conniving before, and she has never *had* to be either. She always prided herself on her honesty. But now, here she was, plotting, scheming, lying, deceiving and even cheating.

I hope you're proud of what you've done to me, Daniel, she thinks to herself as she climbs into the shower.

They say payback is a bitch, but for Nadia, it is an angel. At last, Daniel will get just a little of what he deserved.

After her shower, she takes out her phone and puts into motion the last part of her plan.

Hi Leila, just got back from London, she writes with cool indifference. *Let me know when you're free to catch up xxx.*

28

I sat in the girls' toilets next to the library, my jeans around my ankles and my hands trembling as they held onto the slender piece of plastic that could quite possibly change my life.

The toilets were empty, with most of the students either inside the library studying, or attending lectures and workshops. Outside the stall, a tap dripped, and its precise drops made music with my thudding heart.

I'd seen this scene on TV a million times, but being the naïve teenager that I was, never expected that I would experience it myself. No matter how many times I had witnessed that very same scene however, nothing had prepared me for the sheer terror that was clawing away at my stomach.

I imagined my mother's face when—*if*—I broke the news to her. I wondered if my father would approach me with a belt. Or worse, a one-way Air India ticket to my Grandmother's house in Surat. I wondered if I would be disowned.

I wondered what Jayden would say. If he would stand by me. He may have converted to marry me in secret, but that didn't mean that Islam was in his heart. It didn't mean that he was against abortion like I was. Who knew what he would think if I told him that I was carrying a piece of him inside me?

My phone beeped, indicating that the three minutes of waiting time were over. As soon as I opened my eyes, my life would change. Even if, God Willing, I wasn't pregnant, this experience had scared me enough to vow to change my ways.

I swear I'll be a better Muslim if you help me through this, Ya Allah, I prayed to myself, my eyes squeezed so tightly that they hurt. *I swear I'll change. I'll do anything you want me to do.*

Desperate drops of sweat began to form on my forehead and I inhaled deeply, trying to regulate my erratic breathing. Unable to calm myself down, I took one last deep breath and with *Bismillah*, opened my eyes.

Then I saw my entire world begin to tumble down before me.

That night I sat at the dinner table with my family and pushed around the food on my plate. Mum moaned, Dad grumbled, Ibby chattered, but I didn't hear a word of it. All I could think of was that thin, blue line that had managed to change my entire future in just three minutes.

Mum had made Oondhiyu, a Surati speciality that I usually ravished. I was famous for my hearty appetite, but not even the sweet and spicy fragrance of herbs, vegetables, and chillies infused to create a gastronomical masterpiece, could tempt me to try just one bite.

She watched me as I somehow managed to stuff a morsel into my dry mouth, a frown on her face.

'Hu thuyu? Kem ny khathi?' she asked, the annoyance in her voice masking the concern that lay beneath.

'Nothing. Just worried about exams.' I mumbled, unable to meet her questioning gaze. My stomach churned for the hundredth time that day, and I felt my face turn green with nausea.

'Khawanu hate rama ny kar,' she snapped. 'You need your energy to study properly.'

My family continued eating while I played around with my food, my dad chewing noisily as he always did, and my mum scolding him for his lack of table manners as she always did. My brother, Ibrahim, also known as 'Ibby', droned on about Uni, and as always I was thankful that he went to a different one from me, and therefore, was unable to keep tabs on me.

Despite Ibby's somewhat brash nature, before Jayden came along, we were as thick as thieves. No one took our bickering seriously and beneath the playful fights, real fights, name-calling and bullying, was mutual love and respect. As his elder sister he valued my opinion and would often come to me for advice about Uni, friends, and occasionally even girls.

I wasn't disillusioned though. I knew enough about the warped sense of 'honour' that existed within our community to understand that as much as he could confide to me about pretty much everything, when it came to boys, he was not my confidante. He was my brother and he would do anything to protect our name.

'Mummy, do you mind if I leave the table? I really need to go and study. I might even have to go to Farah's house to borrow her notes if that's okay,' I managed to choke out, trying hard to keep my voice from shaking.

'Just go. I see your mind just isn't with us today.'

'Thanks.' I jumped up from the table, took my plate to the sink and then dashed out the front door, grabbing my coat and my bag as I did.

The cold air hit me like a slap in the face. It was February and the icy air penetrated my lungs with every breath I took. I shoved my hands into my pockets and pulled out my gloves, my fingers already becoming stiff from the intense cold.

The bus stop was empty, but I didn't want to sit down and get even colder, so I hopped from one foot to another, rubbing my hands over my arms in a lame attempt to stay warm. I willed the 243 to hurry; the quicker I got on it, the quicker I'd reach Turnpike Lane and see Farah and hopefully get some decent advice. My stomach rumbled. Looking back, I know it was out of hunger, but at the time I thought it had something to do with the baby.

I started to cry the same time it started to snow. But not even the magical white flakes descending from the heavens could make the tears stop pouring. I just didn't know what to do. I was an Indian girl from an orthodox community, and even talking to a black guy could tarnish my squeaky-clean reputation. If people found out I had become *pregnant*, and outside wedlock, my entire family would be ruined. I imagined the look on my mother's face and started sobbing again.

'Omigod, what's going on, Sugar?'

I looked up and through the blur and saw my cousin Khansaa standing in front of me. How I hated the fact that nearly all my relatives lived in a three mile radius from my house. No wonder Stoke Newington was known as Little Gujarat.

Khansaa was also one of my best friends, and the only one of my cousins who knew about Jayden. Prone to dating the wrong kind of guys and somehow managing to hide it from the male members of our family, she had given me loads of valuable tips on how to sneak around behind everyone's back. She didn't know about our secret marriage though. No one but myself, Jayden and our three witnesses knew about it. And I intended on keeping it that way.

'Nothing,' I sniffed, wiping away my tears with my hands.

'Don't be stupid and tell me what's going on. Did Jayden break up with you or something?'

'No, nothing like that.'

'Well what is it then? Did he cheat on you?'

'No! Listen, my bus is here. I'll see you later, okay?' I got up as the 243 finally approached, wishing it had come five minutes earlier. To my frustration, Khansaa got on with me and followed me to the top deck where I plonked myself down on the first seat. She promptly sat behind me, bending forward on the seat so she could wrap her arms around me in a bear hug. Her warmth caused fresh tears to erupt and soon the whole sordid story came tumbling out.

I never made it to Farah's house that day. My chat with Khansaa discussing my options left me completely and utterly worn out. She was adamant that I terminate the pregnancy and even told me that she knew a pharmy who could give me a killer combo. No matter what arguments she put forward though, the thought of taking a bunch of tablets that would kill a baby—*my* baby—made me feel even worse than I already did.

We stayed on the bus all the way to Wood Green, where we got off and sat at a nearby chicken and chip shop for another hour, talking. By the end of it, I was more confused than ever. Khansaa was insistent that an abortion was the best way forward, but I just couldn't bring myself to even entertain the idea.

My face swollen from the tears and my nose bright red, I stumbled back into the house just before midnight, and crawled into bed without even changing out of my jeans and jumper.

I eventually managed to drift into sleep around dawn, but almost as soon as I did, I was woken by the cry of sirens entering the street. At first I didn't realize what was going on. I remember sitting up in bed, disoriented. Then the banging started, and it felt as if someone was trying to break down the front door. Leaping out of bed, I ran down the stairs that separated my floor from my parent's floor and flung their door open. They were already awake and pulling dressing gowns on.

'What's going on?' Papa asked, panic in his eyes.

'I don't know,' I replied.

'Don't go downstairs,' he called out after me as I ran out of the room and back up the stairs towards Ibby's room.

'Ibs,' I yelled, pushing open his door. As usual, the smell of stale cigarettes masked by deodorant wafted out. To my surprise, Ibby was lying in bed, the pillow over his head, completely dead to the world.

'Wake up! Something's going on!' I hissed, shaking his sleeping body.

'What?' he mumbled from under the pillow and duvet. 'Get lost man, I'm trying to sleep.'

'Something's going on! Just get up when we need you to for once in your bloody life!' My heart still thumping mercilessly, I glanced at Ibby's clock radio. It was just past five in the morning.

Loud voices filled the hall downstairs, and I could hear a mix of men's voices, cockney accents talking over my dad's subtle Indian one.

'Where's your warrant?' I heard my dad shout and my heart got stuck in my throat. As illogical as it was, at that moment, I thought that the feds were after me and it had something to do with the baby. I stood there in Ibby's room, completely frozen, my throat dry with fear.

'What's going on, man?' he finally said, sitting up and rubbing his eyes.

'I don't know,' I choked out, still rooted to the spot.

The sound of footsteps pounding up the stairs could be heard, and Ibby's door was thrown open by two hefty looking men, my dad close behind.

'What do you think you're doing?' my dad protested in fury, following them into the room.

'Ibrahim Sheikh?' the larger of the officers asked, looking around the large bedroom.

'Yeah?' my brother replied, standing up straight. At six feet three, with broad shoulders and a shaven head, to most people, Ibby appeared intimidating, but next to the two bulky men in front of him, he suddenly seemed so small.

'What's going on?' I squeaked and was promptly ignored. I turned to look at Ibby's face, but instead of the defiance I expected to see, there was resignation. Almost as if he had expected this.

'You are under arrest for causing grievous bodily harm...'

My mouth open in sheer shock, I stared at Ibby and then the feds as they read my brother his rights, their words drowning under my mother's hysterical cries.

'What's going on?' I whispered again.

This time my brother looked straight at me with steel in his eyes. 'You should have known better,' he snarled at me in Gujarati as the police pulled his arms behind him and snapped the handcuffs on.

My dad was shouting in English and Gujarati, my mum was wailing prayers in Arabic, but all I could hear were Ibby's words attacking me, and almost immediately, I knew it had something to do with Jayden.

'What are you talking about, Ibrahim?' I cried in Gujarati, following the officers and my brother out of the room and on the landing. 'What did you do to him? What did you *do?*' My breath coming out in heaving gasps, I stumbled down the stairs after my brother and into the freezing street below.

The sun had already risen, but the light was still grey and all around us everything was covered in a thin blanket of snow. A group of neighbours had gathered on the street, some staring at us in horror, others in pity and some with perverse pleasure.

Unable to control myself, I followed my brother and the officers to the car, tears pouring down my face.

'What did you do?' I sobbed over and over again in Gujarati.

Ignoring me, they got into the car and drove away. Feeling as though my life had just been sucked out of me, I fell to the ground, oblivious to the snow, the cold, the people, and screamed until my voice gave way.

29

A million light years away from the magnificent eight-bedroom Jumeirah villa of her dreams, Leila sits alone in her bare apartment staring at the blank wall in front of her. Unable to digest what she has recently come to know, for the past few days she has been feeling weak, stupid, and broken. Although she tells herself that such thoughts are fruitless, she cannot help but wonder what Lady Luxe was thinking all those times she gloated about Moe's attentiveness, his full lips and his big hands; or what she was thinking when Leila boasted about all the gifts she had received and how she would return the favour.

She was thinking you were an old, delusional tramp who could never bag a single man, a cruel voice taunts her, every night as she tries to fall asleep, causing her heart to wrench in shame and agony. *She didn't tell you sooner because she wanted to prove you a fool.*

'Shut up,' Leila mumbles in the dark, *unaware that she is actually speaking out loud to herself. Throwing the covers off her body, she sits up and takes a sip of water, desperate to placate her nerves.*

Rocking back and forth, her knees drawn to her chest, Leila begins to cry. She weeps for herself, her achingly lonely self, who has been made a fool of all over again. She weeps for her heart, in love with a man who is married to her friend. And she even weeps for her friend, stuck in a loveless marriage with a man who brings his conquests to their marital home.

But thinking back of the opulent villa with its marble floors and crystal chandeliers, Leila feels another emotion that slowly replaces the previous emotions of pain. Envy.

She has all of that but she's still not happy, she thinks, her mind taking a more dangerous turn. At least Lady Luxe wasn't alone. She had someone who came home to her at the end of the day. She had someone to look after her. She had someone to raise children with.

I could have made him happy, she thinks wistfully, thinking back to the night they spent together, wishing that she could have woken up beside him the following morning.

And then, a tiny seed plants itself in the darkest depths of her mind, just as she falls asleep.

I can still make him happy.

Leila wakes up on Friday morning with a pain in the rear of her skull that she has grown accustomed to.

Contrary to her earlier predictions, instead of discarding her like a cigarette stub after finally managing to dip his wick, Mohamed has been constantly hounding her with phone calls and messages. In order to avoid awkward confrontations, Leila has been pretending to be too sick to even talk to him, let alone meet him and as a result flowers, Godivas, and teddy bears have been sent to her apartment every day and much to her horror, she hasn't even been wishing the cute tokens were those that glitter instead.

In fact, the more time she spends apart from her ex-lover, the more she misses him and the more she wonders if she is making a mistake by letting him go without a fight. She would be lying to herself if she didn't admit that the thought of blackmailing her once-best friend hadn't crossed her mind. It had. Daily, in fact. Leila couldn't help but wonder what Mohamed would do if he found out that his wife had been playing Show-Me-Yours-And-I'll-Show-You-Mine with half of Dubai and perhaps all of London. She had a feeling that as open minded as his interpretation of marriage seemed to be, the attitude didn't extend to the female members of his family.

It would be so easy to throw subtle threats in Lady Luxe's direction and in return, continue dating Mohamed and of course, continue receiving extravagant gifts from him. Leila realizes that she could actually extract far more from Lady Luxe than her husband's attention. She could persuade him to marry her. She could move into his fabulous villa and make Lady Luxe move out and live in a much smaller villa in some obscure locality like Um Nahd. Perhaps, she thinks, really losing herself to her fantasy, she could force Lady Luxe to give up her red crocodile skin Birkin. Or even better, her Ferrari.

The phone beeps, and Leila sighs as reality snatches her beautiful daydream away from her. As if she would ever have the guts to openly challenge Lady Luxe like that. With her infinite wasta and scheming personality, she would undoubtedly get Leila banned and deported before she even had a chance to pack her diamond necklace.

Rolling over, she checks her phone and is surprised to see that the message is from her new friend Nadia, a North African-British girl who is probably the only Moroccan Leila would ever consider associating with. No matter what people said about the Lebanese, one thing they were never accused of being was trashy. Moroccans, unfortunately, were right up there with Russians in the illegal sex trade business, but unfortunately, not half as glamorous.

Leila reads the message and wonders whether or not to call Nadia back and arrange to go out. She has been hibernating for so long that she has actually forgotten what it feels like to get dressed and make an effort to appear normal. She has even called in sick at work, and has made an old friend who happens to be a doctor issue her with a week's worth of sick notes to justify the absence.

Sighing for the hundredth time that morning, she drags herself out of bed and stumbles into the bathroom. She forces herself to look in the mirror and almost chokes on her own tongue when she is confronted by her dull dry skin, her tired red eyes, and limp, matted hair. She realizes with fear that if she doesn't face the world soon, she will dissolve into a fragment of her former self. She is, after all, Leila Saade, the Lebanese sex bomb. She has never looked *this* hopeless, not since she first discovered the marvels of assisted beauty anyway. No Emirati man *or* woman was going to be the cause of her demise.

Taking out her phone, she sends a quick message to Nadia confirming the appointment. It is time to restart the husband hunt and with a girl as innocent-looking as Nadia—with her headscarf and modest clothes—by her side, maybe for once she would attract the right kind of attention.

A couple of hours later, Leila emerges from her apartment a new person. Not wanting to stand out as the promiscuous friend, she opts for fuss-free jeans and a loose, striped t-shirt that slips off her right shoulder whenever she moves. With no discernible traces of makeup and her hair left loose and messy, she looks like a simple girl-next-door, not a high-maintenance maneater.

'Hi Nadia! Keefik?' she cries out in faux enthusiasm upon spotting Nadia outside Starbucks in JBR, completely forgetting that her companion doesn't speak a word of Arabic. She kisses her on both cheeks and hopes that if she pretends to be excited about life, she will eventually start feeling excited for real.

Nadia smiles and kisses Leila back and they make their way to PQ's, chatting away like old friends, neither aware that all the other really wants to do is curl up in bed and heal.

As they talk about work, men, family, and friends, while sipping coffee and picking at sandwiches, Leila is surprised to discover that she is having a decent time, and if thoughts of Mohamed and Lady Luxe hadn't been looming over her like a heavy raincloud, perhaps she would actually be having fun. Something she never thought was possible without at least a drink or two in her system.

It has been a long time since she has had a girlfriend to confide in. Ever since Moe came on to the scene, she pretty much lost her one and only female friend; a friendship that, in light of recent revelations, was unlikely to be resurrected. Despite her original ulterior motives when she wormed her way into Lady Luxe's life, Leila had actually grown attached to the somewhat crazy, but never boring Emirati, and she feels another pang of self-pity. She has lost far more than just a man; she has also lost her best friend, and all because Lady Luxe decided to deceive and humiliate her in the worst way possible.

'So how's your friend? Sorry, I can't remember her name. The pretty girl who was with you at

Zuma?' Nadia asks lightly, taking a bite out of her sandwich.

'Fine,' Leila snaps, looking away with a frown.

'Are you okay?'

'It's a long story,' the vulnerable Leila replies with yet another heartfelt sigh. 'I wouldn't even know where to begin.'

'Do you want to talk about it? Trust me, I've had my fair share of friendship issues and if you need an unbiased ear, I'm here.' Nadia leans forward and places her hand on Leila's arm, coaxing her to open up.

Leila mulls the offer around in her mind for a moment, and concedes that there is really no harm in divulging Lady Luxe's secrets. It isn't as if Nadia knows anything about her. She isn't Arab or particularly significant. So leaning back in her chair, Leila opens her mouth and finds that once she starts talking she can't stop. The feeling of just emptying out her mind and soul to an almost-stranger is wonderfully liberating and by the end of it, she feels lighter than ever.

'So that's it. I've lost my lover and my best friend in just one week,' Leila concludes almost an hour later, leaning back in her seat and looking at Nadia with sorrow in her eyes.

'What do you mean, "that's it"?' Nadia cries in indignation, completely blown away by Leila's story. 'You mean you're just going to give him up without a fight?'

'There's no point,' Leila says, her shoulders stooping. Her throat dry from talking so much, she takes a sip of cold coffee, and looks at Nadia's horrified expression with amusement. 'He wasn't going to marry me anyway,' she explains. 'And I was in the process of letting him go when I found out that Lady Luxe was actually married to him. So what's the point of bothering?'

'The point is that she lied to you! She let you date her husband without caring to enlighten you. She played with your heart and your feelings just to protect herself!'

'She did?'

'Yes! Why else didn't she tell you the truth? She didn't tell you because she was scared you would tell her husband the truth and then he would divorce her. She obviously wants to stay married to him for her own warped reasons.'

'She does?' Leila whispers, her eyes wide.

'Yes! Why else hasn't she left him? He probably pays for all her expensive things and gives her the financial freedom to do whatever she wants. But you know what will happen if he divorces her, right?'

'What?' Leila asks, leaning forward in her seat, her eyes now bright with enlightenment.

'He'll be lonely, vulnerable, and maybe even a tad bitter. Who do you think he will turn to for comfort?'

Her eyes still wide, Leila falls back against her seat and realizes that it makes perfect sense. She knows enough about Lady Luxe to know that she is strong enough to handle herself, and that no one could make her do anything she doesn't want to. She obviously wanted to remain married to Mohamed so that she could use him. He probably cheated on her in the first place because she was too busy with the countless other men in her life to give him the time and attention he craved. Since when was one man enough for Lady Luxe?

Leila could give him all the time and attention he needed. He had the right to be doted on by a wife who loved him for more than his ability to provide financial security. He had the right to be happy.

'Maybe you're right,' Leila concedes after awhile. 'But I wouldn't know how to start. I'm not very good at plans.'

'Well that's where you're lucky,' Nadia says with a smile. 'Because I happen to be *very* good at making plans.'

30

Ever since she came home to find her brother's lover and her once-best friend in her driveway, Lady Luxe has lost the ability to eat, sleep, or even speak more than a syllable at a time. She has cancelled all of her client appointments, social appointments, and even salon appointments and has spent every minute of every day holed up in her bedroom; either lying in bed watching mindless reality television, lying in the bath reading fashion magazines, or lying on the floor staring up at the ceiling and wondering if she has succeeded in breaking up Mola.

Although she feels guilty for shattering Leila's trust in her friend as well as her boyfriend, the sheer relief of potentially succeeding in putting an end to their ridiculous relationship, far outweighs any discomfort Lady Luxe's lies may have caused her to experience. However, this relief isn't enough to cure her of weeks of mental anguish; weeks of wondering if Leila would discover her true identity and if she would be at Leila's indefinite mercy as a consequence, if she would be subjected to a lifetime of blackmail and bribery, if her double life would eventually be exposed and if one day, she would suffer the same, mysterious fate as Hend.

The sense of relief isn't enough to cloud the reality of the situation either. Just because Leila thought Mohamed was married, didn't mean that the man-hungry, gold-digging Lebanese had withdrawn her claws and given up.

Lying on her thick, fluffy white rug in her favourite, most comfortable Juicy tracksuit, her face bare, and her hair pulled away from her forehead with a sweatband, Lady Luxe closes her eyes and wonders if the emotional instability that has developed as a result of all her escapades and shenanigans, the palavers and pandemonium, the wheeling and dealing, dating and mating, was actually worth it. Was it *worth* the constant stress and fear? Was it worth losing absolutely everything she had ever known just to perfect her bedroom skills, get drunk and high on all kinds of beverages and narcotics, and 'date' whomever she pleased, in whichever manner she deemed appropriate?

She knows that it wasn't just about fun though. It was about freedom. It was about choices. It was about the right to choose her own path, to make her own mistakes, to manipulate her own future, without having to conform to community and familial doctrines. It was about experiencing life without navigating through a maze of endless rules and regulations.

It was about defining her own identity in the sunlight, not cowering under her father's name in the shadows.

There is a knock at the door, but Lady Luxe ignores it, as she has been doing the entire week. She opens her eyes but remains lying in her position on the floor, scowling at the interruption. Couldn't a girl think around here without someone disturbing her every five minutes?

'Sis? Can I come in?' Ahmed asks tentatively from the other side of the door and Lady Luxe's scowl fades away in an instant. She doesn't have the heart to be mean to the only person in her family she actually cares for.

When she doesn't answer, he pushes the door open and sticks his head around it, his eyes squeezed shut.

'Okay, I'm coming in,' he warns, stepping into the room. 'You have about five seconds to become decent if you're not already, and then I'm opening my eyes.'

Almost as if he is afraid of what he may find, Ahmed opens one eye first, and when he sees that things are more or less as they always are in his sister's room, he opens the other and sighs in relief. Unsure as to what to expect, he had been putting off visiting his sister on her self-made island for the past few days, but when she didn't bother attending the Dubai International Film Festival, he knew that whatever was going on, was far worse than he imagined.

Ahmed tried very hard not to imagine what recreational activities his older sister enjoyed. He wasn't stupid, and he knew that she was probably up to more than just smoking the occasional Malborough Light, going for shisha in joints unsuitable for respectable women, or racing men down Jumeirah Road. His sister wasn't like any-one else in his family. Not even his crazy cousins Moza and Rowdha could compare to Lady Luxe, with her surreal ideas of what life should really be like, her sharp tongue, and her complete disregard for traditional Emirati and Islamic values. She was fiery, tempestuous, argumentative and bold, and constantly searching for something more. He dreaded to think what 'more' was.

'What's going on?' Ahmed asks, sitting down next to Lady Luxe on the rug and smiling with bemusement at her appearance. Even when she was trying to slum it in sweat clothes and no makeup, somehow, she still managed to look sophisticated and glamorous.

'Nothing,' Lady Luxe mumbles, giving Ahmed a small smile. 'You?'

'Other than worrying what you've gone and done this time, not much. You know my life's boring compared to yours.'

The two sit in silence for while, Lady Luxe now sitting upright and leaning against the bed with her knees drawn to her chest and Ahmed sitting beside her with his legs crossed. Lady Luxe wonders how Ahmed can be so much at peace with himself. He always has a serene aura about him, and despite being just seventeen years old, he oozes confidence and contentment. Looking at the sharp features he has inherited from his father's side, and the smooth mocha skin he has inherited from his mother, Lady Luxe knows that once Ahmed grows out of his gangly, awkward phase, he will be just as good looking as Mohamed, perhaps more so, for there is kindness in his twinkling eyes—something lacking in every other immediate member of the X family.

'Do you ever wonder if there's more to life than this?' she asks after a while, gesturing at her lavish belongings.

'I know there is,' Ahmed replies simply, giving his sister's arm a squeeze. 'But I know you don't like listening to Islamic lectures so I won't go on about it.'

'It's not as if I don't believe in God or the Prophet,' Lady Luxe says in a small voice, her shoulders slumped.

'I know,' Ahmed says. 'But what I don't get is, if you believe why don't you care about doing anything about it?'

'I don't know,' she replies honestly, looking away. 'I guess in the beginning, I just wanted to try all the things we weren't allowed to try. And once you get a taste of it, it's difficult to give it all up. I keep telling myself I'll stop next year or next month, but I can't seem to help it.'

'Sis, I find it hard to believe that you do things because you can't help it. You are the strongest woman I know. You do what *you* want to do.'

Lady Luxe smiles, knowing that Ahmed is right.

'Yeah, you're right,' she concedes, throwing her arm around his slight shoulders. 'I guess I'm not ready to stop. I'm not ready to give up being me, to give up my personality and live the life others have planned for me just because I happen to be a girl, a Muslimah, and an Emirati.'

Ahmed says nothing, and just listens to his sister with no judgements.

'Those reasons just aren't good enough for me. I don't want to marry a guy who's chosen for me or to live in a place where I have no choices. I want the right to choose, Ahmed. Is that too much to ask for?'

'No one has the complete freedom to choose everything in his or her life, sis. They may think they do. They may think they're choosing those jeans because they like them or that house because of the location, or that car because of the speed, but the reality is, they choose the jeans because some celebrity wore them, they choose that house because they needed to live near the kids' school, or that car because it was the only one they could afford that could live up to their social standard.'

Lady Luxe gives Ahmed a hug and ruffles his hair playfully. 'Since when did you become so wise?'

'Since when did you become so jaded? You're Lady Luxe. You have the world as your oyster. You can do anything you want.'

Ahmed's face is earnest and Lady Luxe can see that he truly believes that things are that simple. For a second, she wishes she also had his staunch faith. Perhaps things would be easier if her religious convictions were stronger.

'Thanks munchkin. Whoever ends up marrying you is going to be the luckiest Emiratiya in the UAE. Just make sure you let me choose her, because if you let the aunts do it for you, you'll suffer the same, sad fate as our cousin Obayd, who married a hopeless bimbo who giggles like a hyena at absolutely everything.'

'As if I would ever get married to a girl my sister didn't handpick from the orchard herself,' Ahmed laughs, before leaving his sister alone with her thoughts once again.

Curling up on her white leather bed Lady Luxe mulls over what Ahmed had said. It is true, she doesn't lack self-control. Everything she does or says, is always for a reason. Rarely does she utter something she regrets later. She has chosen to live the fun life that she has been leading, based on a more Western interpretation of fun.

If she wanted to, she *could* give it all up, and live the life her father wanted for her. Would it really be that difficult? Would she really become that miserable? Could she contain her spirit, her soul, her vibrancy, within the narrow walls and minds of her community? Could she find happiness in a kind word or a beautiful photograph, or a delicious meal? Could such an existence satisfy her?

In her heart, Lady Luxe knows that it cannot. She wants more than just a rich husband, more than a successful business, more than a respected family. She wants success beyond her wildest dreams. She wants to travel the entire world and meet people in the most bizarre places. She wants to eat, smell, breathe, and taste every single corner of the Earth. She wants to meet the perfect man, wants him to sing Bruno Mars' songs to her, she wants to fall in love with him, and spend the rest of their life together learning and growing. Not choosing second wives. Not serving his family. Not giving birth to countless children.

Her BlackBerry rings and Lady Luxe rejects the call as she has been doing all week without even looking at it. Until it rings again, almost immediately. With a sigh, she picks it up to check if whoever it is, is important enough for her to bother answering.

Then, her heart skips a beat and the flame within that had almost been extinguished, reignites. Her pulse racing with excitement, Lady Luxe sits up straight, clears her throat, tosses her hair over her shoulders and answers with the biggest smile she has smiled all week.

'Well hello there, Mr Delicious,' she says, her voice as smooth as freshly churned qishta. 'I was wondering if you would ever be resourceful enough to track me down.'

31

Nadia looks around the apartment and for the first time since she moved to Dubai, feels a sense of home. Although the spacious studio is completely barren, she can already picture her brown suede sofa settled into the corner, her Persian rugs adding a splash of colour to the white tiles, and her photographs decorating the walls. She can finally see herself making a home.

'I'll take it,' she tells the estate agent with a wide smile. 'It's perfect.'

With only a couple of days left before Daniel returns to the UAE, Nadia knows she has to act quickly. She has already organized the various facets of her scheme—the financial crippling, the public humiliation, revenge on his prostitute of a girlfriend. All she had left to do was send out a couple of emails from an internet cafe, move into a new place, take absolutely everything with her, and then sit back and enjoy the show.

Her access to Daniel's emails still intact, Nadia has learnt that her husband is planning on satisfying more than just one woman during his trip home. And with every innuendo that passes between him and his various ex-girlfriends, her resolve to get even strengthens.

'Are you sure you want to go through with all this?' Jayden asks her during their marathon Skype session later that evening, the night before she is due to move to her new apartment.

They have been Skyping and exchanging text messages constantly for the past three days, and as thrilled as she is that he is still a part of her life despite the ocean between them, Nadia cannot help but feel frustrated. She enjoys Jayden's company, but although they are claiming to be 'just friends', the scenario smells vaguely like a long-distance relationship, something she vowed never to embark on again.

'Of course,' she replies sharply. 'Why wouldn't I?'

'You could always try to be the better person and let Karma do your dirty work for you,' he says, looking worried.

'No way,' she says with determination. 'He has made me go through hell. He has stripped me of everything—my life, my family, my self-respect, my hope. There's no way I'm letting him get away with it unscathed.'

'Okay, if it makes you feel better...'

'It does,' she says firmly, closing the subject.

As much as she enjoys Jayden's presence in her rather miserable life, she wishes he would stop lecturing her. Why is it that Daniel can do whatever he wants with whomever he wants and she is supposed to walk away with her tail between her legs? She is tired of men always having the upper hand, and women submitting to their every whim.

'I'm sorry,' Jayden says after a while. 'I know you know what you're doing and you can look after yourself, but I can't help but worry about you. You're so far away that if anything happens, there's not much I will be able to do from here.'

'Don't worry, I'll be fine,' she replies softly.

Nadia is unaccustomed to having a man in her life who actually cares enough about her to worry. Her father has been absent for more than half of her life, and her first love let the ocean between them numb him of the sense of duty he should have felt towards her. Even Daniel, when he first fell in love with her, never, ever worried about her. He wooed her, he pursued her, but he never walked her right to her door and waited for her to go inside. He never gave her his jacket. He never told her to call him when she reached home. She finds Jayden's concern unnerving, and wonders if it is just a tactic to draw her closer. She shakes the thought out of her mind and scolds herself for being so paranoid.

'So have you moved your stuff out yet?' Jayden asks, stretching.

Nadia watches his shoulder muscles flex and looks away. Even on the webcam he looks handsome and Nadia wishes that she also looked as good.

'Almost. I've packed pretty much all my things and the movers are coming tomorrow to take it all to my new place,' she says, trying hard not to look at him.

'You gonna leave anything behind for him?' he jokes.

'Nope. What I'm not taking, I've sold already,' she answers with seriousness, oblivious to the surprised look in his eyes.

'Bloody hell, remind me never to cross you!' he says, raising his eyebrows in mock fear.

She smiles at the exaggeration but feels an odd niggling sensation in her guts. 'Now you know what'll happen if you lie or cheat,' she half-jokes.

That night, Nadia lies on the sofa and looks around at the cold, empty apartment, at the countless packing boxes, the bare walls, and shivers. She wonders if she will ever be able to fully trust a man again.

The next evening, as the movers bring the last of her boxes to her new apartment, Nadia sits down on the sofa and examines the amount of work yet to be done. Instead of feeling stressed at the sheer load of unpacking that remained, she feels excited. At last, she is out of Daniel's home. She wonders how he will feel when he comes home to find every single thing, including his clothes, gone. He will have no suede sofa to sit on, no forty-two inch TV to watch, no iPod docking station to listen to music on, no bed to sleep in, or even a kettle to boil water in. It was all with her, sold or given away.

And then, when he thinks the worst is over, he will receive another unpleasant surprise. And another.

He deserves it, Nadia tells herself, forcing any guilt she is experiencing to a place she cannot reach. *Look what he did to you. He deserves it.*

Without warning, tears start falling from her eyes. This is it. After just a year and a half of marriage, it's all over. Right now she was supposed to be happily married, perhaps pregnant, perhaps content. Instead, she has become everything she hoped she would never be; nearly-divorced, lonely, insecure, and bitter. After all that effort, all the prayers, she is no different from the rest of the Ziani women. Why did she bother begging God to give her a happy marriage all of these years if she was only going to suffer the same fate as everyone else?

'Hello?' she sobs when her phone rings an hour later, her packing boxes still untouched all around her.

'Nadia? What's going on? Are you okay?' Jayden asks, his voice full of concern.

'This is it, J,' she sniffs, wiping her nose with her sleeve. 'I've officially left Daniel. My plan to ruin him is in motion. But I feel awful. I feel so alone. I can't even bring myself to pray.'

They speak for an hour, but instead of feeling comforted by Jayden's kind words, Nadia feels worse.

Morning comes, as it always does in Dubai, with a brightness that hurts your eyes. Nadia who cried herself to sleep on the sofa in her jeans and trainers, wakes up only to remember the emptiness that is her life. She doesn't regret her decision to leave Daniel. She just wishes that her reality was different.

Getting up and making her way to the bathroom, she realizes that she doesn't actually know where any of her things are. She doesn't even know where the toothpaste is, let alone face wash or comfortable clothes. Cursing herself for doing nothing but lament the previous day, she begins rummaging through her things until she finally finds a tracksuit to change into, together with her toiletries.

Stuffing her earphones into her ears, she turns up her iPod and starts unpacking, forcing herself to think positively.

Six hours later, Nadia collapses on to the floor, surveys her apartment and smiles. Her rugs lie on the floor, colourful cushions relax on the sofa, her plants smile at her from the balcony, her clothes hang in an orderly fashion in the huge fitted wardrobes, and her books sit comfortably on the shelves. Her kitchen appliances and utensils have been arranged and her toiletries and cosmetics have taken their places in the bathroom.

Hoisting herself up from the rug, she takes a quick shower, changes into a comfortable pair of jeans and a cardigan and leaves the apartment, her stomach growling in hunger. She had forgotten she would need to go to Carrefour and stock up on all food essentials, and she doesn't have any takeaway numbers on her phone either.

As she waits for a taxi outside her glossy new building in Jumeirah Lakes Towers, her phone rings and she pulls it out. She realizes she hasn't even glanced at it all day, and numerous icons fill the screen indicating missed calls and unread messages.

'Hello?' she answers as she climbs into the taxi that pulls up in front of her.

'You bitch! You took it all!'

'Oh hi, Daniel,' she says as calmly as she can, forcing her voice not to betray the fear that he instantly injects in her.

'That's all you have to say? You fucking two-faced conniving bitch! You took it all! You took all my stuff! You cleared out my bank account! When I see you...'

'But you won't see me,' she interrupts smoothly, feigning confidence. 'I've even left my job so you won't have any way of getting to me. It's a good thing we never registered our marriage, right? We don't even have to go to court.'

'You self-centred bitch! How could you do this to me? We were supposed to be working things out! You came back from London acting like everything was okay and then you fucking stabbed me in the back!'

'Yes, we were. Only you hooked up with your girlfriend when I was in London, and then you went off to the States and spent the last week hooking up with all your exes, didn't you?'

There is a silence on the other end of the phone and Nadia finally unclenches her free fist, as she struggles to keep her voice steady.

'Listen, Nadia, let's talk...' Daniel begins, and she sniggers involuntarily.

'Okay, what shall we talk about? How about we start with the pornographic picture you took with Jennifer? Don't even pretend it wasn't her. Her face may have been hidden but I'd recognize that hair anywhere.'

There is another silence.

Unable to bear talking to him for a minute longer without exploding, Nadia hangs up and throws the phone to the floor, much to the surprise of the taxi driver.

'Sorry,' she whispers, catching his eye in the rear view mirror. She closes her eyes and inhales deeply, trying to regulate her breath. Her hands are shaking and her mouth is dry with fear.

Despite her show of confidence, Nadia begins to feel scared. What if he tries to track her down? What if he somehow manages to find her?

What will he do to her once he finds out what else she has done to him?

32

It's been a while since I've dreamt of Jayden. Of his fresh, cool, scent, his slender fingers, his long, smooth neck, his warm, laughing eyes. But this morning, I woke up feeling as if his presence were right beside me. I even looked over to the other side of the bed, half expecting him to be there.

It used to happen all the time when I was in India. Every night I'd wake up before dawn, my entire body damp with sweat, and my heart thudding after yet another nightmare. I'd stare up at the ceiling fan, watching it rotate with calm precision, praying that the repetition would lull me back to sleep. But more often than not, it wouldn't. So I'd clamber out of bed, a feat that became more and more difficult the bigger I became, struggle out of the mosquito net and make my way to the kitchen to make myself some chai. Gita, our maidservant, would usually wake up and finish making it for me.

At the beginning of my stay in Karol Bagh, I felt guilty about getting Gita to help me out with my washing and ironing, so I tried to tip her as much as possible without my cousin getting wind of the way I was 'spoiling' her. After a couple of months though, Gita and I actually became friends. I still continued tipping her, but more for her ability to listen to me ramble on and on about my issues without judging me, than for her meticulous ironing skills.

'Maybe he died, didi,' Gita whispered over a cup of steaming, fragrant masala chai as we sat in the living room that also doubled up as her bedroom during the night.

'Don't say that,' I whispered back, my heart aching. 'Please don't say that!'

'Well why else hasn't he written to you or anything? He loved you so much!' she reasoned with childish innocence.

Her naiveté was both endearing and irritating. It was true though. Why hadn't he?

After my brother was cleared of all charges due to the lack of evidence and his iron-strong alibis, I was too scared to contact Jayden myself; too scared that if he wasn't already dead, he would be if Ibby found out that we were still in touch. So I forced myself to let him go, and to let him be. And when I did, yet another part of me died.

He didn't even know about the baby.

My phone rang as I lay there in bed, my head still swimming in the past. I answered, my throat still a little croaky from having just woken up.

'Hello?'

'Sugar! Wake up! It's me!'

'Nadia?' I squinted at the time. It was only nine in the morning, and I scowled. I hate people waking me up in the morning, especially at ungodly hours. 'What's up? Is it an emergency? It had better be a bloody emergency!'

'Sorry, sorry,' Nadia giggled, her enthusiasm irritating me further. 'I know it's early but I wanted to catch you before you made plans for the day. You haven't got any plans have you?'

'I'm meeting Goldenboy in the evening, but that's about it,' I grumbled.

'Oh cheer up you moody cow,' Nadia replied dismissively. 'Look, I have some news I want to share with you, and I have to do it in person. Meet me for lunch at the Marina? I'll treat you to Thai...'

'Gosh, you must be in a good mood if you're treating me,' I teased, smiling at last. 'Sure, see you at one.'

Hanging up, I snuggled back under the covers and fell asleep.

'Sugar, we agreed. We've signed the papers. You *know* how much this means to us!'

Samira, my cousin, stared at me with fear and confusion in her eyes. I stared back in defiance and clutched the baby closer to me, feeling vulnerable in my cotton nightie, my face greasy and my hair matted to my forehead. My body still aching from the eighteen-hour labour, I looked down at the bundle in my arms and felt my breath get caught in my throat.

'Sam,' I began, my voice shaking. 'I just don't know if I can do this...'

'You don't *know*,' she cried, her voice rising and her arms flailing as she spoke, 'You've been living in *my* house for the past *seven* months for this! We've seen lawyers, we've signed contracts, we've even painted the nursery for God's sake and now you don't *know?*'

'Well I'm sorry if my confusion has interrupted your home decor plans!' I retorted. 'I know we agreed okay, but I...look at her. She's my baby Sam. *My* baby, not yours. I've been carrying her inside me for the past nine and a half months, and now she's in my arms. She's real. I don't know if I can let her go.'

'You don't have a choice, Sugar. She may be yours biologically, but legally she's ours. The sooner you come to terms with that, the better.' Her face hard and her eyes narrowed, Samira stared at me for a second and I stared back. With her dark skin and jet black hair, she looked nothing like me, but oddly enough, she looked more like my daughter than I did.

Turning around abruptly, she choked back a sob and then stalked out of the room. I listened to her footsteps retreat, her heels clacking along the marbled floor.

For the next few hours, I spent every second staring at my beautiful daughter's face, at her soft mocha skin, her almond shaped eyes, her tiny button nose and in the evening, I packed my things and waited for the driver to come and collect me to take me back to Karol Bagh.

Instead, Samira came, accompanied by her husband Sulaiman, who glared at me as I climbed into the car. It was obvious she was too scared to face me alone. It was clear that they were worried I was going to pull something dodgy if they let the driver collect me.

I spent the remainder of the day and most of the night, pacing up and down the room with the baby, unable to let her go. Whenever I left my room, Samira would stare at us, and I'd clutch the baby to me and stare back, my eyes full of fear. Sometime before Fajr, I must have fallen asleep with her beside me on the bed, and when I woke up in the morning, the baby and Samira had gone. Gita handed me a note with tears in her eyes, and explained that they had gone to the village to introduce the baby to their family as their own and that they didn't want any trouble.

I didn't even get a chance to say goodbye.

I wake up a little before midday to find my pillow wet with tears. Wiping my nose on my sleeve, I get out of bed and climb into the shower. Turning on the cold water, I stick my head under it, anxious for the cold to numb the pain.

I get ready to meet Nadia slowly. My limbs just don't want to co-operate and I have to redo my eyeliner three times before it's actually straight. I finally finish getting ready, and when I look in the mirror to check out the results, I am a bit taken aback at how good I actually look. I don't look like a person who has nightmares that result in soaked pillows.

I've unintentionally managed to lose weight while I've been here and my skinny jeans aren't skin tight anymore but slim and flattering, making my legs look thin and toned. The loose grey jersey dress hides my slightly wobbly tummy completely, and the silver sequins along the neck brings out the silver eye shadow I have applied on my eyelids. I slip on a loose black cardigan to cover my arms and stick my feet into my new black heels. Giving my hair one last brush, I saunter out of the apartment, feeling beautiful and confident.

'Oh my God, Sugar, you have *so* been Dubai-fied,' Nadia squeals as I walk up to the table. She too is looking better than I have seen her in ages. Her usually pale complexion is slightly sun-kissed and she has a strange glow to her. She's wearing a turquoise hijab with a loose white shirt-dress and pale blue jeans, the bright colour of the scarf highlighting the gold in her skin.

'What do you mean?' I ask, slipping into my seat and grabbing the menu.

'Remember that first time we met in MOE when you first moved here? You kind of looked like a mess. You were in that awful cotton top thing, and you looked like you hadn't slept in a year. Now look at you, you look fantastic. You're all manicured and even your makeup is different. You really are a true Dubai diva now!'

'Well you're looking better than you've looked in ages yourself,' I reply with a laugh, pleased at the compliment. 'What's your secret?'

'I'll tell you in a minute. What's yours?'

'Goldenboy and I have kinda patched things up,' I admit with a smile.

'What? For real? That's amazing!' Nadia cries out, stretching over the table and giving me a quick hug.

'Yeah, it is isn't it? He didn't call me for about three days after that awful conversation we had that ended in my slamming the phone down on his face, but he called in the end and we've seen each other every day since then.'

'So have you told him the truth about your past?' she probes, leaning forwards. 'I don't know why you won't tell me what went down. I'm sure it's not that bad.'

'No I haven't,' I reply. 'And it is that bad so I'm not telling you anything!'

'Well, don't you think you should tell him if things are getting serious?' Her questions hit a raw nerve and I look down in shame.

'I know I'll have to tell him if things get any more serious, but right now, I don't know what's going on. I don't see the point of telling someone my sins when nothing may even come of it in the future.'

'Well whatever it is, I'm sure he won't care if he's into you that much.'

'I don't know, Nadia,' I admit, finally looking at her innocent expression. 'Things are better than they've been in *so* long. I haven't felt this happy since...I don't even remember the last time I felt such peace in my life. I just don't want anything to mess it up. I finally feel like I can move on from the past and try and focus a little on the future.'

We sit in silence for a few minutes and I ponder what I have just admitted. It's true. I do feel better than I have in a long time. I still feel that niggling sense of guilt, but instead of it plaguing my every thought and following me around like a bad smell, it's just there. In the background. Not at the front of my mind like it was before.

The time I've spent with Goldenboy is also unlike anything I have ever experienced. It's just so...normal. We go to the cinema, dinners, walks in the park or the beach. We go shopping, we hang out with friends. There's no sneaking around, no lying, no tiptoeing home at midnight, worried about what to tell my mother.

It's not technically all kosher, seeing as men and women aren't supposed to interact on an intimate level outside wedlock in Islam. But the fact that I'm not constantly looking over my shoulder in case someone spots us together, is wonderfully refreshing.

I've also been praying regularly, which has helped my general state of mind. I finally feel as if God actually cares about me, and I feel pretty in-tune with my spiritual self. I also think that I'm almost ready to take the plunge and start wearing hijab. I tell Nadia this and she squeals and gives me a hug, and we talk about the concept of hijab and she explains to me that it's a lot easier than people think.

'So, what's your news?' I ask Nadia, taking a bite out of my Phad thai.

'Well...' she begins with a mysterious smile on her face. 'I've left Daniel.'

'WHAT?' I screech in mid-chew, almost choking on my food. 'I can't believe you've finally done it!'

'I know, I can't believe it either,' Nadia admits with a shrug. 'I just couldn't take it anymore. I've had enough of his bullshit. I've even moved to my own apartment and everything.'

'Wow, you're in a much better state than I imagined you would be.' The last time I saw Nadia was before she went to London, when she looked like a fragile old woman. This Nadia looks confident and strong. It is amazing how time can heal wounds.

'Yeah I know, I'm actually surprised at myself. It's just dragged on and on and I'm sick of it all. It's not a shock to the system anymore. I'm not even mildly surprised by his behaviour. I just want to get out with the little dignity I have remaining.'

'So why now?' I ask, curious as to why it had taken her so long.

'That brings me to part two of my announcement,' she says with a smile so wide it belongs in a toothpaste ad. 'I've kinda met someone.'

'NO!' I shriek, almost choking for the second time that day. I take a gulp of sparkling water and stare at Nadia in admiration. 'That was quick work! Who's the lucky man? And more importantly, does your bastard ex know of his existence?'

'Daniel doesn't know anything. He's just a random guy I met in London, but, Sugar, he is *so* amazing. He makes me feel all light and fluffy inside, you know? He's so different than any guy I've ever dated. He's fun, vibrant, and absolutely hilarious. He actually reminds me a lot of you.'

'He sounds perfect,' I say, beaming. I am thrilled that Nadia has finally had the guts to leave that cheating low-life, and even happier that she's met someone who may be worthy of her. 'So how does it work with him being in London at stuff? Let me guess, naughty web dates?'

'Sugar!' Nadia gasps, turning pink. 'I'm not that kind of girl. As a matter of fact, we spent almost every minute together when we first met in London and he's coming to visit me here in Dubai as well.'

'When?'

'Today,' she confesses with a mischievous grin.

'Today! Bloody hell, you move fast don't you!'

'He's just so spur-of-the-moment. I was in a bit of a mess after I moved out, you know, crying and all that, and next thing I know, he's booked his ticket.'

'Listen, Nadia, I don't want to be a wet blanket,' I begin nervously, looking down at my plate. 'But...isn't all this moving a bit fast? You've only known the man for a couple of weeks and he's already visiting you here in Dubai when you're at your most vulnerable? Don't you think you need a little alone time to figure out what you want without any men clouding your vision?'

Nadia laughs, brushing aside my concern.

'Sugar, we're not about to get married or anything. We're just having a bit of fun and getting to know each other.'

'I'm sorry,' I say, feeling guilty. 'I'm just worried about you that's all. You've just made the toughest decision in your life and I just don't want to see you hurt again.' I lean over and give Nadia a hug.

The awkward moment subsides and we spend the rest of the meal laughing and joking as we usually do. After dessert, we drive to Nadia's new apartment. I notice her hands shake as she fumbles with her keys and I realize that she's not as okay as she claims to be.

The apartment is a lot smaller than her old one, and it feels weird not to have Daniel's basketball on the sofa, or his trainers by the door. I glance at Nadia, and her face is paler than it was earlier. She notices my concerned look and tries to smile.

'It's hard coming home to an empty apartment,' she says quietly, looking down. 'Thanks for coming back with me.'

'Don't be silly, that's what I'm here for,' I reply, giving her another hug. She begins to cry and I just hold her, saying nothing. I know what loss can do to a woman.

She pulls away after a few minutes and gives me a watery smile. 'I'd better go and wash my face.'

As Nadia disappears into her bathroom, I glance around her new apartment and her new life, wondering what things she had taken from the old place and what was new. Nearly two years of marriage and all she had to show for it was some furniture and a broken heart.

The doorbell rings, interrupting my thoughts and I get up from the sofa to open the door while Nadia finishes up in the bathroom.

For a moment, I think I'm hallucinating. My head spins, I look around me wildly, wondering if somehow, my dreams are fusing into reality.

'Sugar?' he whispers, taking a step forward. I stumble backwards and open my mouth to speak, but words fail me and not even a croak escapes my lips.

He looks exactly the same as he did the last time I saw him. I feel the blood drain from my face. I stare at him, and he stares back at me as if he has seen a ghost.

'Jayden! You made it! Why didn't you call me from the airport? I would have come to collect you!' Nadia comes out of the bathroom, smiling from ear to ear.

I look back at her and then again at Jayden.

The dots finally connect and I fall to the floor.

33

Leila paces her apartment, hoping that the constant movement will eventually release the knots of fear clenching her stomach. But half an hour of pacing, and a packet of Marlborough Menthols later, she still finds no signs of relief.

Her stomach contracts again and she wonders if she should go to the toilet and force herself to throw up the contents of her meagre lunch into the toilet bowl. But she doesn't look as good as she usually does, and puking will undoubtedly make her countenance worse than it already is. The last thing she wants is Mohamed to take one look at her and wonder what he saw in her in the first place. But although she has piled on more makeup than most women wear in a year, the apprehension she is experiencing somehow shows on her face. She looks tired, worried, and if she is brutally honest with herself, old. It doesn't help that the brown fake fur hat she has worn in order to disguise herself a little, hides her hair completely, giving more emphasis to her face. She is also wearing a pair of thick glasses to change her look further, and decides that without her hair on display, and with thick glasses covering half of her face, Lady Luxe will never recognize her if she spots her from across a room.

'Don't worry so much,' Nadia had said to her when she popped over to see her in the morning. 'Even if Mohamed somehow works out that you orchestrated the encounter he has no reason to be upset with you. In fact, he'll probably be thrilled that you showed him his wayward wife's true colours.'

Leila hoped to God, Jesus, Mary, and everyone else in the Bible that she was right. That no matter what happened that night, she would be safe, Mohamed wouldn't be angry with her and Lady Luxe would finally get what she had coming ever since she escaped her mother's womb. If Mohamed happened to turn to her for a shoulder to lean on after the horrifying truth was exposed, well that was just the syrup on the knafeh as far as she was concerned.

She wished she had learned a thing or two from Lady Luxe in the plan-executing department but alas, Leila lacked the creativity and innovation to implement a flawless scheme. She had placed all of her trust in Nadia to ensure that everything went according to plan, and she hoped with every part of her that Nadia was as good as she said she was.

Her phone beeps with a message from Mohamed telling her that he is waiting outside. Her heart about to go into cardiac arrest, she hurriedly sprays perfume all over herself and her hat to mask the odour of smoke and leaves the house.

Please please please let everything go smoothly she thinks, as she waits for the lift, her mouth dry with trepidation. Upon entering, she glances at her reflection, thankful that her body looks good even if her face appears slightly haggard and her hat looks ridiculous.

'Habibat albi! Ya Omri! Ya aini! I missed you!' Mohamed exclaims as Leila exits her building and walks up to his car. She can't help but smile at his over-enthusiasm, and realizes with sadness that she missed him too. So much for vowing never to let her heart become entwined with an Emirati's again.

'I missed you too,' she says, kissing him on the cheek and then sliding into the car as he holds the door open for her. She glances at him from the corner of her eye as he starts to drive, admiring his sharp cheekbones and smooth neck, and wondering if this will be the last time they are together.

'Shu? How have you been then? And I wasn't going to say anything but...what's up with the hat and glasses?' Mohamed says as he joins Sheikh Zayed Road and then starts weaving between the cars at one hundred and sixty kilometres an hour. As always when confronted with high speeds, Leila feels her stomach plunge and she grips onto her seat, knowing quite well that should they ram into the barriers, she will be crushed to pulp instantly.

'Well you know I had the flu and I'm still recovering. The doctor said I should cover my ears otherwise I might get an ear infection, and he also told me not to strain my eyes too much, so I thought I should wear this hat and give my eyes a break from having to strain so much you know? Anyway, I haven't been up to much lately.' Leila knows she is rambling but cannot help herself as she shifts around in her seat and tries not to look at the blur of scenery as they speed down the monstrous motorway.

'Hammoudi,' she says after a while, frowning as they pass the Um Suqeim exit and continue racing down Sheikh Zayed Road. 'Weren't you supposed to take that exit? We're going to

Mall of the Emirates, right? To the Moroccan restaurant there?'

'I don't feel like Moroccan food. I thought we could go somewhere else instead,' Mohamed replies indifferently.

Leila stares at him in horror, cursing him for being so frivolous with her wishes and then cursing Nadia again for practically shoving this ridiculous plan down her throat and forcing her to choose Momos as a venue. Who eats in the mall anyway?

'But I really wanted to go there!' she says, trying not to let her voice rise to an unattractive whine. 'I've been craving a good tagine all week. Could you turn around please?'

'I really don't want Moroccan food,' Mohamed replies, frowning. 'In fact, I don't like Moroccan food at all. I hate couscous. What kind of name is couscous? Do you know what that means in Arabic?'

'If you don't like Moroccan food, why did you even agree to take me there?' Leila ignores his question, her voice rising as her nervousness grows.

'Because you kept going on about it and I wanted to see you! What's the big deal?'

Leila swallows, unsure of what to say that will justify her behaviour. She knows that she is crossing a line by being so annoying, but if she doesn't manage to drag Mohamed to the restaurant, everything—all her and Nadia's hard work—will be completely ruined. Who knows when they will get an opportunity to coerce Lady Luxe into venturing out as Jennifer again?

'The thing is,' she begins, blinking rapidly as she tries to think of a plausible reason why it is imperative she consumes Moroccan food tonight. 'The thing is, today is my late best friend's birthday. She was Moroccan and she died in a horrible car accident three years ago, right here in Dubai. Since her death, I've made it a point to go to a Moroccan restaurant every year on her birthday to pay my respects to her. I know it sounds strange, but it makes me feel closer to her. I had never had a friend like her, and no one has been able to take her place since.'

Leila feels so saddened by her made-up story that tears spring to her eyes. She looks at Mohamed and when he looks back, he is surprised to see the water clinging to her eyelashes.

'Yalla, Momos it is then,' Mohamed grumbles, taking the next exit until he is back on Sheikh Zayed Road but heading south.

Trying hard not to let her immense relief show, Leila looks away and tells herself to snap out of it. She needs to maintain her cool. She can't let herself be flustered by every obstacle. After all, the night has only just begun.

'Thank you, habibi,' she whispers, leaning over and planting a kiss on Mohamed's cheek.

Surprised by her sudden display of affection, he grins and puts his arm around her shoulders. Maybe a little Moroccan action wouldn't be that bad after all.

The restaurant is quieter than usual and Leila feels another surge of panic as she surveys the people around them. How on earth is she supposed to hide among the masses if there are no masses available? Lady Luxe is sure to spot her as soon as she enters, with her eagle eyes and uncanny ability to sniff out a secret a mile off.

They choose a table in the far back, Leila ignoring the curious stares from passersby as they observe the faux fur creation atop her head. Her hat would look more at home in the Serbian mountains than in a Dubai mall and Leila readjusts it with embarrassment, wishing she had just worn a hijab instead. Mohamed sits down next to her and flings his arm around her shoulder and she snuggles up next to him, glancing at the entrance every five minutes.

They talk and laugh, catching up on the past week and Leila feels another pang, hoping that this isn't their last date. Unlike her earlier predictions, Mohamed's behaviour is exactly as it was before they sealed the deal. She had expected him to either disappear entirely or at the very least, start ignoring her, but so far he is just as gentlemanly, affectionate, and attentive as he has always been. Leila guesses it's because he is planning to use her for her time, company, and, of course, body, for as long as he can before he bores of her; before a younger, more attractive, more interesting version comes along to catch his attention. The idea of being a temporary fling hurts her and she wonders if she really does want to marry a man like Mohamed. A man who is married to a beautiful, successful, vivacious young woman and yet seeks excitement elsewhere.

Trying hard to let her uneasiness go undetected, Leila glances down at her watch and almost chokes on a plum when she realizes that it is 10 pm, and Lady Luxe will be arriving any moment now.

'How's your food?' she asks Mohamed distractedly, her eyes focussed on the entrance.

'It's actually pretty good,' he replies sheepishly. 'I guess I should apologize for my earlier reservations.'

'No apologies necessary. Just leave some room for dessert,' Leila flirts with as much warmth as she can muster.

Mohamed laughs, taking another bite of his roasted lamb and Leila leans into him, her eyes still glued to the door.

When Lady Luxe, aka Jennifer, enters wearing Mr Delicious on her arm like a designer handbag, a grin etched from one ear to another, adrenaline pounds all through Leila's body. She stares at her ex-best friend, her eyes narrowing in anger. Everything about Jennifer—from her expensive wig to her provocative designer ensemble—screams money. She is everything Leila wants to be. And she is married to the man Leila wants by her side.

Jennifer laughs as Mr Delicious says something to her, and as they walk over to their table, Leila cowers in shadows, her heart pounding with fear. But then Lady Luxe never gave much credit to Leila's grey matter. She would never guess that it was Leila who was behind Mr Delicious' sudden phone call. She didn't know that Leila had memorized his number when they in the restroom that night at the Cavalli Club. And that she was thirsty for revenge, and had a friend—a *real* friend—who had helped her orchestrate the entire plan without gaining anything from it. No, for once it was Leila who had the upper hand.

Jennifer and Mr Delicious sit at a table just a few metres away, their backs to Leila and Mohamed and Leila can hear their quiet laughter from where she is sitting. She glances over at Mohamed, who is completely oblivious that the blonde sitting in front of him is his wife. Leila tries to feign normalcy, but the blood is now pounding in her ears and a part of her aches to yank that ridiculous wig off Jennifer's head. Lady Luxe is so close, Mr Delicious is so close, retribution is at her fingertips, yet Leila still has no idea how to make Mohamed look at her long enough for him to realize who she really is.

'Isn't that couple cute?' Leila asks Mohamed, as Jennifer whispers something in Mr Delicious' ear while stroking the back of his neck with her finger.

'No, their behaviour is vulgar,' Mohamed mutters, frowning as he watches Jennifer giggle and whisper in Mr Delicious' ear again. As he looks at her razor sharp profile, blurred by the shadows dancing in the room from the countless Moroccan lanterns hanging from the ceiling, he feels a sense of unease come over him. Although he hasn't been able to see the girl properly, he is certain he knows her from somewhere, but he can't quite work out where. Ordinarily, he wouldn't have given it a second thought—or the girl, a second glance—but something doesn't feel right, and Mohamed is determined to find out what it is.

Lost in his thoughts, he is startled when his phone beeps, interrupting his thoughts. He glances down at it, his face impassive.

'Listen, I just need to pop out to take this call, I'll be back in a minute,' he says to Leila. Before she can protest, he walks away and Leila watches his retreating back with growing agitation. Why hadn't Nadia briefed her on what to do if Mohamed just didn't notice Lady Luxe in the restaurant? If no amount of coaxing could make his gaze linger on his wife's disguise for more than a couple of seconds?

Sighing, she begins to wonder if the whole plan was a huge waste of time. Of course, she could always walk up to Lady Luxe and say hello with Mohamed by her side, but that would undoubtedly cause Lady Luxe to do everything in her power to get her deported with a ban stamped on her passport, and possibly even a prison sentence. No, she couldn't openly defy Lady Luxe like that. Even if she was in the right, Mohamed would protect his name before anything else, and he would settle his family matters away from the spotlight.

Leila stares at the door, willing Mohamed to come back to the restaurant soon and when he does, she sees him glance at Jennifer and Mr Delicious. His gaze lingers on Jennifer for a second longer than necessary and Leila's heart jumps in anticipation as she stares at his face, trying to gauge whether or not he has recognized his wife. Mohamed looks away, his expression impassive and joins Leila at their table.

'You haven't eaten much since I left you,' he smiles, scooping up a spoon of couscous and lamb and date tagine and feeding her. Her mouth full of food, Leila almost gags in frustration, wishing he would hurry up and notice who Jennifer really is. He must have had a clear view of her when he re-entered the restaurant and she had seen him look at Jennifer with her own two eyes. But nothing in his expression or body language revealed whether or not he had realized who the blonde in the tiny black dress was.

'I thought you didn't like public displays of affection,' Leila says, desperately trying to make his mind move back to the couple in front of them. Unless she manages to make him notice his wife, the entire evening will have been a gross waste of time and she looked like a fool in a fur hat for absolutely no reason.

'I don't,' he says. 'But feeding my girlfriend some food is hardly the same as slobbering all over her,' he says amicably, still smiling.

'Like those two, you mean?' Leila says in a final attempt to force him to look at Jennifer again.

'Exactly,' he says, glancing at Jennifer, the distaste evident in his eyes. 'People who openly disrespect the traditions and religion of this country must know that their actions will eventually bear unsavoury consequences. And then they will have no one to blame but themselves.'

Leila swallows nervously and looks at Mohamed from the corner of her eye. His expression is cold and steely. A ripple of fear suddenly runs through her as she realizes that the last person whose mercy she would choose to be at, was his.

'Habibti, I am coming down with the most horrendous headache,' Mohamed says as they finish off their meal with Moroccan mint tea. 'Would you mind terribly if I excused myself and went straight home?'

'Of course not,' Leila lies, annoyed that he is about to let her go home in a taxi just because of a silly little headache. She wonders if he is excusing himself early because he made the connection between Jennifer and his wife, but knows that it is unlikely that he did. Surely he would have reacted in some way or another if he had. Or perhaps it had something to do with the mysterious phone call he received. Either way, there was no way to know for sure if her plan had succeeded, or if he really did have a headache.

'Thank you, my angel. You really are the perfect woman. Beautiful, sexy, kind, understanding, kinky. What more could I possibly ask for?' Before Leila can respond, he tosses a thousand-dirham note on the table, kisses her hand, and then walks away.

Unsure whether or not to be offended by the parting of cash for her services, Leila gestures for the waiter and slumps down in her seat. She supposes she will find out sooner or later the result of her and Nadia's excruciating plan. After all, every earthquake has its aftermath. She could only hope that none of the tremors would reach her.

34

Nadia is determined to make more than just lemonade with the lemons life has given her. She is tired of being depressed, tired of moping around with a scowl on her face, but more than anything, she is tired of feeling worthless.

She tells herself that is because she is still acclimatising to her new surroundings, but deep down, she knows it's because she is terrified that she will be alone for the rest of her life. Everyone knows that Dubai is a haven for men wishing to sow wild oats, and is absolutely the worst place in the world to find a husband. And when you are a practising Muslim woman, not to mention a divorced one, it is virtually impossible.

From what Nadia has heard from her single Muslimah friends, Emirati men are just out to have fun, the other Arabs—Jordanians, Palestinians, Syrians and the like—usually refuse to marry outside of their culture, and the ones who do, often Lebanese, are usually the 'modern' type who drink alcohol and don't pray. The practising

Arab men are often far too traditional to marry independent women who have been living in strange countries without their families, who are likely to have questionable pasts, and who have modern ideas about marriage that are incompatible with their traditional ones. As for the handful of non-Arab single Muslim men in Dubai open to marrying divorcees, how many were of the right age, right personality and right wage?

Jayden's arrival in Dubai was supposed to prevent Nadia from completely losing her mind to such desolate thoughts, and for a while, it did. The initial thrill of having Jayden a mere phone call away however, has worn off far quicker than she expected. Although she still enjoys spending time with him, and there are moments when she catches a glimpse of what attracted her to him in the first place, there is something odd about his behaviour and it unnerves her, making her feel even more confused and disorientated. The Jayden in Dubai is somehow different from the carefree, easygoing Jayden she had met in London. This one is quiet and brooding, almost as if he is in some constant anguish and Nadia has no idea why. She's not sure she wants to know either. After all, if he wanted to tell her, he would have. The fact that he has kept his problem to himself probably means that it's something she won't like and right now, Nadia cannot stomach any more ugly surprises.

Nadia is also hurt that Sugar has suddenly disappeared from her life. She doesn't answer Nadia's calls or even bothers to return them. Text messages have gone unanswered, emails have been ignored and Nadia is convinced that she is being avoided by her best friend.

Sugar's absence, together with Jayden's drastic personality change, is making Nadia's brain go into overtime, and for the past two days, she has been suffering from paralyzing headaches. She hopes to God that whatever it is that Jayden isn't telling her is something that will not crush her all over again.

As well as constantly wondering about what is plaguing Jayden's mind, Nadia is also consumed with curiosity as to what is stewing in Daniel's life. With no money, no furniture, no TV, no anything really, she can only assume he is going crazy, and what's more, it is about to get worse.

Nadia's phone rings and she jumps when she sees Daniel's name on the caller ID. The last time he called her, she was with Jayden, who answered it for her before she could protest.

'What?' he had growled into the phone, his eyes narrowed. They were in her apartment, and he had been hanging her paintings and photographs on the walls while she unpacked more boxes and organized the rest of her belongings. Music blaring, he danced and sang along to all the R&B and Hip Hop songs on her iPod, and she laughed at his antics, glad to see him relaxing at last, and wished she was brazen enough to sing and dance along with him.

The phone call, however, killed the atmosphere like a stake to a vampire,

'Nadia? Yeah she's here,' he said, his voice hard. 'What do you want?'

There was a pause and Nadia could almost see the fury in Jayden's eyes as he listened. 'I don't think she wants to speak to you right now, bruv,' he replied, feigning politeness. 'In fact, I don't think she ever wants to speak to you, so how about you stop calling her before I come and break your hands so you can't call *anyone*?'

Nadia stared at Jayden, her mouth hanging open in shock. He tossed the phone at her and smiled at her expression.

'What? Don't look at me like I'm some kind of thug,' he teased, coming over to her and giving her arm a squeeze. 'He needs to know you're not all alone out here and he can't intimidate you anymore.'

She smiled back at him weakly, partly glad that he had stood up to Daniel, but worried that he may have made the situation even worse.

Now, with no Jayden by her side to jump to her rescue, Nadia is unsure as to whether or not she should answer the phone. Although she wants nothing further to do with her ex-husband, she cannot help but wonder if he has found out about what she has done to him. As always, curiosity gets the better of her and she answers, bracing herself for the worst.

'I thought you were told not to harass me again?' she says, keeping her voice steady and neutral.

'You think you can scare me with some fake boyfriend?' Daniel hisses and Nadia swallows nervously, her heart rate picking up pace. 'Like it or not, we're married, and you're not going to get rid of me that easily until you stop being such a bitch.'

'Whatever, Daniel. I take it you haven't heard of the concept of "khola"? I'm well within my rights to get a divorce whether you agree or not. Now leave me alone.'

'Wait!'

The desperation in Daniel's voice stops her from hanging up and she curses herself for responding to his agony. She waits for him to speak, silent.

'Look Nadia, I know you're pissed at me and I deserve it, but please just let it go now. You left me, you took my money, you took all our stuff and left me with nothing, don't you think you've done enough? Whatever it is you're planning, can you please just drop it? You made your point. I get it, okay?'

Nadia almost laughs at how ridiculous he sounds and wonders for the millionth time what she ever saw in him.

'No I don't think you do Daniel,' she replies coldly. 'You put me through hell and you haven't even had the decency to apologize. So no, I will not let it go. There's a lot more coming to you and I just wish I could see your face when it does.'

'You little bitch,' he snarls, his venom almost making its way down the line. 'If you think this is over, you're more stupid than I thought. I will make your life miserable and I won't stop till you kill yourself. Do you hear me?'

Her mouth dry and her body trembling, Nadia hangs up, unable to listen to anymore.

She knows his threats are empty, but the way he spoke to her sent chills down her bones. Why did Daniel still have the ability to crush her with just a few words? Why did she even answer in the first place?

The nervousness slowly wears off, and Nadia forces herself to get up from the sofa and change out of her pyjamas before Jayden arrives, thankful she no longer has a job to go to. As the fear dissolves, her resolve to get even strengthens. Just who did he think he was, threatening her like that after everything he put her through?

After she finishes getting ready, she takes out her laptop and sits for a moment, wondering if she should go ahead with her plan or really just let it go. She had waited this long before she did it only to see if Daniel would express any sort of remorse over what he had done to her. But he hadn't. Instead, he insulted her and threatened her. He deserved everything that came to him.

And so, as Jennifer dines with Mr Delicious at Momo's, Nadia begins composing the email that will—if all goes well—send Daniel packing back to the States where he belongs. When she is finished, she skims through the email to ensure all the information is there, and then hits 'send'. She then composes the second, and minutes later, it's done. All she can do now is wait.

***

'What's up? You seem distracted,' Jayden asks her as they sit together at the Mall of the Emirates food court having lunch.

As always, the mall is crowded and Nadia finds herself looking at the milling throngs wondering if Daniel is among them and what he will do to her if he sees her.

'I guess I am a bit,' Nadia admits, pushing her plate away. 'But then, so are you.' She looks straight into Jayden's eyes and to her surprise, he looks away, almost as if he is hiding something. She feels her stomach contract and instantly, she knows that something she will not appreciate is happening in his life.

Ever since they met at midday, Jayden has been jumpy. He looks tired and nervous and his mind is clearly elsewhere. So much so that he has missed half the things Nadia has said to him.

'Jayden,' she begins, frowning. 'What's going on?'

'Nothing, I'm just worried about you,' he replies, smiling at her. But his smile doesn't reach his eyes and Nadia thinks back to the odd behaviour he has been displaying ever since his plane landed; the constant text messages, the absentmindedness, the edginess, the pain in his eyes when he thinks no one is looking.

It is, Nadia realizes, as if he is cheating on her. But she knows that he isn't, he can't be. They're not married, they're technically not even in a relationship, although the way he flew out to Dubai when she needed him spoke volumes in itself. He has no reason to be with her unless he absolutely wants to.

'You're lying,' she says on a whim, staring at his face for a sign. He flinches and her heart plummets. 'There's someone else, right?'

When he doesn't reply immediately, Nadia feels a surge of anger, hurt and stupidity, course through her body. 'God, what is it about me that just isn't enough?' she spits out, standing up and grabbing her bag.

After everything he knows that she has suffered through, she cannot believe that Jayden would do this to her. Not him. Not now. He was the only thing that inspired her to wake up every morning. And now, even that was gone. She truly had nothing.

Her mind racing and her head about to explode, she walks away from the table, stumbling as she does.

'Wait Nadia it's not what you think,' Jayden calls out after her, grabbing her arm and steadying her. 'Look you need to sit down, you've gone all pale.'

Nadia shakes his arm away and collapses into the nearest chair. 'What the hell is it then?' she asks quietly, tears filling her eyes. 'All I know is that you're acting *exactly* like Daniel used to when I first moved to this place. Can you please just tell me what's going on?'

She looks at Jayden, who is looking everywhere but at her and waits for him to begin. *Allah please, don't let him break my heart*, she prays to herself, over and over again, as she watches different emotions show in his expression one after the other.

His voice coarse and his eyes bloodshot, Jayden finally looks at her and clearing his throat, begins to talk.

35

Lady Luxe walks through Mall of the Emirates with Mr Delicious on one arm and her tiny Hermes clutch on the other, a huge smile on her usually expressionless face. Burberry trench back on and her daring outfit hidden from the public, (in respect of the 'modest dress code' policy all malls in Dubai promoted), she cannot believe how much of a geek she's being in such a delicious man's presence. However, despite her best efforts to try and force her mouth into a straight line, she cannot seem to prevent the corners from lifting into a perpetual grin. Not only has she met a man who has managed to capture and subsequently *retain* her attention for more than a couple of hours, but she has met someone who maybe, just maybe, she may have a future with.

Mr Delicious is everything, no, *more* than everything she ever wanted in a man. He is funny, intelligent and witty, he holds doors for her, pays the bill, listens attentively, and makes Lady Luxe feel as if she is the only girl in the entire world.

As they walk through the mall hand in hand, laughing at other people's outfit choices, she gets the distinct impression that she has finally found a man who will sing Bruno Mars' 'Just the way you are' to her.

Yeah. Just the way you are...as Jennifer, an annoying voice reminds her, causing her smile to fade as quickly as it did the time she stepped on dog poop in Hyde Park.

Trying not to let Mr Delicious sense her sudden change of mood, Lady Luxe swallows the rising lump in her throat and wonders if there is any possible way to get around the teeny issue of him not actually knowing who she is so they can develop some kind of relationship that isn't entirely based on lies and disguises. But only time will tell whether she will ever be able to trust him enough to reveal her true identity. And the longer she lied to him, the longer she pretended to be a Syrian raised in the UK working as a marketing executive in Dubai, the harder it would be to eventually enlighten him.

And who knows, despite being half Lebanese and half French and therefore probably the least traditional Arab man in Dubai, there was a huge chance that he wouldn't want a future with a girl who had forged horizontal alliances with more men than she could ever possibly mark on her two metre high bedpost. As reluctant as Lady Luxe ever is to question her lifestyle choices, she wonders if God has brought Mr Delicious to her life to show her the error of her ways; to show her that if she had just placed her trust in him, perhaps the only notch on her bedpost would have been that of conquering her soulmate.

Look, just calm down and stop acting like a besotted teenager, Lady Luxe tells herself with annoyance. For all she knows, Mr Delicious is just another one of the plentiful players that roamed Dubai's streets, preying on unsuspecting women desperately searching for husbands. She has only known him for a few hours and she was practically designing her wedding dress in her head. She needed to snap out of it before she not only damaged her reputation as being incredibly difficult to woo, but did something that she would invariably regret.

'So what does a classy lady like yourself like to do when the date is nearing an end? A walk on the beach? Coffee at mine? A lift to the metro?' Mr Delicious jokes as they browse through shops aimlessly, enjoying each other's company.

'A lift to the metro? Are you serious?' Lady Luxe asks with a laugh.

'Yeah, why not?' he replies, a cheeky glint in his eyes. 'Some girls don't deserve a lift home after they burn a hole in your pocket just for the pleasure of their company. When all they managed to do was bore you senseless for a few hours.'

'Are you trying to tell me something?' Lady Luxe asks in mock offence, stopping in the middle of the mall and placing her hands on her hips.

'No, if I were, I would have just dropped you off at the station without offering other options. So I take it you'll prefer a walk on the beach then?'

Laughing, they make their way to the car park and when Mr Delicious stops outside a white Audi R8 with black trims and rims, Lady Luxe looks at him in surprise.

'Is this your car?' she asks, raising a perfectly plucked eyebrow. There is something about Mr Delicious mannerisms that makes her believe that he is not wealthy, and she was half-expecting him to stop outside a piece of tin with wheels. Otherwise known as a Japanese car. She certainly wasn't expecting a 750,000 dirham one.

'Yes,' he says with a slightly defensive tone in his voice. 'Why?'

'I don't know, I just wasn't expecting this,' she says, sliding into the tiny passenger seat and pulling on the seat belt, wishing she hadn't said anything. She knows that with readily available credit up to ten times one's salary from more than one financial institution, in Dubai an expensive car is no testimony to wealth. But there's something about him that makes her certain that he is feigning wealth, regardless of his descriptions of skiing holidays in the Alps and summers at the Hamptons.

Lady Luxe's instincts are almost always right, unlike Leila who always gets it wrong. She suddenly misses Leila and her warped sense of how the world should work, the way she rarely finds anything funny, but when she does, she lets out the most infectious, hiccup-inducing laugh. Lady Luxe wonders if their friendship is destroyed beyond repair or if they will ever be able to put the Mohamed debacle behind them and move on.

'A dirham for your thoughts?' Mr Delicious asks as they drive down Um Suqeim Road and join the regular Jumeirah traffic.

'Trust me, they're worth a lot more than that!' Lady Luxe laughs, unsure whether to look out the window at the Maclarans, Bentleys, Porsches, and occasional Lamborghinis and Ferraris cruising past them with their windows half open as the drivers look for girls to race and chase, or whether she should savour the sight of Mr Delicious' toned arm as he holds the steering wheel with one hand. She opts for the latter and gulps as her eyes scan over his strong jaw, slender neck and then further down.

'What's wrong?' Mr Delicious asks, turning to look at her as they wait at a traffic light.

'Nothing!' Lady Luxe croaks, looking away. His eyes are beautiful; not too big, not too small, rimmed with thick, dark brown lashes, and even his hair sits in a perfect mess on his perfectly shaped head, which is neither too flat, nor too eggy. Everything about him, Lady Luxe realizes, is perfect. Right down to his clean, trimmed nails. She has dated a lot of good looking men in her relatively short life and although some of them were, admittedly, even better looking than Mr Delicious, none of them had managed to elicit such a profound reaction from every part of her being.

There is something different than usual about her longing for Mr Delicious though. For the first time since she left London, she has connected with someone on a level deeper than that which is purely physical. She feels connected to him emotionally and even spiritually, despite the short amount of

450

time she has spent with him. Even his part-Arab, part-European heritage, and the time he has spent in the West, attracts her like a moth to a flame.

Her heart pounding with excitement and her blood racing with anticipation, she wonders if this is what love at first sight feels like. Perhaps it wasn't just a gimmick created to make you want what you could never get, to keep you eternally unsatisfied, to force you to seek gratification elsewhere. From the second she saw him at the Cavalli Club with Leila, she knew. From the second he sauntered over to them and they spent the evening talking, laughing and dancing, she knew.

And now, months after that first, mindblowing meeting, he is back. She doesn't even care how he managed to find her, she is just thankful that he wanted her enough to find a way to do it.

'So....we're here. Shall we go for a walk?' Mr Delicious says quietly, turning off the engine to look at her. The windows in the car are tinted so heavily that Lady Luxe can barely make out the cars on either side of them and she knows for certain that no one can peep in either. The location, the darkness, the chemistry between them begs for more than a walk in the sand. She licks her lips unconsciously and turns to face him.

451

'Okay,' she whispers, trying hard not to look at his lips.

'You don't sound very interested in walking,' he teases, leaning over to brush a golden strand of hair away from her face. As he does so, his fingertips graze her cheekbone, and she swallows nervously. 'I'm not,' she manages to squeak, cursing herself for being such a bundle of nerves. No man had *ever* made her feel so powerful and yet so weak, and until that moment, she never attributed either of those adjectives to herself.

Lady Luxe finds that she cannot continue looking into his eyes without pouncing on him, so she looks away and reaches for the door handle. But before she can swing the door open and let the sound of the ocean remind her of where she is, Mr Delicious reaches out to stop her. She turns to look at him, and as she is about to ask him what's wrong, he leans over and presses his lips to hers.

The next few minutes are a blur as both Lady Luxe and her lover struggle to unite within the confinements of the car's snug interior, the atmosphere charged with longing. Completely oblivious to their risqué surroundings, they tug at each other's clothes with an urgency that fuels Lady Luxe's desire further. Scared that pulling her dress over her head will also result in the removal of her wig, Lady Luxe twists her body to let Mr Delicious pull down the zip, her eyes sleepy with desire. He tugs at the tight dress until it sits around her waist.

Even his touch is electrifying and Lady Luxe lets out a sigh and opens her eyes. As she does, she is confronted by a face peering in through the windscreen.

Letting out a horrified scream, Lady Luxe tries to pull her dress back on to cover her exposed bra, her heart in her throat.

'Is the door locked?' she hisses to Mr Delicious, but before he can press the button to check, the passenger side door swings open and Lady Luxe is yanked out of the car. She stumbles, unable to steady herself while trying to cover her exposed body with her arms, the blood draining from her face.

She knew this day was bound to come, but she never expected it to be like this. She never expected to be so vulnerable, so exposed, so completely at the mercy of her heartless brother.

'Get in my car,' Mohamed says through clenched teeth, his eyes burning with rage. Lady Luxe stares at him in horror, her mouth so dry she can hardly swallow. For a second, she wonders if she is dreaming, but the sheer terror she is experiencing is like nothing she has ever felt. Her heart thuds furiously and her palms begin to sweat as she struggles to breathe. She desperately tries to pull her dress back on and looks all around wildly, the scenery, the cars, all a blur.

'Who the hell are you?' Mr Delicious jump, out of the car and runs over to the pair, the bewilderment evident in his expression.

'Stay out of it,' Lady Luxe croaks, and as she does, Mohamed raises his hand and slaps her so hard across her face that she almost falls to the ground. Her head spinning, she staggers and Mr Delicious runs over to her, shouting at Mohamed in Arabic.

'She is my sister and this is a family matter.' Lady Luxe hears Mohamed say to Mr Delicious, his voice cold and hard. 'I will deal with you later. As for *you*,' he turns to look at his sister, his eyes alight with rage, 'get inside the car before I break your face.'

When she doesn't move, Mohamed grabs Lady Luxe by the hair and her golden wig slides off her head. Cursing in Arabic, Mohamed tosses it to the ground and grabs hold of her arm, instantly bruising it by the strength of his grip. Too ashamed to turn to look at the shocked Mr Delicious, Lady Luxe lets her brother drag her to the car and shove her inside, thumping her in her face as he does so. As Mohamed gets in and starts the engine, Lady Luxe struggles to contain the tears forming in her eyes. She will never give him the satisfaction of seeing her cry.

They drive towards Lady Luxe's fate in silence.

36

'What's wrong , habibti?'

Startled, I glance over at Goldenboy to find him staring intently at me. I was completely unaware that he had been watching me and not the creek in front of us, and I feel a stab of guilt as I smile and mumble 'nothing', before looking away. After all, what was I supposed to say? That I was torn between him—the beautiful breath of fresh air in my life—and my ex-husband, the father of my child, the ex-love of my life?

It has been just three days since Jayden descended on Nadia's doorstep, three days since I collapsed in the hallway of her apartment, and three, long, painful days, since our haunting conversation on the beach.

The shock of seeing Jayden standing there, in the flesh, close enough to touch, knocked my soul out of me. Nadia called an ambulance, and they took me to Rashid Hospital, where I spent the next few hours in absolute agony with both Nadia and Jayden by my side. Not because I was hurt physically, but because of Jayden's proximity. After all the crying, pining, loving, regretting, for every single day for two years, there he was, right in front of me. I could even smell him, but I couldn't even smile at him or talk to him, much less hold him.

As neither of us admitted knowing the other from the get go, the longer we kept our mouths shut, the harder it became to confess the truth. I kept feeling his gaze on me and I tried hard to avoid all eye contact with him. I just couldn't bear to see what was lurking in his eyes. What was he thinking? What was he feeling? Was he hurting as much as I was?

I got out of the hospital as quickly as I could, and let Nadia drop me off at JBR. I didn't let her come up to the apartment though. I was too scared that once we were alone, she would read my feelings in my expression and somehow, work it all out.

That night I stared at my phone, waiting for Jayden to call. I knew he'd manage to get my number from Nadia somehow and then call me. As I expected, a little after two in the morning, no doubt as soon as he had bid Nadia a good night, my phone began to ring.

'Hello?' I answered, my voice shaking so subtly that if you didn't know me, you'd never guess that anything was wrong. Jayden, of course, knew me better than anyone.

'I'm outside your building. Plaza. Come down.' It was a demand, not a question. And just like the Sugar from two years ago, the one who used to get secret phone calls in the middle of the night, and then sneak out of the house while everyone else was sleeping, I got up, threw on a hoodie over my vest stop and cotton PJ bottoms, slipped my feet into sandals and made my way down to the plaza level of my building.

But I didn't want to be the Sugar from two years ago.

Instead of going straight down to meet him, I went to the prayer room instead, pulled up the hood to cover my hair and prayed two rak'ah to God to help me, guide me, and protect me. My nerves more settled, I was finally ready to face him.

He had his back to me and stood staring at one of the many fountains that decorated the common area. I walked up to him and stood beside him, my entire body trembling. Without uttering a single word, he took my hand and we started walking towards the beach. The warmth of his skin surged through me and wrapped itself around my heart.

With the exception of the gentle lapping of the water as it caressed the shore, the world was completely silent. All the shops along the promenade were closed, and the pavement was empty. It was just us.

We took off our sandals and walked along the cold, damp sand, both of us unable to break the silence first. What could I possibly say that could justify what happened? No words or apologies could make it okay.

'Sugar,' Jayden spoke first, stopping in front of the ocean. He turned to look at me, and I looked down, still afraid to meet his eyes and see what was lurking in their depths.

'What?' I mumbled, kicking the sand, my hands stuffed into the pockets of my top.

'What happened? You...you disappeared. I looked for you for ages. I sat outside your house in my cousin's car for months but you never came in or went out. I was...I thought they had killed you.'

The crack in his voice made me look up at his face. A single tear rolled down his cheek. The pain in his eyes was unbearable to look at, so I looked away.

'J...' I began, reaching out to him.

He turned away from me abruptly and I could hear his breath coming out in deep, rasps. 'What the hell, Sugar,' he exclaimed after composing himself, whipping around to face me, anger blazing in his eyes. 'I loved you! I loved you more than anything in this world. I became a Muslim and I *married* you. I had the shit beaten out of me but I didn't care! I was ready to fight the world for you.'

His voice broke again and this time he fell to the sand with his head in his hands, and began to cry. Unable to stop my own tears, I joined him and together we wept with no inhibitions, clutching on to each other as if we were afraid that the other would suddenly disappear again.

'Jayden,' I began, taking his damp face in my hands and forcing him to look at me. 'I loved you too. More than you know. My parents forced me to leave London and made me move to India for a while. I checked my email every day hoping that you'd contact me, but at the same time, I didn't want you to. I was certain that if we got in touch with each other, my brother would find out, and this time, he'd actually kill you.'

'That's why I never emailed you,' he said softly, looking sideways at me. 'When I never saw you leave your house, I wasn't sure if you were hurt, alive, or being kept a prisoner. I didn't want to leave behind any evidence in case he found out and did something to you this time, instead of me.'

'You must really hate him,' I mused out loud. 'I bet you wish he had ended up in prison like he deserved.'

'He's your brother, Sugar,' he replied softly, looking away. 'I didn't tell the police it was him. I couldn't do that to someone you love. I couldn't break up your family like that.'

I started to cry again; the realization of what Jayden suffered just for loving me was beginning to suffocate me all over again. Leaning over, he engulfed me in a bear hug and stroked my hair until I stopped.

We sat together for ages, our knees drawn to our chests, talking about everything that happened over the past two years. Everything except the baby. Each time I tried to tell him, I felt the words get caught in my throat and my heart begin to pound all over again. In the end, I gave up trying. There was no point. All it would do was hurt him even more.

'So....Nadia, huh?' I said with a wry smile. 'She's really an amazing woman. Don't break her heart, okay? She's been through a lot.' I kept my tone light, but my heart ached just saying those words.

'Are you telling me that we're over, just like that?' he asked, his voice hard and controlled.

'I don't know, J,' I admitted, hugging my knees closer to me. 'It's hardly "just like that." We've been through a lot in the last couple of years. We've put our families through hell and back. It's taken me a really long time to get to where I am today. For months and months I spent every night crying. Every part of me missed you, yearned for you. I don't know if I can go through all this again.'

'But what if you didn't have to go through it all again?' he replied, his voice rising with excitement. 'I could move here, we could be together, no one would even know, Sugar. Think about it...you, me, the sun, the sea. It will be amazing!'

'We're not the same people we were back then,' I said softly, taking his hand in mine. 'What happened to us happened because of all the lying. I can't do that all over again. It would mean that I've learnt absolutely nothing after everything we've been through. I'm trying to be a different person. A better person.'

'Why can't you be better with me?' he interrupted earnestly, his eyes shining with excitement. 'Sugar, we were great together. Maybe your parents will actually bless our relationship once they see that we still love each other despite everything.'

The sun began to rise, casting warm, pink hues all across the sky and I stared at the ocean in wonder. It was so beautiful,sparkling with life and hope. I thought about what Jayden had said. He was right. It would be so easy.

But what about Goldenboy? When I was with him, I felt like a queen. I felt as though the world was at my feet and I could do anything or be anyone. With him by my side, I felt ready to take on any challenge that came my way. Until Jayden arrived, I had begun to believe that Goldenboy held the key to my future.

'I really don't know,' I whispered, staring at the sea, hoping it would give me some answers. 'Do you know for the first time in my life, I've actually started praying five times a day without anyone even reminding me? That I actually believe Allah loves me, and he's looking out for me. I've started turning to him, J. Not just when

I need help, but to thank him when I'm happy as well. When we were together, I didn't even fast, let alone pray.'

'So you're saying that you were a bad Muslim because of me?' he asked quietly.

'No! I'm not! I'm saying that when we were together, I was the worst person I've ever been. It wasn't because of you , but because of our situation. All the lying and sneaking around really affected me. It made me into someone I wasn't proud of.'

He said nothing.

'Look Jayden, let me think about it okay? But until then, *please* don't say anything to Nadia about our past. She doesn't know anything. I've never told her and I can't bear to have yet another person who respected me look at me with disdain.'

He agreed and I bid him a hasty goodbye, dragged myself up the stairs to my apartment, and then collapsed into bed, so exhausted that I fell into a deep sleep as soon as I closed my eyes.

'Sugar, are you *sure* nothing's wrong? You seem like a million kilometres away.'

He says it with such seriousness that I can't help but burst into laughter.

'What? What did I say?' Goldenboy asks with a frown. 'If you're going to laugh at my English, I'll only speak to you in Arabic.'

'Miles! It's million 'miles' away, not kilometres, you geek,' I gently shove him and he looks so crestfallen that I can't help but give his arm a squeeze.

'It's nothing, really. Just some family stuff,' I lie, feeling guilty. I really didn't want to meet up with Goldenboy, not until I had decided what to do, but he called me this morning and was so insistent about meeting me that in the end, when he turned up at my doorstep bearing gifts, an adorable woebegone expression on his face, I felt obliged to agree.

It has been four days since we last saw each other. We were supposed to meet the night I was taken to the hospital, and although Nadia tried to make me call him, I refused, and sent him a text message pretending I was sick.

I've had the 'flu' every day since then. And every morning, I've been waking up to a message telling me to look outside. The first day, I found a bunch of flowers and a thermos of chicken soup. The second, I found the latest *Desperate Housewives* box-set with a note that read, '*I hope this makes lying in bed a bit easier, habibti xxx.*' The third day, yesterday, I found a box of chocolates and a little teddy bear. But this morning, I when I opened the door, I found *him* standing on the other side looking slightly embarrassed.

'Oh no, you do look terrible,' he exclaimed, taking in my sunken, red-rimmed eyes, my dry skin and greasy hair.

'Thanks,' I muttered, giving him a dirty look.

'Look, you'll feel better if you come out and get some air. It's been three days now so you should be fine. Go and change, I'll wait for you downstairs.'

I'm kind of glad that I've left the house, as the change of scene has definitely raised my spirits, and showering obviously helped as well. But I wish I hadn't gone with him. I have no idea how I'm supposed to behave in his presence. I am at a loss as to what to say that won't make me feel completely hypocritical. I know that my confusion, my inner turmoil, is written all over my face, and I don't know how I can possibly justify it to him without telling him the truth.

We go for cheap shawarmas somewhere in Deira and then drive to the creek, where we're sitting on a wall and munching our dinner, talking about nothing and watching the dhows slowly sail by, illuminated by the twinkling lights from all the buildings on the other side.

Being with Goldenboy is so easy. He's funny, easygoing, and very easy to talk to. He makes me feel as if everything will be okay even though he hasn't said anything particularly profound.

But things aren't okay. You saw how he reacted when you wouldn't tell him if you had a boyfriend in the past. Imagine what he would say if he knew about Jayden.

'Goldenboy,' I begin, swallowing nervously and taking a sip of Laban Up, 'why do you like me?' I know it's a stupid question and I feel stupid for asking, but I have the sudden urge to know exactly what he likes, or doesn't like, about me. I need some kind of reassurance that giving up Jayden for him will be the right decision.

He looks at me and raises an eyebrow. 'Is that a trick question?'

'No.' He takes in my lost expression and realizes that I'm actually serious. Rearranging his legs, he turns to look at me and smiles a smile so genuine that it lights up his entire face.

'Erm, okay then. I love the way you are with people,' he begins, a little shy, unable to meet my eyes. 'You're so friendly, and polite to everyone, You have such a sweet heart. People don't realize that because you're always making jokes and you can be quite sarcastic, but you're actually generous and kind.'

'Good answer,' I grin, feeling a tad embarrassed by the compliments.

'I'm not finished, Miss Big Head,' he jokes, playfully shoving me, 'I like the way your mind works. You're clever and quick-witted, and you know how to take care of yourself. But you also let others take care of you, and I like that too. Sometimes you are hard, sometimes you're soft, but you're never weak.'

I'm surprised by his analysis of me and with every word he utters, I feel warmth spread over me and I watch his face as he talks, wishing I had asked the question sooner. I wasn't expecting such a deep answer. I remember the time I had asked Jayden why he loved me and he said he liked my laugh, my hair, and my crazy spontaneity. At that time it felt enough, but listening to Goldenboy speak makes me feel as if there is more to me than just doom and gloom.

'I also love the fact that you're so honest and upfront about everything. What you see is exactly what you get. No games, no lies, just the truth. And that's the most important thing of all.'

He stares at me with uninhibited respect and adoration, his face as open as a child's book and I stare back in horror, my heart sinking to the bottom of my sandals. Of course it is important.

That evening, I sit in my bedroom, aching to have someone to talk to. But I have no one. The only real friend I have in this country can't know about any of this. She's only just beginning to recover from her bastard husband's betrayal, she's only just starting to smile again. How can I possibly tell her that the guy she is falling for is my ex-husband.

He's not your ex-husband, Sugar. Technically, you're not even divorced. Maybe, Islamically, you're still married.

Sinking down onto the floor, I rest my head on the bed, aching for advice from someone who actually knows me and can help me decide what I'm supposed to do.

With a sudden jolt of realization, I take out my phone and call my best friend, Farah, feeling silly for not having thought of it before. Just because I have no friends in Dubai doesn't mean I have no friends at all.

'Oh my God! Sugar! Assalaamu Alaikum!' Farah squeals through the phone, her excitement immediately lifting my mood.

If there's one person in this world I can rely on to tell me the truth as it is, without sugar-coating it, it's Farah. Bold, brassy, beautiful, and brainy, she is great at giving advice simply because she doesn't believe in lying just to make someone happy.

We make small-talk for a couple of minutes before I launch into my dilemma. Farah, being one of the witnesses to my marriage with Jayden, knows my sordid story up until I moved to Dubai, and I don't have to waste time explaining what happened in the past. Instead, I tell her about Goldenboy, the way I feel about him and the way he makes me feel. I confess that he has no idea about my past, and will probably run a mile if he did.

When I get to the part about coming face-to-face with Jayden and discovering that he is Nadia's object of desire, Farah gasps and I can imagine her hazel eyes popping out of her head.

'Bloody hell Sugar, it's like something out of a Hindi movie,' she says. 'What are you going to do?'

'I was hoping you would tell me,' I say weakly. 'Jayden and I have a history together and a part of me will always love him. And if I'm honest with myself, another part of me thinks I should get back with him because I feel guilty about everything that happened.'

'That's a shitty reason Sugar, and if he heard you say that, he wouldn't want you anyway.' See what I mean about her brutal honesty?

'I know. I wonder if maybe it was just our timing that was wrong. Maybe this time, we have a chance to be together.'

'Maybe?'

'I don't know, Farah. At the same time, I'm not the same Sugar I was two years ago, when I was willing to compromise my family, everything, for a guy. I think I've changed for the better. I *want* to be better. But getting back with Jayden will make it hard for me to change. When I'm with him, I'm crazy and reckless, and that's what he likes about me. I don't want to be like that. I don't like who I become when I'm with him. It's taken me almost two years to work it out, but it's true.'

'So what's stopping you from just ending it with him, once and for all?'

'I don't know. We have so much history, it seems unfair to end things, and...' I stop, unsure of how to phrase what I'm feeling. It's something

I've never said out loud, or even thought about properly. But the feeling is there, in my head, even if I haven't articulated it, even in my head.

'Is it because you're afraid that when Goldenboy finds out about your past, he won't want you, and then you'll be left with nothing and no one?'

Hearing the words said out loud, even though they are by someone else, makes another surge of guilt course through me, and I feel my face turn red.

'I'm really awful, aren't I?' I whisper, hanging my head in shame.

'Not really,' she replies softly. 'No one wants to be alone. But no one wants to be second best either. You need to let him go Sugar. Let him get on with his life.'

'Do you think I should tell Goldenboy the truth?' I'm scared of what Farah's answer will be, worried that if she says yes, I will feel even guiltier than I already do until I oblige.

'To be honest, no. He doesn't need to know, and in Islam, we're supposed to hide our sins, not publicize them, especially to someone who is little more than a friend right now. But if things get serious between you guys and he asks you any questions then tell him the bare minimum. If he doesn't want you after that, screw him Sugar. You've suffered enough for your mistakes without being with someone who'll continue to make you suffer.'

We talk for a little longer and when I eventually hang up the phone, I actually feel okay. Talking through my dilemma has made me realize that there is no dilemma. I don't want to let the past dictate my present *and* my future. As much as I will always love and respect Jayden, we're just not right for each other anymore. Too much has happened in the past two years.

As for Goldenboy, if things take a more serious turn, I'll tell him. But right now, it's too soon. We've only known each other for a few months. Why should I tell an almost-stranger my deepest, darkest, secret?

I change into my pjs, crawl into bed and turn on *Desperate Housewives* to cheer myself up a bit, my mind tired of constantly going through my dilemma. My phone beeps and I look down to see a message from Jayden. I'm reluctant to open it and when I finally force myself to do it, I wish I hadn't.

Nadia knows everything. She took it worse than I expected. Call me.

37

Leila hasn't heard from Mohamed for four days. There have been no phone calls, no text messages, and no gifts either. Although she has been mentally preparing herself for this moment since the time she began enjoying his company almost as much as his gifts, Leila feels far emptier than she imagined she would. His absence from her life has suddenly made her existence seem even more meaningless than it previously did.

Looking around her scant apartment with its cheap furnishings and tatty finishing, she realizes for the hundredth time that she has absolutely nothing. All the effort she had exerted as a teenager in order to persuade her parents to allow her to study abroad, all the trauma she experienced when sneaking off to Dubai behind their backs, all the years she spent fending for herself with no family to welcome her home every evening, has resulted in nothing. All she has managed to achieve is extensive plastic surgery, extreme cynicism, and a few hundred thousand dirhams in her savings account. Oh, and a handful of expensive gifts. She has nothing real to show for herself after ten whole years of supposedly going after her dreams.

And, with Lara's wedding just three months away, Leila is still no closer to finding a fiancée as she was the day she found out that her younger sister would be usurping her in their race towards the altar. Maybe if she had tried hard enough to find a suitable groom for herself, instead of wasting time with Moe, right now, she would be in a more prosperous position.

Who are you fooling, she tells herself with a short laugh. She has been trying ever since she left Lebanon. She tried throughout her year in the States, but the only marriage offers she received were those bestowed on her by ageing, beer-bellied monstrosities. Not even a green card could compensate for *that.* Then she had worked her way through Mohameds and Johns, Fahds and Michaels, she had undergone rhinoplasty and breast enhancements, collagen fillers, and horrendously expensive maintenance treatments, all to market herself as the bride of choice.

Of course, she could have sought her mother's help. But not even Leila was that desperate. Admitting defeat to her mother was tantamount to digging her own grave and jumping in it. She could have looked for options in Lebanon, but for Leila, that too stank of defeat. She had to prove to her mother, her sister, everyone who scoffed at her for leaving Lebanon for a better life, that she actually *had* a better life. That she made the right choice in leaving all those years ago. That she was far better off than all of them, with their lazy afternoons drinking arak, their big hair, their constant fear of war, and litter of babies running amok.

No, she was better than them all. She had escaped the drudgery. She had forged her own future. She had stopped waking up to her alarm clock with her heart pounding, thinking it was a siren or worse, a bomb.

As she sits at her dining table in nothing but a baggy, tattered T-shirt, uninterested in even searching for something to eat, she wonders why she was stupid enough to believe that Moe would turn to *her* after discovering his wife's dual identity. If he did actually realize, that is. With no word from Lady Luxe since their confrontation outside her home and no word from Mohamed since their dodgy date, she is none the wiser to her ex-best friend's marital status. She is sizzling with curiosity, and has to sit on her hands to prevent herself from calling either of them to find out what happened. Did he know or not? If he knew, were they still married? Had he kicked her out and sent her back to her father's house?

Pulling herself off her chair to try and take her mind off what was happening in her lover's marital home, Leila makes her way to the bathroom and stares at herself in the mirror. Her face, thanks to botox, is almost wrinkle-free, but despite the regular glycolic peels she undergoes, the pores in her skin are becoming more visible every day, adding years to her. In three weeks, she will be thirty-three, hardly a spinster by Western standards, but in the Arab world she was rapidly approaching her sell-by date. She had a year, at the most, to be considered by *any* Arab man who wasn't previously married. As for the Western ones, most of the men older than her already had families of their own. Her best bet would be to move to a Western country, lower her standards, and marry the first half-decent, half-wealthy man that showed any interest.

Tearing her eyes away from her reflection Leila washes her face and goes back to the living area, her mind still on Mohamed. The torture she endured last week trying to get him to notice

Jennifer has undoubtedly aged her a few more months. She is certain that the origins of the tiny line she found on her forehead could be traced back to that terrifying evening. After everything she suffered through last week, after the pain she experienced when she discovered he was married to her best friend and after losing her best friend because of this, should she really give up *this* easily? Should she really be wallowing in self pity in her horrid little apartment wearing a grotesque t-shirt that smelt vaguely of jibneh?

Making her way to her bedroom, she changes into a pair of jeans and a plain black vest, combs her hair and pulls it back into a ponytail. Rubbing moisturizer on her face, she sprays on a little perfume and tries to smile.

'Leila, you are *not* giving up,' she says out loud, hoping that the more she pretends to be positive, the more positive she will actually feel. 'You are *not* a quitter,' she says, adopting a chirpy American accent and enjoying the sound of her voice echoing through the apartment. Sitting down on her bed, her mind drifts to Mohamed again and she knows that she won't be able to move on with her life until she finds out exactly what is happening and where she stands.

Swallowing her ever-diminishing pride, she decides to call Mohamed, bracing herself for whatever it is that is about to happen. She doesn't know whether he will bother answering, reject her outright or act completely normal and offer excuses of business, travel, or sickness.

None of this happens. Instead, the call goes straight through to voicemail. Surprised but also relieved, she leaves him a brief message asking him to call her back and then puts her phone down on the table.

Wondering what to do with herself, Leila eventually gets up and decides that she may as well clean her dusty apartment and perhaps even go the extra mile and organize her closet. Her cleaner is due in a couple of days, but Leila decides that that is no reason to live like a haiwana, waiting for a woman to come and clean when she is perfectly capable of doing it herself. Switching on the TV to MTV Arabia, she grabs the brush and starts cleaning, laughing inwardly at the thousands of working class expatriate women who come to the Gulf and develop airs and graces that are akin to royalty. In their home countries, many of them don't even know someone who has a part-time cleaner, let alone a full-time, live-in maid; yet they move out to the Gulf on ridiculously high salaries, get a maid or three and spend their days lunching, brunching, and relaxing at the salon as though they have been doing so their entire lives.

When Leila finally takes off her rubber gloves four hours later, she is pleased that her apartment is sparkling and somehow, just by moving the furniture around and using colourful scarves as table runners and wall hangings, she has managed to make it look more homely than it ever has before. She wonders if she made a mistake never investing in pretty things for her home. But she never expected to be living alone in her own apartment for a decade. She had assumed she would get married and move into a nice villa in Jumeirah within a couple of years.

Collapsing onto the sofa, she glances at her phone and realizes with a start that Mohamed hasn't called her back. After Fahd, she swore never to call a man more than once until he returned her phone call, but the longer she doesn't hear from Mohamed, the more determined she is to know whether or not he caught his wife. For the second time that day, she pushes her pride aside and calls him, but again the phone goes straight to voicemail. Without leaving a message, she hangs up and thinks for a few moments. The reasons for his silence could boil down to anything, starting with his desire never to see her again. He could have found another playmate to roll around in the sandpit with. Or he could be pre-occupied with his marital issues. Whatever the reason, Leila aches to know what's happening and knows she will be unable to move on with her life until she does.

She knows what she has to do, but she is too scared to do it. She is afraid that Lady Luxe will know by her voice that she was the traitor behind her husband's realization of her alternate identity. *If* he knew, that is. And if he didn't and everything was just dandy, she will have to pretend to want to reconcile their friendship. Leila doesn't know if she is a good enough actress to be able to pull that off without the perceptive Lady Luxe gunning her down in one sentence.

Taking a deep breath and sending a quick prayer to God she calls Lady Luxe, flinching as she does so.

'Alhatifu al mutahhariq allathi talabtahu mugh-laq', a computerised voice says almost immediately, indicating that the phone is switched off. Leila immediately tries Lady Luxe's 'dodgy' line, only to get the same response.

Panic beginning to take over, Leila's mind races as she tries to work out why Mohamed's phone is constantly going through to voicemail and Lady Luxe's is switched off. Numerous scenarios run through her mind; from Mohamed being imprisoned for killing his wayward wife, to Lady Luxe running away in the dead of the night to escape her husband's wrath. Whatever it is, Leila knows that the only way to find out is to go to Mohamed's home.

Without pausing for another thought, she jumps up and rifles through her closet until she finds her novelty abaya, sheyla, and niqab, purchased for a fancy dress party many, many years ago. She throws it over herself and then spends half an hour trying to secure the scarf on her head, but no matter how many times she wraps it around her head the way she has seen Lady Luxe do it a million times, it just slides off her head. In the end, she pins it together using large safety pins, and then ties the niqab around her face until only her eyes are exposed.

Blanching at her unattractive and completely inconspicuous reflection, Leila slips her feet into plain black ballet pumps, grabs her keys and heads for the door.

As she drives down Sheikh Zayed Road towards Jumeirah, doubts begin creeping into her mind. She knows enough about Moe to know that if he spots her in his house, he will be absolutely livid. But with her genius disguise, and the fact that the male and female quarters will be entirely separate, the chances of bumping into him are next to impossible. As for Lady Luxe, Leila feels safe in the knowledge that there is no way her friend will rat her out, not with all that Leila knows about her alter ego.

Upon reaching Jumeirah Road, Leila turns into one of the side streets and parks her BMW outside a different villa just to be on the safe side. Fixing her niqab and struggling to breathe under the constricting cloth, she stares at the wrought iron gates, her nerves static. There is no mistaking the imposing villa, with its white columns and fountains and as she walks up the long drive with as much confidence as possible, she stops for a moment and stares at her surroundings. In the daylight, the grounds are even more beautiful than when lit up at night and once again, she is reminded of all that Lady Luxe jeopardized for a little fun.

'Can I help you?' The Filipina maid says in Arabic, her young face expressionless.

'I've come to visit my friend Lady Luxe,' Leila says in English, her voice haughty.

'I'm sorry, ma'am, but she's not here. Can I take a message?'

'Will she be long? It's quite important so I don't mind waiting for her.'

'I'm sorry, ma'am, but she may be a while.'

'Do you know when she'll be back?'

'She's travelling, ma'am.'

'Travelling? Where did she go?'

'I'm sorry, ma'am, but I really can't help you. Goodbye.'

The huge wooden Berber style door closes quite literally in Leila's face and she stands there in stunned silence for a few moments, composing herself, before trudging down the long drive back to the main gates. Her mind spinning, she wonders if Lady Luxe really is travelling, or if it was a pre-arranged spiel designed to hide the truth. That Mohamed had divorced her and sent her packing to her familial home.

As soon as she is back on Sheikh Zayed Road, Leila pulls the niqab off her face and wipes the perspiration trickling down her cheeks. She tries to tug the sheyla off her head, but it has been secured with five safety pins and refuses to budge.

Turning the AC on full blast, Leila wonders how Muslim women can bear the extra layers in such stifling heat. Not to mention the way it strips them of most of their beauty. If her hair and body had to be covered up, and if she didn't look or feel half as sexy as she did, how would she ever manage to flirt or coerce her way into getting what she wanted?

Before she reaches the Discovery Gardens exit, Leila's phone beeps and she almost crashes into the old Toyota pickup on her left when she sees it's from Mohamed. Her car swerves and she tries to steady it, still holding onto the phone. Slowing down, she opens the message with baited breath and holds her phone in front of her in order to see the road at the same time, squinting at the screen.

I know you came near my house today. I saw your car. It's over Leila. Don't contact me again.

Leila stares at the screen, tears filling her eyes. That was it? That was all he had to say after everything? Although she has been preparing herself for this moment, although she believed that she would be able to handle his rejection with cool dismissal, Leila feels an ache in her heart that joins all the other aches until her entire soul feels crushed.

Still staring at the screen with tears pouring down her face, the car veers to the left again, but before she realizes what is happening, before she can straighten the steering wheel, there is the screech of brakes, the deafening crunch of metal, the tinkling of breaking glass, as the entire world begins to spin.

38

Nadia had no idea what to expect when Jayden sat her down in Mall of the Emirates and began his confession. She watched his face as he struggled to find the correct words, and with each second that passed, her panic intensified. Bracing herself for the worst, she clenched her fists in her lap, desperately trying not to let fear overcome her.

She felt as if it was the Daniel scenario all over again. Her life was supposed to be different, better, but somehow, she always found herself back in the exact same situation; with a man interested in more than just her. While she waited for him to start speaking, she thought back to her own behaviour over the past few days. She had been a bit abrupt with him, occasionally moody, depressed, boring. It was no wonder he was sick of her.

'Jayden,' she began. 'I know my moods have been all over the place, but I promise you, I'm not like this all the time. I'm just finding what happened with Daniel difficult to cope with...'

'Nadia stop,' he interrupted, a pained expression on his face. 'It's not you. You remember that girl I told you about?' Fidgeting with his mobile phone, Jayden's eyes were everywhere except on her.

'What girl?' she asked, forcing her voice to remain neutral, staring at his expression for some kind of clue as to what he was about to say.

'The one from England. The one I was in love with and disappeared after her family almost killed me? The Indian girl?'

'What about her?' Frustrated, Nadia stared at him, wishing he would get to the point quickly instead of painfully drawing out the explanation.

'She's back.' He finally looked at her and she felt a charge of electricity at the intensity of his gaze. There was something in his eyes, a darkness that previously went unnoticed by the Nadia who was consumed by her own problems.

'What do you mean, "she's back"? Did she get in touch with you?' She wasn't expecting this and although it was, in the end, about a girl and not her, she felt oddly relieved. This was a girl from his past, not someone he met and cheated on her with. In fact, it wasn't completely dissimilar to her recent liaison with Yusuf. She understood that people had pasts that often resurfaced at the most inappropriate times. That's all it was, a blast from the past.

'Not exactly. I bumped into her,' Jayden replied, his vagueness beginning to irritate her.

'Okay...' she probed gently, trying her best not to lose her temper. 'Look, just tell me what's happening. It's okay, I'm not upset. These things happen.'

'So things are obviously a bit weird.'

Nadia looked at Jayden for another clue in his tell-tale eyes, but aside from the darkness and the pain, there is nothing. There must be more to the story than just him bumping into an old flame.

'Get to the point, Jayden,' Nadia finally snapped, her tone more aggressive than she intended. 'So far, you haven't told me anything weird at all. How do you feel about her?'

As soon as she asked the question, she wished she hadn't. Jayden's eyes said everything before he even spoke.

'I...I'm still in love with her.'

Nadia inhaled sharply, almost as if she has been punched in the gut. This she wasn't expecting. She thought he would be confused or lost but Jayden's voice, though faltering, was one that belonged to a man who knew exactly what he wanted. And it wasn't her.

'I can't help it,' he continued, his voice cracking. 'I don't want to be, but at the same time, I do. It's her. She was the love of my life, you know? We never had closure. And now she's back and I don't know what to do, what to feel or anything.'

Nadia listened to Jayden in silence. Her throat dry, she struggled to keep the water stinging her eyes at bay as she tried to swallow everything he was telling her.

'So why did you bother coming out here if you felt like this?' she whispered after a while. 'It wasn't fair to me, Jayden. I know all about exes and ghosts okay, I don't blame you for that. But how could you come to Dubai as if we were something, if we're not?'

Jayden opened his mouth, and then closed it again and Nadia could see that he was at a loss for words himself. He reached out to touch her hand, but she pulled it away.

'I...' he began, clearing his throat. Nadia stared at him, her pulse thudding in her ears, waiting for the next blow that was sure to be delivered. 'I bumped into her here, Nadia. Here in Dubai.'

'Don't lie to me, Jayden, what are the chances of that? And you've acted weird since the moment you got here so unless you saw her at the airport, I'm not buying it.'

Nadia waited for Jayden to explain further. The initial understanding she felt towards his dilemma wore away the longer he remained elusive. He was deliberately being obtuse. The least he could have offered her was the truth, but even that appeared to be too strenuous a task.

Jayden continued to say nothing and Nadia knew exactly what that meant. He was lying when he said he bumped into her in Dubai. She couldn't believe she had been fooled by a man *again*. Sugar was right to tell her to take things slow. She wasn't ready for this. Her wounds hadn't even had a chance to heal. She wasn't even divorced. Yet here she was, being lied to by a man she barely knew but already meant something to her for the umpteenth time. And she had no one to blame but herself. She knew he carried a lot of emotional baggage and yet she went ahead and fell for him anyway.

'If that's all you have to say, I'll be off then,' she finally said, realizing that he was not ready to divulge further. 'Call me when you're really ready to tell me what's going on.'

Getting up from the table, she examined Jayden's face one last time as a final attempt to understand what was happening. His stricken expression revealed nothing but his own internal battle, and with a sigh, Nadia picked up her bag in defeat, ready to turn away. Jayden's phone began to ring, and as she moved to leave, she glanced down at it without intending to. Nadia's heart plummeted to the soles of her shoes as Jayden grabbed the phone and rejected the call, but looking up at Nadia's bewildered expression, knew he was too late.

'Why is Sugar calling you?' she whispered, desperately hoping that her gut feeling was wrong, that the pieces that fell into place in one, swift, second were horribly misplaced.

Jayden looked down and said nothing. She watched his Adam's apple move as he swallowed nervously, unable to speak.

'It's Sugar, isn't it? She's the girl.' It was more of a statement than a question, and as soon as Nadia said it out loud, the extent of what had just happened to her, and who caused it, hits her like a hammer on her face.

Jayden and Sugar. How could she have not seen it before? Why else would Sugar have collapsed like that in her apartment? Why else would she have moved to Dubai? Now that she realized it, it was glaringly obvious. They loved each other, they had a history together and there was Nadia, the idiot in the middle of it all, thinking she had something special with an amazing guy, when in reality she was nothing but a rebound.

She should have known better than to think that there was a single guy in the world who was capable of being with her, and only her.

That evening, as she sat alone in her apartment, Nadia wept silent tears for the husband, boyfriend, and best friend she had lost in just one week. She tried to make the pain go away by telling herself it was for the best, that it was all part of God's plan, that she would one day see the wisdom behind it. But despite her best efforts to appease her restless soul, she felt a cold chill take over her, inside and out.

Glancing down at her watch, Nadia realized that she had missed the Asr and Maghrib prayers and the time for Isha had already arrived. And then, for the first time in years, she looks away and ignores the call to pray that came from within. She wasn't in the mood to submit.

Although twenty-four hours have passed since Jayden's revelation, the ache in Nadia's heart has far from subsided. It has, in fact, increased with every hour, and now she lies scrunched up in a ball on her sofa, desperately trying to make the headaches and nausea disappear.

Nadia knows that part of her despair comes from the lack of connection she currently has with her creator. Ever since she returned from London, she has been finding it difficult to gather up the desire to pray. At first, she still prayed, but for shorter durations. Then she started praying quickly, going through the motions without pondering over the words or taking the time to make the connection with God.

And now, she either prays late, after the set times or doesn't pray at all. Deep down, she knows that if she makes an effort to reconnect with her faith, she will feel better. But something from within prevents her from doing so. She knows that her revenge strategy goes against her religion and she feels like a hypocrite when she acts like she is placing her trust in God when she's not.

Why was what she was doing so wrong, anyway? She was the victim in the scenario, not Daniel. Not Jennifer. Not Jayden. And definitely not Sugar.

Sugar knew exactly what she was doing when she neglected to tell Nadia the truth behind her relationship with Jayden. When the three of them were there, in the emergency room, she chose to speak to him as if he were a stranger. Not the love of her life, the reason why she left England, the reason behind her dramatic character change.

There was only one act that could make her feel just a little better, and that was the act of revenge. Sugar deserved what was coming.

When the doorbell rings, Nadia ignores it. Jayden has tried calling her several times but she isn't ready to face him just yet. And she is certain there is nothing he can say to her that will make the ache go away. Even if he chose her, not Sugar, it wouldn't be enough. He had lied once. He could easily lie again. She had no desire to waste another moment of her life with a man who would make her suffer due to his inherent nature.

There is another knock on the door and this time, she forces herself to relax her muscles and uncurl in order to walk across the room and check who it is, on the off chance that it isn't Jayden. Straightening her white cotton PJs, she throws on an old cardigan and wraps a creased pashmina around her head in case it is a man.

'Who is it?' she asks and when there is no response, just another knock, she curses whoever designed the place and neglected to put a peephole in the door. She cannot believe she never thought about it when she moved in.

Had Nadia been in London, she would never have dreamt of opening the door without checking who it was first. This was Dubai though, where many didn't even bothering locking up, let alone checking who was at the door before opening it. Something makes her hesitate though, so she chains the door first, just in case.

As soon as she unlocks the door, whoever is on the other side pushes it open but the chain prevents it from opening completely. Nadia jumps in shock and grabs the handle to close it, but the person blocks it with a shoe and heaves his body against the door.

'Open the door, Nadia,' Daniel snarls from the other side and Nadia gasps, momentarily letting go of the handle. He shoves it door again and it strains to break free from the small metal links preventing it from doing so. Nadia stares at the chain in horror, knowing that she had no chance if he managed to get into the apartment.

'I'm calling the police!' she cries, desperately looking for her phone, her eyes wild with terror. She can't find it anywhere and her panic grows with every second that passes as she throws cushions to the floor and rummages through her belongings as fast as she can, knocking over anything in her way. 'Like I fucking care, you fucking psycho bitch!' he screams, slamming his body weight against the door.

Nadia hears a crack and her throat tightens in fear. Her hands shaking, she grabs a knife from the kitchen, and as she does, finally spots the phone on the counter. Almost weeping in relief, she runs into the toilet and locks the door.

'There's someone trying to break into my apartment! I think he's going to kill me,' she cries into the phone as Daniel continues to beat the door down.

'OPEN THE FUCKING DOOR!' he screams again. 'You fucking ruined my life! I lost my job because of you! I'm being *deported* because of you! Jennifer's disappeared and I know it has something to do with you, you evil bitch! I'm going to fucking kill you!'

'Please hurry!' Nadia sobs into the phone, her hands clammy and her face white with fear as she hears the two small screws that were preventing him from entering give way, and the front door flies open and hits the wall.

'Where the fuck are you?' Daniel yells, storming into the apartment. All she can hear is the sound of glass breaking and plates smashing as she cowers against the bathroom door, praying he won't be able to get in.

Her fingers still shaking, she struggles to send Jayden a text message. He is also staying in the JLT area and she hopes to God either him or the police will get there before it's too late.

She shouldn't have sent the email with the pictures of Jennifer to her husband. She knew the family was high up in the food chain but she didn't expect them to have the power to deport Daniel. She should have found a better way to obtain justice. But it was too late, and now, she was going to have to pay the price.

'How could you *do* this to me?' Daniel cries from outside the bathroom, thumping the door with his fists. Nadia jumps again and she squeezes her eyes closed and recites the Shahadah over and over again in her head.

Things continue to break outside the room and Nadia closes her ears with her hands, shaking violently. After a while it stops, and the only noise left is the sound of Daniel's panting.

When the police finally arrive, the same time as Jayden, Nadia feels as if she has aged a century. She hears the handcuffs clink onto Daniel's wrists and emerges from the bathroom where she falls into Jayden's arms, sobbing hysterically. A crowd of neighbours have gathered outside the apartment and they stare at her, with her red eyes and blotchy face and offer words of consolation. But Nadia hears nothing.

All she can see is the wreckage that was once her new home, her new start. The TV lies on its side, a spider crack in the middle and everything else decorates the floor—broken glass, books, plants, pictures. There are tears in the canvas paintings on the wall and even the contents of her fridge have been emptied.

'You can't stay here tonight,' Jayden says to her, his arm around her shoulders.

She leans against him, too tired to stand up straight. 'I have nowhere to go,' she whispers, closing her eyes and inhaling deeply, trying to regulate her heartbeat. She really didn't. She had no real friends, no one she could rely on anyway and the one proper friend she did have was someone whose memory made her want to retch.

'Come and stay with me,' he replies, squeezing her tightly. 'Seriously. I'm not letting you stay here.'

It would be so easy to just go back to Jayden's hotel with him. He would make her tea and hold her till she fell asleep and she would feel loved again. But in the morning, she would remember what he did to her and who he was actually in love with, and then she would have yet another painful memory to erase when she eventually went back to her lonely existence.

Maybe it was time to go back to her family and be with people who loved her for who she was, not what she could offer them.

'Thanks, but no,' she says, pulling away, 'I think I need some time alone.'

39

Lady Luxe stands on her balcony and stares out at the sea, watching it lap against the shore with calm precision. The night air is warm and slightly sticky, as it always is in June and she inhales deeply, knowing that this could quite possibly be the last time she inhales the scent of the Arabian Gulf. She looks around the gardens, at the regal palm trees, the fountains decorated with mosaic tiles, the luscious green grass fresh and plump from being watered three times a day and tiny goose bumps form all over her skin. As soon as her father arrives, it will all be over.

A part of Lady Luxe considers stuffing all her jewellery in a rucksack and then shimmying down the drain pipes and disappearing. But even if she does manage to make it to the ground with her limbs intact and somehow manages to sneak past the watchman, where will she go? Her father will place a travel ban on her before she has the chance to make it to the airport.

As half-hearted escape plots form in her mind, Lady Luxe realizes that she doesn't even want to run. She has spent her entire life running from her duties, her culture, her religion, and now she believes it's time to face the consequences. After all, ever since she moved back to Dubai, Lady Luxe had known this time would come; that all her extra-curricular adventures would one day blow up in her face. Dubai is an incredibly small place, and she was an idiot to think that a blonde wig and some contact lenses were enough to protect her forever.

Walking back into her bedroom, she gently closes the French doors behind her and leans against them, sadness creeping into her usually hard heart. She looks around her room; at her beautiful leather bed, the fluffy white rug, her vast walk-in closet and thinks back to all the fun moments she has had within its walls: smoking her very first cigarette at fifteen with Moza and Rowdha egging her on, watching horror movies with Ahmed while sharing a bucket of butter popcorn, piling on makeup during elementary school sleepovers with her classmates. No matter how unhappy and dissatisfied she was with her life, she couldn't deny that it had been a privileged one.

She wonders if things would have been different if she grew up with her parents still together, if having someone to hug, to love, to show her drawings to when she came home from school would have shaped her personality differently. What if she had had someone who could have helped her navigate her way through her teens with kindness, not with a list of non-negotiable rules, someone who could have explained to Lady Luxe her value as a woman, told her that she didn't need male attention in order to feel beautiful, powerful, successful, desirable?

Whatever. It's too late.

Lady Luxe sits on her bed and draws her knees to her chest, hugging them to her as close as possible. She winces as she accidentally presses one of the many bruises that have formed as a result of Mohamed's earlier explosion and she turns to look in the ornate, brushed silver mirror hanging above her makeup table. A black eye has already begun to form on her right eye, and her lower lip is cut and swollen. She tries to smile, but even that hurts and she sinks back against her pillows, wishing she could call Moza or Rowdha for help. But Mohamed has not only taken both of her phones, but has also turned off the wireless router.

She is lucky that she managed to give Ahmed Mr Delicious' number to warn him to leave Dubai just before Mohamed locked her in her bedroom. She hopes, with all her heart, that he will pay heed to her warning and leave. She doubts he will try to be the hero and save her. When it comes to family honour, no one ever intervenes, least of all Arab men who would probably do the same to their own sisters.

All Lady Luxe can do is wait for her father to arrive and decide her fate.

She knows her father well enough to know that before making a decision, he will weigh every possible option—he will consider disowning her, and leaving her to do as she pleased without making a mockery of him and his beliefs. He will contemplate marrying her off to her cousin, but he will know that she will probably end up divorced in less than three months and then, after being publicly perceived as soiled goods, he will worry that she will have even more freedom to further sully his name. He will think about banishing her to her room and withholding her access to wheels and money, hoping it will curb her desires. But he knows, and she knows, that if she wants to get around the obstacles he sets, she will.

Her body sore from Mohamed's thorough beating, Lady Luxe lets her eyes close and wonders what could have happened between her and Mr Delicious if they hadn't met in a club. If he knew her as *her*, not as Jennifer. If he had been from a prestigious family. If she hadn't.

She wishes she had called him back the night he stored his number in her phone. She wishes she hadn't been so stubborn, so intent on playing the game by her rules, so caught up with playing games, full stop. She wishes she had the chance of getting to know him a little bit more. She wishes she had chosen the 'metro' option at the end of their date.

However, even if she had done things differently, Lady Luxe gets the feeling that she would still have ended up like this. There was no way Mohamed would have known who she was through the tinted windows of a car. He had to have seen her getting into the car at the mall. Or perhaps he saw her at Momos. But Mohamed hated Moroccan food and he never ate in malls.

Lady Luxe thinks back to Mr Delicious' sudden phone call. Why had it taken him so long to call her? How had he managed to find her number in the first place? And then, with a start, she realizes something that, in her excitement, she had missed earlier. He called her on her real phone line, not the dodgy line reserved for indecent encounters. She hadn't realized that earlier as she had stored his number on both her phones in case she lost the other one.

You bloody idiot, you were set up.

The sound of the front door slamming echoes through the villa, and Lady Luxe's heartbeat quickens, her anger dissipating like fire under water. She jumps off the bed and sticks her ear to the door, desperate of some kind of clue as to what will happen. All she can make out is the low rumblings of male voices, and then the door to her father's study is closed and all is silent again.

Sliding to the floor, Lady Luxe sits with her back against the door, wondering what Mohamed is saying to her father. She can imagine the delight with which he explains everything he saw in graphic detail and for once, she cannot even accuse him of exaggerating. After all, he caught his sister wearing not much more than a blonde wig, with a half-naked man.

There is a barely audible tap on the door and Lady Luxe stiffens. 'Sis, are you there?' Ahmed whispers.

Despite the fact that he is barely audible, Lady Luxe can hear the fear in her brother's voice, and her heart aches once more. Unbeknownst to Ahmed, he is about to lose his older sister, and he is probably going to have to witness it all.

'Shu, habibi?' she murmurs, pressing her ear to the door and placing her palm flat against it, imagining Ahmed's palm on the other side.

'Are you okay?'

'I'm fine, don't worry. Did you manage to get through to the number I gave you?' Lady Luxe speaks quickly, knowing that she doesn't have long and any moment now, her brother or father will come storming into her room.

'Yes. But I don't know if he'll listen.'

'I feel like I was set up, Ahmed,' Lady Luxe confesses, feeling more frustrated than angry. 'Not by him, but by someone else. I've been thinking about it and it just doesn't add up.'

'What shall I do?'

'If you get a chance, please ask him how he got my number. Tell him it's a matter of life and death and he's bound to tell you.'

Lady Luxe listens to Ahmed's footsteps disappear down the hall and then slumps back to her position on the floor, her mind spinning so

507

furiously that the blood pounds in her ears and she feels a sense of panic rising through her body. How could she have been so stupid?

Before she has a chance to analyse further, loud, deliberate footsteps make their way up the stairs and Lady Luxe jumps up from her position on the floor and waits on the other side of the door, clenching her fists to stop her hands from shaking. She feels weak and lightheaded, as if the slightest touch will send her crashing to the ground.

The door is thrust open and Mohamed stalks in, swelling in his own importance. Lady Luxe almost laughs out loud, knowing that he is enjoying every second of her agony. He has always been jealous of her relationship with their father, at the respect their father had for her business acumen and success and he must be thrilled at being the one to show their father exactly how misguided he actually was.

'Ta'ali ma'ai,' he says shortly, without even looking at her. He turns and walks away and she pauses for a moment, unable to move from fear. He turns back, his lip curled in distaste and snarls, 'Or do you want me to drag you?'

For once Lady Luxe has no retort to throw back at him. She is in no position to assume airs and graces. Without a word, she follows him down the hall. Her muscles aching from the earlier beating, she falters on the stairs, and clutches the banister to steady herself. She wonders if she should let herself fall, if she should let her head crash against the marble, let the blood ooze out of her skull and decorate the white with splashes of ruby red. But in Islam, one who commits suicide is destined to an eternity in Hell and Lady Luxe has always maintained a shred of hope that God, Al Rahman, Al Rahim, will forgive her for all she has done. If she takes her own life she will lose all chances of gaining his mercy.

She follows Mohamed into her father's study and keeps her eyes down, too afraid to even look at her father. As always the scent of bakhoor is overpowering, making her feel even more lightheaded and helpless than before. She struggles to maintain her composure, but every part of her trembles with apprehension.

'Mohamed, you may leave,' her father says coldly.

There is a pause and Lady Luxe knows that Mohamed is surprised and annoyed at being discarded. But even this small victory isn't enough to stop her blood from drumming violently in her ears. There is a long silence after Mohamed leaves and with each second that painfully passes, Lady Luxe's trepidation intensifies.

'You have disgraced me,' he finally says, his icy voice cutting into the stuffy room like a knife through butter. 'I never expected my daughter, my own flesh and blood, to behave in such a disgusting manner,' he continues drawing out every word slowly and deliberately. 'You are from the X family, you have a lineage that anyone would be proud to be a part of, yet you have been gallivanting around my country, my home, acting no better than a cheap whore.'

Her cheeks burning with embarrassment, Lady Luxe continues to remain silent. Her father, whom she has struggled to impress her whole life, was looking at her like she was nothing. Anything she had ever done to gain his respect had been brutally shattered. And it was her own doing. She imagines Mohamed describing, in painful detail, the way he had found her with her dress around her waist, and her insides shrivel up with shame.

'You are not stupid. You are not naive. You are not simple. I cannot blame your misdemeanors on ignorance or innocence. You think I do not know that this isn't the first time you have disrespected my name and our religion in public like a commoner? You think I do not know how wild you are, how you yearn for everything we hold in contempt? I had hoped that your time in London would cure you of your satanic desires but instead, you have continued your disgusting behaviour here in my home.'

Her father's voice is hard, and she knows that there is nothing she can say that will make him change whatever he has decided to do. She could cry, plead, beg, faint, but nothing will alter his decision. She did after all, inherit her stubbornness from him. She was as in-tune with his temperament as she was with her own.

'I have thought long about what to do with you. I cannot even look at you. You disgust me. You have brought shame on my entire family just to indulge in some fun. You knew what was at stake, yet you chose to disobey me while living under *my* roof, eating *my* food, and spending *my* money.'

His voice rises by a mere decibel, but it is enough for Lady Luxe to notice, and she cowers under the weight of his words. Her father is not a rash man, every action is premeditated, precise, and she knows that he is not speaking merely out of anger.

'I cannot even begin to imagine how many people know what my daughter has been doing while my back is turned,' Lady Luxe's father says, his voice rising once again. 'How many of my neighbours, my family, my community, have been pitying me, and laughing at me? Do you even care?' He slams his fist down on the hard, mahogany desk, and she jumps, sweat leaking out from every pore in her skin.

There is another excruciatingly long pause, and Lady Luxe can hear her heart beat over her father's heavy breathing, the grandfather clock in the corner, and her own shallow breaths.

'You are no longer welcome in my home, or my family. *Ana mitbarri minnich.*'

Although she was expecting something similar, upon hearing the words, upon hearing that she is no longer his daughter, that he is no longer her father, Lady Luxe's knees almost buckle and she holds onto the bookcase to stop herself from falling to the floor.

'You will pack your things. The driver will collect you and take you to the airport and you will board a flight to London. You will never receive a single dirham of your inheritance and you are not welcome at my funeral. Get out.'

Lady Luxe breathes heavily, but none of the oxygen seems to be travelling around her body and she feels weak and lightheaded. She opens her mouth to speak, but not even a squeak manages to escape from her dry lips. She looks up, her eyes brimming with tears, and her gaze connects with her father's. His usually handsome and youthful face looks old and tired, and for the first time in her life, he doesn't look immortal.

'Baba,' she croaks, the tears spilling over and falling down her cheeks. He turns his head away and says nothing and Lady Luxe knows that this is the last time they will ever meet.

40

Despite the strange looks I got from the passengers nearby, I cried through most of the nine-hour flight from Delhi to London. I didn't browse through a single magazine, I didn't switch on the screen in front of me, and I didn't touch a morsel of food. All I did was wonder if I would ever see my baby girl again. She didn't even have a name. I was too scared to name her because the act of being able to call her something other than 'the baby' would only bring her closer to me, and make my actions even worse than they already were.

My dad was waiting for me at Terminal Three. He looked older than I remembered. His hair, which used to be jet black with faint specks of grey, was now almost entirely silver. The lines that decorated his face had deepened and he where he once stood tall, proud and commanding, he seemed to have developed a stoop over the past seven months.

I wanted nothing more than to collapse in his arms, as I would when I was a child and had scraped my knee or lost a spelling competition or broke up with my best friend.

I didn't. And he made no effort to comfort me either. Perhaps he didn't understand how much my heart was bleeding.

In the months that followed my return to the UK, I never left the house more than once a fortnight and even that was because I had to sign on for my Job Seekers Allowance. I wasn't seeking a job of course. I could barely speak coherently, let alone process complex information, but it was the only way I could 'earn' some money. Yes, I was one of those Asians abusing the system.

Food became a necessity rather than a pleasure. My body wasted away and so did my mind. My friends got bored of trying to talk to me, but after a while, they gave up. No one knew how to get through to me.

In their desperation to cure me, my parents forced me to visit countless molana sahibs and pirs, but no amount if incantations or prayers blown into zam-zam could fix me. After everything else failed, they sent me to a counsellor.

It took a while but I eventually learnt how to deal with my pain, my anger, the way I blamed my parents for how they reacted to my mistake.

I'm well versed with the kind of hurt that first turns to frustration and eventually into uncontrollable rage. I understand the feeling of betrayal.

I don't blame Nadia for being angry with me for withholding vital information about my history with Jayden, but I never expected her to be this livid. According to Jayden, she saw my name on his phone and went ballistic. And that's it. She doesn't want to know me anymore, and I don't know how to get through to her to apologize and explain my side of the story.

Nadia's disappearance, together with my dilemma over Jayden and the constant guilt and fear I feel for not telling Goldenboy the truth about my past, is driving me crazy. Even now, although I'm at work, I can't concentrate on anything other than my personal issues and I certainly don't know how I'm supposed to focus on teaching my students anything other than how to screw up their lives beyond redemption.

I've been going to work like a zombie. I usually go out of my way to make my lessons fun and interesting for my students, but for the past few days, we've played no games, had no interesting conversations, or even done a vaguely fun worksheet. Instead, I've given them exams every single lesson under the guise of exam practice, but really so that I can space out.

Today's no exception. I've been blanked out all day. I've barely heard any of the questions my students have asked me, and I can't even concentrate long enough to mark all those bloody exams I made them take.

My phone vibrates with an incoming text message, and I check it with trepidation. It's from Jayden. He's already arrived to take me out for my lunch break.

Jayden basically gave me a grand total of two days to think about whether or not I wanted to get back together with him. After my conversation with Farah, I pretty much decided what I wanted to tell him. But knowing something and actually doing it are two different things. In approximately half an hour, I'm supposed to give him my answer. I already feel nauseous.

Having Jayden back in my life as a friend has been wonderful. We share so many memories and if I could, I'd keep him in my life as someone special. But I know it's not fair to him, Goldenboy, or even Nadia, to keep him to myself just because of our shared history.

When the clock strikes one, I leave my classroom, dread weighing down my body, and I practically have to drag my feet down the hallway. Jayden is waiting for me outside the pink building and as I see him from afar, I feel all nostalgic again. Just watching him lean against the car in his baggy jeans and loose sweatshirt reminds me of all the times he would wait for me outside the lecture theatres and then join me on the train journey home or to the library to study. In that short walk from the building to the car, I have flashbacks of driving through the rain singing along to TLC, strolling hand-in-hand through Hyde Park arguing about music, films, and books, shoplifting token items from souvenir shops in Central London just for a laugh.

My stomach contracts again. Was letting him go really the right choice?

Then I remember everything else. All the lies I told. All the fasts I missed. All the prayers I didn't even think about doing. The petty shoplifting. The continuous clubbing, smoking, the tarty clothes. The drugs.

It is the right choice, Sugar.

I get into Jayden's rental and we drive the short drive from Knowledge Village to the Mall of the Emirates, making small talk all the way. We talk about food, Dubai, London, music, basically everything other than what we're supposed to talk about. We laugh at people's clothes, we mimic their accents, we talk about the silly stuff we used to do like evading fares on the tubes and trains and sneaking into concerts.

When I'm around halfway through my crispy duck, I actually start feeling a little better. I may have changed, but Jayden is still the same and as always, he has me in fits of giggles.

And then right in the middle of the laughter, he asks me what the hell is going on.

I stare at my duck, and the atmosphere deflates. How am I supposed tell him that, after everything he sacrificed for me, and everything we went through, I don't want to get back with him? That I don't think I'm the person I can be when I'm with him?

'What's going on with you?' I deflect, taking a huge mouthful of duck, pancake, and cucumbers, buying myself a little more time while I work my way through the food in my mouth.

'I've told Nadia that I can't be with her,' he says bluntly, looking me straight in the eye.

'Why did you go and say that?' I mumble, my mouth full of food. Jayden gives me a dirty look.

'Because I'm still in love with you,' he says, his voice dripping with sarcasm. 'It's not fair to mess her about. She deserves better than that.'

'So that's why she won't answer my calls, my texts or my emails. Thanks for that.'

Jayden's confession has made what I've been planning to say even more difficult. I look at him, but I don't see the same guy I used to see. He still looks the same of course, give or take a stubble and a few pounds, but it's like the rose-tinted glasses have been taken off. He's become just…a friend. Someone I shared a lot with in the past and that's it. He's not the centre of my universe anymore.

'Can you please refrain from speaking with your mouth full next time?' he replies, a look of distaste on his face. 'I really didn't want to know what crispy duck looks like when it's smashed up with a pancake and some plum sauce.'

'Oh shut up,' I laugh, throwing a piece of spring onion at him. 'Seriously Jayden, I really wish you didn't tell her about us. She's the only friend I've got in this bloody country and now I've hurt her. I came out here for a fresh start, not for my past to go and ruin everything all over again.'

'She had the right to know the truth about why I wasn't going to see her anymore. Should

I have let her think that she had done something wrong?'

'No, of course not, but...'

'I want to get back with you, Sugar. If that happens, she'll find out anyway.'

'Jayden...' I interrupt, butterflies in my stomach, 'You know a part of me will always love you. We've practically been through a war together. You're my first love. Nothing will change that...'

'But?' he asks with a wry smile, looking away as if looking at me is too painful.

'But I have changed. I want something different from my life. I want peace. I want to make my family proud of me. I want to make God happy.' I pour my heart and soul into my words. My voice is thick with emotion and I feel my eyes welling up with tears. I'm desperate for him to believe me and to not take anything I say personally.

'Oh whatever, don't give me that crap,' he practically spits at me, and I'm shocked by the aggression in his voice. 'I'm sick of your religious bullshit, Sugar. You think I don't know about your Arab thing on the side?'

'What?' I gasp, wondering how he has made me feel like a slut and a liar in one second, when I know I'm neither.

'Yes. I know *all* about how you've been spending your time here, so please spare me your little Disney spirituality tale. Nadia told me everything.'

'Nothing's even happened between us! We're just friends!' I exclaim, my heart pounding. Having my spiritual journey shot down to the ground is like a punch in the gut. Is that what he really thinks of me? A liar who is using religion as an excuse to commit sins?

'Like nothing happened between us, you mean?' he sniggers, his face twisted into an expression I have never seen. In fact, I've never seen this side of him before. Maybe I'm not the only one to have changed.

'That was out of order, Jayden and you know it,' I whisper. 'I need God more than anything right now and I've never tried so hard to be a good Muslim and a good *person* before. I don't really care if you believe me or not, but it's the truth.'

'*You* need God more than anything? What the fuck happened to *you*? Did you get the shit kicked out of you? Did you? I was hospitalized because of *you* and now you think you're too good for me or something?'

'You're not the only one who suffered!' I cry out tears spilling out of my eyes. 'Yes, you got beaten up really badly and I didn't, but I suffered more than you know and I don't appreciate you belittling what happened to me. I wish I felt the same way I did two years ago, but I don't. Too much has happened and I'm a different person because of it. So please stop making it harder than it already is.'

'What happened that was worse than what happened to me? Tell me, Sugar, did mum and dad stop your allowance because you were associated with a dirty black boy? Oh yes, I forgot, you were sent off for a holiday to India for a few months. Did the mosquitoes get too much for you?'

Two years worth of frustration pour out of Jayden and he doesn't stop talking. I can't see through the tears blurring my vision, my head is throbbing and it takes all my willpower to stay seated and not get up and walk away. I keep telling myself he's just hurt, that he feels rejected, that he doesn't mean what he's saying.

'People think black girls are slappers. But I know from first-hand experience that it's the Asian girls who are the real slags.'

We stare at each other for a few seconds. Jayden is breathing heavily, his hands shaking from anger. My tears don't stop rolling down my cheeks.

'Jayden,' I begin, praying that I am making the right decision by telling him this. 'I was pregnant.'

'What the fuck do you mean?' he snarls and I flinch, scared that he will start another tirade of verbal abuse.

'The day they found out about us was the day I found out I was pregnant. That's why Ibby went crazy. That's why they sent me off to India. They sent me away to have the baby and then they forced me to give her up. That's why I'm so messed up now, and that's why I want nothing more than to turn my life around. '

I look at Jayden's eyes for what I know will be the last time. He has been stunned into silence and I can almost see the blood drain from his face. Part of me wants to comfort him, and be comforted *by* him. But I know that he can't say anything that will reduce the pain.

I get up and slowly walk away. He doesn't try to stop me.

I phone the school and tell them that I've fallen sick and won't be coming in for my afternoon class. At this point, I don't even care if I lose my job. I feel exhausted and although I'm furious that Jayden could actually say such terrible things to me, I'm hurt more than anything else. How can someone who professed to love me talk to me like that? I knew that he was angry, bitter, and even resentful, but I had never seen this dark side of him before.

I sit in my car, my head resting on the steering wheel, and close my eyes.

If I had to go back in time so I could change my future, what would I change? Would I erase Jayden? Or would I just refuse to give away my baby? Or would I tell my parents about Jayden from the beginning and force them to let us get married. But if I could change history, I would never have come out here and met Goldenboy. I really don't know if I would choose to go back and do things differently.

I do know something though. No man likes being lied to—or even likes to think he has been lied to. What will Goldenboy do if or when he finds out the truth about my past from someone else? Wouldn't he prefer to hear it from me?

Nothing—not even Goldenboy's reaction—can possibly be more painful than what I've already been through. The worst thing that will happen is that he will want nothing to do with me. But wouldn't it be better to end things now before we got in too deep?

Without giving myself time to change my mind, I turn on the engine and start driving towards Bur Dubai. When I get to his complex, I park the car and quickly check my reflection. My eyes are rimmed with pink, my nose is red, and I have black mascara streaks running down my cheeks. I couldn't look more unattractive if I tried, but I don't care. I just want to talk to him. And if he judges me because of the person I used to be, not who I am today, then I guess it just wasn't meant to be.

I don't know which house he lives in, so I call his mobile. It rings and I will him to pick up, my stomach churning with fear. After all, tonight could quite possibly turn out to be the night Sugar Sheikh lost everything she had left.

He picks up on the tenth ring.

'Goldenboy?' I squeak, my heart thudding so loudly that I'm sure he can hear it through the phone.

'Hi,' he replies and immediately, I know something's wrong.

'What's wrong?' My voice is barely audible and I'm too afraid to breathe in case I miss what he says.

'I don't know. Maybe you should ask your friend Nadia.'

His voice is like ice, and my hands start to shake.

'I need to talk to you,' I stammer. 'Please, let me explain.'

'There's nothing to explain, Sugar. You let me think you were honest and open, but you weren't. And you didn't trust me with the truth. What else is there to say?'

The phone goes silent. I look at the screen to see if he's still there. But he's not. He's gone. Just like that, I lose three friends in one day, one of them for the second time. Just how much crap does one person have to go through before she gets a little happiness or peace in her life?

My hands shaking, I turn on the engine and slowly drive out of the compound. I don't cry. I'm tired of crying over people who obviously don't care.

SIX MONTHS LATER

41

The sun is shining as it usually is in the resort town of Zahle, but the December air is refreshing and cold, as if delivered fresh from the freezer. Nestled between snow-capped mountains and set along the steep banks of the frozen Birdawni river, Leila's hometown is pretty and picturesque and she is quite possibly, the only inhabitant who wishes she were somewhere else.

As she sits in the small garden of her family home, a cigarette in one hand and a glass of arak in another, Leila pulls her woollen shawl closer to her. She wishes she were in Dubai with its mild December climate, not fighting against frostbite in Lebanon and being forced to listen to her mother shout down the phone to her friend, her voice loud enough to be heard outside the stone walls of their house.

Not much has changed in Zahle in the eleven and a half years since Leila left home, aside from the widespread availability of satellite television and every other person clutching a mobile phone in their hands. Almost all of her friends still live within a six kilometre radius, albeit in their marital homes, not with their parents; her mother is still wearing the same apron she did when Leila as a child, rolling war'enab, stuffing borek, and chopping bakdounis. Everyone still listens to Fairouz in the mornings and Um Kulthoum in the evenings. Everyone still gets their hair blow-dried every Thursday, they still visit their families for a range of mahshi on Fridays and they still love to litter their sentences with French in order to appear more sophisticated than they actually are.

Only Leila appears to be different. Just by looking at her, it is clear that she has become somewhat of an ajnabi. Leila's mother is pleased that her daughter is prettier but is disapproving of the sudden airs and graces she has developed. As if sticking her nose in the air will help her find a husband. Unknown to Mrs Saade, her daughter has never looked so awful in her entire life. Aside from the unflattering crutches she is forced to hobble about on, she has stopped styling her hair, is barely wearing any makeup, and refuses to wear anything other than jeans and an assortment of old sweaters. After all, there is no one in Zahle Leila intends to impress, and sees no point in making an effort just for her parents.

Unfortunately for Leila, after the accident she didn't really have much choice but to return to her parents' care. Her yearly housing contract was coming to an end and renewing it for another year when she knew she wouldn't be able to work for at least six months, made no financial sense. Then when her company didn't renew her employment contract, Leila realized that she could either shell out a portion of her savings just for the privilege of wallowing in self-pity in her lonely flat or she could sell her car and furniture, withdraw her ten years' savings and go back to Lebanon where her mother could fuss over her.

At least her accident gave her a reason to come home. No one had to know that she never managed to achieve her dreams. With almost a million dirhams in her pocket, she could easily start a business in Zahle and everyone would assume she had chosen a career over marriage, like many modern girls did. They wouldn't know that she was aching to find someone to share her life with.

Unable to travel for three months while her broken leg, broken ribs, and fractured spine had healed enough for the journey, she also had the perfect excuse to miss Lara's wedding. Had Leila been of a more positive disposition, she may have wondered if the accident was a blessing in disguise. Leila being Leila, however, cursed Mohamed for making her take her eyes off the road for that second. She cursed the day she ever laid eyes on Lady Luxe relaxing by the infinity pool in the Burj Al Arab's spa. And she cursed herself for letting all the men she had been in relationships with dictate the entire course of her life.

She had struggled so hard to leave her home town and make something of herself, to find a dashing, wealthy groom. She had been abused, emotionally and physically, she had had her heart broken more times than she could remember, she had made friends, betrayed friends, and lost friends, all in the quest to bag the man of her dreams. She had moved countries twice and had made a life for herself twice. And it was all a complete waste of time, for here she is, eleven years later, back in Lebanon in her parent's quaint house where the highlight of her day is to find out what her mother has cooked for dinner.

The only interesting prospect in her life was her business idea, something she was hoping to discuss that evening with Adam—her geeky and overly-clever childhood friend. Having moved to Beirut the same time she moved to America, Leila hasn't seen Adam for over a decade—their trips to Zahle to visit their parents never coinciding. His mother had told her mother that he was coming to visit, and like any respectable Arab woman, Mrs Saade immediately invited the entire family over for lunch as soon as he was settled in.

The sound of an approaching car engine startles Leila out of her thoughts and she looks up to find a brand new BMW 5 series crawling down the cobbled street. It grinds to a halt outside her house and she stares at it suspiciously, wondering what it's doing there. As the doors open, her mother's friend Julia jumps out of the car and runs over to Leila, engulfing her in her generous bosom.

Somehow managing to extract herself before she is suffocated, Leila smiles as sincerely as she can and greets Julia as her own mother runs out of the house, exclaiming greetings. She turns to look at the rest of the family climbing out of the car and on seeing her old friend Adam, Leila's pulse quickens.

Gone is the short, chubby nerd from her youth, gone are the thick glasses and bad haircut, and in their place stands a man so handsome that for a second she is at a complete loss for words. The warm hazel eyes are still the same though.

Horrified, she wishes she had the sense to dress in something sexier than old, faded jeans and a sweater that was so ugly it looked as if her mother had knitted it for her. Why hadn't she joined her mother for the weekly blow-dry instead of letting her hair sit in a wild mess on top of her head? As for her face, with nothing but a dash of mascara, she feels horribly naked and exposed. Why hadn't anyone told her that Adam had blossomed into a swan? Why hadn't her mother forced her to look more presentable?

'Wow, Leila, you're looking good. Dubai must have agreed with you,' Adam says, looking her up and down and smiling widely. 'I've been looking forward to catching up with you.'

Taken aback by his compliment, Leila stares at Adam and smiles at the sheer irony of possibly meeting someone in the one place she believed she wouldn't. Maybe being home wasn't going to be that bad after all.

Back in Dubai, the sky is a clear, startling blue, without the slightest wisp of clouds interrupting its beauty. The beach is relatively quiet considering the pleasant weather and warm, inviting waters. Children play with buckets and spades, bright reds and greens dotting the sand. A handsome couple jog past on the running track, their eyes straight ahead, seemingly unaware of the exquisite beauty around them.

A lone figure sitting on the wall separating the pavement from the sand, shields her eyes with her hand and looks up at the sky, smiling. She turns and faces the sea again, bending down to scoop up a handful of sand, which she lets slide and fall through her open fingers.

There is a slight wind and the loose end of the girl's colourful headscarf dances in it. She grabs it and tucks it into her long white dress, preventing it from lifting up and exposing her skin. Although her eyes are hidden by sunglasses, her expression speaks volumes. Her smile is easy and her face is relaxed and she carries about her the confident aura of someone who knows exactly who she is.

A boy watches her from a distance, a small frown on his face as if he is trying to work out where he has seen her before. He takes in the tilt of her head, the curve of her back, the smile on her lips, but cannot place her. He hopes she will remove her sunglasses but she doesn't, and he cannot ask her to. So he takes a seat not too far away, and glances at her every so often from the corner of his eyes, wondering why he feels so drawn to her. He hopes she doesn't notice him looking at her.

After a while, the girl takes a notebook out from her bag and begins to write in it. She takes off her sunglasses to see what she is writing, and when he sees her eyes he finally recognizes her. He is shocked by the hijab. He remembers her talking about wanting to wear it, but so do many girls out to make a good impression. He never thought she would actually do it. He has tried hard to forget about her. First he tried immersing himself in activities to get his mind off the sorrow. When that failed, he went on holiday to remind himself that there was an entire world out there beyond his own. Upon returning to Dubai, he found himself playing with his phone and letting the cursor hover over her name. He wondered if what she had done was really that bad. He wondered if he would be able to forgive her for lying to him. The wondering was beginning to drive him crazy, so he tried to date other girls. But even that attempt to move on with his life failed miserably. No one could compare to her.

His heart caught in his throat, all the reasons that kept them apart seemed too trivial now that he finally set eyes on her again. Just looking at her breathe makes him want to hold her and never let her go. But after the terrible things he had said to her, he doubts that she will ever give him a second chance. He doesn't blame her.

He looks at her one more time, memorizing the angle of her face, the slight frown on her forehead as she concentrates on what she is writing, her hand grasping her pen and moving across the page. She looks so peaceful—the hijab really suits her, much more than he imagined. He half wishes that he had the chance to touch her silky auburn hair when he could have. But now it's too late.

The girl senses someone watching her, and for a while she ignores it. She doesn't want whoever it is staring at her to think that the interest is reciprocated. The feeling doesn't stop and she becomes more and more uncomfortable. She picks up her bag, stuffs her notebook into it and gets up to leave, her unspoiled solace well and truly spoilt.

She puts her sunglasses back on and glances around as she makes her way back to the car.

And then she sees him.

He looks exactly the same as he did six months ago. He is wearing a green t-shirt and his golden skin looks smooth and buttery just like it did the first time she saw him almost a year ago on the beach. Her heart begins to flutter. She wonders if she should just turn around and walk away. After all, he made it perfectly clear that he wanted nothing more to do with her.

But before she can, he starts walking towards her, and in just a few seconds he's standing in front of her, a tired smile on his face.

'Mashalla, it really suits you Sugar,' he says, unsure of how to greet the girl who has dominated his thoughts longer than he cares to remember.

'Thanks,' she replies casually, her breath getting caught in her throat. They look at each other for another minute. She wonders if she should walk away before he breaks her heart again.

He has a thousand things to say to her, but pride, shame, and fear, prevent him from allowing them all to spill out.

'Well, it was nice to see you,' she mumbles. 'Bye.' She turns away from him but before she can move, he grabs her arm. She is shocked by the physical contact. It is the first time they have touched.

'Wait,' he says, his voice brimming with uncertainty.

She turns back round to face him, but says nothing. The ball has been in his court for a long time. She refuses to put herself out there again, only to be hurt.

'I miss you,' he says, scared it is too little, too late. 'Can you forgive me?'

The girl looks him in the eyes, and sees sincerity in their depths. The bitterness disappeared a long time ago. She realizes that she can.

'If God can forgive anyone, who are we to hold grudges?' Sugar replies with a small smile. 'It may take a while though.'

'It's okay,' he says, his voice full of hope and his face breaking into a hesitant smile. 'I'll wait.'

A few thousand miles away, Nadia stares out of her bedroom window and watches the trains rush past every ten minutes, their regularity giving her a sense of stability she currently lacks. The sky is grey, covered completely in rainclouds, and splatters of water decorate the window pane. From her position by the windowsill, she can see into her neighbours' gardens and she watches the

Bengali girls in the house on her right playing with a skipping rope, their greasy hair tied back into long, flapping plaits. The Somali woman in the house on her left hurriedly brings in the washing hanging from the line, stuffing the brightly coloured patterned dresses into a basket.

She wonders if saying goodbye to Dubai was the easy way out. Just having her sister close enough to hug is a dramatic improvement from the month she spent entirely alone in a broken apartment in Jumeirah Lakes Towers as she tried to mend the pieces that were her life. It was worth giving up eternal sunshine, long sunset walks on the beach, weekly manicures and pedicures and part-time maids, for the beauty of having family around her.

But she still hasn't recovered, and she still hasn't worked up the desire to pray.

When Nadia looks back at the life she has left behind, she cannot pinpoint the exact moment when everything went terribly wrong. She wonders if her mistake lay in not leaving Daniel as soon as she found out he wasn't who she thought he was. If she had, perhaps she wouldn't have been quite as bitter, perhaps she wouldn't have found solace in the concept of revenge, and perhaps her friendship with Sugar would have remained intact.

Or maybe she should go back a step. Perhaps moving to Dubai was the mistake. The luxurious, sun-kissed lifestyle and the abundance of beautiful, single women seemed to have changed Daniel or at least, brought out the worst in him. But then if she were honest with herself, she would know she needs to go back even further. Perhaps the true mistake was marrying him. Maybe she should have spent more than just six months getting to know him before she took the plunge. Maybe she should have spent time getting to know his friends and family to better understand his character, rather than being swayed by his charm.

Regardless of what it was that brought Nadia to where she is today, she is yet to look back and understand the wisdom in what she has learnt. She is still bruised, still finding the loneliness difficult to contend with, still wary of any new person who ventures into her life.

She thought getting her own back on those who had spurned her would give her solace, but she was terribly misguided. All it did was shape her into a bitter, angry person who turned away from God when she needed him the most to guide her. All it did was create a long list of people who disliked her, or at the very least distrusted her, even though they pretended that they had forgiven her.

Sugar, for example, accepted her apology when she called her the day before she left to return to London, but Nadia knew that things would never be the same between them. Looking back she realizes that she should have talked to Sugar about what happened, instead of calling Goldenboy and telling him his girlfriend's secret in as much detail as possible. But she didn't, and it was too late.

As for Jennifer, according to Leila she had disappeared off the face of the Earth, and Leila feared her to be... Nadia couldn't even bring herself to say the word.

Feeling nauseous, she gets up from her position and moves to the bed. She wonders if she should pray and ask God to help her, to forgive her for all her wrongdoings, for taking judgement into her own hands. But she hasn't prayed since...she can't even remember the last time she did and she feels too ashamed to start now. Besides, after all the pain she inflicted on everyone, after perhaps being the cause of another woman's death, she is certain He didn't want anything to do with her.

She wishes in vain for some kind of divine sign that everything will be okay.

An hour later, Nadia hoists herself up from the bed, tired of waiting for a sign. Throwing on the first headscarf she can find, she grabs her winter duffel coat and heads outside into the sharp December winds.

She walks past rows and rows of terraced houses, each nearly the same as the other, with the only differences being in the colour of the front door or the variety of discarded toys littering the front path. She shivers and walks faster, trying to warm herself up.

Why didn't I listen to reason when they all kept telling me to let it go?

Now that she is back in London, Nadia's experience with Daniel feels like a story she's heard somewhere, not her own personal hell. If she hadn't been left with a hollowness that grew each time she tried to avenge herself, she would have thought the entire affair a figment of her imagination. But that bitter taste in her mouth, the acidic buzz in her stomach, the guilt weighing down on her shoulders, were all far too real to be mere imagination.

She had tasted revenge, but it wasn't sweet like she had thought it would be. It had cast a shadow on her, dimmed the light in her eyes, and forced her back into a stoop. She had betrayed her friend, ruined her ex-husband, and caused the disappearance of a silly girl who really didn't deserve something so severe. And then there was Leila, whom she had manipulated like a puppet, just to serve her own twisted cause.

Nadia continues to walk aimlessly around Holloway, tears streaming down her face. As she waits to cross Holloway Road, for a split second she's tempted to throw herself under a bus to end the misery. Wiping away her tears, she waits for the traffic lights to change, and as she does, her gaze falls on a couple waiting on the other side. The girl is beautiful, with brown shiny hair, hanging down on either side of her face like silk curtains. A cherry red hat sits on her head matching the red of her full lips and she turns to smile at the handsome man next to her, his arm linked in hers. She is wearing a plain black coat, and Nadia struggles to remember where she has seen her before.

The light changes, and she crosses the road, still staring at the girl. As their eyes meet, the girl frowns and stumbles on a step and Nadia too recoils in shock.

It is her. She is okay.

Breaking into a shaky smile, Nadia runs to the bus that is just about to leave the stop and jumps inside just as the doors are closing. Ignoring the curious stares from the other passengers, she continues to smile and cry at the same time, thanking God for giving her a sign when she needed it the most.

The bus stops outside the mosque and she alights, tripping over her own feet as she stumbles into the ladies' section and heads straight for the ablution area.

Thank you, she whispers over and over again as she washes her hands, her face, her arms, her feet with lukewarm water, preparing herself for prayer. The water slides off her skin and falls to the ground, splashing her jeans, but she doesn't notice a thing. Not her soaked trousers, nor the buzz of voices around her. All she can think about is pressing her forehead on to the soft carpet and submitting once again.

Thank you.

The girl looks familiar but Lady Luxe cannot discern where she has seen her before. The girl clearly recognizes her too, for she almost knocks into a passerby as she gapes at her. Frowning, Lady Luxe stares back, desperately trying to work out where she has seen her, if she is someone from her old life or her new one. Lost in thought she trips over her own shoelace, and Khaled steadies her, preventing her from falling flat on her face.

When she reaches the other side of the road, she stops and turns to look back at the girl but she is gone, and Lady Luxe is left with an unsettling feeling in her stomach. It is the same sensation she experiences whenever she comes across a woman in an abaya or inhales the sweet fragrance of double apple shisha, or listens to the sound of the adhaan inviting the faithful to worship.

This feeling often renders her speechless. Unable to articulate the sense of loss and longing to Khaled, she has given up trying. As for him, he accepts it as an innate part of the person he had come to love, just like the fierce independence or the unwavering stubbornness.

She continues to walk down Holloway Road in silence, hand in hand with Khaled, waiting for the despondence to subside. After a while as always, it disappears into the dreary grey sky and when she looks up to see swollen rain clouds hanging over them, Lady Luxe feels as if it is the clouds which keep swallowing her misery.

She blinks back tears and then looks at Khaled, revelling in the warmth of his skin instead of depressing herself with such an insipid temperament. She squeezes his hand and he squeezes it back without saying a word, making her smile. She never realized that a simple gesture like this could give her so much pleasure. She did not expect to enjoy something as banal as a walk down a grimy road dotted with litter and pigeon droppings. But then she never imagined herself capable of living such an ordinary life either and yet here she was in a New Look jacket and H&M boots, navigating herself around dog crap like every other nobody.

The air is cold and Lady Luxe pulls Khaled closer to her, using him as a shield against the bitter breeze. He smiles down at her and hugs her back and she is yet again taken aback by his beauty. She never tires of gazing at the sharp rise of his cheekbones, his aquiline nose, his soft full lips, his generous smile. A shiver runs down her spine and she giggles to herself, completely aware that it has nothing to do with the cold, but everything to do with the man by her side.

Man. How strange it was to say 'man' and not 'men'. How liberating it was to have found someone who was enough for her not to even consider looking elsewhere.

They finally arrive at the Holloway Road tube station and welcome the warm sooty air that greets them as they enter the Westbound platform. Lady Luxe pulls off her coat and slings it over her arm as she struggles to board the train, trying hard not to let her face press into the armpit of a sweaty commuter. She remembers when, almost a year ago, she boarded an EK flight to DXB and kept moaning to herself about having to leave behind London and the anonymity it afforded. She remembers missing the way she had to board the tube with everyone else, the way she was served in restaurants like everyone else, the way no one knew she was the daughter of X.

You must have tempted fate with that one, she thinks to herself, grimacing. *Like you even knew what 'everyone else' meant.*

Just because she bought the occasional dress from Camden Town market or that she didn't mind eating in Wagamama or other common eateries did not make her the same as everyone else. She lived in South Kensington. She flew first

A NOTE ON THE AUTHOR

Ameera Al Hakawati[*] is the enigmatic author of *Desperate in Dubai*, has always known that she was born to be a writer. A natural storyteller, her career began at age three, when she told her very first story to her mother that explained the 'truth' behind the missing chocolate biscuits. Numerous writing projects and a creative writing degree later, the twenty-something-year old Ameera moved to Dubai from London. Inspired by the fascinating lives of the women who dominated the glamorous city, she put pen to paper and created 'Desperate in Dubai', a blog that soon became an internet sensation among the expatriate community in Dubai. *Desperate in Dubai* is Ameera's first novel. She is currently based in Dubai where she lives with her husband and their hamster, Fat Sam.

[*] Ameera Al Hakawati is her nom de plume.

or business. She had tins of quality Caspian caviar in her fridge. She carried an authentic Birkin on her shoulder.

But now she finally knows what 'everyone else' means, and although it isn't impossible to live like she always dreamt of living, it isn't easy. Although Khaled's presence in her life does make waking up in the morning easier, she cannot deny that she misses her Egyptian cotton sheets, her custom designed Ferrari, her vast designer wardrobe. She would be a liar if she claimed to enjoy living in grimy one-bedroom flat in a council estate rife with needles in the stairwells. She would be a hypocrite if she claimed to enjoy eating beans on toast almost every day when, just a few months ago, she had a French chef who cooked up whatever she wanted, whenever she wanted. She would be plain stupid to swear that she enjoyed donning a pair of Yellow Marigolds in order to give the toilet bowl a thorough scrub. No one enjoyed cleaning toilets. That's what maids were for.

No she doesn't enjoy living like a pauper. She doesn't enjoy watching every penny of her personal savings in case of emergencies. But the material possessions she has given up are not nearly as difficult to contend with as the ache in her heart whenever she remembers her brother Ahmed. It isn't nearly as painful as the knowledge that she can never ever return to her birth country. And it isn't nearly as soul-crushing as knowing that aside from Khaled, she has absolutely no one who will notice if she disappears. But then, did she really want anyone seeing her like this?

Lady Luxe wonders if, now that her life is anything but luxurious, she will hold the same appeal to all those who were in awe of her, including Khaled. Or if they will simply disappear, now that she wasn't who they thought she was.

As much as she loves Khaled, as happy as she is for having him in her life, a dark quiet part of her, which only surfaces when he is far too lost in the world of dreams to notice her pacing up and down their tiny bedroom, wonders if it was all worth it.

It is strange how the taste of freedom isn't quite as glorious as she imagined it would be. It had come at a phenomenal price, and everyone knows that the best things in life are free.

Thinking back to the first time she met him and how different she was, she looks up at Khaled and whispers with a wry smile, 'I used to call you Mr Delicious you know.'

He laughs his low, rumbling laugh and strokes the top of her head with a tenderness, which she absorbs as thirstily as a sponge in water.

'That's okay,' he replies with a smile, 'I used to call you Lady Luxe.'

ACKNOWLEDGEMENTS

Baba, thank you for encouraging me to write and for always believing that I would publish a novel one day—although I don't think this is exactly what you had in mind! Despite the slightly salacious nature of this book, I hope I've made you proud.

Hayati, thank you for never complaining when you went without conversation, attention, and occasionally, dinner, as I focused on completing this book. I love you.

Thank you to my friends and family; for your suggestions, your criticism, and your patience as I bounced ideas off you, based characters on you and often gave up nights out so I could sit at home and write. I love you guys too!

Milee and the RHI team, thank you for giving me the opportunity to make my childhood dream a reality and for bearing with me through all my diva-esque moments. You've been a saint during this process. I know it couldn't have been easy!

And of course, a HUGE thank you to my wonderful readers, for motivating me to continue writing when life kept getting in the way. Your support has been immeasurable.